"HAS NO MAN EVER TAMED YOU, MADAM?"

"Many have wanted to, but none has found a way."

He laughed softly, and she looked up to see the softened lines of his countenance in the glimmer of lamplight. "I have a way, lady," he said. "A most effective and pleasurable way."

He lowered his head and touched his mouth to hers—touched her with only his lips. Gentle and warm, they tasted faintly of ale . . . and honey. They moved ever so slightly, fitting more closely. Tasting sweeter and warmer. Hot. Hotter.

Puzzled by the feelings he aroused in her, Jarvia stepped back. He moved closer. His arms slid around her. He pulled her fully against him . . .

LORD OF FIRE

EMMA MERRITT

An Avon Romantic Treasure

AVON BOOKS ◆ NEW YORK

LORD OF FIRE is an original publication of Avon Books. This work has never before appeared in book form. This work is a novel. Any similarity to actual persons or events is purely coincidental.

AVON BOOKS
A division of
The Hearst Corporation
1350 Avenue of the Americas
New York, New York 10019

Copyright © 1994 by Emma Merritt
Inside cover author photograph by F.E. Alexander
Published by arrangement with the author
Library of Congress Catalog Card Number: 93-91643
ISBN: 0-380-77288-4

First Avon Books Printing: January 1994

AVON TRADEMARK REG. U.S. PAT. OFF. AND IN OTHER COUNTRIES, MARCA REGISTRADA, HECHO EN U.S.A.

Printed in the U.S.A.

RA   10 9 8 7 6 5 4 3 2 1

To Paul,
Whom I shall love 'til the twelfth of never

and to
Carol, Elyse, and Kaye

Chapter 1

Village of Wybornsbaer
Norse Kingdom of Southerland
Northern Coast of Scotland
A.D. 625

Dressed for battle, his dirk and long sword strapped around his powerful body, the Highland warlord strode down the main street of the village. In the silence that had descended, the firm thud of his booted feet against the hardened dirt echoed loudly, ominously. Malcolm mac Duncan's unannounced visit struck fear into the hearts of the people.

Jarvia had not seen Malcolm in four years, but he had not changed. His countenance was still dark and brooding, and he exuded the predatory grace of a ferocious wildcat.

Brilliant torch flame climbed the night-darkened sky to touch him with gold. His clean-shaven features, sharply etched angles and planes, looked as if they had been carved from stone. His black hair brushed against his broad shoulders, which were cloaked with a red-and-yellow plaid tartan. The rich material, swirling about his body as he moved, emphasized his blatant masculinity. His physique was hard and indomitable. Everything about him bespoke power, might, and prowess with weapons of war.

The wind caught his tartan and billowed it back to reveal his black shirt, the shoulder placket fastened with three small golden brooches. Tight-fitting black trousers, fastened about his waist with a leathern girdle, revealed legs as muscular as his shoulders. Light glinted off the gold buckles on the girdle. The forest green border of the tartan slapped against his cowhide boots, laced up his legs to the knees.

As he drew nearer, Jarvia moved from the king's house toward her own home across the street. She retreated not

1

from fear of the man, but from fear of her own emotions. Four years ago the Highlander had attracted her; he still did. He would not remember her, but she would never forget him. Wanting to put distance between them, she sought the shelter of her front porch, from which she had a clear view of the proceedings.

Like the people who crowded into the yard of the king's house, she wondered why the warlord was in Wybornsbaer. Since his visit was unexpected, she entertained no hope that he had come to celebrate the spring festival of the Success Sacrifice of Planting Time Moon. His countenance and demeanor suggested this was no pleasure trip.

He halted in front of the porch of the Great House that served as a dais for the seated king and queen of Southerland.

"Welcome, my lord Malcolm mac Duncan, prince of Northern Scotland and chief of Clan Duncan," King Wyborn said, his skald translating his words from Norse into Gaelic.

The Highlander looked around as if searching for something . . . someone.

"Your . . . er . . . your visit is a surprise, lord," Wyborn said.

Malcolm returned his attention to the king. "Is it, lord?" His voice was deep, husky, and sardonic—just as Jarvia remembered it.

Wyborn squirmed nervously. "But it is a . . . er . . . a pleasant surprise. Had we known you were coming, we . . . er . . . we would have planned a reception for you."

Jarvia laughed softly. Though the barbarian had been married to Wyborn's daughter, Hilda, for the past four winters, he still frightened thě king.

Wyborn waved his hand to include those who stood gawking. "We invite you to join our spring celebration."

"I did not come to celebrate, Wyborn," Malcolm said.

Fluent in Gaelic, Jarvia noticed that the Highlander omitted using a title of respect for the king. The skald stammered when he came to translating the king's name. He looked at Malcolm questioningly.

"Translate what I say just as I say it," the Highlander ordered.

The skald nodded and did so, making the villagers gasp and edge away from Malcolm mac Duncan. Wyborn's personal warriors moved closer to him, their hands on their weapons. Jarvia feared this visit boded no good.

Malcolm's gaze moved slowly over the crowd. Again Jarvia had the impression that he was looking for someone in particular.

"I am here on business, not pleasure," he said.

"What is your business, lord?"

Although Wyborn seemed to be composed, Jarvia knew he was not. With one hand he fiddled with the linen furniture covers draped over the arms of the chair. With the other he finger-combed his beard.

"I want another bride from the kingdom of Southerland."

"Another bride!" Queen Adelaide exclaimed, leaning forward in her chair. Her huge bosom pressed against the confines of her dress. One fat hand curved around the armrest: the other tightly clutched a handkerchief. "Is not one wife of Southerland enough for you?"

"Your daughter, my wife, is dead."

Dazed, the king and queen could only stare.

Pain gripped through Jarvia's heart and twisted it until she thought she would surely die. During Princess Hilda's formative years, Jarvia had been a slave in the king's household and had served as Hilda's personal maid and companion. The two of them had become close friends.

"She killed herself," Malcolm said, "and the unborn babe she carried."

The villagers gasped.

The queen shouted, "You lie!"

"Nay!"

Jarvia could not believe Hilda was dead, that she had deliberately taken her own life. But something Hilda had said to her two springs ago, when Jarvia and her then living husband Ein-her had accompanied the king and queen on a trip to Northern Scotland, made Jarvia wonder if perhaps Hilda had indeed been driven to suicide.

Because Malcolm had been away on a hunting trip with other clan chieftains, Jarvia had been able to spend uninterrupted hours visiting Hilda. She had confessed to Jarvia that she hated and feared her husband. She claimed he was unkind to her, prone to frequent outbursts of anger, and often struck her. As proof she showed Jarvia the bruises on her body. Sometimes, Hilda had said, she feared Malcolm would kill her. Other times she feared he would drive her to kill herself.

Wyborn was now saying, "My daughter would never have shamed the names of her father and husband by taking the life of an unborn royal heir. She knew her responsibility as the daughter of a king and the wife of the prince of Northern Scotland. She understood how important it was for her to bear you a son."

"Evidently not," Malcolm said.

"Why would Hilda do this?" Wyborn demanded.

"She was a traitor."

The barbarian's words hung heavily, accusingly, over the crowd. Openmouthed, Wyborn stared at the warlord. Adelaide gripped the armrests so tightly that her knuckles whitened. Jarvia fought to control her trembling.

Even the elements seemed troubled by the fateful events. Thick, heavy thunderheads swirled blackly in the sky to hide the moon and stars. Wind ripped through the village, snapping the tapestries that hung from the eaves of several buildings. The chill of early spring and the impending storm enveloped everyone.

"My lord Malcolm," Wyborn said, visibly struggling for composure, "I am distraught by the news that you have brought. It is difficult enough for us to accept that our daughter is dead, and that she killed herself and her child, but for you to tell us that she was a traitor . . ."

"You may have difficulty accepting what I say, Wyborn," Malcolm said, "but it is the truth. Your daughter betrayed me. She assisted rebels within our kingdom who wished to overthrow my father, the high king."

The queen spoke. "Are you sure, my lord Malcolm, that my daughter was not murdered?"

"Nay, she killed herself," Malcolm answered. "She had run away and was living with the renegades. My clansmen and I captured her. Rather than return to our village to await judgment by the Council of the Chiefs, she ended her own life."

"Your clansmen could have killed her," Adelaide pointed out.

"They could have, or I could have," Malcolm returned, "but we did not. Hilda was more important to us alive than dead. She carried a child who would have guaranteed the alliance between our two kingdoms, and she also had information that we wanted, which would have helped us capture the renegades. She died before she could tell us anything."

The wind blew stronger. Nervous and cold, Jarvia pulled her white linsey-woolsey shawl more snugly about her shoulders and tucked an errant strand of hair beneath her head scarf.

Finally the king spoke. "How did she kill herself?"

"She ate poisoned berries."

"You have proof of this?"

"Aye, my clansmen were with me. All of us witnessed her death. There are also those who will testify that she deserted me to live with a renegade Scot."

"Are your witnesses Highlanders?"

Malcolm nodded. "One is my father, the high king."

"What of Berowalt, my emissary to your kingdom?"

"He knows of Hilda's betrayal," Malcolm said, "but he did not witness her death."

"Where is he? Why is he not here to corroborate your story?"

"I do not know," Malcolm answered, "I expected him to be here, but I am not his keeper."

Wyborn gave a weak nod and leaned back in his chair. "I will speak to him about the matter when he arrives."

"So be it," Malcolm said. A slight movement of his left hand brought two lads scurrying to the front of the Great House to set a huge chest in front of the king and queen.

"Your daughter's belongings," Malcolm said, and nodded to the lads. They opened the chest and removed a large copper urn. "I also bring her ashes for the burial service."

The king and queen stared as the young man approached and set the urn before them.

"I thank you for this kindness," Wyborn said.

"I did it out of necessity, not kindness," Malcolm replied. "Your daughter was remiss in her duties as a princess of

Southerland. She was disloyal to herself, to her people, and to her husband. Her death denied me a son and our peoples a covenant of friendship and peace."

"You cannot blame me for this, Chief Malcolm," Wyborn said. "My daughter is dead, whether by her own hand or not, I have no proof. Either way, I had no knowledge of the situation."

"You are responsible for the well-being of your kingdom, and you do have the power to find another wife for me among your kinswomen, one capable of producing the son I need."

Wyborn bristled with indignation. "But I have fulfilled my duty, my lord, by giving you my only daughter in marriage. Surely you will not break our covenant of peace because of her death."

"Your daughter severed the covenant, not I. It was broken through no accident, nor by an act of God. Hilda deliberately killed herself, and thus the child, denying me my heir. To repair the breach, I demand that you give me another bride."

Adelaide leaned over to whisper in Wyborn's ear. He nodded and raised his hand. Four of his warriors moved forward.

"Do not act in haste, Wyborn," Malcolm warned, "or you will regret it."

By the time the Southerland warriors stood in a semicircle around Wyborn, six Highlanders—best men or heads of the houses that comprised Clan Duncan—had materialized from the darkness to join Malcolm. With the ease of a farmer carrying his hoe on his shoulder, each carried his long, heavy war lance. Fastened about their waists were long swords and dirks. One Highlander, as large and powerful as Malcolm, moved to his side.

All of these warriors were tall and fearsome-looking, yet Malcolm mac Duncan's bearing and countenance were even more thunderous and terrifying. Although he was surrounded by warriors, he seemed to stand apart from all others.

"I did not come to fight you," Malcolm said, "but I shall if it is necessary, and have no doubt, I shall win."

Villagers scurried for protection. Wyborn squirmed in his chair, and Adelaide's eyes grew round. Even Jarvia drew back. More of Wyborn's warriors moved across the yard so that they fanned out behind the Highlanders.

"We have you surrounded and we outnumber you," Wyborn said.

"Perhaps. Perhaps not. You have no idea how many men I have concealed in the darkness." Malcolm's sardonic laughter sent a chill of fear up Jarvia's spine. "You should know, battles are won by courage, strength, and ability, not by numbers."

The Highlanders, their weapons drawn, faced off with the Southerlanders.

"You may kill us," Malcolm said, "but I guarantee Wyborn, you will die before I do."

In palpable silence the two men stared at each other.

Finally Wyborn lowered his eyes, "I will consider your request," he said.

Chapter 2

"Surely, Wyborn," Malcolm said, breaking the ominous silence, "you are a man of honor."

Wyborn sighed. Once more he waved his hand, this time calling off his warriors. "Aye, I am an honorable man."

Malcolm smiled sardonically. "Surely you have a kinswoman of marriageable age."

"Aye." Adelaide blew her nose noisily, then stuffed her handkerchief into her girdle. "The king has many. We shall find you another bride."

Wyborn rolled his eyes. The queen glared at him. He fidgeted in his seat. "It will take time . . . er . . . to select the right one for you."

"I have no time. I want a bride immediately."

"My lord—" Wyborn began.

Malcolm held up a silencing hand. " 'Twould be to your advantage, Wyborn, to do as I bid. Else you will find your warriors standing alone when your clansmen from Northland sail down to avenge themselves for the evil you have brought upon them." With the fury of the gathering storm, the Highlander's words whipped across the villagers.

Wyborn pulled back.

Malcolm laughed, the sound devoid of humor. "Do not look so innocent. Rumor travels through the Highlands as freely as the wind. I have heard why you and your Northmen settled on our shores nine summers ago. I know of your foul deeds."

"How dare you speak to me in such a manner!" Wyborn shouted, his bloated face turning red, the veins pulsing in his forehead. He grabbed the hilt of his sword, but released it when Malcolm raised a brow. "In Northland I am an earl by birth," Wyborn went on. "In Southerland, the kingdom I founded and settled, I am king."

8

"You are king because you usurped your kingdom and your High Seat," Malcolm said. "You did not found or settle it. You took it from unsuspecting Highlanders by force." His gaze flitted over the large group of mercenary warriors who stood to one side of the king. "You keep the kingdom of Southerland only with the help of your paid warriors."

"How I got my kingdom and how I keep it are not a matter for discussion," Wyborn said. "We are talking about Hilda's death."

"Nay, lord, we have finished with that. Now we are discussing what you are going to do to mend the broken alliance between our kingdoms."

Malcolm schooled his features and watched Wyborn squirm.

"I will find you another bride from among my kins-women," Wyborn said, "but, as I said, I must have time."

Malcolm shook his head.

"All of—" Wyborn began, but stopped when Adelaide slapped him on the arm and gave him a warning glare. He swallowed. "The majority of my kinswomen who are of marriageable age live in Northland."

Malcolm crossed his arms over his chest. Slowly he said, "Only the majority?"

Wyborn and Adelaide nodded in unison.

"Then, my lord king of Southerland," he said softly, "that means a few of them are closer by."

"Aye." Wyborn tugged nervously on his beard.

"I ask not for a woman who is a beauty, or one who is blessed with social graces, or one who can give me great pleasure in bed, my lord king. I ask only for one who is young and strong enough to bear me a son."

His blunt words did not surprise Jarvia. He had never hidden his reason for marrying Hilda. And in all honesty, most men married to have sons.

Even in the torchlight, Jarvia could see the Highlander's hard gaze fixed on the king's countenance. Wyborn seemed to have shrunk back in his chair. That was no surprise either, she thought. He had lied to the Highlander. He had no kinswomen of marriageable age—young or old, beauti-ful or ugly, seductive or repulsive—living in the land. All of them resided far away in the Northland, and even there none respected him. If the situation were not so grim for the people of Southerland, she would have taken great pleasure in Wyborn's misery.

What the Highlander had said was true. Wyborn lived in constant fear. Nine years ago, he had been banished from Northland after being accused of murdering his brother and his brother's entire family as they slept in their home. Although Wyborn had protested his innocence, the people of Northland had declared him an outlaw, to be hunted and killed. He had gathered his immediate family and sailed south to the northernmost tip of Scotland.

Migrating with him had been family members and friends who believed in his innocence. Under Wyborn's leadership, these Northlanders had vanquished one small village after another until they had conquered the native people and established the kingdom they called Southerland. So far Wyborn's clan from Northland had not sought revenge, but always the threat of attack hung over the land.

Finally the Highlander broke the silence, "My lord king, I repeat myself. From among the few kinswomen you have here, you *will* find me a bride."

"Aye." Wyborn nodded. "I will, but—"

Malcolm glared.

"I beg you, Lord Malcolm, give me time."

Firelight gleamed on Malcolm's gold helmet, on the gold ring pin that fastened the red-and-yellow plaid mantle about his shoulders, and on the gold torque around his neck— the symbol of his status. Everyone in Southerland knew Malcolm mac Duncan, the Highlander who had married Princess Hilda. He was one of the most feared warriors in the kingdom of the Northern Scots. Nay, in all the kingdoms of the land. He was chief of the largest and most influential clan of the Northern Scots and foster son of the high king, Fergus.

"Chief Malcolm, what say you?" Wyborn peered nervously at him.

Queen Adelaide, speaking in a soft, pleading tone, said, "My lord, the death of our daughter and that of her unborn bairn fills our heart with immeasurable grief."

Having known the king and queen of Southerland for the

four winters he had been married to their daughter, Malcolm doubted their sincerity, but he said nothing.

"I implore you," the queen continued, "be generous and give us time. Time to mourn and time to find the bride you request."

"My lady-queen, I repeat myself for the last time." Malcolm ground out the words. "I do not request. I demand."

Hastily Wyborn said, "We shall get you a bride."

"Aye," Malcolm said, "you will."

Wind rushed around the longhouse, and torch flames spiraled into the dark sky. The Highlander seemed one with the elements, an extension of the flames. His entire body radiated fire. Hot. Consuming. Lord of fire!

Expectantly Jarvia waited for the Highlander to give an answer, as did everyone else who crowded around the Great House.

Finally he said, "You asked for time, Wyborn. How long do you need?"

As the translation sounded, the king squirmed again. He brushed a hand through his hair. Queen Adelaide leaned over and whispered into his ear. Wyborn nodded.

"The passing of two moons," he answered.

"Three days. No more."

Wyborn opened his mouth to protest.

"Three days!" the Highlander repeated, his tone brooking no argument. "If you cannot find me a bride during that time, I will consider the alliance between us destroyed and will seek an agreement elsewhere."

"Three days," Wyborn agreed.

"Good."

Malcolm motioned with his left hand a second time. Three young men, dressed in red slash-sleeved vests that fitted snugly over short yellow tunics, moved from the shadows to stand behind the Highlander. One held aloft in his left hand the iron standard from which fluttered Clan Duncan's colors. A second carried a huge horn. The third held an inflated leathern bag the size and shape of a cow's udder—a Highland musical instrument called the pipes.

"Ho, Jamie," the warlord called to the lad holding the huge horn, "sound the lur."

Gripping the horn in both hands and stepping forward, the young man lifted it to his mouth and blew—a loud, blaring sound that echoed through the village. Thrice he blew before he lowered the lur, resting the mouthpiece against his thigh, the other end against his shoulder.

"Now, Arthur," Malcolm commanded, "the song of the Duncans."

The piper, who was also the bard and interpreter, stepped forward and began to blow on the pipes. A terrible wailing sound filled the air. The door to Jarvia's longhouse opened, and her personal maid and housekeeper, Morag, stepped onto the porch to stand beside her.

"Ah," Morag said with a sigh, "how delightful to hear the sound of the Highlands again."

Jarvia looked to see if Morag was jesting. She was not. A look of bliss on her face, the old woman had shut the door and was leaning against it.

" 'Tis a sound like none other."

"Aye, 'tis that," Jarvia said dryly.

"The Duncans' war song." Morag pushed away from the door and moved closer to her mistress.

Jarvia gave her a puzzled look.

"The song he's piping," the servant explained. " 'Tis the war song of Clan Duncan."

"Aye, you would know," Jarvia said. "Although you taught me to speak Gaelic, I sometimes forget you are a Highlander. You have been with us so long and speak our language so fluently, I think of you as a woman of Northland."

"But I am not." The old woman spoke reminiscently. "As a servant of the Southerlanders, I am known simply as Morag. To my people I was known as Morag nea Rogan."

"Morag daughter of Rogan," Jarvia murmured.

"Aye, and wife of Nuall. My father and my husband were Highland warriors." She paused, then added, " 'Twas a sad day nine summers ago when Wyborn and his Northmen sailed into our loch. Our men were away hunting, else the Northmen would not have captured us women and children and ambushed our men on their return."

The last wailing note of the bagpipes died, and a blood-curdling yell pierced the night air. Jarvia jumped. Chill bumps covered her body. She drew the shawl even more closely about her shoulders, as if seeking protection. The Highlanders were feared warriors, powerful men well versed in the skills of battle, who struck fear in their enemies with their war cries. No more than twelve men had yelled, yet the fearful sound seemed to have come from hundreds.

Morag patted Jarvia's arm. " 'Tis the Duncans' war cry."

"You Highlanders have no need to fight with weapons," Jarvia replied, "as long as you have the pipes, the lur, and that horrid war cry."

" 'Tis a fact." Morag chuckled and bobbed her head vigorously.

"My lord Malcolm," Wyborn said, "I invite you to share my home with me." He waved his hand toward the Great House. " 'Tis newly constructed with special sleeping chambers for privileged guests."

The Highlander nodded his acceptance.

"My people," the king said, "go home. Tonight I shall begin preparations for Princess Hilda's funeral. We shall gather tomorrow to mourn her death."

As Jarvia listened halfheartedly, the Highland warlord turned his head, and his gaze caught hers. Blatantly she continued to stare at him. She could not help it. She would not, could not look away. She lost herself in the mystery of his eyes. She was too far away to make out their color, but she felt their heat and intensity. Golden shadows flickered over his face but did not soften his rock-hard features.

When his mouth quirked at one corner, when he looked as if he might smile at her, as if he might walk toward her, Jarvia realized he must think her brazen. Heat flushed her face. She knew her curiosity could easily be mistaken for flirtation. She could not allow that. True, she was a widow—had been for one winter now—but already she was betrothed again. To be accused of flirting with a man would bring shame upon her name and that of her future husband.

To avoid trouble, she turned her head and pushed back into the shadows. Leaning against the exterior wall of the house, she tried to erase thoughts of the barbarian from her mind. Although she still felt the heat of his gaze, and wanted to look at him, she made herself stare straight ahead at the crowd that was breaking up in front of the king's house.

"Jarvia," a woman called.

She turned to see Gerda, her friend and one of queen Adelaide's slaves, pushing through the crowd.

"I had not anticipated visiting with you tonight," Jarvia said with a smile. "With the lord and lady entertaining the Highlander, I thought you would be needed in the Great House."

"Aye." Gerda pushed the hood off her head and brushed her fingers through her shorn red curls—a symbol of her slavery. "I would have come to see you no matter," she said, then added in a hushed voice, "Madelhari the Trader just returned from the kingdom of the Northern Scots. I overheard him talking about his journey with Lord Kirkja."

Kirkja was one of the most influential lords in Southerland, second only to Wyborn, the king. A strong leader and a just man, he was respected by the people of Southerland.

Gerda whispered, "From rumors Madelhari heard during his travels, he thinks the barbarian was so cruel to Hilda that she could no longer bear being his wife and killed herself. Or mayhap she was murdered. Madelhari also believes that Berowalt has either been taken prisoner or killed. That's why he is not here."

"What does Kirkja think?" Jarvia asked.

"He accused Madelhari of stirring up trouble and told him to keep such rumors to himself. He claimed they are false. In Kirkja's recent message from Berowalt nothing was said to give him the impression that anything was amiss. Certainly nothing to indicate that Hilda was contemplating suicide."

"Yet, 'tis odd Berowalt did not inform us of Hilda's death," Jarvia said. "And 'tis odd Berowalt is not here himself."

Malcolm was disappointed when the woman turned away from him, although he understood that for her to continue to stare so openly would have branded her a wanton. He was even more disappointed when the other women joined her.

He thoroughly liked women and had enjoyed looking at this one in particular. For a matron—and that is what the scarf she wore signified to the Southerlanders, or so Hilda had explained to him—she was quite brazen. For a moment she had blatantly returned his stare.

She fascinated him. She was beautiful and would be even more so without the scarf that completely covered her head and hair. He gazed at the few silver-blond tresses that escaped the binding to spill over her forehead and curl around her cheeks.

The brightly colored tapestry that hung from the eaves of the house behind her was a perfect foil for her beauty, and the light from the torches cast her in a soft golden glow. Like all the women of Southerland, she wore many layers of clothing, including a short pinafore over a long undertunic of sheer white material.

Embroidered with gold and silver floss and inset with precious jewels, the overdress sparkled in the torchlight. Rows of braid trimmed the bottom. The many layers of her dress enhanced the woman's tall, slender beauty and added to her ethereal appeal.

She lightly grazed her bottom lip with her teeth. It was a provocative gesture—and unconscious, Malcolm surmised. A breeze stirred strands of her hair and the sashes of her head scarf.

Malcolm's best friend, Lachlann, standing closest to him, leaned over to say, "I see you are fascinated by her, my friend, and I know your carnal thoughts. You had best control them."

Malcolm laughed softly and turned to look into Lachlann's twinkling brown eyes. "What am I fascinated with?"

"The silver-haired woman."

Malcolm returned his attention to the woman. "Mayhap I am thinking about the smaller woman, the one who recently joined her."

"Nay," Lachlann drawled. "You are letching for the silver-haired one."

"You know my preferences too well, my friend. And my thoughts before I even voice them."

"And you know mine," his comrade-in-arms said quietly.

"Aye, you are interested in the younger woman."

"She may not be for the taking," Lachlann said. "She stood behind the king and his lady-wife on the porch of the Great House."

"She may be a servant."

"Or she may be their kinswoman. Perhaps even your next bride."

"Aye," Malcolm said. "Perhaps she is a cousin."

"She is not to your liking?"

"I want a woman, not a child," he answered.

"You may not have a choice."

"Aye."

Malcolm's foster father, Fergus, was old, and it would soon be time to elect a new high king—an ard-righ. The Northern Scots, warriors accustomed to taking what they wanted by force, eschewed compromise, branding it cowardice. Malcolm disagreed with this philosophy. He believed that unity among the different kingdoms of the Highlands could be brought about by peaceful means, through negotiated alliances and marriage contracts. Because many chiefs of the various clans disagreed with Malcolm's philosophy of peace, they were not convinced that he should be elected king when his foster father died. They were ripe for rebellion.

The first step toward fulfilling Malcolm's dream of unity had been to establish an alliance between the Northern Scots and the Southerlanders. Once Malcolm had married Hilda, Ard-righ Fergus and the Council of the Chiefs had directed him—albeit reluctantly—to begin negotiations with the Northern Picts, a related Highland clan. So far the union between them had been more easily forged than the one between the Scots and the Southerlanders. The Scot and Pict languages were not identical, but each people spoke a Gaelic dialect, and they had many common cultural traits.

Unity among these three kingdoms of the northern Highlands would have been guaranteed by the birth of a son conceived between Hilda of the Southerlanders and Malcolm mac Duncan—who was half Pict and half Scot. This son, whom Malcolm would have taught to live and to govern in peace, would have ultimately ruled over all the northern Highland kingdoms.

Eventually Lachlann said, "Be wary, my friend. The

silver-haired one looks like an angel but may be as cold
as Hilda was."

"Possibly," Malcolm answered.

Hilda had also looked like an angel . . . and at first had
acted and spoken like one. But she had been a Lucifer,
a deceiver. If one judged all the people in Southerland
by her, they were all cold and disloyal . . . people without
honor.

"And she wears the scarf that signifies that she is married," Lachlann pointed out.

"Aye."

"But you are still interested?"

"Aye. This woman looks strong and sturdy of body. She
could bear strong sons."

"Do you mean bear *you* strong sons?"

Lachlann's words cut short Malcolm's imaginings. He
could not squander his time thinking about impossibilities.
As Lachlann had said, the choice of brides was not his
to make.

"Only if she is a royal offspring, one of Wyborn's blood
kin." Lachlann spoke softly. "That was *your* demand."

"Maybe this woman is a relative."

Lachlann shrugged.

"If she were," Malcolm said, speaking as much to himself as to his friend, "I would have heard about her from
Hilda."

Still Malcolm did not—could not—easily give up the
thought of having her. "I want this woman, Lachlann."

"Ah, Malcolm, that could present a problem."

"I did not say I could . . . or would . . . have her, merely
that I want her."

Lachlann shrugged. "Perhaps you can have her. Wyborn
fears an attack by his clansmen and is desperate for an alliance. Desperation will compel him to agree to almost any
bargain you drive. Make this woman part of the agreement.
Highland law allows you to have as many wives and as
many bedmates as you can provide for."

"So does the law of the Northmen." Malcolm smiled pensively. "But no matter how liberal the laws of the Northmen
might be, I doubt they allow a man to take another man's
wife."

Lachlann chuckled. "Probably not. Ah, Malcolm, whether she is angel or icemaiden, I wouldn't want her in my bed. One is too holy, the other too cold."

"I wouldn't want the angel," Malcolm said. "I fear I have too many sins to answer for to feel comfortable with such a heavenly being. But I would take great pleasure in lying with this maiden. I wager that beneath the frosty exterior lies pure fire."

Lachlann threw back his head and laughed. "Mayhap, my friend. Many a married woman is willing to play around if the prize is worth the risk. Perhaps she is one of them. Will you be wise and forgo finding out, or be foolish and lay a wager?"

"If I had time, I would lay the wager," Malcolm drawled, "but I cannot. My sojourn here must be brief and to the point. I have come to collect a bride."

"But I," Lachlann said, "did not travel here for a bride. I have ample time to discover the delights of this land."

Malcolm laughed. "That you do, and knowing you well, I have no doubt you will."

While he and Lachlann talked, wind spewed tiny sparks from a nearby torch against the woman's cheek. As she swatted the embers from her face, she turned her head. Again their gazes caught and held.

By all that was holy, Malcolm thought, the woman was beautiful! Again he was overwhelmed with desire for her.

Her long fingers splayed over the miniver that bordered the scooped neckline of her long tunic. She appeared so pristine and virginal. So cool and aloof. Malcolm understood why Lachlann thought she looked like an angel, but Northland sea raiders did not believe in angels. They believed in Valkyries.

Without being told, Malcolm knew this woman would not take a man to the serenity of heaven but would plunge him into the fiery passion of Valhalla. By all that was holy, he would willingly go with her.

Chapter 3

"'Tis like men—dastardly creatures that they are—to send a woman to do the deed." Morag followed her mistress down the Great Hall of the king's longhouse to the private sleeping chambers at the far end.

"Aye," Jarvia answered.

She glanced up through the smoke hole to see the star-studded sky and realized how tired she was. After two long days of heated argument, the Council of Justice had chosen a second bride for the barbarian. Although the choice was not to Jarvia's liking, she had no alternative but to deliver the message to the Highlander.

"I was a fool to say I had the wisdom to stand up to the Highland barbarian," she said. "It seems that the gods have allowed me to be captured in a trap of my own setting."

"Aye," Morag agreed, her pace slower than Jarvia's. "You've always had trouble with that tongue of yours, mistress. It goes into action much sooner than your mind, and one of these days it's going to land you in a heap of trouble."

Jarvia paused and held the soapstone lamp higher so that light spilled behind her to guide Morag's way.

"Your husband, my master, laughed when your tongue began to run out of control, mistress. Well, he could. He loved you and thought you could do no wrong. Now that he's dead, you must learn to be cautious. The king and queen hate you, but they accept you because the people have elected you to be law-speaker, the position once held by your husband."

Jarvia was grateful that her husband, Ein-her, had educated her by teaching her the reading and writing of the *futhark*, the letters of their language, and by making her his

19

apprentice. She had studied and memorized Norse law and through Ein-her's guidance had learned to lay down judgments accordingly. Many people thought that, like Ein-her, she had been blessed with great wisdom by the god Forsete. Otherwise, she would not have been elected law-speaker after her husband's death.

"Mayhap my tongue shall be responsible for landing me in trouble one of these days, Morag," she said, "but this night I do not accept the blame." She looked over her shoulder at Queen Adelaide, who sat beside the king on the High Seat at the other end of the Great Hall. "I blame that odious woman for this predicament. Truly she is descended from the jotuns."

"She is ugly and uncouth enough to be a frost god."

"Hideous and flabby fat," Jarvia muttered.

She let her gaze rove over the Great Hall. Long benches ran the length of the building. Fitted with thick cushions for comfort and decorated with colorful, embroidered furniture covers, they were placed so the men could be closer to the fire and to the High Seat of the king. Servants scurried back and forth from the kitchen to the scullery and finally into the Great Hall, carrying trays laden with food and pitchers of ale. The *langeldar*, the great fire, blazed in an oblong stone hearth in the center of the hall.

Flames leaped into the air to cast dancing shadows on walls draped with brightly colored and embroidered tapestries; light gleamed on the gold-and-silver gilt shields that hung overlapping to form a border around the room.

The aroma of freshly cooked meat permeated the *stofa*, the house, to remind Jarvia that it had been a long time since she had broken her fast at early morn. Atop slender metal rods lying across the fire, wild boar steaks braised on flat round pans with long metal handles. On raised spits roasted hares, legs of mutton and deer, hams and pork roasts, beef, and wild birds. Two huge cauldrons filled with veal stew, seasoned with cumin, juniper, mustard seed, and garlic, were suspended by chains from the ceiling beam over the *langeldar*.

The heat of the fires, aided by the warmth provided by tankards of ale, dispelled the chill of spring and the dampness of the storm.

"The king and the council have already begun to celebrate the marriage," Morag mumbled. "They believe it is time for the banquet."

Jarvia nodded. Yet the most important matter—the barbarian's acceptance of the bride the Council of Justice had chosen for him—had to be settled before the banquet could begin.

"I fear the king and council are making a dreadful mistake," Jarvia said. She resumed walking, slower this time so that Morag could keep up with her.

"Aye, mistress, so do I."

Loneliness swept over Jarvia. "I wish Ein-her were here. He would know what to do."

"He always did," Morag agreed. "He was a wise man, the only one who could handle Wyborn. You are fortunate, mistress, that you were married to such a man as Ein-her, else your lot might be similar to Hilda's. You might even now be a candidate for the Highlander's bride."

"Aye," she said, then added, "I loved Ein-her."

"He loved you," the old servant said. "You brought him great happiness in the final winters of his life. I'm glad that even in death the master protected you from King Wyborn by stipulating the length of your mourning and betrothing you to his distant kinsman."

"Aye," Jarvia said.

Her thoughts ran to the man to whom she had been betrothed by proxy, Lord Michael Langssonn. Many of the warriors of Southerland, Wyborn among them, laughed and mocked the Northland warrior because he was educated and loved to draw maps of the lands he visited when he went a-viking. But Ein-her had respected Michael and had spoken highly of him.

"King Wyborn and his queen can no longer harm you," Morag said, cutting into Jarvia's thoughts. "Your destiny lies in your own hands."

"We must never underestimate the king." A shiver of fear ran through Jarvia. "No one knows better than I how deceitful he and his lady are, or to what lengths they will go to get what they want."

By now the two women had traversed the full length of the dining hall and entered a small alcove into which opened two doors, one on the right, another on the left. One room belonged to the king and his wife; the other was the sleeping chamber set aside for the king's guests. Such private rooms were rare and attested to the king's wealth. The villagers always knew how important the guest was by his lodgings. If he slept in the special chamber, he was most important indeed.

This is where the barbarian, Malcolm mac Duncan, slept.

Jarvia and Morag stopped in front of the elaborately carved door. Jarvia took a deep breath. Now she would see what her spine was made of, iron that went into the best of weapons or blemished clay that was discarded in the midden pit.

Holding the lamp closer to the door, she glanced at her reflection in the polished bronze panel and wished she had time to retie her scarf and to put fresh cosmetic coloring and powder on her face. She looked over her shoulder one last time to see King Wyborn and the men of the council raising their tankards in yet another toast.

Queen Adelaide, one hand curled around the armrest of her chair, the other hooked around a large drinking horn, looked in Jarvia's direction and smiled maliciously.

Jarvia despised the woman and thought it was much too early for them all to be celebrating. The barbarian had not even heard their proposal, much less accepted it. Yet as much as Jarvia hated their behavior—the drinking and the obnoxious jests shared among the menfolks—she would much prefer to be with them than to confront the Highland warlord.

She believed, as did the council, that her tidings would bring the full measure of his wrath down upon the messenger. The cowardly lot. That was another reason she had been chosen to announce the identity of his next wife.

"Go ahead, mistress." Morag gouged her elbow into Jarvia's side and inclined her head toward the door. "Let us do the deed so we may go home."

Taking a deep breath, Jarvia raised her hand and knocked. On the other side of the door, she heard the creak of the bed, then the sound of firm footfalls on the planked floor. The wrought iron handle rose and the bar rasped, metal abrading wood as it slipped out of place.

Through the door she heard an impatient voice say in Gaelic, "It is about time."

The door opened.

"I wondered if the king forgot his promise to—" His words were abruptly cut off.

Jarvia looked squarely at a broad, naked chest with springy dark curls and clearly defined muscles. Her gaze lowered to the leathern girdle that secured his trousers at his waist. Planted on the floor were two large feet covered in leathern boots—or *cuarans*, as the Highlanders called them.

"Lord Malcolm," she said.

"Aye."

Slowly she raised her head to look into the barbarian's face. Although she had seen him first at his and Hilda's wedding, and several times during the past two days, Jarvia felt now as if she were seeing him for the first time. His rugged face was shadowed by a day's growth of beard and framed by hair as black as Odin's ravens. She watched surprise replace his scowl.

"The silver-haired woman."

She was completely captivated by the barbarian's eyes. They were vibrant and alive, a living breathing blue. The bluest eyes she had ever seen.

They were the color of the village loch, deep and fathomless. She wondered if they were as indicative of danger. One moment the loch could be calm and beguiling, the next as tempestuous as a raging storm.

Was the barbarian like that? If so, Jarvia did not mind. She was not one whose head was turned easily. Yet she found herself drowning in the barbarian's eyes. She felt as if she were swooning, as if in an eye's blink she would be prostrate at his feet.

Morag looked strangely at Jarvia, curtsied, and said briskly in Gaelic, "My lord, my lady—"

"You speak my language, old woman?"

"Aye, I do, my lord. My family and I are Scots. We were taken prisoners when the Northmen colonized this village nine summers past. I became servant to Ein-her, the law-speaker and husband to Lady Jarvia." Morag stepped aside. "My mistress, Lady Jarvia."

"Lady Jarvia," he repeated, his voice deep, his brogue rich and lazy.

Jarvia enjoyed hearing him say her name. He caught her hand and raised it to his mouth, his lips brushing softly against her skin. All this time she looked into Malcolm's eyes. Like his voice, they were rich and lazy and seductive.

Fleetingly she wondered if Hilda had submitted to the seduction of these eyes. How many other women had?

How many enemies had Malcolm mac Duncan lured into traps with his deceptive eyes and beguiling voice?

Hilda perhaps, but not her, Jarvia vowed.

He turned to Morag. "How may I be of help to the Lady Jarvia?"

Jarvia moved forward to say softly in Gaelic, "You may speak directly to me, sire."

He raised a brow. "You, too, speak Gaelic?"

"Aye, lord," Morag answered proudly. "I taught her myself. She, the master, and I used to converse frequently in my native language."

His eyes were for Jarvia only. "I am pleased, lady."

"The council thought you might be," Jarvia said. "That's one of the reasons why they sent me to you."

"May I inquire what the other reasons were?"

"That would be best explained in the privacy of your room." Jarvia spoke in her best official tone. She would make her people proud that they had elected her to such a worthy position.

The news she had to tell him was delicate. She certainly did not wish him to pitch a raging fit in full view of the entire council. Mayhap she could control his reaction better in a small private room.

He smiled; his eyes shimmered. "That is good, madam."

He stepped aside. Only then did Jarvia look into the room to see the bed. There was a slight indentation on one side of the mattress as if someone—probably he—had been lying there. Quickly she averted her head, her gaze going to his clothes that lay atop a large chest at the foot of the bed.

The intimacy of the room, the friendliness of the man, undermined Jarvia's resolve. Mayhap she could control his reaction, but what about her own? She had not expected her emotions to run truant.

Flames from the cauldron lamp standing close by illuminated his clothes—the red-and-yellow plaid mantle, the colors brilliant and alive like him; his smock, woven from a brightly colored twill fabric, striped and trimmed with braid. Next to it lay his linen shirt. His tan leathern gloves. His gold helmet. Several gold brooches. The gold torque was a subtle reminder that he was a Highland prince.

"Let me set this down for you, lady." Jarvia started when Malcolm took the lamp from her.

He went to a table set against the far wall and placed the lamp beside a serving dish filled with dried fruit and nuts. Next to this was a canister of honey and a vase of flowers. Their fragrance mingled with the scents of fruit and nuts.

Malcolm returned, caught her hand, and led her into his room. He closed the door behind her, shutting Morag out in the hallway. The bar slipped into place. Palpable silence followed. Jarvia was alone with the half-dressed barbarian in his sleeping chamber.

"My—my maid," Jarvia said.

"We have no need of her, madam."

He moved to stand mere inches in front of her. When his breath fanned her cheeks, she realized exactly how big he was, how daunting, how overpowering. Although she was taller than many of the women in the village, this man dwarfed her.

She sidestepped and mentally chided herself. She was the law-speaker and a matron, not an impressionable young girl seeing a half-dressed warrior for the first time. She was here for one reason and one reason only. She had a message to deliver to the barbarian.

"Are you . . . are you finding us hospitable, lord?"

"Aye, madam, most hospitable." His gaze moved slowly over her face, down her shoulders to rest on her cleavage. "Beyond my expectations."

Although she was fully clothed, the barbarian's gaze disturbed her. It was much too direct. She deliberately looked away and concentrated on the room, on the bed with its mussed eiderdown covering and head cushions.

The bed made Jarvia remember something else Hilda had told her about Malcolm, two springs ago when Jarvia had visited with her in the Scottish Highlands. "He is an animal with a carnal appetite that is insatiable. You would not believe the things he expects me to perform to satisfy his letching."

"Does my room meet with your approval, madam?"

A tone in his voice caused her to look at him. A lazy smile still curved his lips, but his eyes were filled with . . . amusement. Yet he did not mock her; rather he enticed her.

"I did not mean to stare," Jarvia apologized. She quickly averted her gaze from the bed to the decorated chairs on either side of the table. " 'Tis my first chance to see the guest chamber."

"It is well furnished, lady, and truly suited for a king. For comfort, the bed far surpasses any I have ever slept on."

Although the conversation was innocent, Jarvia felt as if the Highlander spoke on a more provocative level. At the moment he did not seem at all the dark, brooding man she had supposed him to be.

"Lord, I have been sent here to—"

He raised a hand. "Let's not rush, lady. Surely the news will wait a moment."

Surprised, her mouth yet open, she watched the High-lander go to the table. He reached into the serving dish to select a dried plum from which the seed had already been extracted.

"Would you care for some refreshments?" he asked.

"No, thank you."

"Pardon me if I indulge myself, madam. I find this most tempting."

Lifting the lid of the honey canister, he dipped the plum into it. Never had food looked so inviting to Jarvia, so shamefully desirable.

He opened his mouth and took the piece of fruit into it. His tongue wrapped around it. Honey droplets glistened on his lips. She watched the tip of his tongue devour even those. She had never known that the eating of food could be so visually fascinating. She could almost taste the sweetness on her lips.

He chewed slowly, thoroughly, and swallowed. Then he licked the tip of a finger. "This is delicious, lady." Again he settled his gaze on her. "I insist that you share one with me."

He picked up a second plum and dipped it into the honey jar. He cradled the delicacy with one hand as he moved to stand before her. As if in a daze, she reached for it, but he shook his head.

"It is sticky, lady. Let me." He held out the fruit.

Acutely aware of him, she opened her mouth and received the plum into it. She closed her lips. His fingers lightly brushed them as he released the fruit.

Although it was an inadvertent caress, his touch sent sparks of pleasure throughout her body. The feeling intensified when he raised his hand to his lips and licked honey from the fingers that so recently had been in her mouth. Unable to look away from him, Jarvia chewed the plum, feeling as if she were trapped in a sweet web of magic. He held her entranced.

Malcolm mac Duncan's eyes were for her alone. Even if she had been standing with hundreds of other women and this man spoke to her, if he looked at her, his gaze would have been for her and her alone.

He caught her hand and ran his finger around the gold band on her third finger. "You are married?"

The question disconcerted her. "I was."

His touch, not meant to be provocative, also disconcerted her. Shards of fire leaped through her body.

"My husband died one winter past."

"My condolences, madam."

"Thank you, lord."

"You wear the ring of marriage and the head scarf."

"We are allowed to do so, lord, until our mourning period is ended."

"I thought perhaps your heart was still heavy with grief over the death of your husband."

"I loved my husband greatly, lord, but he was ill. Life had become too painful for him to want it to continue. I am past the time of deepest sorrow. If my period of mourning had not been legally stipulated by my husband,

I am sure the council would have demanded that I remarry immediately."

Malcolm's eyes sparked with an undefinable emotion. "I am grateful that the council sent you to me tonight, lady. While I expected to enjoy a succulent feast with the king and his lady, I never expected the added pleasure of your company."

"Thank you, lord."

He stepped closer. "Your scarf, madam, is made of a beautiful and delicate fabric. It is quite lovely, but it covers far too much." He caught the ends and rubbed them between his thumb and index finger.

" 'Tis silk. We bartered for it," Jarvia said, surprised and pleased that he had noticed.

He tugged and the knot slipped free. The scarf fluttered to the floor. His action jolted her back to reality, back to why she was there.

Before she could voice a protest, he spoke. "Pardon." Bending, he retrieved the scarf. He straightened, but did not immediately release it to her. "Your hair, madam, is the color of pure silver, more delicate and infinitely more beautiful than the scarf."

Much to her chagrin, Jarvia's entire body burned with sheer pleasure. She did not understand the conflicting emotions that assaulted her. On the one hand, she distrusted this Malcolm mac Duncan, who might have driven Hilda to take her own life. On the other, she reveled in the sensations he aroused in her.

She must be wary of the man. He was cunning and crafty. He knew how to deceive and to entice. And she must not be lured into a trap of his setting.

He returned the scarf to her and walked to the chest at the end of the bed, where he unfastened the first buckle of his girdle.

"Lord, it is past time for us—"

"Aye, madam, I agree."

The leather fell open to reveal his lower abdomen. Flat, taut muscle glimmered in the lamplight. Hastily Jarvia averted her gaze, only to encounter his scabbard, his knife . . .

"Lord," she began, puzzled by his actions, "if you must undress now, I shall quit myself and wait in the hall."

Undoing the second buckle, Malcolm gave a self-satisfied smile. "Are you shy, madam?"

"Nay, lord, but I am modest."

"Shall I extinguish the lamps?"

Her confusion growing, she shook her head and backed away. "Nay, I shall . . . I shall wait in the hall while you change your clothes."

His hands ceased their movements. "I was not changing clothes, lady. I was taking them off."

Dumbstruck, Jarvia stared at him.

"Madam, I am confused." His black brows drew together. "Did you not come here to wench with me?"

Chapter 4

The wallop of a cudgel to the side of the head could not have rendered Jarvia more senseless. Thoughts completely vanished as she looked into his darkly handsome face.

"Well, madam?"

"Nay, lord." Her voice was a croak. She swallowed as she composed herself. "I was . . . sent here to discuss your second bride."

He stared at her.

She wished he would refasten his girdle.

Finally he said, "I beg your pardon, madam."

"I—I tried to speak to you, lord, but you—"

She fell silent at the realization that she had not tried very hard. Instead she had succumbed to his wiles.

His hands still rested on the parted leathern garment. His countenance was growing darker.

"A woman comes to a man's bedchamber for one purpose, lady." His voice was abrasive with irritability. "All facts led me to this conclusion. Your council had promised me female entertainment; they sent you to me. You were in a rush to be secluded inside my sleeping chamber with me. You are not an innocent. And, madam, for a modest matron, for one who likes to talk about propriety, you spoke openly about intimate subjects, as would a man. I assumed you were here to give me carnal pleasure."

Jarvia felt as if her face were on fire. She turned slightly so that she was looking at the bouquet of flowers on the table rather than at him. "Considering your argument, lord, I can imagine how immodest my visit must seem."

He sighed. She heard the dull clink of metal against metal as he refastened the latchets of his girdle.

"You may look at me, madam," he said. "I am as fully clothed as I was when you entered the room."

She turned to see the warlord standing beside the cauldron lamp at the foot of the bed. The light emphasized his still-naked chest and shoulders. He walked over to the table, picked up a funnel-shaped glass beaker—a trading item reserved for the most distinguished guests—and filled it with ale.

"Why did your council send you to discuss my bride? Was no man willing to do the task?"

"The king was willing, sire, but the council did not think it would be fitting for him to do so. They chose me because I am the law-speaker and because I can converse in your language."

Taking a swallow of ale, Malcolm seated himself in the chair, stretched his long legs out, and looked at her. "Make haste and speak, lady."

His voice had hardened, as had his features. His eyes no longer twinkled. Perhaps now she was seeing the warlord that Hilda had described to her, the man she had feared.

"As I said, lord, we have chosen a wife for you."

He took another swallow of ale, holding the beverage in his mouth as if savoring the taste before he swallowed. "A *native woman* of King Wyborn?"

"Aye, lord, so the king says."

His eyes fastened to the rim of his beaker, Malcolm murmured, "It would not be you, mayhap?"

"Nay, lord, it is not I."

In one long drag he finished off the ale.

"The king openly claims another as his bastard daughter," she said.

"A bastard daughter!" Quick, smooth motion brought him to his feet.

Jarvia added, "The council has also recognized her as such, but to insure her birthright the king is going to adopt her."

The beaker landed on the floor with a dull clang. He glared at her. "Adoption!"

His eyes glittered cold and hard like iron; his jaw tensed. He flexed his hands. "The entire lot of you think to play me the fool, madam!"

Not the lot of us, Jarvia thought. *Only King Wyborn.*

"Nay, lord." She backed away from his angry gaze. "We—we have a law that allows us to recognize bastard children as our legitimate heirs. It also allows a married couple to adopt a child. If the ceremony is carried out correctly, the adopted child is accepted as family. The same blood that flows through the parents' bodies is considered to flow through the child's."

"I want a wife now." His fist came down on the table, the dishes rattling from the impact. Ale sloshed out of the pitcher and beaded on the linen covering. He stepped closer and demanded in a hard voice, "Is this child of marriageable age?"

Trembling, Jarvia remained where she was with effort. "The child whom King Wyborn intends to adopt, sire, is a woman who has seen ten-and-six winters."

"Christ and him crucified!" he swore. "The one who stood on the porch with you night before last? The small one dwarfed by the hood and cloak?"

Jarvia nodded.

"She is hardly more than a child, madam."

"She is a woman, lord."

The Highlander's anger filled the room. It was not directed toward Jarvia herself, but she was frightened nonetheless. She wished now that she was not locked tightly in this small space with him. The more she was around this man, the more she understood Hilda's fear of him. His moods vacillated, taking her unawares. One moment he was teasing and warm, the next angry and implacable.

"I am a hardened warrior of thirty winters, madam, not a laddie who has yet to earn his sword. I need a woman."

He curled his hand into a fist. The muscles in his arm bulged. He did not touch her, did not threaten to, yet she felt the power in his hand.

"If you will give Gerda—"

A black brow rose in question.

"Gerda, lord. The—the woman we are talking about."

As if he were a caged beast, he began to prowl the room.

"Give her time, sire. She will learn the ways of a woman. It will be your pleasure to teach her."

He rounded on her. His hard eyes gazed into hers. "I have not the time or the patience to teach her. Christ's blood! The last thing I need is a child cowering fearfully in my bed."

Jarvia rubbed a moist palm down the side of her dress.

"Lord . . . lord, if you were not so easily provoked, mayhap women would not cower . . . in . . . your . . . bed."

"Women!" Softly he spoke the word as he crossed his arms over his massive chest, rocked back on his heels, and stared at her. "What makes you think *women* cower in my bed?"

His low tone did not fool Jarvia. Her entire body trembled with fear.

"What do you know about the intimacies of my life that you can speak so?"

Jarvia swallowed.

"I await an answer."

"I was a close friend to your wife."

He lowered his lids until she saw only a slit of iron-gray color. "She gave you such insight into my private life?"

Jarvia shook her head. "When I visited with her two springs last—"

"When I was away hunting to the south?"

Jarvia nodded.

"What did my wife say that made you think she cowered in my bed?"

Jarvia could not speak. "Lord, I—I—"

He closed the distance between them. His fingers bit into the tender flesh of her upper arms. "Answer me, madam."

"She—she told me that you frightened her. I saw the marks where she had been beaten."

Jarvia cried aloud as his grip tightened.

" 'Tis said"—she gasped and blinked against the pain that shot up her arms—"that fear of you drove Hilda to take her own life."

Thick black lashes swept down to cover his eyes. When he lifted his lids again, his eyes were devoid of emotion. Abruptly he released her. She stumbled back from him.

"Most of the time, madam, rumors are rooted in the truth."

He made no attempt to refute her accusation.

She rubbed her arms.

"You believe this," he said, "yet still you encourage me to marry this woman . . . this child?"

" 'Tis the king and the council who encourage, lord. 'Tis they who compelled me to bring such tidings to you. Such is my duty as law-speaker."

His mouth twisted sardonically. "What if I drive this child-woman to take her life, lady?"

"The council cares not. She is a woman and a slave—"

"*A slave?*" He bellowed the words.

His black brows pulled together. His blue eyes burned like fire. His voice softened ominously. "The bastard your king wants me to take to wife, madam, is also a slave?"

Unable to speak, Jarvia nodded, then shook her head.

"Lady, do you know that wars have begun over smaller insults than this?"

She nodded. He moved closer. Her palms grew clammy.

"Please, lady, explain."

Jarvia swallowed and drew a deep breath. "She-she was a slave, sire. A dedicated and loyal—"

"Get to the heart of the matter," he shouted.

"She—she is to be freed, and adopted by the king and queen."

A nasty smile twisted his lips. "I am sure, lady, that the king and his wife love her like a daughter."

Jarvia wiped her hands down her skirt. "She is . . . he says she is his bastard daughter."

"Aye, a bastard daughter that no one knew about until this day?" He glared at her. "Do all of you think I am dim-witted?"

"Nay." Jarvia's voice was hardly more than a whisper. "Like all of us, lord, Gerda must do as the king and the council command."

"Are you afraid of me, lady?"

She glanced down at her arm, her gaze lingering on the reddened imprint of his hand.

"Aye, lord. You are fearsome, and you bellow like a bull."

She looked up to find him also staring at her arm.

"Am I so fearsome that you would kill yourself and your unborn babe?"

As if she were a cauldron lamp receiving oil, Jarvia felt resolve flow through her. "I give no person that power over me."

He walked to the chest at the foot of the bed and picked up his shirt.

"I do fear for Gerda, sire," Jarvia added. "As you said, she is a tender woman—"

"Ofttimes, lady, slaves are a calloused lot."

"Not this one, lord."

"I will discuss this matter with your king."

"Since this marriage affects the entire kingdom of Southerland, sire, it is no longer a matter for the king alone to decide. If you wish to discuss it, you must speak to the Council of Justice."

"Then, madam," he said impatiently, "I will speak to your Council of Justice."

He dropped the shirt over his head. "You are indeed a spirited woman."

"Aye, I have been accused of that many times, lord."

His arms raised, the shirt bunched around his shoulders, his tousled head poking through the neck opening, he stared at her. A lock of unruly hair fell across his forehead. He straightened his arms, and the garment slipped down his torso.

After he tucked it into his trousers, he moved his jewelry about on his chest, pulling his shirt taut across his back and making Jarvia all the more aware of his muscles. He reached for a small gold ring, which he slid onto the little finger of his right hand.

"I pity the next man you marry," he said.

"Why? My intended is a strong man, well able to handle a spirited woman like me."

Malcolm turned. "You are spoken for?"

"I am betrothed to a warrior of the Northland. When my mourning is completed, he and I are to be wed."

"Why not to a man here?"

The barbarian was being quite personal in his questioning, but Jarvia did not mind. Now that she had stated her business, now that he understood her purpose in coming, she saw no reason to hide the truth.

"My dying husband arranged this marriage for me."

Malcolm nodded. "What do you think of this warrior to whom you are betrothed?"

"I have never seen my intended," she said. "He has been a-viking for three winters past. He is a kinsman to my husband, and we were betrothed by proxy. My husband chose him for my second husband, and I trusted Ein-her's judgment."

Malcolm nodded. "Your husband was a wise man, lady, to provide for your welfare after his death and to keep his estate within his clan."

He slipped an armband around his left wrist. "How long do the people of the Northland mourn the death of their mates?"

"My mourning period is for two more winters, sire . . . so stipulated by vote of our council." She paused. "Were you speaking one question but asking another?"

He lifted his head to gaze at her, admiration gleaming in his eyes. "You are astute as well as bold, madam."

Jarvia smiled at his praise.

"I truly wanted to know how soon you plan to wed this Northman."

"That, lord, is none of your concern."

"True," he agreed, "but it is of interest to me. You, Lady Jarvia, are of interest to me."

His gaze moved over her shoulders to linger on the upper swell of her breasts revealed by the low neckline.

"I am of interest to most men," she said, "and have been since my husband died and I became a woman of property. Otherwise, they would have nothing to do with me because I have seen many winters, lord, and my childbearing days are quickly coming to an end."

"How many winters have you seen?"

"Twenty-and-five."

"And you have born no children during this time?"

Jarvia shook her head.

Picking up a brooch, he walked to the alcove on the wall beside the door. Next to it was a small wrought iron rod on which hung a drying cloth. Pushing aside the curtain, he revealed a small washing station. A basin and ewer occupied the bottom shelf; above that, a bronze mirror hung on the wall. A soapstone lamp was suspended from the ceiling. Looking in the mirror, he worked to fasten the shoulder placket of his shirt.

"Aye, madam, I can understand—" He caught both of the small loops on either side of the placket with one hand and held the brooch with the other, but he could not thread the pin through them.

"Hell's fire and brimstone!" he muttered.

Amused, Jarvia smiled. "You were saying, lord?"

"I can understand a man's not wanting to take you to wife." A second time he secured one loop but missed the other one. A second time he swore, the words more emphatic. "The law of life . . . of survival . . . demands that a man sire sons. Especially a king. He *must* have a son to bind him to the land and to his people. The cycle of life must be fulfilled for all men. Most surely the cycle of sovereignty must be fulfilled for the king."

Still frowning, he made a third attempt to secure the shoulder placket. "Lady, why on earth do seamstresses design clothing that is so difficult to fasten? It is not enough that I must wear three brooches on my shoulder, but I must thread this pin through these tiny loops."

"Once you have fastened it, lord, you will be most stylish, and the brooches do testify to your wealth and position."

His frown deepened. "Lady, cease prattling and fasten my shirt."

"Nay, lord, I must return to the Great Hall," she said. "I shall summon a servant to help you."

Her scarf in hand, she moved to the door and lifted the wrought iron handle. But before she could leave, Malcolm said, "The longer I must await a servant, lady, the longer your council must await my answer."

His soft, beguiling voice stopped her. Their shoulders almost touched, but she did not look at him. She must not let him seduce her senses again. Truly the man was more practiced in this art than she.

She wanted to be away from him. He did strange things to her, aroused sensations she had never experienced. While she was attracted to him, she was also frightened. Hilda's warning haunted her. As law-speaker, she kept reminding herself, she had a duty to the people of Southerland. She must persuade this warlord to marry Gerda.

That was her duty.

"Turn toward me, sire."

This was her preference.

She laid down her scarf and caught two of the small loops in one hand. With the other she rubbed out the wrinkles. She liked the feel of his warm, firm flesh beneath her palm.

"A new alliance would be good for your people and mine," she said.

"Better for your people than mine."

She leaned around him to pick up the brooch he had lain down. Inadvertently her breasts brushed against his chest. As if she had touched one of the heating stones at the fire pit, she pulled away. Feeling his gaze on her breasts she slowly looked up to encounter his knowing smile. The man intrigued her, unsettled her. She jabbed the brooch latchet through the linsey-woolsey.

"Ouch!" He scowled. "The purpose, lady, is to puncture the material, not me."

"I apologize, lord." Jarvia had difficulty suppressing a smile. She reached for the second brooch.

"Does this woman whom you and your Council of Justice offer to me have any other qualities that would endear her to me?" he asked.

"She is small and beautiful."

"I care not for small women."

This pleased Jarvia. She locked the pin in place on the second brooch.

"She is highly intelligent."

She held the third brooch over his shoulder.

"I am more interested in the condition of her womb, madam, than in her intellect."

Jarvia intentionally jabbed the pin into his flesh.

"Lady," he barked, "did I not—"

"Did I hurt you, lord?" she said with feigned sweetness.

A moment of silence was followed by soft laughter. "Methinks, lady, you are mocking me."

"Lord, your accusation wounds me."

"Aye, I feel certain it does," he answered dryly, yet laughter lingered in his eyes.

Jarvia smiled. "Gerda will be a good wife for you, a good mother for your children."

"She sounds like a woman of impeccable virtue," Malcolm said, his tone a little bored.

"Indeed she is," Jarvia agreed. "The very woman you need, lord."

As if the warlord were her husband, she reached up to brush a hand over his shoulder, to make sure the placket was neatly secured.

"I pray, lord, extend her a little patience and gentleness, and she will be a good, obedient wife."

Jarvia reached behind his neck to straighten the neckline of the shirt. Her hand brushed against his hair; it was thick and silky and soft. His quick intake of breath alerted her to what she was doing. She jerked her hand away, but he caught it.

"I enjoy your touch, lady."

His hand wrapped around hers and held it against his neck. She felt the warmth and texture of his skin, the strength of his muscles, the pulsing life within him.

"I would have you touch more of me."

Looking into his face, the dark brooding face that was so near hers, Jarvia yanked her hand from beneath his and stepped back. This was Malcolm mac Duncan, not Ein-her. This was the lord of fire, and he had singed her. In another second he would have burned her.

"I touched you, lord, without thought. I apologize."

"Mayhap one day, lady, you will do so . . . with thought."

Jarvia took another step backward. "Lord, promise me that you won't hurt Gerda. You have the reputation of being a . . . a—" she drew in a deep breath—"of being a lusty warrior."

Again Malcolm's soft laughter echoed through the room; again the sound caressed Jarvia.

"I am glad I am considered lusty, madam, but I am hardly a warrior in bed. Again I think perhaps you have gotten your tales twisted. Mayhap you heard that I am a lusty lover."

Jarvia's cheeks burned. Although she had been married, had discussed such subjects openly with her husband, discussing them with Malcolm mac Duncan unnerved her.

"My lord, please promise me that you will marry Gerda and that you will treat her kindly, that she will have no cause to fear you . . . unduly."

His features suddenly seemed set in stone; his eyes turned the color of molten iron. "Madam, I owe you no explanation."

"I care for her, lord, as if she were my own sister."

"Why so?"

"She has been in my keeping since she was a wee babe. When my husband bought my freedom so that he could wed me, he also offered for Gerda, but the king would not sell her. Even so we have remained close."

Malcolm's expression did not soften, but his voice did. "According to the law of the Highlands, an *unfaithful*, *unkind*, or even *careless* husband is looked upon as a monster and is treated as such. I was not unfaithful, unkind, or careless in regards to my wife, Hilda. I cannot and will not be blamed for her death. I refuse to feel guilty because she took her own life. I do feel rage and anger, madam, that she denied me a son."

Abruptly he turned and, picking up his torque, went to the mirror, where he slipped it about his neck, situating the terminuses at the front. Lamplight shone on the warrior; it glinted on the gold band around his neck.

Fire, Jarvia thought. Ever-living fire. The Highlands warlord was one with the flames. Even his neck ring was symbolic of fire. *Lord of fire!*

Malcolm picked up a comb and raked it through his hair several times, but always an unruly lock fell across his forehead. He strode to the trunk to pick up tan gloves. He slid his left hand in first, and finger by finger smoothed out the soft leather. Only when the second one was on did he look up at her.

"You wish to extract a promise from me, madam? A promise that I shall treat the child tenderly?"

She nodded.

"Do you know that in my country all promises require a promise in return? Are you willing to grant such?"

The way he looked at Jarvia caused an ache to thr deeply within her. "What would that be?" Her voice sounded wispy.

"Law declares I must have a first wife to be the lady of my home and the mother of my children. If I should choose this woman for that position, will you agree to become my second wife?"

Chapter 5

"Your second wife!"

"Aye." His gaze never wavered from hers. "I find you highly attractive, Lady Jarvia, and would like you to share my bed."

"You insult me, my lord. You make such an offer knowing that I am already betrothed."

"Betrothals can be honorably ruptured, madam, as well you know." He stepped closer to her, his blue eyes peering intently into her face. "I would insult you if I did not offer the honor of marriage, yet I make this offer knowing full well that you are not Wyborn's kinswoman and may never give me sons. After you have had time to consider, I am sure you will see that my proposal is generous."

"Sons!" Jarvia's eyes smarted with angry tears. Her anger at life's injustices boiled over. "Is that all a woman means to you?" While Jarvia longed for a home and family, she also longed to be wanted and loved for herself . . . as Ein-her had done.

She stared at the barbarian. "I will not marry you under any circumstances, and never . . . *never* will I bear you a child."

Jarvia turned and caught the door handle. Her anger was directed not just toward the barbarian but also at herself. She was so angry that she lost her composure. She had spent her entire life learning to hide her emotions so that others could not use them to their advantage. Yet this barbarian, this man whom she should despise, considering that he might have forced Hilda to take her own life, had managed in a few minutes to make Jarvia lose control. Hot, angry tears spilled down her cheeks.

The bar on the door grated against wood and metal. A big, callused hand covered hers.

"Nay, mistress."

The Highlander was so close she felt the touch of his breath against her neck, as warm and soft as a caress. His body surrounded hers, yet he touched nothing but her hand.

"Let me go, sire."

"I spoke the truth, lady, when I said I meant you no insult."

He caught her shoulders and turned her to face him. She was acutely aware of his hands on her flesh, of his strength, his warmth, the power of life that emanated from him. Yet he did not hurt her. Embarrassed that he should see the effect he had on her, humiliated that she responded to his every touch, she struggled to escape him.

"Cease fighting, lady," he said quietly.

His arms completely enveloped her, locking her hands between them. Her palms and cheek rested against his chest. She heard the beating of his heart, only slightly fast to indicate that he had exerted little effort to quell her struggle.

"Please unhand me, lord, and distance yourself," Jarvia said. "I am a lady of quality, not one to be trifled with."

He tucked his hand under her chin and raised her face so that she was forced to look at him. With his thumb he smoothed a tear from her cheek. His somber eyes pierced hers.

"You are a lady of quality, but I like trifling with you. I enjoy holding you. For a verity, you are a large woman—"

Jarvia gasped. His soft chuckle wrapped itself around her senses. She stiffened against him.

"But," he added softly, "methinks you are a delightful armful, delicate despite your size."

Jarvia shoved back in his arms so forcefully that one of the combs loosened from her coiled hair. Tresses tumbled about her face and shoulders, yet still she was unable to free herself from his embrace.

"Compose yourself, madam, and I will let you go. Already your people have branded me a murderer. I do not want them to think I despoiled you."

He reached behind Jarvia, and she felt the brush of soft material on her back and shoulders. She felt it on her cheeks as he blotted the rest of her tears with a cloth.

"I am a warrior, madam, not a gentle man, not one who is content to sit in his Great House and feast and entertain with tales of bravery of bygone years. I also speak what I think, what I believe. I assumed you were the same."

"Lord Malcolm," Jarvia said, "we have addressed all that I wish to discuss, all that I was sent to discuss."

He held her firmly but not roughly. "But we have only begun to address that which *I* wish to discuss."

"Unhand me!"

Moving one arm, he threaded his fingers through her hair. "I find you attractive and would greatly enjoy sleeping with you. I believe you feel the same way about me."

Again Jarvia trembled, from anger at herself because she could not help but respond to his touch, his voice, his scent.

"Lord Malcolm—" She placed both palms against his chest and pushed, finally freeing herself. "I came here because of my duty to my people. I have no kind feelings for you whatsoever."

"I want not kindness, madam," he said softly. "I can get that from grandmothers and children. What I want from you is the passion shared between a man and a woman when they mate."

Composed now, Jarvia could more easily evaluate her feelings, more readily put her thoughts into words. "All people experience this passion you speak of, lord, to a greater or lesser degree. If they did not, procreation might not take place. I believe that any man can arouse me—"

"Lady, listen to yourself speak!" The Highlander's eyes gleamed darkly.

Her composure nearly fled. She drew in a breath, refusing to let him daunt her.

"I believe that if I allow any man liberties with my person, he can arouse me. But I do not choose to do so . . . not with you or any other man."

Malcolm pulled a strand of her hair through his fingers. He stroked it back from her temples, letting his palm rest against her cheek, gently rubbing her face with his thumb. The silence was as seductive as his caresses.

"Mayhap you are correct, lady." His voice was a low

mesmerizing drone. "Any man can arouse a woman. But not every man can light the fires of passion deep within a woman, or share this passion with her to take her beyond satisfaction to bliss."

Jarvia's heart pounded thunderously in her chest. "You can, lord?"

"Aye, lady, this is the way you stir my blood. I am on fire for want of you, and I would share this fire with you."

His thumb stroked her cheek . . . the tip of her nose. "Have you ever experienced bliss?"

Struggling to bring air into her chest, she shook her head. "If we are ever able to achieve bliss, it can only be after death."

"A Highlander can give you bliss before death . . . many times before death." His breath, warm and scented with a mixture of ale and honey, touched her face, her shoulders, her breasts. His voice, like a silk shawl, wrapped around her to bind them together. "Let me take you there, lady?"

Aye, she wanted to cry, *take me there, Highlander. Give me the bliss that we of Southerland may find only after death.*

Instead she said, "I could not marry you, lord, even if I should desire it. I am already betrothed."

"Aye, I have given that some thought. I am willing to purchase your liberty from the betrothal. I want you, lady."

His last statement jarred Jarvia. How many times as a slave had she heard men say it? "Even your wants have bounds," she replied. "I am out of those bounds. No amount of gold or silver can buy me. I am a free woman, not chattel that you may barter on a whim."

A shadow flickered in his eyes. "If only what you are saying were true, lady, but it is not. I have learned that all things are for sale, if one is willing to pay enough."

"I will not marry you," Jarvia repeated.

"Would your answer be different if I asked you to be my *first* wife?"

"Nay, lord. I do not wish to be your first, your last, or any wife to you. You are a harsh man."

"Am I being judged by what Hilda told you?"

"She was my friend," Jarvia said. "I mourn for her."

"You think me cruel. You blame me for her death."

"For a verity, I think you are overbearing and hard, lord." Jarvia chose her words carefully. "I should not be happy married to such a man."

She turned slowly, clasped the door handle, and pulled the bolt. As the door slid open, Malcolm caught her upper arm. She tensed, but his fingers did not bite painfully this time.

"Your comb." He pressed it into her hand.

"Thank you."

Realizing how tangled her hair must be, she eased the door shut and crossed the room to stand in front of the mirror. She had stroked her hair a few times when the Highlander moved so that his image was also reflected in the gleaming bronze.

"Are you finished?" he asked.

She stared at his reflection.

"You have stopped combing your hair."

"Aye, I'm finished." She pulled her hair back and clasped it with the comb.

"Then, Lady Jarvia, it is time for you and me to meet with the Council of Justice."

In the mirror she watched Malcolm move to the table. He took a flower from the vase and walked toward her. She turned.

"Will you receive a gift, madam? One that says thank you for visiting me tonight, for giving me the pleasure of such beautiful and stimulating company."

His deep voice compelled her to look into his face. She lowered her gaze to the pale yellow flower instead. She took the blossom. Small though it was, its fragrance filled her nostrils.

"Thank you, lord."

She touched the soft petals to her nose. The gentle fragrance reminded her that today was the beginning of spring, of the rebirth. She surreptitiously looked at the man standing before her.

"When I visited Northland many winters ago," he said, "I saw a flower that reminds me of you, lady. A tiny white flower that grew in the mountains."

"The Balderblom."

"It was beautiful, lady, but you are much more so. If I could, I would pluck that blossom for you."

"Thank you, lord."

As Jarvia gazed into his eyes, she knew she had allowed the man to beguile her. She had allowed herself to be seduced.

True, Malcolm mac Duncan exuded confidence. He was daunting and overpowering. He admitted he was not a gentle man. But Jarvia had witnessed a facet of his personality that she found puzzling.

He seemed to express what he wanted without subterfuge. This was something she had previously experienced only with Ein-her, and she appreciated it in the Highlander. It touched her deeply. He was a wealthy man and had no need of her estate; he wanted her to be his *second* wife because he did not expect her to produce sons.

"If you are ready, madam," he said, "I suggest we meet with your council."

When Malcolm held out his right arm, she hesitated, then said, "This one, sire?"

"My right arm, madam," he said shortly. "Must you question all my actions."

"My apology, lord." She laid her left palm over the top of his hand. "Your custom is strange to me. In my country a man escorts a woman on his left arm."

"If you knew me better," he said, "you would know that I rarely follow custom."

"I have no need to know you better, lord."

He laughed, and she looked up to see the softened lines of his countenance in the glimmer of lamplight.

"Has no man ever tamed your tongue, madam?"

"Many have wanted to, but none has found a way."

The words were scarcely out of her mouth before the Highlander breathed, "I have a way, lady. A most effective and pleasurable way."

He lowered his head and touched his mouth to hers. Touched her with only his lips. Gentle and warm, they tasted faintly of ale and honey. They moved ever so slightly, fitting more closely, tasting sweeter . . . and warmer. Hot . . . hotter.

Puzzled by the feelings he aroused in her, Jarvia stepped away from him. He stepped closer. His arms slid around her and pulled her fully against him. She braced her palms against his chest and pushed, but her struggles were ineffective. The Highlander did not hurt her, but he kept her secure in his embrace. His tongue pressed against the seam of her mouth. She twisted her head, her mouth brushing his cheek.

"No." Her bosom rose and fell with her labored breathing.

"Yes." His voice was low and raspy.

His lips captured hers again. Taking advantage of her surprise, he slipped his tongue inside. He pressed his large, hard frame closer to hers. Desire shuddered through her.

He asked for more. She gave it. That surprised and frightened her. Frightened her so much that she fought anew to free herself from his embrace.

Jarvia was a large woman, but even so, Malcolm easily controlled her flailing. Now that he had a taste of her, he wanted to know more of the mysteries that made this woman. She kindled a new and exciting desire in him, one he had not felt in a long time. His hands spread across her back. He pulled her closer yet. Her breasts, large and firm, thrust against his chest. He felt the erratic pounding of her heart. He moved his leg. She spread hers slightly to accommodate him.

"Your leg, my lord—" Breathing deeply, Jarvia twisted her mouth from his. She pushed back in his arms. "Remove it—"

"Is that what you wish, lady?"

His manhood hardened and thrust against her lower body. She trembled in his arms.

"I like the taste of you, madam." His lips moved over hers as he insinuated himself more securely against her, so that she could feel the fire of desire that licked through him. "I would have more of you."

"I—" She sucked air into her lungs. "I would have less of you than I have—than I have had."

He laughed softly and straightened.

"Remove your leg!" Her voice was sharper.

Although he had no wish to do so, Malcolm stepped

away. Her eyes, framed by long lashes, sparkled. Her lips were parted, her face filled with rosy color.

It mattered not to Malcolm whether anger or desire caused the shine in her eyes, the pouting of her lips, the heightened color in her face; he wanted to sweep her into his arms and lock her in his room. He wanted to take her to bliss and keep her there.

"Duty calls both of us, lord," she said, her voice even, composed.

"Aye," he drawled. At the moment he could not give in to his carnal desires. He must bow to the laws and customs of this land. He had journeyed here in peace; he wanted an alliance with these people.

"Shall we go?" she asked.

Puzzled, Malcolm stared at her for a long while before he nodded. At one point he thought he had touched a secret part of her and set her on fire. If he had, she had quickly reverted to the staid law-speaker of moments ago.

In silence Malcolm escorted Lady Jarvia into the Great Hall. Her shoulders erect, her back straight, she looked forward. But she still carried the flower he had given her.

Lamplight shone on her long silver tresses. Only then did Malcolm notice that she had not replaced the scarf on her head or coiled her hair into a knot. He wondered if she had forgotten . . . or if she had kept her hair loose intentionally. He found the second possibility intriguing.

He could remind her to bind her hair but he chose not to. He liked it loose. He wanted to look at it.

Small, wispy tendrils curled around her face to brush against cheeks that were flushed a delicate pink. He had thought her beautiful the other night when he first saw her. Now she was more than beautiful.

From the moment he had first seen her, he wanted her. Now he ached to possess her.

Chapter 6

Malcolm was so caught up in his thoughts that he had taken many steps through the Great Hall before he noticed the silence. Only moments ago he had heard the low rumble of voices; now he heard nothing. The people's countenances were drawn, their tension obvious. Only the snap of his cowhide cuarans against the planked floor and the gentle swish of Jarvia's tunic about her ankles broke the heavy hush that hung over the people.

Lachlann rose from one of the benches on the far side of the room. Lamplight glittered on the copper-and-jewel-encrusted helmet he left on the table, and his hand rested lightly on the hilt of his sword as he moved toward Malcolm. "I am glad to see you, my friend. King Wyborn's guard would not let me pass to your sleeping chamber. I have been worried about you." Lachlann glanced at Jarvia, then grinned at his chieftain. "I see I have had no reason to be anxious. You were entertaining a woman."

"More correctly, my friend, the lady was entertaining me." Malcolm winked at Jarvia.

"How dare you!" she exclaimed in a low voice, appalled at his sexual implication.

"I dare more, lady. Well you should know," he answered in the same undertone.

To his amusement, Jarvia's cheeks turned an even deeper pink.

"I thought you told me you had no time for pleasure," Lachlann teased.

"We discussed business," Jarvia said in Gaelic, staring straight ahead.

Lachlann regarded her in surprise.

"Aye," Malcolm said, "she speaks our language. She was taught by a Highlander servant."

Lachlann fell into step with Malcolm and Jarvia.

"Where is Arthur?" Malcolm asked.

"Outside," Lachlann replied. "Our warriors are not allowed to enter the Great Hall until the meeting is ended."

"Get him," Malcolm ordered. "I want him here to translate for me."

"Our skald speaks your language," Jarvia said. "He will interpret, and so will I."

"Thank you," Malcolm said, "but I prefer to have my own bard with me. I know where his loyalties lie."

As he had been trained to do as a warrior, Malcolm observed the entire Great Hall without moving anything but his eyes. He noted the benches and tables that lined both sides of the building. On these tables sat small soapstone oil lamps, which were also hung throughout the room on long metal hooks attached to ceiling support beams. A cauldron lamp, supported on a three-pronged metal rod about four hands high, stood on the floor at each end of every table.

The tables were resplendent with food and set with tankards, drinking horns, and pitchers; spoons and knives were of gold, silver, and bronze. Ornately carved wooden serving and eating bowls and plates, decorated with jewels and precious metals, lined the tables.

By counting tables and benches, he quickly tabulated how many of Wyborn's warriors would be on each side of him.

"How long is the Great Hall?" He asked Lachlann.

His friend grinned. "If you and my lady were indeed discussing business, you would have remembered to count your footfalls."

Malcolm scowled.

" 'Tis sixty long ones to the center of the room," Lachlann answered. "About forty from the great fire to the entrance door." He looked around. "You are right to be wary of the Southerland king, but I would predict we will have no trouble from him this night. From the look of the feast, the old king and his wife are intent on impressing you."

"They will succeed only when they present me with my bride . . . with a woman of my choosing."

Twenty more footfalls brought them to the center of the room.

"I'll get Arthur," Lachlann said. He strode from the building and returned soon with the bard.

"Stand by the door, Lachlann," Malcolm instructed. "You know what to do if need be."

"Aye."

Malcolm turned to Arthur. "Wyborn's bard will interpret. Listen carefully and inform me if he makes any mistakes."

The lad nodded and followed as Jarvia led Malcolm to the High Seat of the Great House. The large, ornately carved wooden settle faced east, opposite the hole in the roof through which the moon shone. On either side of the settle burned a cauldron lamp. Their soft light formed a glowing canopy for the ruling lord and lady who sat here. Below them, and in a much smaller chair, sat Gerda, her hands nervously twined together in her lap.

Although all the color was gone from her face, Gerda was still beautiful. Her mantle hung across the back of her chair to reveal her fine clothes and jewelry. Her sleeveless underdress was long and pleated, with a small train. The neck string was drawn loosely so that the material scooped low to reveal her shoulders and nearly all of her breasts.

The delicate overdress, a pinafore, consisted of two rectangular panels of decorated silk. Sewn to the upper corner of each piece of silk were long, slender straps that met at the top of each shoulder and were fastened together by large gold brooches. Clearly Gerda's dress had been designed and sewn for a wealthy woman. Only rich women displayed their beauty in such a provocative manner. Only they wore such vivid colors.

Like all unmarried women, Gerda wore her hair uncovered. Like all slaves, it was cut short. It curled about her face in a bright red tangle.

"Lady Jarvia. Lord Malcolm." Wyborn's shout drew Jarvia's attention from Gerda.

The king waved to the smaller settle. "Escort Lord Malcolm to the High Seat reserved for Southerland's most distinguished guests."

Jarvia translated for Malcolm as she led them to the place of honor. She lifted her hand from his and took a step away, but he caught her wrist.

"Sit with me."

"Nay, lord." She tugged free of him. "It would not be proper."

"Propriety is not my concern. My wish is to have you beside me."

The skald quietly interpreted Malcolm's words.

A scowl on his face, Wyborn lowered his drinking vessel and shouted, "Gerda, move to the settle to sit beside the barbarian. That is your place now."

Gerda stared blankly at Jarvia and Malcolm. Jarvia's compassion went out to her friend, who had no voice in the proceedings, no voice in her destiny. Jarvia saw not the woman of ten-and six winters, but the bairn whom she had loved and reared in the king's household, the girl King Wyborn was willing to sacrifice for his own ambitions.

"Unhand me, lord," Jarvia said. "I must return to my place."

Malcolm's fingers tightened about Jarvia's wrist. "Your place is where I want you, lady," he murmured, then added more loudly, "I want the law-speaker to sit with me, lord."

Wyborn's eyes slitted.

Malcolm shrugged. "The Lady Jarvia and the one called Gerda are comely women, lord. Let both sit with me."

Jarvia speared the barbarian with an angry glare. "I have no desire to sit with you, lord."

Wyborn leaned back in his chair, smiling smugly, and crossed one leg over the other. Lifting his tankard, he drained it in several sloppy gulps. He raised his arm to brush it across his mouth, drying his beard with his shirtsleeve.

"Lady Jarvia, if the chieftain desires you to sit with him, do so."

Jarvia was furious. The barbarian had played loose with her earlier, when he had kissed her. Now he did so again . . . in front of the people, and Wyborn as well.

"Gerda," the king shouted again, "move to sit with the barbarian and Lady Jarvia."

While Gerda slowly made her way to the settle, Queen Adelaide poured ale for the guest of honor. Malcolm pulled Jarvia down next to him as Gerda assumed a seat on his other side.

Wyborn rose. He brushed his mantle back to expose a myriad of gold and silver jewelry and many strings of green beads. A deliberate move, Jarvia thought, since a man's wealth was reckoned by the number of beads strung on his necklaces.

"Tonight, lords and ladies of the Council of Justice, we salute the marriage between Malcolm mac Duncan and Wyborn's daughter. We seal the alliance between the kingdoms of the Northern Scots and the Southerlanders."

He lifted his drinking horn, the gold-and-silver gilt gleaming in the firelight. All other tankards and drinking horns waved in the air, save one. Malcolm mac Duncan did not touch his. Slowly Wyborn lowered his arm.

A worried frown on his countenance, he asked, "Why do you not accept my hospitality, lord?"

"I accept your hospitality, lord, but I will not salute my betrothal until I have spoken to the council."

As Malcolm's words were interpreted, drinking horns and tankards thumped to the tables; men slid onto their benches.

"Speak," Wyborn commanded.

"I am prepared to marry this woman whom you are adopting as your daughter. I will accept her as my first wife, as the mother of my children, of my inheriting son."

The skald translated. Sighs of relief were audible; smiles lightened expressions.

"But—"

Apprehension returned.

"I would have more, since I am not getting the kinswoman I demanded."

"But I am giving you more than a kinswoman, lord. Did not Lady Jarvia explain that my adopted daughter is also my bastard daughter? My blood issue?"

"She did. A claim for which you have no proof. She also told me that until today Gerda was a slave in your household."

Queen Adelaide lowered her drinking horn. Her tiny eyes, devoid of eyelashes, flashed like polished amber. Color flushed her jowled cheeks. She leaned forward to block Wyborn from view and an ugly smile crawled across her face.

"You have my lord-husband's word, my word as well."

"That is so, madam," Malcolm said. "Surely a man's and a woman's honor rests upon their word."

Adelaide nodded and leaned back.

" 'Twould not be pleasant for any of us, lord and lady, if you were trying to deceive me."

"Nay, lord." Wyborn shook his head vigorously. "The gods of Asgard forbid!"

The Aesir gods might forbid, Jarvia thought, but not Wyborn and Adelaide. Only they would dream up such a scheme and expect people to believe them. Only they would so underestimate their enemy, potentially their ally.

Malcolm spoke. "For three winters I lived with your daughter as my wife, and she spoke not once of this bastard daughter."

"No one knew," Wyborn answered. "I did not wish to own up to her, sire, to save my lady-wife embarrassment. Had Hilda not taken her life and that of her unborn babe, I would not have acknowledged Gerda's parentage."

Malcolm nodded. "Then, lord, I ask for more to seal this alliance between us."

Kirkja, second in command and authority to the king, had been elected by the members of the Council of Justice to officiate. Stroking his unruly red beard, he rose and walked to stand beside the *langeldar*. He had been Ein-her's closest friend, and during the law-speaker's marriage to Jarvia, Kirkja had become her friend also. After Ein-her's death, Jarvia had grown even closer to Kirkja and his family. They and Gerda were the nearest to kindred that Jarvia had.

"What would you have, lord?" Kirkja asked Malcolm.

"I would take Lady Jarvia as my second wife."

Surprise registered on Kirkja's countenance.

Wyborn and Adelaide scowled.

Flames of anger lapped through Jarvia until she felt as if she were the *langeldar* itself. Her hand curled into a fist, and she crushed the flower Malcolm had given her. He insisted on having his way. He cared not whom he hurt in the process.

Kirkja, rubbing his chin, looked from Jarvia to Wyborn and back to Jarvia. Finally he addressed Wyborn. "My lord king," he said, "this is a private and delicate matter, one we should discuss among ourselves."

Wyborn nodded. "Lord Malcolm, we ask you and your bard to excuse yourselves."

Malcolm protested.

Kirkja sought to placate him. "It is not wise for you to hear our argument. You may remain here in the hall or retire to your chamber, but your bard must go. If you leave, we will summon you as soon as we have reached a decision."

Malcolm considered the words, then answered. "I will send the bard away, but I shall remain here, my lord. Though I hear not the interpretation, I shall be able to study your expressions as you discuss the matter."

With a curt nod, Kirkja dismissed Arthur, who slipped unobtrusively from the *stofa*.

Wyborn said, "The warlord drives a hard bargain, one we must consider."

"He drives no bargain at all," Kirkja argued. "We cannot agree to every demand he makes. All concessions are going to him, none to us."

"But we need this alliance," Wyborn argued. "We are a small kingdom surrounded by enemies who may turn on us at any moment. We need an alliance with a kingdom as strong as the Northern Scots."

The council members looked grave.

Wyborn wiggled nervously in his chair. "We must always consider the possibility that our clansmen from the Northland will some day seek retribution. We must bow to Malcolm mac Duncan's demands."

Lord Kirkja locked his hands behind his back and slowly paced the *stofa*. "Although 'twas Ein-her who betrothed Jarvia to his distant kinsman, Michael Langssonn, the betrothal and the coming marriage have created an alliance between Lang's clan and ours. In bowing to the Highlander's demands, my lord king, you will destroy another important alliance."

"Aye, my lord king." Jarvia leaped to her feet. "Listen to the wisdom of Lord Kirkja. If we break our agreement with Lord Lang, our honor will be called into question." She paused. "Our honor, King Wyborn, yours and mine."

The settle creaked beneath Queen Adelaide's shifting weight. Her deep, gravelly voice echoed through the *stofa*. "You speak without thinking, law-speaker.

Betrothals can be ruptured . . . honorably . . . so that no one is shamed."

"True, my lady-queen," Kirkja said, moving to stand in front of the High Seat, "but we are talking about more than breaking a betrothal. Through Hilda's marriage we made a firm and lasting alliance with the Highlanders. Lady Jarvia's marriage to Michael Langssonn would give us an alliance with a strong clan of the Northmen."

He spread his hands out. "Once you and King Wyborn adopt Gerda, she will become your legal daughter. According to our law, she is the same relation to you as Hilda. She is the guarantee of our covenant with the barbarian. We need not give him two of our women simply because he lusts after them."

"At present, Kirkja," Queen Adelaide said, "we have no alliance with anyone. Hilda is dead, and Jarvia is not married to Lang's son."

"And she will not marry him if we are not careful, lady." Kirkja turned to the lord of the *stofa*. "Wyborn, what say you?"

"The alliance with the Northern Scots is more important. If we are attacked by our enemies here, or by avenging clansmen, the Scots can come to our aid more quickly than Lang, who lives in Northland over the sea. We will rupture Lady Jarvia's betrothal."

"No!" Jarvia shouted. "I will not let you do this to me. I am not your slave. I am a free woman of property. I am a rune master."

Wyborn slammed his fist on his armrest. "Woman, you have no voice when it comes to your marriage. No woman does, whether she be freeborn or slave, of royal or peasant blood. This decision rests with the council."

Jarvia stepped toward the High Seat. Kirkja caught her shoulders and held her back, but she would not be hushed.

"Before my husband died, he was my spokesman," she said. " 'Twas he who negotiated the terms of my betrothal to Michael Langssonn through Lord Lang of Ulfsbaer. 'Twas he who declared that after his death I would become my own spokesperson. When the council members clanged their weapons together in what we call the *vápnatak*, they sealed the agreement to make it law. Only I, King Wyborn, can honorably break the betrothal."

"Are you telling the council that you are in love with your betrothed?" Queen Adelaide sneered. Her jowled cheeks flapped, reminding Jarvia of a dog with a square muzzle and loose skin. "A man whom you do not even know? Have never seen?"

"Nay." Jarvia pierced her with a hard glare. "Nothing has been said about love. But I deny that all of you have the right to decide my destiny without at least listening to me."

Jarvia paced back and forth in front of the council members.

"Hear me, men of Southerland. Hear me well. I am betrothed to Michael Langssonn and shall remain so."

"Lady—" Though Wyborn spoke softly, his voice was full of fury. "You try my patience. You do not dictate to me or this council what we can or cannot do."

"Nay," Jarvia replied, "but we believe in our law, sire, and by vote of this council, my fate has long since been decided. Only I have the power to rescind my decision."

"Aye, Wyborn," Kirkja said, his calm voice welcome in the tension-filled room, "Lady Jarvia speaks the truth."

Wyborn rose, his face purple with rage. "*I* am the king of this land. *I* am the final authority."

"Even so, my lord, you are bound by the law," Kirkja continued. In a placating voice, he added, "As the High Ruler of Southerland, you must consider the consequences should you or the council decide to break the betrothal . . . without the lady's permission."

Jarvia allowed Kirkja to escort her to the settle where Malcolm and Gerda were sitting.

Kirkja continued, "Already our people live with the constant threat of revenge because of your deeds in Northland. Do we wish to bring further grief upon our heads by angering and dishonoring a lord such as Michael Langssonn? Do we want to invite his revenge?"

Wyborn threw back his head and laughed.

"None of us has met this kinsman to Ein-her, but I have heard much about him," Wyborn said scathingly. "Michael Langssonn is not one to be feared. He is a dreamer, Kirkja, not a warrior. He sails a trading vessel, not a warship."

Several of the council members laughed.

Malcolm caught Jarvia's hand and whispered, "What is so humorous, lady?"

She shrugged. "It would be of no import to you, lord."

"Methinks it would, lady." A smile eased across Malcolm's face before it blossomed into a soft chuckle.

An eerie feeling skirted up Jarvia's spine.

Wyborn continued. "Lord Michael is not to be feared. He records routes to the lands where he travels so others may follow. He spends his time drawing! 'Tis said that his arms are not strong enough to hold up a warrior's sword or battle-ax. By those who know him best, Michael Langssonn is called a *nithing*."

" 'Tis not wise to mock the rune masters, Wyborn," Kirkja said, "or to call Lord Michael a coward and make light of his reprisal."

"Aye, lord," Jarvia said, returning her attention to the matter at hand. "You know without my telling you what our law says about vengeance."

No one spoke.

"Honor is sacred, infinitely vulnerable, and is to be defended at all times, at any cost," Jarvia recited, her voice carrying through the *stofa*. She rose and moved to stand in front of the council. "According to the code of the Northmen, vengeance is a moral imperative. We have no honor without vengeance, no life without honor."

She paused, looking at each one individually, then said, "I am already betrothed to Lord Michael Langssonn, who is a-viking. I will not marry Lord Malcolm because I have no desire to go against my deceased husband's wishes. I will marry Michael Langssonn. Despite what King Wyborn says, he is a brave and fearsome warrior."

Jarvia spun around and strode to stand in front of Malcolm mac Duncan. Looking directly into his face and refusing to be drawn into the spell he could so easily cast, she translated what she had spoken.

She paused and tossed the crushed flower at his feet.

In Gaelic she added, "A man of honor would make no such demands. Since neither you nor any of these men"— she waved her hand to include all who sat in the hall— "have honor, lord, let this woman have it for you."

Chapter 7

The loudest noise in the *stofa* was the spit and sputter of the fire. Each of the Southermen, an expression of disbelief on his face, sat stiffly, as if the howling cold of an icy winter had frozen him in place.

Yet Jarvia, watching the Highland warlord, felt anything but cold. She had seen men's faces turn thunderous in anger. Now she saw a face that was dark and smoldering, one that promised to unleash all its hellish fury . . . on her.

Malcolm mac Duncan rose, his movements so smooth that his clothing scarcely rustled. The soles of his boots made a muted thud as they hit the floor, as one foot completely covered the small blossom Jarvia had thrown down. With a deceptive lack of hurry, the Highlander pulled his mantle aside and rested his hand on the hilt of his sword. With that one move, he also made visible his dirk—a deadly weapon in the hands of a Highlander.

Tall, broad, and formidable, he blocked from Jarvia's vision all else in the room. Her entire body shook. She wanted to run as far and as quickly as she could from the barbarian, but she stood fast. It was not uncommon for men to strike women for less than she had said and done. Clearly she had overstepped the bounds of propriety. But she meant what she had said and would say it again.

"You accuse me of having no honor, madam?"

His soft words snapped across the room like a bowstring that had been nocked too tightly by an arrow and had broken. The skald, his face white, his eyes wide, sidled closer to King Wyborn and mumbled the interpretation.

"Aye." Jarvia raised her head to look fully into the warlord's furious countenance. " 'Twas what I said."

To her side, the *langeldar* crackled and spit. Flames, beautiful but dangerous, leaped into the air in a burst of golden red sparks, as if they too were in league with the warlord.

"King Wyborn"—the barbarian raised his voice and moved his hand, the red-and-yellow mantle billowing about him like flames—"do you allow women to speak to your honored guests in such a manner?"

Though the skald spoke the translation softly, his words echoed through the inordinately quiet *stofa* with the intensity of a shout.

Lord Malcolm turned. Again the swish and swirl of the mantle reminded Jarvia of fire. It seemed that the warlord was shrouded with flames, that he himself was fire.

"King Wyborn!" he shouted.

Jarvia grimaced.

The barbarian's shout melted the men in the *stofa* out of their frozen trances. Wyborn blinked and pushed to the edge of the settle. Queen Adelaide shook her head, strands of hair escaping her hair-wrap to fall limply about her face.

"My-my apologies, lord," Wyborn stammered.

Heaving a sigh, Kirkja laid both hands flat on the table and rose. He lumbered to the center of the *stofa*. "Lord Malcolm, in a meeting of the council, all members are allowed to voice their opinions. Lady Jarvia is not only a member of this council, but is also our law-speaker."

Hardly had the skald ceased translating than Wyborn stood. He cleared his throat and declared, "But we do not allow anyone to speak to an honored guest as Lady Jarvia has done. She has insulted Lord Malcolm. I shall banish her from the *stofa* while we attend to business."

"Aye!" the council cried in unison. The ring of metal against metal had hardly died out in the room before the warlord spoke, his voice soft. "You would banish her from the *stofa*, King Wyborn?"

Both the king and his lady nodded in unison.

Still the barbarian did not raise his voice. "Is that not much too gentle a punishment for a crime so grave, lords of the Council of Justice?"

The palms of Jarvia's hands grew moist.

Kirkja eyed the man warily. "What punishment would you deem appropriate, lord?"

"If she were a man"—Lord Malcolm moved his gaze from Lord Kirkja to Jarvia—"I would challenge her to a duel to the death." His expression unreadable, his eyes narrowed, he continued to stare at her. "Since I cannot do that, I suggest that the lady be banished from the kingdom."

"Banished!" Jarvia murmured, barely hearing the skald speak the interpretation. She rushed to Kirkja. "Surely, lord—"

"If she were outlawed for a crime of such magnitude," the Highlander continued, "she would not be a suitable wife for the Northman. Aye, lord, you would save his honor by breaking his betrothal to a woman of this sort."

Jarvia could not believe her ears. For four years she had been a woman of quality; she owned her own home, had her own servants, was a member of the Council of Justice, with equal rights and privileges. Now, suddenly, she was in danger of losing everything!

Anger, bitterness, and fear gave her renewed strength and resolve. She removed her hand from Kirkja's arm and strode over to the barbarian. With no one to champion her, knowing the council would acquiesce to the warlord's demands in order to protect Southerland, she had to fight for herself.

Not wanting anyone to be privy to her conversation with Malcolm, speaking softly to him alone, she said in Gaelic, "I am not going to allow you to take my freedom from me without a struggle. Ein-her bought me and released me from servitude. Not trusting King Wyborn, my husband took great care to ensure me a safe future. I will not let you steal it from me!"

He spoke softly also, but with equal force. "Can I not, lady?"

"I am not chattel!"

"Nay, I would not want you if you were chattel, madam. I want you because you are a desirable woman."

"Yet you would make me your chattel."

"I would make you my bedmate. I see a big difference between the two."

"You would go to such lengths to have a woman who despises you, lord?"

"When provoked, aye. I go to any length to get what I want," he answered. "And while our mating would be all the more enjoyable if you liked me, it is not a requirement."

"By Thor's hammer, I would that I were a man!" Jarvia glared at him, her hands balled into fists at her sides. "I would challenge you to a duel to the death, and I would see that you met your end. Then, lord, I would decapitate you so that your body would not rest in the other world, and then—"

Malcolm laughed softly and moved closer to her. Again she inhaled the scent of the man—leather and iron and the herbal water that subtly clung to him. She saw the texture of his skin, the crinkles at the corners of his eyes. She watched his lips move as he laughed, as he spoke.

"Ah, madam, you are brazen indeed."

He reached out to touch her cheek, but she pulled her arm back and swung with all her strength. It was the first time someone had so riled her that she completely lost control. With a quick and sure motion, the Highlander grabbed her wrist before her hand connected with his face.

"Be glad I stopped you." His blue eyes glittered dangerously. His fingers bit unmercifully into her flesh. "Else I would be forced to flog you publicly, madam."

"Aye, you like flogging women, do you not, my lord?"

His facial muscles tensed. "To think Lachlann believed you were made of ice, madam."

"Would that I *were* descended from the frost giants! I would freeze you to death." Jarvia twisted her hand but could not free it from his grasp. She glanced down his body. "Nay, lord, I would freeze certain parts of your body and render them useless."

Malcolm threw back his head and laughed, the deep, rich sound echoing throughout the room. He wiped the corners of his eyes.

"I think you would try, madam."

"I will do it, lord. I promise."

Malcolm released her hand and moved away from her. Jarvia turned to the men of the council. Since she and Malcolm had been conversing in Gaelic in low voices, they had not been privy to their conversation. Yet they were curious. They speared both of them with hard, inquisitive gazes.

"To appease my honor," Malcolm said more loudly, "I demand that this woman be banished."

The interpretation ended, and King Wyborn shouted, "Aye."

He raised his fist, but before he could hit the broad armrest, Kirkja called out, "Hear! Hear!" A troubled expression on his face, Kirkja stroked his beard. "Do you know what banishment means, Lord Malcolm? She would no longer have a home, lord, could no longer reside in Wybornsbaer or in Southerland. She could be hunted down and killed like an animal."

"Or, lord, she could be ransomed," Malcolm pointed out. "She could be used as a condition of agreement between your people and mine."

"Nay," Jarvia said, speaking in Gaelic. "I will not be used by you or anyone else, barbarian. If you banish me, I shall take my chances in the wilds of the Highlands. If I live, I live a free woman. If I die, I die the same. I belong to no one but myself."

Tears blinding her, her heart pounding furiously, she moved back to her seat, picked up her shawl, and clasped it about her shoulders. "I retire to my *stofa*, Lord Kirkja. There I shall await the decision of the council."

Her head held high, her heart breaking, she strode from the king's house.

Angrily, nervously, Jarvia paced back and forth in the large *skáli*, the single room of her small but comfortable home. A fire burned in the circular hearth in the center of the room, and two cauldron lamps flickered on either side of the upright loom propped against the outer wall. Holding the handle of the shuttle with both hands, Morag sat on a three-legged stool in front of the frame and wove.

Left to right flew the shuttle.

Right to left marched Jarvia.

"Stop that pacing," the old woman said, "I don't want to have to add more floor bracken before it should be needed."

Jarvia paused and looked down at the fern floor matting for the first time. She sighed, inhaling deeply of the clean, fresh odor.

" 'Twas only this morn that I laid the covering," Morag said. "I traded one of your silver rings, else I could not have gotten the load I did, mistress. The villagers were making large demands on the bracken harvester and were willing to barter for it. 'Tis the time of the Planting Moon, when the world comes alive again."

She paused in her weaving and leaned forward to study the design.

"Methinks, mistress, I would have a hard time finding more bracken so soon. The villagers have cleaned their homes and clothes in honor of the Success Sacrifice of the Planting Moon. 'Twill be a while before we shall see another harvest."

With the toe of her shoe, Jarvia kicked a piece of the fern. It flew through the air to land beside four small stave barrels.

"Be careful, mistress," Morag admonished, the shuttle winding across the loom once more. "I spent long hours gathering the lichen and tree bark for the coloring of fabric. In an eye's blink you will have put to naught all my hard work this winter."

She stopped weaving to lean down and straighten one of the triangular-shaped warp weights of fired clay. Once she had untangled the threads, she picked up the weaving comb that hung on a long chain from one of her shoulder brooches.

"What do you think of this pattern, mistress?"

"May Thor land you a blow to the head, woman, and strike some sense into you!" Jarvia marched to stand beside the loom. "Have you gone daft? The king and queen are adopting Gerda so that she can marry the barbarian. The council is considering the warlord's demand that I be banished from Southerland. And you sit here talking about your floor mats and weaving."

"Acht!" Morag clicked her tongue. Without looking up from her work, she slid the teeth of the comb between the threads and pushed them upward. "I'm more concerned about your fate than you think, madam, but I fear there is little you and I can do about it, other than pray and keep a level head. I swear by the holy mother and her wee babe, destroying the house is not the answer."

"If the barbarian has his way," Jarvia said, and she had no doubt that he *would* have his way, "I shall not have a home much longer."

Sighing, folding her arms over her breasts, she walked around the fire to stand in front of the cushioned platform in the corner of the room. It served as her bench during the day and her bed at night. She felt helpless. At a time when Gerda needed her most, she was unable to help her. At the time of her own greatest need, she was unable to help herself.

If only she had not allowed her anger to get the best of her; if only she had not lost control. If she had kept silent, she would yet have a voice in the council's decision.

A knock sounded on the door.

Mistress and servant exchanged anxious glances.

More insistent raps echoed.

Morag spun around on the stool, knocking over the yarn-winder leaning against the bottom leg of the loom. She grumbled as she crossed the *skáli* to press the iron lever that released the latch. She cracked open the door.

"Bertha!" she exclaimed. "What be your business at the law-speaker's *stofa*? Why are you not tending to the banquet at the king's house?"

"I must see Lady Jarvia," said Queen Adelaide's housekeeper. "It is most urgent, Morag."

"Let her pass," Jarvia called.

The short, stocky woman pushed open the door with such force that Morag stumbled backward. "Gerda needs you, lady."

"Gerda!" Jarvia exclaimed, all other thoughts fleeing from her mind. "What is wrong?"

"She's having a tantrum, she is." Bertha caught Jarvia's hand and tugged. "Please hurry. I fear for her life, and mine, if I am unable to get her dressed."

Not taking time to obtain a mantle or hood, Jarvia ran out of the *stofa* behind Bertha. They wound their way among the smaller homes that belonged to the warriors, artisans, and freemen.

"What has been happening in the Great Hall?" Jarvia asked.

"The council and the barbarian are still arguing," the housekeeper called over her shoulder. "Mistress sent Gerda to change her clothes. She says that in time the council will convince the barbarian to accept Gerda as his bride. After they adopt Gerda, the wedding will take place, and the banquet will become a celebration feast."

Out of breath, Bertha stopped in front of a small building.

"Why is Gerda in the food store then?" Jarvia demanded, her anxiety growing.

"She was running away. Mistress caught and bound her so that she could not escape. If I did not fear for my life, I would let Gerda go, but Queen Adelaide has made her my charge."

Jarvia nodded.

"Gerda," Bertha called softly as she knocked on and opened the door. " 'Tis me and Lady Jarvia."

Jarvia pushed past the servant but paused for a moment, letting her eyes grow accustomed to the near darkness. In a corner the light from a lone soapstone lamp sputtered to reveal the outline of barrels, casks, baskets, and bags of stored food. From behind one of the barrels she saw the fringe of a mantle. Disregarding her own clothing, Jarvia hurried over to Gerda who was lying in a heap atop sheepskin bags filled with herbs and eiderdown.

Jarvia caught her young friend by the shoulders. "What is wrong?"

Huge sobs racked Gerda's body. "I cannot marry the barbarian."

"Aye," Jarvia said softly, sadly, "you must, little one. You have no choice."

As I have little choice about my own future.

"I must wait for Sven to return home," she cried.

"Do you have tender feelings for him?" Jarvia asked, surprised to hear of Gerda's loyalty to a man who had gone a-viking.

"Nay, but he has already begun to give payments to the king for my freedom. He promised to marry me."

" 'Twill be many winters before he returns home with enough money to buy your freedom," Jarvia said. "Once he accepted the iron arrow of war, he gave his loyalty to the ship's captain, a man who spends many winters on his raids." Gently Jarvia reminded her, "You will be an old woman by the time Sven returns."

She tugged Gerda's shoulders, trying to get her to sit up. "If you have no tenderness for Sven—"

"Nay, I only wanted to be quit of Queen Adelaide."

"Then, you shall be." Jarvia sounded brighter than she felt. "The Highlander will be a much better choice of husband for you than Sven. Lord Malcolm is wealthy and influential. He will take you away from Wybornsbaer, away from Southerland. You will find that he will not be much different from our villagers."

Gerda buried her head deeper into the bag of eiderdown and moaned. "Oh, Jarvia, what shall I do?"

"What will you do!" Jarvia repeated. "How many maidens in this land envy you, and you lie about bemoaning your fate. I will tell you what you are going to do. You will marry the barbarian. You are a stronger woman than Hilda was, and will make the Highland warlord a good wife. It will not be long before you present him with a son, and—"

Gerda's moan turned into a wail; her body quaked all the more.

"Please, Gerda," Bertha begged. "Do sit up and let me dress you. If you're not ready in time, Queen Adelaide will beat me."

"Gerda, you must control yourself." Jarvia dug her fingers into Gerda's shoulders and forced her up, but Gerda kept her head down. "Behavior like this will not help your cause."

She slipped a finger beneath Gerda's chin to raise her head. The light flickered over the girl's tear-streaked face. "You will fare much better if you look pleasing to his lordship."

"Aye," Bertha agreed.

"Certainly he will not appreciate your cheeks being streaked with tears and your eyes swollen."

"He won't appreciate me whether I be a-crying or not," Gerda wailed. "I cannot be pleasing to the barbarian."

"Aye, you can and you will."

Two more tears rolled down Gerda's cheeks. "You are speaking the way Queen Adelaide speaks."

"Although I hate to admit it," Jarvia said, "in this instance the queen is correct."

"Nay," Gerda whispered, and sighed deeply.

"You should have already changed your clothes," Jarvia said. "Where is your dress?"

"I'll go get it," Bertha volunteered. "It's in the house."

Gerda closed her eyes and went limp in Jarvia's arms.

"Make haste," Jarvia told the housekeeper. "Also get her casket of cosmetic paints and powders, and her combs. And some sweet-smelling herbal water."

By the time Jarvia had unpinned a brooch and released the straps on one side of Gerda's silk-paneled overdress, the door had closed behind Bertha. Jarvia quickly unfastened the other brooch, then untied the neck string of the undergarment and pulled loose the gathering. She struggled to pull the long tunic over Gerda's shoulders.

"You must help me," Jarvia said. "I cannot get your clothing off if you lie here like a sack of flour. I cannot help you if you do not help yourself."

"Jarvia . . ." Gerda's voice sounded far away. "My moon . . . my moon has not come upon me."

Jarvia dropped her hands and pushed back on her shins. She felt as if her heart had stopped beating. "Do you know a reason—other than that you are with child—why your moon should be late, Gerda?"

"Sven and I, we-we were going to wed."

"May Odin in his wisdom protect us!" Jarvia shook her head in disbelief. "If only you had told me sooner."

"I did not know that they were going to claim before the council that I was the king's bastard daughter, or that they were going to adopt me. I did not know, Jarvia. I swear."

"I believe you." Jarvia rubbed her forehead.

"I wanted to tell you about the child. That is why I came to your *stofa* earlier today. But I said nothing because I was afraid of what you would think of me."

"Does Sven know you are carrying his child?"

Gerda shook her head.

"What are the king and queen going to say when they learn about it?"

"They know," Gerda whispered.

"They know?" Jarvia repeated. She picked up the lamp

and held it closer to Gerda's face. "King Wyborn and Queen Adelaide know that your moon is late and that you may be with child?"

Gerda nodded. "I told the queen when she brought me into her chamber a little while ago. She was so angry, it was all she could do to keep from striking me."

Gerda's body shook. Renewed tears raced down her cheeks.

"Why did you wait so long to tell Queen Adelaide?" Jarvia asked.

"I was scared she would kill me," Gerda gasped between hiccuping sobs. "I didn't know what to do. I thought if I let her and the king adopt me, they wouldn't be so quick to hurt me." Gerda shook her head and rubbed both sides of her forehead. "I didn't know. . . . I never thought they wanted me to marry the barbarian. I did not know . . . I could be . . . could be . . . a *native daughter.* . . ." Her voice trailed into silence.

Then she lifted her head with a jerk. "When I told the queen about the bairn, Jarvia, she ranted and raved. I swear the *stofa* shook as she marched back and forth. Then she sent for the king. They talked together and were soon convinced the gods had smiled on us. They claimed the barbarian was going to have a son much sooner than he expected. They threatened to kill me if I told anyone the truth, or if I refused to marry the barbarian."

Jarvia felt like a sheepskin wineskin that had been emptied of its contents in one pouring. She laid down the lamp and rested her head in her hands.

"Jarvia—" Gerda leaned forward and curled her fingers over Jarvia's shoulders. "You don't despise me, do you?"

"Nay." Jarvia sighed.

"Queen Adelaide told me I must marry the barbarian. Only I can save the people of Southerland. She said he would be so drunk by the time we . . . we went to bed that he would not know if I was a virgin or not. She said we could hide a bladder of blood between the draping and the mattress. He would not know the difference."

"The Highlander is more astute than the queen believes,"

Jarvia said dully. "King Wyborn may not know the difference between blood from an animal bladder and a broken maidenhead, but the barbarian does."

That the king and his wife had underestimated the barbarian's intelligence was to be expected. That they had lied about Gerda being the king's bastard daughter was not surprising. But to further deceive the Highland warlord by marrying him to an impregnated woman was beyond Jarvia's comprehension.

Gerda bolted up and grabbed for Jarvia. "I am afraid. He wants to have you banished because you accused him of having no honor. My crime is far worse. The lord will kill me should he learn that the babe I carry is not his. I know he will."

Jarvia also feared this was true. When the Highlander was wooing her to be his concubine—or as he called it, *his second wife*—he had been charming. But all the while Jarvia had sensed a dark side to this wild Highland lord. She had felt the iron will that flowed through his being. A sword could be gilded with gold, silver, bronze, and precious jewels so that it became a work of art and beautiful to behold. Yet despite all that, it remained deadly. The same was true of the Highland barbarian. Had he not proved it when he demanded that she be outlawed from the kingdom?

"You're not going to let the barbarian take you," Gerda said, her words coming in a rush. "You said you wouldn't. If the council banishes you, you're going to leave Southerland. You'll be on your own. Take me with you, Jarvia. Please, take me with you. With Sven gone, I have no one here."

"If I'm banished to a life as an outlaw," Jarvia said, "it will be a hard one." She brushed the curls from Gerda's face. "Harder than what you could endure."

"But we'll be together. We'll take care of each other, Jarvia. We'll be like sisters."

"Now we must think about the baby."

"I must go with you, else my baby and I are doomed. If Lord Malcolm doesn't kill me, the king and his lady will."

The door to the food store opened, and Bertha entered. "Here is the wedding dress."

"Oh, Jarvia," Gerda wailed. "What am I to do?"

"Get dressed," Jarvia said. She crossed the shed to take the wedding garment from the servant.

Gerda brushed the hair out of her eyes. "You'll take care of everything?"

"Aye," Jarvia murmured. *If she could.*

She had promised the barbarian she would not marry him under any circumstances, and she would never bear him a child. She had to admit her behavior since then had not endeared her to Malcolm mac Duncan. Yet the only way she could save Gerda and her baby now was to convince him to marry her as his first, and only, wife.

Chapter 8

"What do you think of the dress?" Morag asked, stepping back.

Jarvia stared at her reflection in the large bronze panel in the front door of her *skáli*.

" 'Tis the best we can do on such short notice," Morag said.

"I feel as if I am naked," Jarvia replied.

"Far from it." Morag dismissed Jarvia's comment with a wave and a click of her scissors.

Except for tiny straps, her arms and shoulders were bare; her undergarment—a long, dark green tunic made of sheer material—was fastened by brooches to her paneled overdress so that the upper swells of her breasts were exposed.

Standing to one side, Bertha moved closer and held out a tray filled with tiny jars and metal canisters. "Let me apply the cosmetic coloring to your face." She lifted the lid of the small jar. "How about this one for your upper lid?"

Jarvia nodded.

" 'Twill bring out the color of your eyes."

Jarvia stood still as Bertha applied the colored salves and powders to her face. A cream for her skin. Subtle shading for her eyes. A berry blush to her cheeks and lips. A powder to take the shine off the tip of her nose and to hide her freckles.

"There now. You are quite a beauty." Bertha surveyed her work with satisfaction.

"Indeed." Morag bobbed her head and with her scissors, snipped another loose thread from the tunic.

Jarvia glanced at her bared arms and shoulders. She hoped the slender straps that held up the overdress did not slip loose from the clasp, else her entire bosom would be revealed.

73

"Morag, surely we have a thicker tunic," she said. She had never worn such a sheer undergarment. "Look how the light filters through this one."

"Aye," the servant answered, combing Jarvia's hair. "That is why I chose it. If you stand with the light to your side, the outline of your body becomes clearly visible."

"Morag—"

The old woman shook her head. " 'Twas you, mistress, who decided to play this game. Against my better judgment, mind you. But you've begun. Now you must see it through."

Jarvia sighed.

"Now, lady, it is time to tend to your duty."

"I would put on a hair covering," Jarvia said.

Morag shook her head and spoke impatiently. "I think not, mistress. We must unwrap your beauty, not hide it." She smiled and patted Jarvia's arm. " 'Tis time, lady."

Morag joined Bertha at the door. "We will stay with Gerda until we hear from you."

The two women slipped through the door, but before it closed, Morag poked her head through the crack.

"God bless and take care of you, mistress."

Someone needed to, Jarvia thought. Left alone in the *stofa*, she nervously paced, not caring that she packed the freshly laid bracken. She wrung her hands and wondered how she would get herself and Gerda out of this situation . . . alive. And the baby. She had to think about the baby as well.

A soft knock sounded on the door.

She took one last look in the bronze door panel, peering closely to see if she had any black smudges where her lashes touched her cheeks. She brushed away a curl, which as quickly fell back against her temple.

"Lady Jarvia," Lord Kirkja called.

She raced to the small chest beside the bed and rummaged until she found the containers of cosmetics. She opened one, chose a berry powder, and brushed it liberally over her lips. She dabbed more herbal water behind her ears and on her wrists.

Kirkja knocked again.

Hurriedly she returned the containers to their casket, closed the chest, and rose. Taking several deep breaths, she walked across the *skáli* to open the door.

"Lady, I have adjourned the council meeting and have brought the Highlander to you as your servant, Morag, instructed me," Kirkja said.

"Thank you, my lord."

"With a heavy heart I did your bidding. Before you go further in this plan of yours, do you think perhaps you and I should talk? Tell me what you are planning."

Jarvia shook her head. "Nay, my friend. This is something I must do alone."

"I have argued for you," the old lord said, "but I fear there is nothing else I can do. But, lady, I bid you, do not act hastily. The council will not quickly banish you."

"Perhaps not the council, but King Wyborn and Queen Adelaide will see that the black deed is done." Jarvia laid her hand on his forearm. "You have been a true friend to me, lord. Trust me now to do what is best for me, for Gerda, and for all of Southerland."

"I trust you to do what is best for Gerda and Southerland. I am not sure what you will do for yourself. That is my worry, lady." He leaned over and placed a fatherly kiss on her cheek. "May Thor lend you strength."

May Thor grant me the ability to control my emotions.

"I am going to need him."

A hand clamped over Lord Kirkja's shoulder. Out of the darkness, the Highland barbarian materialized. At first he was a shadow, then the light of the torch illuminated him and Jarvia once again saw him as the lord of fire.

"You sent for me, lady?" he asked in Gaelic.

Swallowing the apprehension that knotted in her throat, struggling for composure, Jarvia nodded and waved him into her *skáli*. When he stood in the center of the room, she closed the door and leaned against it, glad for the cool sheet of bronze on her back, giving her support.

"This is your home." Finger by finger Malcolm stripped the leathern gloves from his hands.

"Aye."

"The house you shared with your husband?"

Jarvia nodded.

He tucked the gloves into his girdle. When he laid his right hand on the hilt of his sword, she saw the glimmer of the small gold finger ring. The red-and-yellow plaid mantle swinging about the calves of his legs, he turned and surveyed the room.

Jarvia wiped her moist palms down the sides of her dress. The *skáli* had been large enough to comfortably accommodate her and Ein-her. But now that Malcolm mac Duncan had entered, the walls seemed to push in on her.

He unsettled her as he took his time studying the furniture: the trestle table and its two benches, the large storage chest set against the entrance wall, the smaller chest beside the sleeping platform, the tapestries that hung on the wall to canopy the bed . . . especially the bed.

Eventually he asked, "What would you discuss with me?"

He walked to the bed and pressed his hand against the mattress. The coverlets were thick and comfortable to lie on; in the winter they provided extra warmth. Jarvia had traded many of her fine pieces of jewelry for eiderdown to fill the mattress, the bed cushions, and the coverlets.

She had spared no expense to tend to her husband during their marriage. He had been a frail man in body but strong in mind and purpose. She wished he were here now to be her champion, to speak for her . . . to guide her.

Malcolm turned and looked at Jarvia. "Have you nothing to say, madam? Am I not going to learn why you interrupted the council meeting to summon me to your house?"

Jarvia nodded, hastily collecting her wits, her thoughts. "Your purpose here, lord, is to—"

"Pray, lady, cease hovering about the door." He crooked his fingers at her.

Reluctantly Jarvia pushed away from the entrance, out of the shadows, into the full light of *langeldar* and cauldron lamps. Deliberately she kept some distance between them. She also made certain she did not stand sideways so that light could filter through the panels of the sheer material and reveal her body to him. She did not trust him, but even more she did not trust her physical reactions to him.

Malcolm's gaze moved from her face down to the tips of her soft leathern shoes and back up again.

"You are indeed beautiful, madam."

"Thank you, lord."

The soft words and smoldering blue eyes unnerved Jarvia further, made her more conscious of her state of undress. She quelled the urge to reach up and tug her clothing higher about her neck.

She walked to the small chest beside her bed. When she made sure she did not touch the warlord as she passed by him, he grinned, a smug, knowing grin that she deliberately ignored. She picked up a pitcher and poured him a tankard of ale.

He accepted it. "I shall drink only if you drink with me, lady. I have no desire to be plied with such strong brew and rendered witless."

Jarvia poured herself a tankard.

The Highlander lifted his in salute; Jarvia did the same. He held it to his mouth but waited to take a swallow until she had done so.

"Now, madam, formalities out of the way, let us be down to business."

For a moment Jarvia stared at the thick, potent brew in her cup. Then she raised her head to gaze directly into those fathomless blue eyes. "You returned to Southerland for a bride, preferably one who is King Wyborn's kinswoman."

With the toe of his boot, Malcolm tapped the low chest on one side of the bed, then walked to the larger storage trunk set against the wall next to the door. This, too, he tapped, then leaned over to examine the metal lock and hinges.

Irritated because he was not giving her his undivided attention, wondering if he were listening to her at all, Jarvia continued. "When you discovered there was no kinswoman to be had, you settled for an adopted daughter."

"I accepted the adopted daughter on condition, madam, as well you know." He ambled over to the trestle table and lifted the lid of one of the iron canisters. Dipping his hand into it, he brought out a dollop of cheese on the tip of his finger.

"Would one adopted daughter serve your purpose as well as another?" Jarvia asked.

Sucking the cheese from his finger, he replaced the canister lid and raised his head to look at her.

Finally she had his full attention.

"Tell me more, lady."

"Since it is in the best interest of the kingdom, the council is determined to find you a bride, sire. King Wyborn chose Gerda because she was his slave and he could do with her as he wished."

Picking up his tankard, Malcolm strolled toward the High Seat. He set the tankard on the broad armrest of the settle and unfastened the gold pin that held together his cloak.

She went on. "Any woman whom the king adopts and declares his legal heir before the council will have the same rights as that of a native daughter. That is Norse law."

Having slung his mantle over the back of the settle, the warlord sat down and stretched his legs toward the fire.

"I have no time, lady, to listen to riddles."

"I suggest that you return to the council and recant your demand that I be banished from the village. Instead, sire, demand that I honorably break my betrothal to Michael Langssonn and that King Wyborn adopt me and give me to you in wedlock . . . as your first and *only* wife."

"Ah, madam"—the warlord drank deeply of his ale—"you drive a hard bargain."

He spoke smugly . . . arrogantly.

Malcolm looked down as he crossed his legs at the ankles. He wiggled his feet in front of the hearth. Jarvia despised the self-satisfied smile that played at the corners of his mouth. As he gazed at his feet, his lids lowered. Thick lashes lay in a black crescent on his sun-browned cheeks.

"Your desires now are different than they were when you spoke before the council," he observed.

"Circumstances have changed," she replied.

He raised his lids, then his head. They exchanged gazes.

"You have no desire to be an outlaw?"

"What do you think of my proposition?" Jarvia countered.

Finally he sighed. "I wish life were so simple, lady, but it is not. I must have a bride from your kingdom because I want a son who will reign over both your kingdom and mine in due time."

"What you desire, lord, is eventually to make our kingdom part of yours."

His gaze once more moved slowly over her body. "You are comely, madam, and most desirable, but you have seen twenty-and-five winters. During this long time, you have not conceived. I am concerned that you will give me no son. Although I would much prefer to bed you, I shall have to marry the younger woman."

"Nay, lord." Jarvia set her tankard on the chest. Her palms were moist and her heart was beating rapidly. "Gerda's moon is late in arriving, and she believes she may be with child."

"By Christ's blood!" The barbarian leaped to his feet and tossed the tankard across the room. He paced angrily. "What will King Wyborn say when he learns of his slave's duplicity?"

"Nay, 'tis not Gerda's doing." Jarvia had the strong urge to shrink from the man, but she did not give way to her fears. "The king and queen know of this. On threat of death, they forced Gerda to do their bidding. She is frightened."

"Well she should be!"

"Lord—" Jarvia took courage and moved closer to him. "You admitted earlier that you found me desirable."

"Desire is not a prerequisite for the marriage bed." He snapped the words. "It is an added pleasure."

"Perhaps I can give you all you want in the marriage bed with additional pleasure."

He looked at her curiously.

"I must have your word, sire, that what I am about to tell you, you will not divulge to anyone."

"Ordinarily I am cautious about making such promises, lady. To you and your people I have learned not to make them at all."

Jarvia licked lips gone suddenly dry; she breathed deeply, hoping to settle the churning in her stomach. "I-I—" Her voice was a croak. She cleared her throat. "I am a maiden, lord."

He stared at her in disbelief.

"Although my husband had lived through forty-and-eight winters, he was yet of child-producing age." Jarvia wanted desperately to have something to do with her hands. "Einher loved me, and I loved him, but he was—he was impotent. We never consummated our marriage." Jarvia chewed her bottom lip. "But Ein-her was also a proud man. I would have no one know that he did not—that he could not—"

"You lie, lady! All of you lie."

"I do not lie."

"Then I would have you prove it."

"I expected that you would."

His eyes narrowed. "I have not found one Southerlander who has any honor. All of you practice deceit. All of you are hellish fiends and sons of Deil. The lot of you!"

"I may be a hellish fiend, sire, and a child of the devil, but I speak the truth."

Deep in thought, Malcolm prowled the room, kicking bracken about. Eventually he picked up his tankard and went to the chest beside the bed. "Lady, if what you say is true, mayhap we shall strike a bargain."

"I have more to say."

After refilling his tankard with ale, he set down the pitcher and turned to face her. "Speak."

"When I agreed to talk to you about accepting Gerda as your bride, the king gave his word before the council that if you declined to wed Gerda, he would set her free. But he has the power to bind his freeman to a particular village, in this case Wybornsbaer. You must insist that Gerda be part of our marriage agreement."

"And why would I wish to make her part of our agreement, lady?"

Jarvia paused and took a deep breath. The Highlander's expression was guarded. She could not tell if he were receptive to her demands or not.

"Because I ask it, lord. Please insist that she be removed to Lord Kirkja's farmstead. I will not leave her here with the king and his wife. If they do not kill her, they will torture her. At Lord Kirkja's she can await the return of Sven, the man whom she would marry."

"Lady," Malcolm said, "your audacity continually surprises me. Do you not know any bounds?"

"I would have your word, sire, that you will protect Ein-her's reputation and Gerda, or I shall not marry you."

Malcolm took a swallow of ale. The tankard hardly removed from his mouth, he said, "Now that you have confessed, lady, you have no choice but to do as I demand. You are not in as great a bargaining position as you would like me to believe. Whether it is to your liking or not, your destiny now rests in my hand."

Jarvia did not like it.

He set the tankard down on the chest nearest him and walked to her. Easing his hand behind her neck, he tugged her closer until their faces almost touched. He bent to kiss her, but Jarvia turned her head away.

"Lord—"

"What now, lady?" Clearly his patience was at an end.

She felt the steady beat of his heart against her breasts . . . the rise and fall of his chest as he breathed.

"Your demand is a son, lord." She paused, then added, "After I have borne you a son, I will remain to be his mother, but I ask that you release me from conjugal rights."

His fingers tightened at the base of her neck. Warm, ale-scented breath touched her forehead. "Lady, I cannot credit my ears with what I am hearing."

"Your word, sire."

"The word I swear to you, lady, is this." Although he spoke softly, his voice was hard. "I will release you from my bed when I am finished letching for you. Then and only then. I will give in to your demands only as it pleases me to do so."

Jarvia stared into his implacable countenance, knowing he would not change his mind.

"Now, it is time for you to prove you are a maiden."

Jarvia twisted her head from his grip and moved away from him. "Shall I—shall I send for Morag?"

He looked puzzled. "Your servant?"

"Aye." She picked up her mantle, swinging it over her shoulders, as she went to the *stofa* entrance.

Long strides brought him between her and the door to block its opening. "Nay, madam."

Jarvia backed away. "But you would have proof of my maidenhood. Morag has been with me since Ein-her and I were wed. She stayed with us in the *stofa* and will swear—"

"Word from your servant will not suffice to prove your innocence. She will be tempted to lie for you."

Jarvia shook her head.

"I might accept the word of a midwife should she examine you and declare that your maidenhead is intact."

"If you say so, lord, but I find the thought of undergoing such an examination humiliating and embarrassing. We shall have to swear the woman to silence, but even with the swearing we cannot be sure she will keep the secret."

"I do not care that the entire kingdom knows," he said. "Do you care so much for a dead man, my lady, that you would go to such lengths to protect his reputation?"

"I loved Ein-her with all my heart," Jarvia replied. "His impotence did not keep him from loving and taking care of me. It did not keep us from talking and sharing knowledge, from becoming the best of friends." Sighing, she turned to grasp the door handle. "I shall send for a midwife, lord."

Again he stayed her movement. "A midwife of my choosing and from my people. I would know where her loyalties lie."

"Do you have such a person traveling with your company?"

"Nay, and I would not return with you to my kingdom without knowing your true state of innocence."

Jarvia strove to maintain her composure. She had sent for him; she was the one who must bargain.

"For a verity, we have only one other recourse." Malcolm smiled ominously.

"Surely . . . surely . . . we can prove my"—Jarvia's voice grew tentative as he shook his head—"virginity another way."

"Nay, lady." His smiled widened.

He stepped closer. Her gaze fell on the golden torque around his neck. Only now did she notice that the neck ring was shaped like a burning torch. Golden flames encircled his neck, but heat emanated from the man. If she gave in to his demand, he would consume her. He was not touching her, yet still she burned.

"I-I must have time to think this over, lord. I had not anticipated your asking this of me."

" 'Tis a fair request."

"I am sure you believe that," Jarvia said, "but I do not. I think it is weighted down on your side, lord. I am the only one who stands to lose—my virginity, my dignity, possibly my integrity. Of the three, lord, the loss of my dignity and integrity concern me most."

"I am surprised by your reaction." Malcolm's tone was underscored with irritation and scorn. "From your behavior in the *skáli*, lady, I would not reckon you to be put off by any situation, certainly not one so forthright as this one. For a verity, madam, what I ask is not unreasonable."

"Asking for the proof is not unreasonable, but your way of determining it is. I request time to ponder your demand."

"You are not frightened because you are lying to me about your innocence?" he asked.

"I am not lying, but I am wary." She gazed openly at him. "What happens between us will greatly alter my life, my future."

"As it will mine."

Jarvia said nothing.

"Lady, you have gone too far. There is no turning back."

Chapter 9

"**N**ay, there is no turning back," she announced with a heavy heart. "So be it."

Smiling, Malcolm mac Duncan clasped her hand. The snug warmth of the clasp stirred Jarvia's senses.

"You have made a wise decision, madam."

"I hope so, lord. Only time will tell." She drew a deep breath, and her next words were more sharp than she intended. "Now, how shall we do this?"

Malcolm regarded her skeptically. Heat flushed Jarvia's cheeks.

"For a verity," she said, "I know about the act of mating, but I-I am not quite sure, lord, how you wish to . . . er . . . to begin."

"Like this, lass." Turning her hand over, Malcolm lightly stroked her palm with his fingers, sending tingles through her body. His voice was low and soothing. "Coupling is more than an act. As I told you before, it is a journey to bliss."

Jarvia closed her mind to the joy of his touch. "For me it is only a duty. Nothing more."

"Ah," he drawled, "so the lady throws down the gauntlet."

Unable to look any longer at the dark blue eyes that gently mocked her, Jarvia lowered her lids. "I know it is best if we mate with our clothing removed. Do I undress myself, or do you? Or shall I divest you of your clothing first?"

Malcolm laughed. The deep, rich laughter, devoid of mockery or sarcasm, caused Jarvia to lift her head. The Highlander was truly amused. His eyes twinkled; his expression had softened.

"Whether you are innocent or trifling with me, lass, I care not. You delight me."

His smug arrogance irritated Jarvia. "Thank you, but we have little time for jesting and soft sayings. We must make haste to prove that I am a maiden. I know Lord Kirkja adjourned the council, but Wyborn can force him to reconvene. Even now, they could be making their decision—"

His hand tightened around hers, the smooth coolness of his ring caressing her flesh. "We have no need for haste, madam. I gave the council and Wyborn instructions to make no decision until I return."

He drew her closer to him with strong but gentle hands.

"Even if the council were about to make a decision, we have no need for haste. Mating is best when done leisurely."

Her irritation growing, as well as her nervousness and embarrassment, Jarvia twisted away from him.

"Do not play coy with me, mistress," he said. "You dressed to seduce me."

She looked up to see him smiling lazily, his eyes hot with desire.

"Did you not?"

Only then did she realize that she stood with the light of the fire to her side, her body clearly revealed through the thin underdress.

"Aye." She turned so that the front panel blocked out the light.

A while longer he held her gaze, then he walked to the door and secured the latch. As if it were an everyday occurrence with him, as if the *stofa* were his home, he returned to the platform.

Suddenly the room seemed too small, too warm, too full of the barbarian.

He slipped the gloves out of his girdle and tossed them on the low chest beside the bed; off came his weapons, each to be laid beside the gloves, all within his reach should he have need of them.

"Where are your furniture drapings?" he asked.

Jarvia pointed. In three strides Malcolm stood in front of the large storage chest close to the *stofa* door. He lifted the lid and rummaged until he found a large linsey-woolsey coverlet, which he held up. He threw it over his shoulder and returned to the bed, giving it a thorough examination, running his hands beneath the layers of covers, even beneath the mattress itself. Finally satisfied, he spread the white linen cloth.

Jarvia's face . . . nay, her entire body . . . burned as she considered what the warlord was doing . . . searching for a hidden bladder of animal blood. He did not trust any of them, and she did not blame him. Wyborn had done nothing to earn the barbarian's confidence.

Satisfied, he straightened. She had offered herself to him, and while she would not change her decision, she was overwrought.

That he possessed the skills to seduce a woman, Jarvia did not doubt, but she had always hoped for more than mere seduction when she coupled. She would have preferred less skill and more warmth and emotion.

But she was mating with him because it was her duty. She must do this in order to save herself and Gerda and Morag . . . and the baby. Yes, she must save the baby.

The Highlander extinguished the cauldron lamps, leaving the *skáli* in the muted glow of firelight. Then he went to Jarvia and caught her hands in his.

"Lady, if this is truly your first time with a man, you may experience a little discomfort, but I shall make the taking as gentle as I can."

"I-I am ready," Jarvia said.

Malcolm tucked a wayward curl behind her ear. "Mayhap."

He bent and brushed his lips across her forehead, his breath warm.

He kissed the skin around the small sphere of gold on her right shoulder. His beard stubble on her flesh, gently abrasive, was as arousing as the soft forays of his lips. "You fastened my brooches earlier. How fitting that I should unfasten yours now."

His lips continued to skim over her shoulders and her collarbone. Pleasure rippled through her body, but she held herself rigid. She would allow him to prove her virginity, but she would not lose control.

"How, lord—"

He brushed his lips over the swell of her breasts, the softness followed immediately by the raspy touch of his beard-stubbled cheek. As if the gentle abrasion were a fire starter, flames streaked from the tip of her breast to the juncture of her thighs. She sucked in her breath sharply and felt her stomach muscles quiver. She closed her eyes against the onslaught of sensation. Fighting the sheer joy of emotion that filled her, she tensed and balled her hands into fists.

"Relax, mistress." Malcolm caught both her hands and pried her fingers loose; he twined his fingers through hers. " 'Twill be much better if you do."

"I seek not pleasure," Jarvia breathed as his mouth softly touched her closed lids.

"But you will receive it."

"I but do my duty and hope that I give you pleasure."

"Duty is not always a burden, lady. Sometimes it can be a delight. So it will be today." His voice lowered. "But you must relax."

He unpinned one of the brooches on her dress and loosened the strap.

"You are most desirable, lady."

The front and back panels of the overdress, still suspended about her body by the other strap, fell to one side. He untied the neck string of the tunic and pushed his hand beneath it and the other strap to slide the clothing from her shoulders. The material fell in a pool around her feet, leaving her naked.

She opened her eyes; he was looking at her breasts. After what seemed a long time, he lightly rubbed the tip of his fingers over the top of one breast, down to the areola, across the nipple. She trembled . . . and knew her control was slipping away. . . .

"You are even more beautiful than I imagined." He stepped closer, and again she inhaled the scent of the man—the freshness of garden herbs and the warm musk of leather. He lifted his arms, the sleeve of his tunic brushing against her cheek. He caught her face between his hands.

Strong, callused hands, accustomed to wielding weapons of war, held her gently, as if she were the most delicate piece of glass among the household goods. His touch warmed and soothed her body as the glowing coals in the *langeldar* warmed and soothed the house in eventide.

He pressed the heels of his palms against her cheeks and threaded his fingers into her hair. Closing her eyes, Jarvia luxuriated in the sensations he aroused in her.

Earlier she had thought he was a spell caster. How much more she believed it now. She was completely entangled in a web of his spinning. She forgot that mating with him was a duty. She did not care that she had been warned by Hilda of his wickedness, of his insatiable carnal appetite; she did not care what the man had been accused of. She conveniently forgot that he was a Highland warlord who wanted a woman for one reason only, that only moments ago he had been willing to see her dishonored so that he could take her into his bed.

"I have seen your naked flesh," he murmured. "Would you see mine?"

"Nay, lord," she lied. "I will be more comfortable in the dark. Please extinguish the fire in the hearth."

"Nay, I would see you while we couple."

"That is barbaric, sire."

"Barbaric?" Malcolm repeated. "Nay, lady. 'Tis part of the ritual of mating." He rubbed the tips of his fingers against her temples, sending tingles down her spine. "Since you have never mated, you would not know. For mating to be best, the man and woman must share all its aspects. They take pleasure from each other; they give pleasure."

"As you say, lord, I cannot say."

"I pray that be the truth, lady."

"It is."

Malcolm raised her hands. Holding them imprisoned in his, he pressed them flat against his chest so that his body heat infused her. Primal need stirred in her as she felt the steady beat of his heart and the hardness of his pectorals.

"You are a strong woman, Lady Jarvia. Whether you are what you say or not, I shall enjoy bedding you."

Jarvia did not answer.

"You defied not only me, lady, but your entire council. When none of your warriors would tell me that King Wyborn was offering me an adopted daughter, you did so. When none of your warriors would stand up to me—the feared barbarian—you did so. Yet now you tremble in my arms. Why? Is it from fear or eagerness?"

"Both. I am eager to have this done and over with, but I am also frightened. This is my first time, and you have a dreadful reputation, lord."

His brows pulled together in a frown. "Are you thinking about Hilda?"

"Nay. As I told you earlier, lord, you have a reputation for being a lusty warrior—"

"Lover."

"Aye," she murmured.

As if her body had a will of its own, Jarvia moved the tips of her fingers through the thick, black hair that fell about his temples.

"And I, lord, am not known to be a lusty woman. Honestly, I-I do not know what to do."

"I *do*."

He drew her into his embrace and lowered his head to claim her lips. His mouth touched hers at the same time that he pressed her body against the length of his. His hands moved down her back. They glided to her waist, where his fingers splayed across her buttocks and kneaded her flesh. She shivered, yet his touch ignited flames of desire throughout her body.

"Put your arms about me," he said.

Duty forgotten, passion her impetus, Jarvia did so.

She had always been fascinated with this man, this barbarian . . . ever since he had arrived in Southerland four winters ago to marry Hilda. Jarvia had wondered even then what it would be like to be wanted by such a brazen man. Her curiosity had not diminished with the passing of time or with the tales of his wickedness.

He raised his head slightly. "Open your mouth."

"Wh-y . . ." Her question was lost as his lips claimed hers again, as his tongue swooped into her mouth to fill her with the essence of him—with abrasive warmth and the taste of ale. Weakness permeated her body, and she felt as if her legs would no longer support her.

His hands pulled her closer to him, closer still, so that she felt a hardness against her pelvis. Her eyes flew open, and she pushed her arms between them to fight free of his embrace. She glanced down to see the impression of his erection, then looked up at him.

"Aye, madam," he said. "It is time for us to know each other fully."

"Lord—"

He placed a finger over her mouth to silence her, then swept her into his arms. He carried her to the bed and laid her on the white coverlet. He sat next to her, his blue eyes smoldering. His hand, big and strong, now tenderly stroked her.

"You are the most beautiful woman in this village, lawspeaker. I was proud of the way you stood up to the men of your council."

"So proud, lord, that you asked that I be banished," she whispered.

"You are much too good for these people," Malcolm said. "If you had been banished, I would have ransomed you. You belong to a proud race like the Highlanders. If indeed you are innocent, madam, and I marry you, my people shall be happy to see me return with such a spirited woman. A woman like you will bear strong sons."

"And daughters," Jarvia said, her words lost in the flood of emotions that inundated her being as the warlord caressed her body, building a heat of desire in her so hot that she felt she would explode into scores of tiny sparks.

Each stroke heightened her excitement. It whetted her yearning to know the intimate secrets shared between a woman and a man during mating.

"I have wanted to make you fully mine ever since I first saw you," he confessed.

Jarvia, too, had felt a primal attraction to him. She still felt it and was frightened by it. His cool lips touched her breasts, causing the fire of desire to burn more hotly. She felt sensations in places she had never dreamed possible. Awareness tingled; desire throbbed through her.

"Ah, lady, this is more than a duty, is it not? You desire me."

Breathing deeply, drowning in the delicious emotions, Jarvia said, " 'Tis a duty, sire. One that I shall perform well."

"Be truthful, lady. You have a letching for the barbarian." His lips captured the tip of her breast, and he suckled.

"Aye." She felt another flame of ecstasy sear her body. "But wanting, lord, is not loving."

"Nay." Without moving his mouth, he said, "I want not loving, now or ever, nor do I offer love."

His warm breath spread across her already flushed flesh. Jarvia pushed her hand through his hair, delighted by the soft strands between her fingers. His hand cupped her breast to ease the nipple farther into his mouth. She gasped and closed her eyes, feeling the prick of tears behind her lids.

She knew how hard a man the barbarian was; she knew his purpose. One part of her despised what he was doing to her, what he had done to Hilda. She consoled herself and justified her actions by arguing that she was only doing her duty.

Yet another part of her—a primitive part that she had not known she possessed until she had been alone with the Highlander in his chamber—this part of her wanted him. It craved his touch. She wanted him with the same intensity, the same fervor that he wanted her.

"Madam," he said, "unfasten the brooches on my shirt."

Slowly Jarvia sat up. Through passion-laden eyes she sought the brooches and fumbled to undo them, until his shirt was open.

She lay down. Malcolm rolled off the bed and began to undress. First he took off the torque and his armband, and placed them on the small chest beside his weapons. Then he pulled the tunic over his head and tossed it onto the settle. He sat down on the small stool in front of the loom to unlace his cuarans. Standing, he unfastened one by one the latchets of his girdle. He stepped out of his trousers.

Ein-her was the only man Jarvia had seen naked, and his frail, aged body looked nothing like the Highlander's. Muscles rippled from this man's chest to his feet, and his body gleamed in the firelight. Visually she traced the hard line of his stomach to his erection.

He strode toward her, and she pulled back from such blatant masculinity, such blatant desire.

"You said you would take me in tenderness," she reminded him.

"Aye."

He returned to kneel on the bed. Bending, he took her nipple into his mouth. He sucked it gently and Jarvia felt the excruciating pleasure of desire pierce her body afresh, taking residence in the lower part of her stomach.

"Earlier you wanted to make haste, madam," Malcolm said. "Indeed there are times when a man and a woman come together in fierce, urgent matings. But not the first time. Only after the woman has been taught the secrets of seduction, after she has grown accustomed to receiving a man."

His lips moved against her breasts, his warm breath blowing against her stomach. He brushed his mouth over her other breast, his tongue exploring the areola.

"Hilda said that you were—"

Malcolm tensed.

Instantly Jarvia regretted her words.

"You were saying?"

"Hilda said you had an insatiable carnal appetite," Jarvia murmured. "That you degraded her with your demands, lord."

Malcolm laughed heartily. "Aye, madam, I am a lusty man. I enjoy carnal pleasure. And so will you when I am finished with you this night."

As he spoke, he spread kisses on her cheeks, her hair, and her temples. So intense was the joy that she shivered.

"Somehow, madam, I don't believe mere mortals could have conceived of mating with their limited minds. Soon you will understand that what can be shared between a man and a woman far exceeds the bounds of this kingdom—yea, the bounds of all known kingdoms."

He said nothing about wanting her to perform degrading acts, and as he caressed Jarvia, Hilda's accusations against him began to seem untrue. Or, trapped in his spell, was Jarvia just deceiving herself?

But his loving soon wiped the thought from her mind. Giving herself up to the pleasure of the moment, she closed her eyes and ran her fingers through his hair, massaging his scalp. He pressed her down on the coverlet and stretched out beside her, aligning his lean body along the length of hers. His lips closed over hers.

He moved his hand to her thighs, then between them. His fingers had no sooner touched the sensitive area than Jarvia tensed and felt her body throb. She arched against him.

"Methinks we are moving with too much haste," she mumbled.

He laughed softly. "Nay, lady, yet I understand your fears. You must learn to receive the pleasure I give so that you can give it in return."

"You would make a wanton of me, lord?"

"I believe you are already a wanton, lady."

He brushed his lips down her throat, across the collarbone, back and forth in whisper-soft motions that teased and tormented.

"Let me show you how wonderful mating can be. Let me carry you to bliss."

His mouth reclaimed her breast, his tongue seeking the swollen tip. His other hand brushed over her breasts, down her stomach, around her navel. Then his fingers touched once again the soft triangle of hair.

"Enjoy this, lady."

Slipping his fingers into her secret place, he kissed her mouth, her neck, her breasts. He slid his fingers deeper within her, moving them in and out, each stroke lifting her higher and higher, away from reality into a world of . . . bliss. Jarvia bit back her cries, but they would not be contained. She groaned and threw her head back against the bed cushion. She had never known such feelings. And though she pleaded for fulfillment, she wanted this wonderful moment never to end.

Malcolm removed his hand. Bereft, rendered a beggar, she opened her eyes and reached for him. He lifted himself over her, his knee spreading her legs farther apart. Gently he pressed the tip of his hardened manhood where his hand had been.

Time and again he stroked her, whispering soothing words, until she relaxed, until she began to feel the heat of his arousal against her flesh.

"Do not be frightened," he said.

He did not remove his shaft but neither did he enter her. He continued to stroke her with his hands; he kissed her; he whispered reassuringly to her. Gently his arousal probed between her thighs to make her ready; it massaged the opening of her femininity, hot flesh caressing hot flesh, asking for entry.

Always he touched and played with her body. The gentle forays soon alerted Jarvia to her emptiness, and she wanted more of him. She was giving herself to his kisses, taking his tongue fully into her mouth, taking him fully into her embrace, arching against him to take him fully inside of her.

He was surrounded by warm tightness.

She stiffened.

He encountered the barrier.

She gasped.

The maidenhead!

"Lord," she murmured, breathless with wonder. Her body trembled with awe at the change she felt within herself on having received him. "You—you are so big."

He stopped. "Am I hurting you?"

"Yes . . . no—I do not know." Tears ran down her cheeks.

"Lady," he said, "if I am hurting you, I will stop."

"Nay, I don't want that."

"Am I too big for you?"

"Nay."

In the warm glow of the firelight, he looked dark, huge, and mysterious, but also concerned. This was the first time she had seen his features truly softened by caring. Her awe and wonder joined with a sense of her power as a woman in that ancient ritual of coupling.

"I-I did not know what to expect."

"Is it better or worse than you thought?"

"It is better," she murmured. Much better, she thought, feeling his magnificent endowment inside her, filling her, promising her a wonderful journey to bliss. A deep, clenching thrill seized her. It felt good to be stretched and filled by a man's desire.

He laughed. "And it will be even better."

He kissed her and moved in her at the same time. Jarvia thought surely she would die from happiness. As he had promised, he brought her more pleasure than she had ever dreamed she could feel.

"Is this bliss, lord?" she whispered.

Chuckling, Malcolm nuzzled his face against her cheek, as if he deliberately sought the tender spot beneath her ear. He found it.

"Nay, sweet lady. We have only begun our journey."

Jarvia closed her arms around him, her fingers digging into his back. She clung to him, and he began to move faster and deeper. She received him . . . all of him. His hands, his lips, spoke of his needs and desires. They told her of his pleasure in touching her. The friction of his thrusting was such that a marvelous pressure began to build.

She caught Malcolm's rhythm and rocked with him, their tempo increasing. The pressure built to permeate her entire being. She felt as if she were a fragile glass beaker that had dropped onto a stone and shattered into countless tiny, sparkling jewels. She tore her lips from his and rolled her head to the side. She arched to receive his last thrust.

She tensed and shuddered.

He stiffened and groaned.

He spilled his seed inside her.

She received it.

He lifted the bulk of his weight off of her, pulling her with him, his head on her bed cushion. She buried her face against his shoulder, feeling the beads of perspiration on his hot skin. In the firelight she saw the glistening sheen on his splendidly bronzed body. She rubbed her cheek against his damp chest.

"Aye, Lady Jarvia," Malcolm said. "Already my seed is inside you."

Already his seed was inside her.

"Now you belong to Malcolm mac Duncan."

Aye, she feared she did indeed belong to this dark Highlander.

Chapter 10

His eyes grown sultry, the Highlander gazed into Jarvia's upturned face as, propped on an elbow, he soothed a hand over her hip and down her thigh.

"You are as passionate as you are beautiful," he murmured, "and your skin feels like the finest silk."

He lowered his head and nuzzled the sensitive area below her ear before his lips placed kisses down the column of her throat. "For a verity, madam, you have given me great pleasure this night."

His mouth gently touched hers. Jarvia's lips quivered beneath his. She opened them slightly, still hungry for the feel of him. How quickly resumed was her longing for the barbarian! She was sated, yet unsated.

Had this man awakened within her an insatiable carnal appetite that matched his own? The gods forbid! The idea of not being able to control her emotions frightened Jarvia to no end.

He lifted his mouth from hers. "Did I hurt you?"

"Nay."

Not physically. But the unfamiliar emotions he had aroused in her were as disturbing and overwhelming as a physical affliction.

His eyes were midnight blue, with black at the center. Eyes that cast a spell over her so that she did not want to think. She wanted to be locked away forever in her *stofa*, in her bed, with this man.

She ran her fingers over his cheeks. The raspy feel of beard stubble beneath her skin sent flickers of renewed arousal through her body.

Malcolm smiled at her. "I will give you what you want, my lady."

Vaguely Jarvia knew she should feel humiliated or angry or frightened by what had passed between them, but she was still wrapped in his warmth, bound to him by threads of desire that transcended rational thought. The glowing flames of the *langeldar* shone up on them, etching their contours in a blaze of gold. She was captivated by this man who had carried her to bliss . . . who promised to do it again, and again.

Malcolm bestowed a kiss on the tip of her nose. "Give me but a moment, mistress."

He rolled away from her, the movement jolting Jarvia from her dream world and tugging her back to reality. Through languid eyes, she watched as he rose from the bed and walked to the washing alcove. He pushed aside the curtain and filled the basin with water, with which he cleansed himself. After he tossed the dirtied water into the stone-paved drainage ditch that ran through the *stofa*, he refilled the basin and set it on the small chest next to the bed.

He sat beside Jarvia, dipped the cloth into the water, and wrung it out. He handed it to her. As she accepted it, knowing what it was for, her cheeks burned. She shoved up on the bed, acutely aware of her nudity, equally aware of his. He turned his head to allow her privacy as she cleaned herself. Yet still she felt self-conscious.

After a moment, he said, "For such a wanton—"

Jarvia tensed.

"For such an opinionated woman, you have little to say about your first coupling."

She dropped the soiled cloth into the basin. " 'Twas the coming together of a man and a woman. Surely it is the same everywhere."

"Nay, lady, sadly it is not. I gave you pleasure as well as receiving it myself, but it is not always that way."

He drew his fingers along the outside of her thighs, over her hips, and dipped low on the tender skin of her stomach. Jarvia's muscles quivered, and she sucked in her breath. Although she felt the quickening of sensation, a renewed yearning, she rolled away from the Highlander.

If she did not, she would give in to his demands. It had been necessary to mate with him once, to prove she was a maiden. But there could be no purpose in a second mating except to appease their carnal lusts, and that would compromise her integrity.

"Where are you going?" he asked.

Rising from the bed and grabbing her clothing, Jarvia held her green tunic in front of her and turned to face him. " 'Tis time for us to announce our intention to the council."

A languorous smile creased Malcolm's face as he regarded her through slitted eyes. He reached out, caught the material in her hands, and jerked it from her. "Nay, madam, I am not ready to depart from your *stofa* . . . or your bed . . . so soon." With his hand he beckoned to her.

The Highlander's suggestive gaze quickened a cord of longing in Jarvia that embarrassed her. She bent to retrieve her clothes and hastily retreated to a shadowed corner of the room, where she began to dress.

Softly he called, "Return to the bed, madam."

"Nay." She drew the string of the tunic tightly so that the neckline rose until the material fully covered her breasts.

He spoke more sharply. "Madam, return to the bed."

"The purpose of our coupling, lord"—Jarvia quickly fastened the pin of one brooch—"was to provide proof of my maidenhood. You have proof."

She fastened the other brooch, then brushed out the wrinkles from her overdress.

"There is no need for us to go through the ordeal again. And we shall not until we are properly wed."

"Ordeal!" Malcolm bolted up. But immediately a smile wiped the anger from his countenance. "Ah, madam, you were deliberately goading me. Something you should be wary of doing. I do not like playing games with a woman who belongs to me."

Jarvia moved back into the full light of the *langeldar* and sat on the small stool. The Highlander's words reminded her of her days as a slave, when she had belonged to Wyborn.

She had promised herself that if ever she were free, she would allow no one to dictate to her again. Even after that day had arrived, she had hidden her emotions so that no one—*no* one—had been able to touch her real self—the soul that resided in her body. That belonged to her and her alone.

Now she had met a man who she feared would be able to reach that secret self she had hidden and protected all these years.

"I do not *belong* to you, Lord Malcolm," she told him. "And our marriage will not take place until my betrothal to Michael Langssonn has been honorably dissolved. At that time—and only at that time—shall I consent to become betrothed to you."

Malcolm flipped off the bed, his hard physique glimmering in the golden firelight. He reached for his trousers.

"Mistress, do you think to play me for a fool?"

"Nay, but neither do I intend to let you play me for one."

Jarvia concentrated on putting on her shoes, unwilling to let her body play truant to her mind. It was so tempting to return to the Highlander's bed and beg for his caresses, but she would not do so this night.

She heard the rustle of material followed by the dull clank of metal. What her eyes did not behold did not stay her imaginings. In her mind she saw him step into the black trousers that fit his legs so snugly, saw him fasten the latchets of his girdle—the leather slowly covering his long, now flaccid manhood and his flat, taut stomach.

Pushing such tantalizing thoughts aside, Jarvia went to her clothing chest and found a linen scarf. She did not care if it matched her clothing. As she straightened, she noticed the mussed bed coverings, her blood on the white coverlet.

She stopped and stared at the token of her innocence. The loss of her maidenhead did not concern her; that she had given in to the barbarian's demands did. Aye, it could be argued that she had done so willingly. But she had had no other choice.

"Do you need the linen as proof that you were the first man to lie with me?" she asked.

"Nay, madam, but I wanted to be sure that you were not deceiving me with little tricks."

Jarvia caught the piece of material and jerked it from the bed. Turning, she tossed it into the *langeldar* and watched the flames greedily lap around the cloth, completely consuming it. At first it was a thin black sheet; then it shattered, tiny particles of black intermingling with the flames. Soon nothing remained but the scent of burning linen. She looked at the Highlander and wondered if he too would consume her, leaving nothing but the ashes of herself.

With a heavy heart, she moved to the bronze panel in the door and began to bind her hair with the scarf. She was holding her head down, tying the bow at the nape of her neck, when she felt the jerk of material. Pins and combs and hair tumbled about her face. She spun around, almost colliding with the warlord.

"I hate this damnable rag," he spat out.

She stared at his naked chest.

"I do not wish you to wear it."

White-hot fury swept through Jarvia. She lifted her head and glared into his fiery countenance.

"You do not dictate to me what I can or cannot do," she said with soft vehemence, "You are marrying me for one purpose only—to have a child."

"A son, madam. A son!" The considerate lover of only moments ago had once more become the harsh Highland warrior. "No matter the purpose, we are to be married, and I *shall* dictate what you can or cannot do. Know, madam, that you are mine."

A woman full of cold fury glared into the face of a man inflamed with rage. Both were equally strong and determined. Both were consumed by their purpose.

"I am not yours yet. I am marrying you to save Gerda and her unborn child. You do not own my person and never will. You will treat me with respect, lord. That I demand or I shall not honor our bargain."

"No matter how I treat you, lady, you will marry me. You and I both know that I hold your destiny in my hand."

The harsh but true words pained Jarvia deeply. But she did not give in to tears or hysterics. Her only defense against this man was her composure. Her aloofness. Her coolness. She must never let him know how deeply he affected her.

"Now, lady, you shall send word to Lord Lang that you wish to dissolve your betrothal to his son."

"What if he does not—"

"He will," Malcolm said. "Every man can be bought, lady."

"Aye, lord, perhaps you are right." She spoke quietly, keeping the anger out of her voice.

"I am right." Malcolm caught her left hand in his. "Although that cloth you wear on your head signifies that you are married, I give you permission to wear it until we are wed. But you shall not wear it afterwards. And this"—he tugged the marriage ring from her hand—"you will cease wearing now."

Words of protest leaped to Jarvia's lips, but she swallowed them as she looked into his hard eyes. The Highlander was acting within his rights. She had no reason to wear the scarf or the ring any longer. Ein-her was her past; Malcolm mac Duncan was her future.

"I would keep the ring, lord," she said softly.

"So that you can remember the man?"

"Nay, I have no need of touchable objects to remember Ein-her. I have memories of him locked in the coffers of my heart. This was a gift, a special gift from him to me. It signifies my freedom from slavery."

Malcolm nodded curtly and dropped the ring into her extended palm. "Keep it, madam."

Jarvia lifted the lid of her clothing chest and dropped her ring into a small jewelry box. Her back to him, she said, "I have observed that you wear only one ring. Most men of your wealth and stature wear many."

"I have no need to bear my wealth for all to see," he answered.

Jarvia turned, her gaze going to the three brooches and the shirt lying on the chest.

He shrugged. "I allowed myself this luxury, lady, because I was going to woo a bride." He held out his hand. "This ring, like the one you wore, has a special meaning for me."

Jarvia stepped closer to him and studied the ring. Because it was worn smooth, she could tell that it was old.

"It is in the shape of a sickle," she said.

"Aye, a religious symbol for those of us who are born on either the summer or the winter solstice. The gold symbolizes the sun, the crescent shape the moon."

Jarvia touched the ring with a fingertip. "We have such a symbol in our religion, too. The golden sickle represents the twin deities, Light and Darkness."

"It is the same for us," Malcolm said. "Night rules over the autumn and winter, and Day rules over spring and summer."

She looked at him. "On which solstice were you born?"

"The summer."

Aye, she thought, it had to be. He was the lord of fire.

"My birth father had the ring crafted prior to my birth," he said. "My mother presented it to me when I was in my tenth winter, when I became a warrior. I have worn it ever since."

He paused as if lost in thought. "As I grew older and bigger, I changed the finger on which I wore it many times until now it fits only the smallest one."

Dumbstruck, Jarvia stared at him. If he had told her the gods had hewn him out of Highland mountain stone or that gnomes had forged him in their magical underground furnaces, she would have more easily believed that than she believed he had been conceived by mere mortals.

"My father had the ring crafted for my older brother."

Before Jarvia thought, she murmured, "The gods forbid that there should be two of you loosed upon us."

Malcolm smiled slightly. "Nay, lady, have no such fear. When my brother was but a child, he was killed by Northland sea raiders. My father, too." He rubbed his fingers over the ring before adding softly, "My mother calls all Northmen barbarians, lady, and she hates them with passion. They deprived her of the man whom she loved with all her heart and soul, and of her eldest son."

"I am sorry, sire," Jarvia murmured.

"There is no need for sorrow, good lady." The Highlander spoke sharply, and his eyes were unreadable. "Birth and death are the cycle of life. For some the cycle is longer than others."

Jarvia closed the lid to her storage trunk. In the small jewelry box, she had locked away her past. Now she must look to her future.

She walked to the center of the *stofa* and picked up her scarf. She did not wish to wear the head-wrap any longer, but felt that she must. She had given up the ring, but this scarf was now symbolic of her independence. At the moment she needed to feel that she was her own person. She threw the cloth over her shoulders and quickly rearranged her hair into a coil at the nape of her neck.

"Although you have decreed that we shall be married, that my betrothal shall be broken," Jarvia said, not caring that she spoke sarcastically, "we shall have to go through with the formal ceremony."

"We shall have to hold two ceremonies, lady. One here to conform to your laws and customs, another when we arrive in the Highlands to conform to my laws and customs."

"We shall truly be bound in matrimony," Jarvia said dryly.

"I would have it no other way."

"You should know, the penalty for rupture is heavier for the woman than for the man. While I live comfortably, I do not possess great wealth, certainly not what Lord Lang, my intended's father, would require as the rupture endowment. Someone will have to pay that penalty."

"I suspect so," he said.

She felt his eyes on her back.

"Are you asking me to pay it, lady?"

She shrugged. "I would rather you did than King Wyborn."

"Why?"

"He once owned me as a slave. I do not wish to be beholden to him again. Since you will own me as a husband owns a wife, the debt should be yours."

"You ask this favor of me," Malcolm said, "yet you would refuse me the pleasure of your body until we are wed."

" 'Tis for the best, lord. I would have no shadow on either your name or mine. I would make sure that our child's birth is well secured in wedlock. I will not take the chance that you might yet refuse me your name."

"Lady—" His voice went soft; his lashes lowered until his eyes were slits. "You are indeed audacious. I count the days until you become mine."

He reached for his shirt and the three brooches. Handing them to Jarvia, he said, "Fasten this for me."

Only hours earlier she had at first refused to perform this menial task. Now circumstances had changed. She fastened his shirt, but did not brush out the wrinkles. She stepped back.

"The people will demand that we hold the betrothal ceremony," she said.

"I would insist. I would have you legally bound to me. And that, lady, will be the only reason why I do not mate with you again until you are severed from your betrothed. Understand well, lady, you are mine."

He strode to the small stool she had recently vacated, sat down, and put on his cuarans. "If I remember, lady, your betrothal ceremony consists of my bestowing on you a ring, a kiss, and a gift."

"Aye," she answered. "A gift of great importance to you."

He laughed sarcastically.

Jarvia felt a tinge of irritation but continued, "The people of Southerland must know that you are sincere in your desire to have me as your bride."

Malcolm tied off the leathern thongs that bound the boots to his leg, then walked to the chest to pour himself a goblet of ale.

"In addition to the bride-gift, lord," Jarvia said, her heart beating wildly, "I shall expect a morning-gift."

Malcolm nearly choked on the ale.

"Why should I give you a morning-gift? Everyone would then know that you surrendered your virginity to me. I thought you wanted to keep that a secret."

"I do want it to be a secret. But I would like you to give me a morning-gift in private, to acknowledge just between us that I have given you the gift of my virginity."

"Have you any particular gift in mind?" He set the goblet down.

"Since I am the one who is breaking the betrothal, I shall have to surrender all my possessions to Lord Lang. And he will demand even more than what I own."

Malcolm cinched his weapon belts about his waist with quick, sure movements.

"Not knowing what the outcome of our marriage will be, lord, I want you to bestow on me as my morning-gift land enough to build my own farmstead and a small chest of gold and silver."

"How big a chest?" he asked dryly.

She pointed to one in the corner.

He gasped. "Lady, do you have any idea how much gold and silver it would take to fill that?"

"That is my price."

"A warrior is not valued so highly, madam!" he snapped.

"Nor can he give you the son you seek." Feeling rather smug, Jarvia went on, "Formal consummation makes the marriage, sire, and the morning-gift is its seal. Although I am not reckoned a virgin by my people, they will expect to see proof of our marriage."

He picked up his gloves and slipped them on.

"Do you agree to my terms?" she asked.

Jarvia had seen the passionate side of the barbarian. Now he stared at her with ice-blue eyes.

"I shall think on them, lady."

He strode across the *skáli* toward the door.

"Also, sire, I would have your promise that if I do not bear you a son, you will give me an honorable divorce."

He stopped, turned, and stared at her. "Madam, you are new at this game. I am not. Know for a fact, letching runs its course. In most instances the course is short. At the moment you are in my favor. My desire for you runs hot. Thus, I overlook many of your faults. But tread softly. Cease pushing. I will not be made to look like a fool in front of others."

It was the Highland warlord speaking, not the man who had only moments ago been her lover, her tutor in the subtleties of mating. He was a hard man, indomitable, hewn out of the Highlands themselves, and would crush anyone who prevented him from getting what he wanted.

"Aye, lord," she answered, "I am new to the game, but I am not dim-witted. Because the course of letching is short, I must make all my bargains while your desire for me is strong. I cannot afford to wait longer."

His thick, dark brows came together in a frown. "Until we are married, I am content to let you lay the boundaries of our relationship . . . within reason. Once married, you will belong to me. I will set the rules."

His hand curled around the wrought iron door handle and lifted the latchet.

"Lord"—Jarvia despised herself for sounding so tentative—"you have not forgotten Gerda, have you?"

The door opened; cool, damp air blew into the *stofa*. The Highlander held out his hand. "Lady, accompany me. I would have you present when I make my demands before the Council of Justice."

Chapter 11

The rain had stopped. Moonlight washed the village in soft shades of blue, gray, and silver. A cool wind blew against Malcolm as he and Jarvia stepped onto the stone porch of her house.

In the distance Wyborn's warriors surrounded the entrance to the Great House. Malcolm could see none of his men, but he knew they were close by. In the next moment several Highlanders stepped into the torchlight.

Lachlann, his helmet tucked under his arm, joined Malcolm, and the two men stepped aside so that they could speak in private.

"It went well?"

"My search has ended," Malcolm answered. "I have found my bride."

"I presume she is not married," Lachlann said. "Or is this a *small* problem you shall have to overcome?"

Malcolm grinned at his friend's dry wit. "Nay, she is not married, only betrothed. Our only problems are seeing that she becomes the king's native daughter and that her betrothal is honorably ruptured."

Lachlann's thick brows rose. "Knowing you, I'm sure you have these small details worked out."

"Aye. Southerland law is much like ours. Lady Jarvia will become a native daughter when she is adopted."

Lachlann chuckled. "This is a pleasing solution to your problem then. You have had a letching for the woman since you laid eyes on her." He paused, then added in a low, serious voice, "Be wary, my friend. I trust none of these Southerlanders and wish before God you had taken your bride from elsewhere."

"I remember Hilda's treachery," Malcolm replied. "I shall be careful."

Jarvia said nothing, but Malcolm knew she was curious

about the conversation. He would not enlighten her. The less she knew, the better she would serve his purposes . . . and the safer she would be.

"What about the younger woman?"

Malcolm clapped his best-man playfully on the shoulder. "You have found no one to ease the ache in your loins?"

"Aye." Lachlann lowered his lids. "I was just curious."

"I shall take care of her," Malcolm answered, his glance straying to Jarvia. "I promised my lady."

Malcolm knew he had not appeased his friend's worries. Later when they were alone, they would talk more freely.

"Ghaltair and Thomas recently rode in," Lachlann said.

"Ghaltair?"

"Aye."

"He should not be here!" Malcolm exclaimed. "I left him back home to care for the breeding mares."

"He said he came on an urgent matter."

"No message is so important that he should leave his post and bear it himself."

"Aye, Malcolm, it is. Ard-righ Fergus sends word that while we are honoring the peace agreement between us and the Picts, they are not. They have continued their raids on us, daring cattle and pony raids deep within our territory."

Malcolm swore softly. The burden of his kingdom weighed heavily on his shoulders. He needed to be home. He needed to be here. He had felt—and still felt—that he had had no choice but to come to Southerland himself. At the moment his marriage was his most important concern. He wanted this peace alliance with Wyborn, but more, he wanted a son who would be a blood heir and first claimant to the High Seat of all the northern kingdoms of the Highlands.

Lachlann said, "Lady Sybil wants us to declare war against the Picts."

"Aye, she would. She warned me that the Picts would not keep their word."

Sybil, Malcolm's foster sister, had also accused him of being hungry for power. He would never forget her jealous rage the day the Council of Chiefs had elected him heir to the king. Malcolm touched the torque he wore about his neck, the symbol of his rank. He knew—and deep down so did Sybil—that his desire to bring these kingdoms together was not for his own glory. Unified, the Highlanders could accomplish much more than they could separately. Time that was spent fighting and killing could be put to better use . . . tending crops, hunting food, trading for goods. Peace and a better life for his people were what Malcolm mac Duncan wanted.

He told Lachlann, "As soon as I have spoken to the council, I shall speak with Thomas and Ghaltair. Until then, see to their needs."

Lachlann nodded. "Do you want Arthur to return to the meeting with you?"

"Nay. Wyborn's bard has been truthful so far, and I have Lady Jarvia with me."

"Take care," Lachlann admonished, then eased back into the shadows.

When Malcolm was alone with Jarvia, he extended his right arm. She lay her palm lightly over his hand.

"Now, madam, we shall be on our way."

"Your outriders bring bad news?" she asked.

Malcolm looked at her. The silver glaze of the moon softened her beauty and highlighted the curls that escaped her head scarf.

"Why do you ask?"

"Your arm is tense beneath my hand," she answered. "Your brows are drawn together in a manner that indicates your displeasure."

Jarvia's observation surprised Malcolm. Although he was glad she spoke his language, he did not trust her and knew he could not speak freely in front of her. Now he realized he must also be careful to guard his facial expressions and body gestures.

"I am concerned about my kingdom, lady," Malcolm said. "Always when a chieftain is away, he fears trouble. He has enemies without . . . and within."

Malcolm did not wish to say too much. Perhaps Jarvia knew more about the turmoil in the kingdom than he had thought. Since Hilda had been involved in a conspiracy and Jarvia had been Hilda's friend, she might be involved also. She possessed more soul and passion than Hilda; she was more intelligent, more capable of harming him. She could be craftier than several enemies put together. He must be cautious and observant. He would disclose nothing.

"Who is Lady Sybil?" Jarvia asked.

"She is my foster sister."

"Is foster kinship among your people like ours?" Jarvia asked. "Fostered brothers and sisters are considered related in the sense that they bond families and clans together, but they are at liberty to marry each other."

"Aye, 'tis like our fosterage," he answered.

They took a few more steps before Jarvia said, "Exactly what is the relationship between you and Lady Sybil?"

Surprised by her question, by her astuteness, Malcolm did not answer.

"You might think it forward of me to ask," Jarvia said, "but since I am consenting to be your wife, I want to know."

Malcolm grinned. "Jealous, my lady?"

"Nay, curious."

"At one time, Lady Sybil and I were lovers. But that was long ago."

"Did you ever wish to marry her, lord?"

"You are most inquisitive," Malcolm said.

"Aye," Jarvia replied.

"At one time we thought of marriage."

"Does the Lady Sybil grieve her loss?"

"Me?"

Jarvia nodded.

Malcolm laughed. "Nay, she does not consider me a loss."

Jarvia was quiet for a long while, then said, "Did she hurt you, lord?"

"Nay, lady, I do not entertain the idea of hurt. That is a weakness no warrior, much less a king, can afford. Most times what one loses, one can replace with something better."

Malcolm's grip tightened on the door, but he did not open it. "I have one desire. That is to unite Southermen, Scots, and Picts so that Highlanders are one, and to have a blood heir, a son who is first claimant to all three High Seats. Every other thing is second."

"Are you hungry for power, lord?"

"I have been accused of it."

He pushed open the door and motioned for Jarvia to enter.

She shook her head and pointed to the closed door next to it. "I must enter there. It is the women's entrance."

Customs varied among people. When Malcolm was being diplomatic, he adhered to them. Tonight he was testy. Wyborn had taken him for a fool. Thomas and Ghaltair brought ill tidings. He was uncomfortable with the direction his conversation with Jarvia had taken.

He was unsure of this woman he was taking to wife. He could not allow himself to become too interested in her, else she would become his weakness. Already he had given her too much freedom, had succumbed to her demands too easily.

He stopped Jarvia from opening the women's door and waved at the men's entrance. "Enter with me."

She gazed at him before inclining her head.

Malcolm swept her down the aisle of the *stofa*. He was pleased that she held her shoulders back, her head high. They did not stop until they stood before the king and queen.

"King Wyborn, I have returned to your house to make known to you and the council my demands," Malcolm said.

Queen Adelaide's small, glittering eyes fastened on Jarvia, who raised her chin higher and returned the stare. Malcolm smiled. So far his bride-to-be was holding her own. But she was with her own people. How would she fare when pitted against his devious foster sister?

Like Jarvia, Sybil was a large woman. She was also beautiful. Because she loved gaming, she wore her dark auburn hair in a long, single braid down her back. Often she dressed in trousers. She could wield weapons with a skill and might equal to many warriors.

But Sybil was also a woman, soft in all the right places. How well he knew. His first lover, she had schooled him in the fine art of seduction. Like Malcolm, Sybil wanted a united Highlands, but she intended to conquer the different tribes by force for the sheer pleasure of the fight. When she had proposed marriage, and that they jointly govern the Clan Duncan and someday the kingdom of the Northern

Scots, Malcolm had refused. He had been enamored of her and had wanted marriage, but he knew it was impossible for them to rule jointly.

He wanted unity, but he wanted it for different reasons. So much more could be accomplished for the people if they could turn their energies from fighting to building a peaceful civilization. Malcolm had chosen to follow the Christ and to blend the good of Christianity with the good of the old ways. Sybil rejected the new god, she fully espoused the ancient dieties. The older she grew, the darker her magic became. Malcolm did not fear the Ancient Ones or their magic; he feared Sybil's magic, which she used for evil purposes.

His rejection of Sybil had driven her into a rage. A strong woman, one who fought for what she wanted, she screamed for revenge. She was determined to regain what she believed Malcolm had taken from her . . . her birthright, her clan. Filled with bitterness, she still sought to humiliate him by disputing his right to lead Clan Duncan. The number of her followers was growing each day.

"What are your demands, lord?" Wyborn inquired.

Malcolm turned his thoughts back to the business at hand.

He escorted Jarvia to the smaller settle. His hand on the hilt of his sword, his mantle snapping about his ankles, he strode to the tables where the members of the council sat.

"I, Malcolm mac Duncan, chief of Clan Duncan of the kingdom of the Northern Scots, do this night declare that I desire Lady Jarvia to be my wife."

As the interpretation sounded through the *stofa*, eyes widened; council members looked from one to the other and murmured among themselves. They shook their heads in surprise and indecision.

When the skald hushed, the queen slapped the arm of the High Seat. "This cannot be! Gerda is my husband's bastard daughter." Her coarse voice grated through the room as she gouged her husband in the ribs with her elbow. He jumped as if coming out of a trance. "Tell him, husband."

Blinking, Wyborn stammered, "She-she is. She is the native daughter you demanded, lord."

"And hoped I would take," Malcolm said.

He paused a long while, letting the translation echo into silence. "Your law-speaker convinced me, Lord Wyborn, that according to Southerland law an adopted child is recognized as a native child."

"Yes, lord." Wyborn bobbed his head.

"Then, I request that you adopt Lady Jarvia."

The queen's mouth fell open.

"Also the slave whom you call Gerda."

Malcolm saw the color drain from Jarvia's face. Her hand tightened around the end of the settle so that her knuckles whitened. She had wanted him to save Gerda from Wyborn and the queen, but she had not expected him to demand that they adopt Gerda so that he could marry her also.

Jarvia's visible reaction worried him, but he could not allow himself to give in to soft feelings for the woman. As he had told her earlier, the tenderness that came from letching always ran its course. While he would enjoy Jarvia and would accept her as his first wife, he could not allow passion to rule his head. He would have his son. If Jarvia did not produce a male heir, he would divorce her and marry Gerda.

As the king listened to the skald's translation of Malcolm's words, his nostrils flared in anger. His brow furrowed; his face turned a sickly shade of yellow.

"Lord—" He brushed a hand down his beard. "Do you know that this woman has lived twenty-and-five winters, four winters of which she was married? During this time she did not conceive a child."

"The lady has told me that, and I am still determined to take both women back with me, making Lady Jarvia my first wife. If within a stipulated period of time, she does not bear me a son, I shall marry your second daughter. If Lady Jarvia does bear me a son, I shall arrange a suitable marriage for Gerda."

Wyborn shook his head. "Lord, I-I—"

"My original demand has not changed," Malcolm went on smoothly. "Only the order in which I shall marry the two women."

The queen yanked her husband's shirtsleeve and leaned over to whisper in his ear. Tugging nervously on his beard, he nodded.

His hands twitching, he said, "I must give this request some thought. I-I—the council—we had counted on you marrying Gerda."

"Aye." Malcolm laid his hand on the hilt of his sword. He lowered his head and pretended to ponder. Then he settled his gaze on Wyborn. "It has come to my attention that your bastard daughter may be with child—her own *bastard* child."

Gasps of disbelief went up all over the *skáli*. Wyborn paled. Queen Adelaide shrank back on the settle as if in a swoon.

"May Odin help us!" Kirkja exclaimed. "Wyborn, what do you know of this?"

Wyborn swallowed, his larynx bobbing up and down. Sweat beaded on his face. His hand shook.

"By the gods, Kirkja," he answered, "I know nothing of this treachery. Loki in all of his evil and mischievousness is loosed among us. We must invoke Odin's help. Only he can control the god of evil."

Wyborn's rambling answer released pandemonium in the *stofa*. The babble of many voices raised in protest filled the room.

Malcolm, walking up and down the center aisle, held up a hand for silence.

"If you double your marriage endowment, lord, I shall take Gerda no matter that she be with another man's child."

Wyborn looked suspiciously at the Highlander, as did all who sat in the *skáli*, Jarvia included.

"Taking her is to my advantage" Malcolm went on. "For a verity, I know she is capable of conceiving a child. While Gerda is living in my household, I shall keep an eye on her to ensure that she wenches with no other man."

Once more Wyborn and Adelaide conferred in whispers.

"Wyborn"—Kirkja sounded weary—"accept the Highlander's offer and be grateful that he is not demanding revenge for your deceitfulness."

"Aye," rose a rumbled murmur through the room.

The queen again spoke privately with her husband.

Wyborn said, "If I meet your demands and you should divorce Lady Jarvia because she is barren, what compensation would I receive for taking her back into my home?"

Malcolm looked over his shoulder at Jarvia. Her face was pale, but she remained rigidly straight and stared at him without flinching.

"You will receive no compensation," Malcolm answered. "Justly so. You have practiced great deceit today."

Unease fell over the people.

"But I feel magnanimous, my lord king," Malcolm continued. "I must consider the fate of my kingdom as well as yours."

Malcolm recognized the sacrifice Jarvia was making. It deserved recognition. He had promised to provide well for her should she agree to be his second wife. How much more would he do now that she was to be his first.

"Under no circumstances will Lady Jarvia be returning to your household. I shall endow her with a morning-gift that will make her a woman of substance. She will answer to no one but herself and will be free to live wherever she chooses. What you give me as a marriage endowment for Lady Jarvia will also be considered a marriage endowment for Gerda." He paused. "Considering all that has transpired, my lord king, I want double the amount you and I originally bargained for."

Lord Kirkja rose but did not move from the table. "There is one matter we have not discussed, Lord Malcolm. What of Lady Jarvia's betrothal to Michael Langssonn?"

"She has agreed to rupture the betrothal, lord," Malcolm answered.

Jarvia nodded reassuringly to Kirkja.

"Lord Malcolm," he said, "are you satisfied that we have fulfilled our agreement? This will suffice to bind our peoples together in an alliance?"

"Aye," Malcolm answered.

Nodding, Kirkja slid back onto the bench.

The council talked, they debated, but their shock and outrage over the Highlander's demands and Gerda's pregnancy did not last long. All quickly acquiesced to Malcolm's requests. Lord Kirkja spoke once more to confirm Jarvia's decision. Again she assured him she approved of these arrangements. Forthwith, a messenger was dispatched to Lord Lang across the sea. An answer was expected back in four weeks, by the passing of Planting Time Moon.

"Now," King Wyborn shouted, "it is time for the final *vápnatak*. Then we shall rejoice and celebrate!"

"King Wyborn!" Malcolm called. "One other matter I wish to discuss."

Apprehensive eyes from all over the *stofa* were pinned on the Highlander.

"I request that you move Lady Jarvia into your home."

Jarvia regarded him in surprise. Malcolm could imagine what was going through the minds of the councilmen.

The king grinned. "You want the Lady Jarvia to occupy your chamber with you, lord?"

"Nay," Malcolm answered. "With your permission I shall occupy Lady Jarvia's home."

At the king's house Malcolm had no privacy for himself and his warriors, no place to plan strategy, to receive or send messages. Jarvia's house would provide that. He would have preferred to keep her with him there, but she was too fluent in his language. He dared not take the chance that she knew how to read and write the *ogham*, the letters of his people as well.

He was bound to stay in Southerland until he married to make sure no other man touched his bride, that any child she conceived was indeed his. But he also had to talk with his warriors, had to be free to receive and send dispatches without anyone being the wiser. This included written as well as oral messages.

"I do not understand," Wyborn muttered.

"Lady Jarvia is a matron, lord," Malcolm said. "She has no way of proving her virtue since her maidenhood has been ruptured."

Malcolm noticed the flush on Jarvia's cheeks and was grateful he could not read her thoughts. He could well imagine how scathing they must be, and with just cause.

"I want to be sure that any child she bears is mine. I would have her stay in a safe place until such time as I can claim her for my wife."

"I understand your concerns, lord," the king answered. "And your needs. The Lady Jarvia shall return to my household under the watchful eye of my lady-wife. Lady Jarvia's house and servants are at your disposal."

Nodding, Malcolm sat down next to his intended bride.

He reached for her hand, but she deliberately moved it from him. He caught it in a tight clasp anyway.

"Thank you, *my lord*, for publicly humiliating the law-speaker of Southerland in front of her people," she said sarcastically, trying once again to pull her hand from his. He clasped it all the harder.

"How so, madam?"

"You have announced to the entire community that you do not trust me, that I need a watchdog in order to retain my honor."

"Surely you can appreciate the situation in which I find myself, lady. The first woman your king would have had me marry was pregnant with another man's child. I will not risk such a thing again."

"You do not trust me, lord?"

"I trust no Southerlander."

"I do not trust you either. I have no doubt you shall use my home to carry on with women until we are wed."

"So it is with men, madam." Malcolm laughed softly. "Is my bride-to-be jealous? You do not wish me to have other women?"

"Jealous, lord? Nay, I am not jealous. To be so would indicate that I have tender feelings for you. I do not. I care not what you do if your actions affect only you. When they affect my honor, I care deeply. I also resent that you have taken my home and my freedom from me."

Malcolm heard the words. He also heard her courage.

"I want you here in the lord's household, lady, so you can keep an eye on Gerda. As you said, she is tender and innocent. She needs a firm but loving hand to mold her into a proper wife."

"For you."

"You speak Gaelic well enough to know what I said. Now, let this silly discussion end. I would celebrate this evening. Fill my goblet with ale."

"I would much rather fill your gut with rot!"

Malcolm laughed. "Ah, lady, be grateful that I have a letching for you. Otherwise, I might not find your audacity amusing."

"Be grateful, lord, that I am intent on saving Gerda and her baby, else you would not be getting me for your bride.

Mayhap, lord, before this marriage is over, you will rue the day we met."

Malcolm reached out to catch her chin in his hand and brought her face closer to his. She tried to jerk away, but he held her fast.

"I do not want your affection, lord."

"I told you, I have no affection to give, only caresses."

"I do not want them."

His lips brushed hers. "Shall I prove to you, and to all the people in this building, how unwanted you find my caresses?"

"You would not!"

"No?" His lips touched hers softly.

Chapter 12

❝**A** possible rebellion!" Malcolm's exclamation of disbelief hung in the air. He sat in the High Seat at Jarvia's house, his legs crossed, and stared into the flames of the great fire. Although revelry would continue throughout the night at the Great House, he had retired early. His world seemed to be crumbling around him. "Surely Angus is not leading a rebellion."

"Aye, he is, lord," Thomas answered, ruffling his graying hair with a distracted hand.

Moving past the best-men who lounged on benches they had dragged close to the High Seat, Morag set a roasted leg of lamb on the table in front of the two outriders who had recently joined them. Thomas and Ghaltair nodded their appreciation.

Cutting a slice of meat with his dirk, Thomas continued, "We left the day after he and Lady Sybil wed."

"I cannot believe that Angus and Sybil are wed," Malcolm muttered. " 'Tis so soon after the death of his wife."

"Aye, and Lily's death was a strange one. She was a young thing," Ghaltair said. His straight black hair, hanging to his shoulders, framed his long, gaunt face. His expression was melancholy.

"Aye," another of the best-men agreed. "No one would have expected her to go to sleep one night and never awaken."

"But I can't say I am surprised that Angus married Sybil." Brian, a burly warrior about the same age as Malcolm, and best-man of one of the largest houses of Clan Duncan, shoved back on the chest on which he was sitting. "Any man would if given the chance. She's one of the fairest—"

"Nay, *the* fairest," Ghaltair interjected.

"Well, mayhap the second fairest woman in the entire kingdom," Brian conceded, "my lady-wife being the first."

After a moment of silence, Thomas resumed his story. "We left the day after Angus accused you of bringing the evilness of the Picts on us. I fair shivered as I listened to his ranting and raving."

Ghaltair laughed. He reached into his shirt and drew out a small gold medallion suspended on a chain around his neck. "You should wear a good luck talisman like I do."

Brian leaned over and peered more closely at it. " 'Tis like the one your father wore," he said.

" *'Tis* the one he wore," Ghaltair said. "He gave it to me just before he died, and I have never taken it off. It had great magic. If it will make Thomas feel better, I shall let him borrow it."

"Nay." Thomas threw up both hands, as if warding him off. "Not I, Ghaltair. No man can borrow another man's luck. He must seek his own."

The men laughed and Thomas settled down to his eating and talking.

"Angus claims it's your fault, Malcolm, that the Picts are raiding our villages and stealing our cattle." Thomas waved his knife. "Why, they even stole your breeding mares."

"Christ's blood!" Malcolm swore, straightening in his chair. "My selected breeding mares?"

"Nay," Ghaltair answered, "not your special ones."

Thomas swallowed a mouthful of food. "Angus and Sybil are blaming you for the trouble. And many of the chiefs are ready to believe them because you have departed from the old ways and have embraced the new god, because you don't allow us to be warriors and win glory in battle."

"Aye, Angus mocked the Christ and said the way of peace was the way of cowardice," Ghaltair added. "Angus and several other chiefs want to go on raids into Pict territory, but Ard-righ Fergus won't allow it. He awaits your return. When Fergus collapsed the other day, Angus said—"

"My father collapsed!" Malcolm bolted out of the chair and rounded on his warriors. "Why was I not told of this?"

" 'Tis no big matter, Malcolm," Thomas said quietly, cutting his eyes reproachfully at Ghaltair. "The ard-righ made us promise not to upset you with the news. He was exhausted. He had been meeting with the chiefs for several days and nights, listening to them argue. And he is old, Malcolm."

"Aye," Malcolm agreed, and sat back down.

"In part," Thomas continued, "Angus is right. Fergus is too old to be burdened with all these problems. 'Twill kill him if he's not careful."

Ghaltair speared a piece of meat with his knife. "Aye, 'twas exactly what Angus was saying, Malcolm. Fergus is too old and sick to lead the people. Going by the law of the Ancient Ones, he said Fergus would disease the land with his illness and bring a curse upon the people. Angus called for an election."

Malcolm sighed, rubbing the back of his neck. "What does the Lady Sybil say?"

"That she loves her father, but agrees with Angus. She believes Fergus should step down, for his own good and the good of the people, and let someone else rule."

"Sybil would say that," Malcolm muttered. "She wants the High Seat for herself, no matter how she must get it."

Ghaltair held up his goblet, and Morag refilled it with ale. "Malcolm, you have no time to waste here in search of a bride."

"The search is over, but I cannot leave yet," Malcolm said. He twisted the gold ring around and around on his little finger. "The messenger asked for the passing of a moon to make the journey to Northland and back, to arrange for the rupture of Lady Jarvia's betrothal."

"Nay." Brian rose and went to the High Seat. "Let's go home now and settle this. Then you can return for the wench."

"I will not leave without a bride."

"Christ and Him crucified!" Lachlann, standing across the room, slammed his fist against the wall. "Have you gone daft, mon?"

Malcolm glared at his friend.

Lachlann moved to the chest where his weapons lay. "We will sit here and wait for four weeks and quite possibly Lord Lang will not see fit to rupture his son's betrothal. What then?"

Malcolm gazed at the copper-and-jewel-encrusted hilt of the sword—the Highland sword—that Lachlann had won the first time he captured the silver fox in the annual summer chase. Malcolm's gaze went to the helmet nearby. Lachlann had been so proud of his trophy that he had had the helmet crafted so that it matched the sword in materials and design. Both sword and helmet were easily identifiable with Lachlann mac Niall.

Malcolm did not answer.

"When you finally decide to return home," Lachlann said, "will we have any kingdom left? You heard what Thomas and Ghaltair reported. Both Angus and Sybil are calling for Fergus to give up his High Seat. They're pressuring the clans to go to war against the Picts. The two of them together could easily make the clans rebel against Ard-righ Fergus . . . and you."

Thomas pushed back from the table and brushed his sleeved arm across his mouth. "Even now, Malcolm, it is rumored you have promised Pictish tribes some of our territory if they swear fealty to you, as you have already done to the Southerlanders."

"I have given no one any of our territory and have made no such promise," Malcolm replied.

"Aye, we know that," Ghaltair said, "but rumors are still circulating. And many people believe them. They have a tendency to believe the worst."

Malcolm noted Ghaltair's melancholy expression, his shadowed eyes, and knew he was remembering his father's tragic downfall. He was having a hard time accepting his father's death.

Egan, a headman of one of the houses of Clan Duncan, had been much older than Malcolm, but they had been good friends nonetheless. Malcolm had trusted him, but the old man had been unable to break from the old ways. Eventually he had joined with warriors from other clans in an attempt to overthrow and replace Fergus. Egan had been captured and tried by the Council of Chiefs, been found guilty of treason by Scottish law, and been publicly beheaded.

A young impressionable warrior, Ghaltair had refused to believe his father's guilt. He had spoken in his father's defense, had tried to convince the council that his father had been fighting *for* the king rather than *against* him. Even when Egan had confessed his crimes, Ghaltair had shut his heart and mind to the truth.

Understanding Ghaltair's inner conflict, Malcolm as clan chief had taken the young warrior under his wing.

"Ghaltair, you must put the past behind you," Malcolm said.

"How can I?" he demanded. "I am my father's son. He died in shame, and I, his son, bear that same dishonor."

"You are your own man first, an honorable warrior."

"I know that and so do you," Ghaltair said. He waved his hand to include all the best-men sitting in the room. "So do they. But many of our people remember that I was so distraught when I was not allowed to become best-man after my father's death that I entered the monastery and studied to become a priest. I turned away from the warrior's code and for a time wore the vesture of the priest."

"But when you were finished with your grieving, you returned to the world that suited you best," Malcolm said. "You wanted to be a warrior, and you are."

"But unlike you, our people distrust me because I, too, can make and read the marks of the *ogham*."

Malcolm said nothing, but he knew Ghaltair spoke the truth. Although Christianity was growing in acceptance among the tribes of Scotland, the majority of the people, steeped in the tradition of the ancient gods, still eschewed the written language. Reading and writing the Scottish alphabet, the *ogham*, was reserved for only the learned, a chosen few, among them.

"What is considered fine for you is considered unacceptable for others . . . especially me," Ghaltair continued.

" 'Tis the way you perceive it," Malcolm said. "Think less of what you consider to be your failures, Ghaltair, and concentrate on your successes. You have a special way with ponies. That is why I have put you in charge of the herds, especially the breeding mares and stallions."

Many times since Egan's death, Ghaltair's frustrations had surfaced, and he and Malcolm had had this same argument.

"A warrior." Ghaltair rose and slammed his hand on the tabletop. "Because of my father's dishonor, I am now a warrior, not best-man, not heir to the chieftainship of the clan. That distinction belongs to Brian."

"Aye," Malcolm said, "that is true."

" 'Twas a fair election," Brian said softly, though his countenance was hard.

"Aye, I do not dispute that you were the one selected by the clansmen, Brian. I dispute that anyone but me should have been selected." Ghaltair's eyes, blazing with anger, burned into Malcolm's. "Why did you not let me become best-man when Egan died? 'Twas my right. *I* was guilty of no crime."

"Best-men are elected by members of the family, not appointed by the clan chief."

"But clan chiefs can sway an election; they can let the people know whom they consider the best warrior." Ghaltair doubled his fists and pressed them against the tabletop. "They should have elected me. They would have, if you had spoken on my behalf. If you had convinced them I had nothing to do with the plot against High King Fergus."

"I spoke for you," Malcolm reminded him. "But I refused to speak against other deserving warriors who were being considered by the members."

"Brian, you mean."

"Aye, I had to speak for Brian. He is a worthy warrior." Malcolm rose, and moved to stand behind Ghaltair. "You are yet young and must prove yourself. Given time, you will become best-man."

Malcolm gripped his shoulder reassuringly. "Do not be impatient, Ghaltair. You have come a long way toward restoring the integrity your father lost. Your house looks up to you with respect."

"But there is always the chance that I will never be elected best-man, that another champion will rise to take my place and will eventually be elected as clan chief."

"That would be true even if you were best-man."

"If I were best-man of my house, I would have more of a chance of becoming chief of Clan Duncan. I swear, Malcolm, one day I shall be clan chief. One day I will be ard-righ."

Malcolm was silent for a moment before he answered. "You shall have the opportunity, if you do not let your bitterness destroy you."

Brian, an ale goblet in his hand, began to pace in front of the fire. " 'Tis time you returned home, Malcolm. All of us are testy, and we fight amongst ourselves. 'Tis plain to see from what Ghaltair and Thomas report that the clan chieftains do not question their loyalty to you. They question yours to the new god and the new ways. You must return and set things in order."

Malcolm did not speak for a long while. The only noises in the room were the spit and sputter of the fire and the occasional movement of the Highlanders as they shifted in their chairs or moved about the room.

Finally Malcolm stretched out his legs, crossing them at the ankles. "Thomas, have your heard anything of Wyborn's emissary?"

"Berowalt?" Thomas asked.

Malcolm nodded. "I was surprised to learn he had not informed Wyborn of Hilda's death. It was to my advantage that he had not, but . . ."

Thomas shook his head. "Have you heard anything about him, Ghaltair?"

He also shook his head.

"Send a rider back to the kingdom to investigate the man's whereabouts," Malcolm ordered. "His absence causes me great concern."

Thomas nodded. "Aye, Malcolm."

"Also, Thomas, I shall give the rider an *ogham* marker."

"You are sending a written message?"

"Aye, to Chief Fibh of the Northern Picts."

" 'Tis a dangerous thing to do, is it not?" Thomas asked.

"Aye," Lachlann agreed. "You know how our people tend to suspect words written on markers. They would be doubly suspicious if they knew you were writing to a Pict, a man whom many consider to be our enemy."

"I must find out more about these cattle raids," Malcolm insisted. "And I shall be sending my most trusted outrider. Thomas has perfected my pony relay system."

Thomas grinned. "With your help, Malcolm. I chose the men; you chose the ponies. Only after long, grueling hours in the saddle did our men find the fastest and safest routes."

Malcolm moved to the table to refill his goblet. "Aye, only by working together can we succeed at anything . . . especially the governing of a kingdom." Gazing into the fire, he took several swallows. Eventually he said, "Someone must be agitating the Picts. Surely they would have honored our agreement otherwise."

"*Someone?*" Ghaltair exclaimed. "One of us, Malcolm?"

"It could be."

Lachlann moved to stand before Malcolm. Shaking his head in disbelief, he said, "Have you more faith in the Picts than in our own people?"

"Some of our people feel they have much to lose by honoring our alliance with the Picts," Malcolm said. He chose a piece of wood from the bin, removed his dagger, and began to whittle a small, flat marker onto which he would carve the *ogham*, the Scottish letters.

Brian finished off his ale and set the goblet on the trestle table with a thud. "Mayhap Sybil and Angus are stirring up the trouble, Malcolm."

"Mayhap."

"Then," Lachlann said, "we surely have reason to return home immediately."

Malcolm returned to the High Seat. "I have said all I intend to on that subject."

Lachlann scowled. "Sometimes, Malcolm, I wonder if you are deliberately letting that woman take your kingdom piece by piece, as I believe she—"

Malcolm pushed up from the chair. He had taken as much from Lachlann tonight as he intended to take. In low, menacing tones he said, "What are you saying, Lachlann?"

Lachlann met his gaze without flinching. "She's a witch, Malcolm, filled with evil magic."

Thomas laughed. "But a beautiful witch."

Ghaltair smiled. "Aye, Thomas, a beautiful, seductive witch."

"Once she sinks her fingers into someone—" Lachlann broke off, shaking his head.

"Have no fear, best-man, Lady Sybil does not have me in her clutches yet. Nor does she have my kingdom. I shall deal with her when I return."

Ghaltair laughed. "As you dealt with the Lady Hilda?"

Thomas cast a scathing glance at the younger man. "You know as well as I do that Malcolm did not kill the Southerland wench. She killed herself. I was there when she died."

"When she died," Ghaltair emphasized, "but not when she ate the berries. That's why rumors that Malcolm killed her are rife. We have no one but our own clansmen to testify on his behalf."

"The word of a clansmen is all we need," Lachlann said.

His brow wrinkled in thought, Thomas rubbed his chin. "Ghaltair is right. It is not enough to stop the rumors. Our enemies will probably use Hilda's death against Malcolm and the king."

"I should have taken her threats of suicide more seriously," Malcolm admitted. "But I had no idea she would—"

"You were careful enough," Thomas said, "but you don't practice the evil magic that Sybil does. Maybe Hilda did not poison herself. Maybe Sybil cast a spell on her. Sybil has stirred the muddy waters before, and she'll do it again."

"Aye," Ghaltair murmured.

Thomas nodded. "Sybil knew that rumors about Hilda's death would help to undermine your authority. Murdering an unborn child is a horrible offense. Sybil's powers are great, Malcolm. She is to be feared."

"Aye," Lachlann agreed. "Beware of her, Malcolm. She will let no one stand in the way of getting what she wants, not you or her father. And she wants the High Seat of the Northern Scots."

The truth of Lachlann's words cast an uneasy silence over the Highland warriors.

Planting Time Moon slowly passed. During the first two weeks that Jarvia and Malcolm awaited word from Lord Lang regarding the rupture of her betrothal to Michael, Malcolm had remained in the village of Wybornsbaer, living in Jarvia's house. She returned to live at the Great House. Because of Malcolm's passionate nature and his professed desire for her, she expected him to make sexual demands on her, but he did not. He actually seemed to prefer to be with the warriors. During the day he jousted, hawked, and hunted.

She worked on filling her bridal chest with household goods. The nights they spent together at the Great House in revelry, but they were never alone and she always retired earlier than he did.

At the end of the second week King Wyborn announced that he was taking Lord Malcolm on a tour through Southerland. Jarvia took advantage of the two-week separation to sort through her feelings, but she was no nearer to understanding them now than she had been earlier.

At dawn a runner arrived at the village with the news that the king and his entourage had completed their tour, spent the night in the nearby forest, and were hunting today. They would be home by afternoon with enough food for a banquet. The queen and other ladies were busy preparing for the returning warriors, but not Jarvia. Since the day was warm and sunny, she decided to picnic in the meadow.

She and Morag sat on a spread coverlet beneath a tree. Morag was sewing Jarvia's wedding dress, and Jarvia was gazing at the rushing water of a nearby mountain stream. This glen had always been her haven, this particular inlet her refuge. This is where she came when she wanted to be alone to think.

She awaited word from Lord Lang with mixed feelings. A part of her, the woman who was fearful of change, the freed slave who was fearful of renewed bondage, would have been relieved if Lord Lang had rejected her request. Another part of her, the protective and maternal self, knew she had made the only choice possible.

"For a verity, my lady," Morag said, breaking into her thoughts, "you will indeed be the most beautiful bride Southerland has ever seen. Your dress is lovely." Morag lay out the shimmering green material.

Jarvia glanced down.

"The color will show your eyes to their best advantage," Morag continued.

"So the barbarian said."

"And he is right."

So he had also said! Jarvia thought, vividly recalling the heated argument between her and Lord Malcolm with regards to the selection of fabric for her wedding dress. In the end she had acquiesced to his wish. The possibility that she would always be acquiescing to his wishes worried her.

"This shade of green will do more for you than the traditional red," Morag added.

"We must have another ceremony once we reach the Highlands," Jarvia said.

"Aye, he told me as much."

Jarvia laughed softly. "He has forgotten much about our Southerland wedding ritual. After we are showered with the firstfruits, our clothes will not be wearable again."

Morag laughed also. "The grain is not so bad. 'Tis the ale, mead, and beer that ruin them."

Jarvia flopped over and plucked a blade of grass. "Before Lord Malcolm left with the king, I saw women coming and going from my house."

She deliberately said "women" when, in fact, she had seen only one *woman* leaving, the village whore.

Morag chuckled. "Methinks, mistress, you are jealous. You would be hard put to convince me that you hate the Highlander."

"I am not jealous!" Jarvia spoke more sharply than she intended, but Morag's assessment upset her. Ever since she had agreed to marry the Highlander, ever since they had mated, her entire world had changed. And the changes frightened her.

Quietly she said, "I do not like being put out of my own house and back into the king's, always under the eye of that odious woman."

"Don't fret. Soon you and the Highlander will be wed."

"That calls for celebrating," Jarvia said sarcastically. "I shall be moving from the watchdog to the hawk. I have a feeling the Highlander will be far more dangerous than Queen Adelaide."

"But also more entertaining," Morag said.

"Were you at the house when he entertained *her*?" Jarvia's thoughts had returned to the whore.

"Nay. The Highlander knows I am your servant, mistress, that my first loyalty is to you. He does and says nothing in front of me that I can report. He arranged a chamber for me in the storage hut behind your *stofa*."

Once again Morag settled down to her sewing. Jarvia forced herself to relax.

She admitted her feelings confused her. Before the High-lander had returned to Southerland, she had been in control of her life, of her future. Ein-her had helped her build her self-confidence by educating her, by loving and pro-viding for her. When he had realized he was dying, he had searched until he found her a gentle warrior as her second husband, a man who would cherish and protect her as he had.

But Lord Malcolm had brought the winds of change, and they had blown Jarvia's well-organized life into disarray. She had no doubt that the three Fays of Destiny, the Norns, had spun a life thread of gleaming gold for Malcolm. He was a hero, a prince. He had only to speak a word and others rushed to obey. Even she did.

Her reaction to the barbarian frightened her. Before he had entered her life, she had thought herself self-sufficient, dependent on no one. With his coming and mating with her, she had discovered that he aroused her passions to the point that she could neither control nor resist them. She was becoming so entangled with his life's thread that she began to wonder if she had a thread of her own anymore. The thought that she might be losing her self-identity to this man disturbed her greatly.

"We should be hearing from Lord Lang soon," Morag said.

"I hope so. The waiting makes me nervous," Jarvia murmured. She breathed deeply, moving away from the basket of food and drink she had packed at early morn. She stretched and propped herself on an elbow. Sunlight touched the stream, making it glitter like blue jewels. She thought of Malcolm's blue eyes.

Morag adjusted the wooden hoop and continued embroi-dering. In and out of the material went the bone needle, the gold floss gleaming.

"Jarvia!" Gerda's voice suddenly called.

Her figure appeared across the mountain meadow, a small black dog nipping at her heels. Since she had gained her freedom and Jarvia had returned to the king's house to live, Gerda had changed. She laughed more frequently. Her face glowed with color and excitement. With the passing of Planting Time Moon, she had missed her flux a second time. She knew for sure that she was with child, although she had not yet begun to show.

"The warriors have returned, and the barbarian is looking for you," she announced.

"Let him keep looking," Jarvia said. "I have no desire to be found."

"Why are you running free this time of the day?" Morag asked. "Shouldn't you be helping Bertha?"

Gerda nodded. "Queen Adelaide sent all of us out of the house. She is entertaining guests."

Jarvia did not care what the queen was doing, but now she understood why Adelaide had agreed to her proposed picnic in the meadow. Morag, as usual, expressed eager and open curiosity.

"Who might the guests be?"

"Madelhari the Trader and several strangers," Gerda replied. "Warriors and artisans."

"Perhaps the queen is getting Jarvia's bridal trunks ready," Morag said.

"I sincerely doubt that," Jarvia replied. "She thinks only of herself. If anything, she is filling her own trunks and will put as little as possible into ours."

"Makes no matter to me," Gerda said, "as long as I have this beautiful day to enjoy."

Morag returned her needles, scissors, and tweezers to her needle case and folded the tunic. "I must make haste, mistress. His lordship might have need of me."

"Do you mind being the barbarian's servant?" Gerda asked.

"Nay," Morag answered. "I have enjoyed conversing in my own tongue. Although I was born here in this village, it ceased being my home when it became Southerland. I enjoy hearing the Highland warriors talk about their families. It brings back old memories for me. And the warlord is demanding but not overbearing."

Jarvia disagreed with this last statement but made no comment.

"Do you want me to help you?" Gerda asked.

"Nay." Morag set off in the direction of the village. "I do better by myself. If I do not see either one of you again this evening, I shall see you in the morn. May you rest well."

Hardly had Morag gone than the dog, Nott, barked. His tone alerted Jarvia and Gerda that someone was approaching.

"Who can it be? The Highlander?" Gerda asked, then answered, "It cannot be. You are well hidden here."

Jarvia did not underestimate Lord Malcolm. She reached for her head scarf and searched the horizon.

Out of the stand of trees appeared a warrior. A hazy impression against the glorious sunlight at his back, he walked toward them. Blinded by the glare, Jarvia could not distinguish his features, but she knew from his stature, from the way he carried himself, that it was the Highlander.

When the path turned, he was no longer silhouetted golden by the sun, and Jarvia could make out his features. Her heart skipped a beat, then pounded rapidly. Blood rushed through her body. Her breath caught in her lungs.

He was so handsome! Not as many counted handsomeness, with long flowing locks and a neatly trimmed and combed beard, but with a ruggedness that was one with the Highland kingdom from which he came. His skin, kissed by the sun, caressed by the wind, was a golden bronze. His thick black hair did nothing to soften the angular hardness of his face with its bold, square chin.

His lips were deceiving. They managed to be both hard and sensuous at the same time. His broad shoulders and wide chest looked to be hewn out of Highland rock. His thick, muscular legs were reminiscent of tree trunks in the forest.

The barbarian was elemental, earthy.

A gentle breeze ruffled his hair, blowing a few strands across his forehead. His mantle billowed away from his body, and his shirt and trousers pressed against the flexed muscles of his chest and legs as he climbed the incline toward the meadow.

As if the elements understood that this man was one with them, as if they recognized his importance, the sun glinted on the gold torque about his neck. It shone on the gold pin at his shoulder and on the gold band on his wrist. He stopped, propped a foot on a small boulder, and held one hand up to shield his eyes from the afternoon glare. The other hand he kept behind him.

"Here you are, Lady Jarvia." The words easily carried the short distance, but with an ominous undertone. "I expected you to be in the village, as were the other women, awaiting my return."

"I don't know what the barbarian is saying," Gerda whispered, "but he does not look happy." She leaped to her feet and brushed twigs from her skirt. "I had best be going."

Putting two fingers in her mouth, she whistled, and Nott scurried over to her. Both bounded away to leave Jarvia alone with the Highlander.

Chapter 13

Lord Malcolm walked slowly toward Jarvia. Like a strand of Morag's gold floss, time spun out between them. All the while he studied her with his intense sea-blue eyes. She rose to meet him.

"The women of the village welcome home their weary warriors with a bright smile and open arms, lady." His voice was soft and full of censure.

Fleetingly Jarvia wished that like Gerda she could take flight. "As of this moment, lord, I have no warrior to welcome home. My warrior is a-viking."

"As of this moment, lady, you are looking at your warrior."

They stood for a moment, unmoving, analyzing.

The color of his eyes darkened, their expression softening as he took in every feature of her face.

"I missed you, lady. These two weeks away from you have seemed like two years."

Jarvia's legs felt as incapable of supporting her as the oil in a soapstone lamp. Malcolm's words had obliterated her irritation, her anger . . . even her jealousy. A small smile touched his lips, his eyes.

"I missed your smile." He paused. "And your stimulating conversation."

Jarvia had no doubt Malcolm mac Duncan, an expert at manipulating people and their emotions, knew exactly what he was doing. Even so, he made her feel wanted . . . cherished. That he could do it so easily was proof of his power to beguile.

He stood so close she saw the bronzed texture of his skin, felt the heat emanating from his body. As if compelled by an external force, she looked at Malcolm's lips, expressive and finely shaped. She remembered the feel of them on hers.

"What of you . . . Jarvia?"

It was the first time he had called her by name. It was an invitation for her to speak his name aloud. She wanted to; she would have. But when he held out his hand to her, she remembered seeing the village whore leaving his house. She would not let this man captivate her as he had done others. She would not become victimized by him.

She was stronger than Hilda! *She was*.

"Did you not miss me?"

She ignored his hand. "I had no chance to miss you." Her voice did not betray her inner turmoil. "I have been busy since I returned to the king's house. The queen has given me many duties."

His black brows drew together. Displeasure colored his countenance. "Too many?"

"Nay. I can take care of myself."

"I am your champion, lady. I take care of you."

She stared unflinchingly into his eyes. "Not yet, lord."

His scowl deepened; his blue eyes glittered.

Jarvia knew she was provoking the Highlander, and a certain exhilaration ran through her. A part of her dared to push him further; another part urged caution.

"I have a gift for you." He brought his hand from behind his back and held out a bouquet of flowers.

Awestruck, Jarvia stared at them, overwhelmed by this unexpected gesture, by this complex man who continually surprised her. One moment he was scowling and censuring her for not greeting him, the weary traveler; the next he was smiling and giving her a gift.

"Do you not like them?" He searched her face.

"Aye. They are beautiful."

As she reached for them, she saw a badge of scarlet and lavender flowers pinned to his mantle. The same flowers he had picked for her. One color denoted bravery, the other skill; the number of flowers corresponded to the number of game killed.

"You did well in the hunt today," She commented.

"I have provided well for our table."

"You also made the most daring kills, else you would not be wearing the badge." Lifting the bouquet and lowering her face, she smelled the fragrant flowers. "I am proud of you."

" 'Tis what I am trained to do, madam. 'Tis a good warrior who protects his people. 'Tis a good man who provides for his family." He spoke without a trace of arrogance. "Some of the meat I shall keep for my table while I sojourn here. Another portion will go to the less fortunate and to the widows. The remainder I give to you. Also I give you the furs. They will serve well for clothing and blankets."

"I am grateful for your generosity, lord." She lowered the flowers. "How did you know where to find me?"

"I am a hunter."

She was the prey.

"You have yet to call me by name, madam."

He had not forgotten. . . .

Wanting to, yet not wanting to, Jarvia once more buried her face in the flowers, pretending renewed interest in the bouquet.

"I would have you do so," he insisted.

Countless were the times she had called his name in her thoughts and murmured it aloud for her ears alone. Even more times she had wondered about his relationship with Hilda, with Lady Sybil, and with the village whore! Warriors—Highlanders, she had supposed—had come and gone from her *stofa* now that Malcolm resided there. She never questioned them. The woman she did.

"I would look at your face, madam."

He caught her wrist and lowered the flowers. A smile flitted across his face until it erupted into soft laughter. He brushed the tip of her nose.

Puzzled, she looked at him.

"You wear the yellow flower dust, the blessing of your god Balder, or so your skald sings."

She lifted her hand and pressed it against her face. "Oh."

His eyes twinkled. "I would hear you say my name, madam."

Bemused, Jarvia stared at him. The man did not cease to amaze her. She had accused him of being harsh and unyielding. A hard warrior. A barbarian. All of these he was, and more. But he could also be thoughtful, almost gentle. Jarvia must always keep her guard up; he was seductive and beguiling.

"I am waiting, mistress." Soft was the command.

Soft was the answer. "Lord Malcolm."

"Shall we dispense with 'lord'?"

Jarvia leaned toward him, inhaling his scent—that herbal scent she identified with him, that musky odor of leather and metal. She drew to her the heat that radiated from his body.

"Malcolm."

"Lovely Jarvia." He touched his finger to her mouth and drew the tip along the full lower lip.

A slight flare of his nostrils and a parting of his own lips told Jarvia that he desired her. His gaze still on her face, he removed her head scarf and pulled the combs and pins from her hair. It spilled over her shoulders and down her back.

"Your hair is beautiful," he murmured, "but I especially enjoy seeing what the light does to it, madam." He caught a strand and pulled it through his war-hardened hand. "It spins it into the purest silver floss."

"Thank you." Jarvia's entire body seemed to melt and pool at the barbarian's feet.

His gaze lowered to linger on her breasts. They tingled to life.

"I am glad I found you," he murmured.

His kindness was her undoing. An answering hunger leaped in the pit of her stomach.

"I must be going, lord. The sun is sitting low in the western sky."

He glanced down at the spread coverlet. "Let us not depart so soon. I would visit with you quietly. We have been hunting since before the rising of the sun, and I am aweary."

"Aye." She dropped to her knees at the edge of the coverlet, placed her flowers so they would not be harmed, and opened the basket. "Are you hungry, lord? Or perhaps you would like a glass of beer?"

"For a verity, lady, I am hungry." His eyes greedily roamed her face.

He sat down beside her, moving the food basket and the flowers to the other side of his body, so that nothing lay between them. He looked at her. She looked at him. Both knew the significance of the gesture.

"I would have a good bath this night, lady, and someone to rub my aching muscles."

Jarvia's body became a cauldron of emotion as she imagined bathing the Highlander and massaging his shoulders, his back, and . . . lower.

"Did you ever bathe your husband?" he asked.

She nodded.

Malcolm released the gold mantle pin and loosed the plaid cloak from his shoulders. He unfastened the belts that bound his weapons to him and laid them close by.

"When we are wed, madam, I shall expect you to bathe me and rub my body with strawberry water and scented oils."

Jarvia kept her head lowered as she ran her fingers over the food basket. "Will we not have servants for that purpose?"

"We will have servants, madam, but your duty will be to see to my needs, my wants, and my comfort."

Stretching out on the blanket, he propped himself up on an elbow, lying in much the same position as he had that night after they had mated. So vividly did he awaken memories in her that Jarvia visualized his hand as it smoothed over her hips and down her thigh. Her emotions fully aroused, she wanted to bathe the Highlander, wanted to feel the hard muscles of his body beneath her hands.

"Time has passed since we mated," he said.

He opened the basket and lifted out a small canister, then tore a piece of bread from the loaf. He dipped a spoon into the jar and liberally laved *skry*, a tasty cheese curd, onto the bread.

"Has your moon come upon you?"

The thrill of the barbarian's visit faded. Jarvia's desires waned into dull frustration. "This is why you sought me out, lord?"

Chewing, he nodded, then swallowed. "I would know if you are carrying my babe."

His eyes fixed on her face, he held the bread at his mouth, ready to take another bite. She shook her head. Sighing, he lowered the food.

"I had hoped."

She bent her legs and brought them up to her breast.

Locking her hands around them, she rested her chin on her knees and stared into the distance. "Mayhap, I shall not conceive."

"Mayhap," he answered absently, "but I would say we have not given ourselves fair opportunity, lady. When we are wed, we shall mate aplenty. If you do not conceive then, you will have reason to be concerned."

He washed down the bread and cheese with beer. After he returned the tankard to the basket, he caught her hand, turned it over, and rubbed the callused tip of his thumb slowly over the center of her palm, sending shivers of pleasure through her body.

"You tremble," he said softly.

His thumb brush-stroked her palm and moved to the sensitive skin of her inner wrist.

She gazed into his dark blue eyes, fighting to free herself from the spell he cast over her. If she did not, she would be asking for her own seduction. She would not forget her vow to remain separate from him until they were wed, and she would not let him forget either.

"I am chilled," she murmured. The chill, coupled with his caresses, caused her to quiver. "In the mountains when the sun begins to set, the wind blows cooler."

"Where is your shawl?"

"I did not bring one. I thought I would be home before the cold set in."

Malcolm threw his mantle over her shoulders, bringing the warmth she needed, overwhelming her with his scent that lingered in the cloth. She felt him all around her.

Breathlessly she said, "I must return to the king's house."

Gripping both edges of the mantle in his hands, cradling her in the garment, he held her prisoner and drew her close. She pressed her palms against his chest.

"Please, lord—"

He transferred the edges of the mantle into one fist and lifted his other hand to cup her chin. She shook her head, but could not free herself. Although a big woman, she did not have the strength to budge his strong, callused fingers. She resented being reminded of Malcolm's size and strength, even if it made her feel less of a giant herself.

"Remember your promise, lord," she murmured. Even as she uttered the words, she felt her resolve turning to mush.

"Aye." He leaned closer; his breath blew on her cheek. "I promised I would take you to bliss many times in this life."

A hot, melting sensation stirred her secret parts. "N–nay."

She could say no more. All she was aware of was hard muscle and sinew as her hands slid down his chest and around his waist. Black hair brushed softly, seductively, against her cheek as she raised her head.

"Aye."

His mouth claimed hers, warm lips playing with hers to make her giddy with desire. He rekindled flames that he—only he—had lit inside her. Fire reached to the very core of her being and burned away her resentments, her resolutions.

He lifted his lips slightly. "I have wrapped you in my tartan, madam, and am warming you with my body, yet you tremble. Mayhap, you have a hunger for me also?"

"From the wind," Jarvia murmured.

"Ah, yes," he drawled. "The wind."

"Please, lord, leave me."

"I cannot, lady. I have thought of nothing else but you since we mated."

Unbidden, mental flashes of the beautiful whore leaving her house came to Jarvia's mind. It took little imagination to visualize the petite beauty in Malcolm's arms, in *her* bed with him. Abruptly Jarvia shifted in his embrace, her hands digging into his muscled forearms. His arms tightened around her, but she did not cease twisting.

"If you thought of no one but me," she said scathingly, "why did you have need of the village whore? Why did you see fit to parade her openly in front of me and the entire village?"

"Lady, I did no such thing." Malcolm grinned. "Methinks you are jealous."

"Nay, lord." She breathed heavily from exertion. "Angry, yes. Jealous, never."

A strand of hair fell across her face. She tried to blow it out of her eyes.

"I remind you, lady, that my warriors, none of whom are celibate, share your house with me."

The words thrilled Jarvia, but she would not set aside her anger. "Still, you will not use me until I am legally yours."

She blew again, but the curl refused to budge.

"If you have need of a woman, do as your men do. Go to her."

Holding her securely with one arm, Malcolm pushed the tendril out of her face and tucked it behind her ear. "If I had need of a woman, madam, I *would* seek out a whore." His eyes glittered. "But I have need of you . . . only you."

Her heart pounded. The man disconcerted her when she least expected it.

" 'Tis indecent," she sputtered. "I am still betrothed to Lord Michael."

Malcolm sighed deeply, impatiently. She felt the rise and fall of his chest.

"Lady, do you not know by now that you will be mine . . . one way or another?"

Afternoon sunlight slanted down on him, emphasizing the harsh lines around his eyes and mouth.

"I will take you any time, any place that I desire. And I shall take you here, madam. Now."

As quickly as he aroused Jarvia's passion, he aroused her ire. She refused to be treated like chattel ever again. His grip slackened. She wiggled free, her hand trailing over the hilt of his dirk.

"Cease your silliness," he commanded gruffly.

Silliness! Jarvia could never be accused of being silly! Her hand closed over the hilt, and she freed the dirk from its sheath. She twisted away and pressed the blade against his stomach, taking care not to puncture him.

"I will be yours one way and one way only, lord." She hissed the words. "You will honor your word and not mate with me again until I am legally yours."

"Lady," Malcolm said quietly, "I do not understand. You are the one who suggested that you become my first wife, that you bear the son I seek, yet you fight me at every opportunity. You create the situation, then get angry without provocation."

"You accuse me of being angry without cause?"

"Angry, because of *imaginary* causes."

Strong fingers clamped onto her wrist, pulling her hand down and away. In two quick movements, the dirk was sheathed.

He stared at her.

She squirmed beneath his scrutiny.

" 'Tis no harm done to you," she finally said to break the silence. "I did not mean to hurt you, lord, only to let you know how serious I am."

"Madam, I assure you, I take this situation as seriously as you do, perhaps even more so." Though gently spoken, his words were sardonic.

"Then do me no harm, sire."

"Nay, lady, that is far from my intention. 'Tis true, I am asking much of you, but I will give you much in return."

Jarvia pushed away from him, but his arm lashed out and caught her. His fingers bit into her arm.

"I will provide well for you, lady, and I will cherish you. As my wife, you will have an honored position in the clan and in the kingdom."

"I am reconciled to my future with you, but I am speaking of this moment, lord."

Malcolm's hand slid down her body. She caught her breath.

"This—this moment when my betrothal is not yet ruptured. You prom—"

His hand rested at the juncture of her thighs.

"Do you not know when to cease your prattling, madam?" The color of his eyes deepened to an intense blue; his voice softened. His fingers pressed gently against her secret part, creating an intense longing in her.

"Have you ached for my strength between your legs?"

Aye, she had.

Even through her clothes, Jarvia felt the warmth of his flesh. Desire raced hotly through her to take residence beneath his fingertips. She closed her eyes and begged the gods for the strength to resist. But her body did not want divine interference. It hungered for his caresses. She exerted all her will to keep from arching into the warmth and movement of his hand, but her body won the battle.

She stopped thinking and totally absorbed the pleasure he gave to her.

"This feels good, does it not?" he taunted.

Yes, she silently confessed.

His hand continued to give her great joy as his mouth touched her forehead, her eyelids. "We are going to begin our second journey to bliss, lady."

Yes, they were. She stared at his lips. How could they look so soft and strong at the same time? How could herbal water mixed with his sweat smell so wonderfully masculine?

She felt the warmth and strength of his fingers around her waist. She tilted her head back to look up at him. His impassioned features filled her with awe.

His whisper, "Jarvia," pushed aside the last vestige of her resistance. She dissolved willingly against him. His lips captured hers in a kiss that began sweet and warm and tentative, but soon became hot, demanding, and urgent.

Jarvia felt as if she burst into flames as she answered his hunger with her own. He cupped her head with one hand, banded her waist with the other. With both he pulled her closer to him; she writhed against him, clinging to him and drinking in the pleasure from his mouth and his strong, muscular body. She pushed her fingers through his hair, loving the feel of it against her flesh. She reveled in his arms about her. He was much stronger, more overpoweringly virile than she had remembered.

"I like to look at you, Jarvia."

She felt his words as much as heard them. He used his wonderful voice to caress her, making her feel alive and beautiful and excited. She moistened her dry lips.

"Please." Her plea had changed.

Malcolm understood and nodded.

Looking deep into each other's eyes, they moved together. Malcolm's lips touched hers; Jarvia's mouth opened in welcome. She received his fire. It cleansed, kindled desire, blotted out thought. Aye, Malcolm mac Duncan was the lord of fire.

His hand, both gentle and urgent, moved over her body. She responded as a lur horn did to a master player. She let him have his way, for his way was her deepest pleasure.

Somewhere in the haze of heat and desire, she heard him speak.

"Touch me, madam."

Reluctantly she lifted passion-laden lids. "You're dressed for the hunt, lord."

He rolled away. "And the hunt is over."

"Aye." *The hunt is over*.

He undressed her first and lay looking at her, simply looking, adoring her with his eyes, taking in every detail. Then he rose and undressed himself. They gazed at each other in the hazy glow of sunset. The flames in his eyes mesmerized her; she could easily, willingly surrender to their fiery beauty, though she would be burned to cinders by doing so.

He caught her to him, their naked bodies touching to rekindle the fire that burned between them. He claimed her lips, his tongue slipping into her mouth. Before, she had wanted to sink into him; now she wanted him to sink into her.

As he asked, she touched him. She moved her hands across his torso, exploring his hair-covered chest, the smooth ridges of muscles and warm flesh. He received her caresses, moaning and murmuring his delight. She moved her mouth from his to strew soft kisses down the strong column of his throat. She licked teasingly at each nipple resting in a nest of black chest hair. Need drove her to give and to take pleasure.

Then she was lying on her back. He hovered above her. She wanted him; but he did not settle himself on her. He continued to make love to her with his mouth, with his hands. She gloried in it, but a longing was burning in her lower body, a yearning that kisses and caresses would not assuage. No pride left, she cried for more, more of him.

She tried to pull his buttocks against her, but he resisted. His lips grazed the tips of her breasts; his hand rested at the juncture of her legs. Sweet temptation. Her thighs opened willingly to the slightest pressure. His fingers began to tease and stroke, while his tongue and lips played over her breasts. She cried out with pleasure.

Still she wanted more of him.

Her hand slid to the warm and rigid maleness that pressed

against her. Her fingers closed around it, and she began her own tantalizing game. She teased and stroked, setting up a rhythm to match his. His hips moved; he groaned softly against her breast, caught her nipple and suckled greedily.

"Now, Malcolm," she urged.

His breathing was ragged, his skin wet, hot and flushed. His eyes blazed with need as they gazed into hers.

"Malcolm," she pleaded.

He took her mouth once more, a gentle touch, then covered her body with his. She welcomed him with a sharp cry, trembling and shaken with the power of her response as he sheathed himself deep inside her.

White-hot pleasure shot upward from the center where they joined to sear her entire body. She gasped; she raked her hands up and down his back; she nipped his shoulder with her teeth. His smooth, turgid shaft pierced her with deep, demanding strokes. Her hips rushed up to meet him. She would have all of him.

They reached the ultimate pleasure together. Their bodies deeply entwined, they cried out their completion. Then they collapsed on the pallet, while gradually their heartbeats and breathing slowed. Rolling to one side of the coverlet, Malcolm drew her into his arms, pillowing her head on his chest.

She stroked the long hair from his shoulder, running the black strands through her fingers. She gazed up at the violet evening sky.

"Lord—"

"Malcolm." His warm breath tickled her bosom.

"Malcolm." She loved the sound of his name on her lips.

"I like to hear you say my name." Sweet joy rushed through her as his lips moved against her breast, still swollen and sensitive from their mating.

"I like to say it . . . Malcolm."

She continued to brush her fingers through his hair.

"When I first saw you," she said, "I wondered what mating with you would be like."

"And I you. You looked lovely standing in the torchlight."

Jarvia wrapped a strand of hair around one finger. "Long before that."

He raised his head and peered into her face.

"When you came to get your first bride."

He said nothing.

"You did not notice me, lord. I was already wed and was one of many matrons gathered for the ceremony. You had eyes only for Hilda." Smiling, she released the strand of hair to trace his thick black brows. "I noticed you, and I wondered."

"Now you know." He kissed her gently. "Twice you know, lady. Has your opinion of coupling changed since the first time?"

"I like mating."

"I am glad, because we shall be mating frequently."

"You said . . ." Jarvia hesitated.

He waited.

"You said you had a letching for me."

"Aye." His callused hand stroked tendrils from her face. "Is letching all that it is?"

Jarvia wanted to believe that he desired her for more than sex, that he desired more than her body to bear him a son. She doubted that he loved her, that Malcolm mac Duncan could ever love a woman, but she wanted him to feel a lasting tenderness toward her. It would make marriage to him and the bearing of his children more palatable.

"Do not press for what I cannot give you," Malcolm said softly. "Let us take what happiness we can find. I want you more than any woman I have ever known."

If Jarvia had learned anything during her lifetime, it was to take happiness where she could. She would extract no promises from a man who would give none. She had made a marriage agreement with him. He would honor it. So would she.

In a husky voice he said, "I want you again."

Feeling a warm desire for his hardness begin deep inside her, she did not want to talk anymore. She turned to receive his kisses and caresses, to give them back with equal ardor. This time when they reached completion, her entire body felt as if it were in flames. She became one with the fire that was Malcolm mac Duncan.

Later, he gave a gusty sigh and muttered, "Ah, Lachlann, if only you knew."

Startled, Jarvia stiffened. "What did you say, lord?"

Malcolm tangled his hand in her hair and pulled her face to his. "I am well pleased with you, Jarvia. My best-man warned me off you. He predicted that you would be like a berg of ice."

In the violet haze of twilight, Jarvia gazed into the warrior's face. Irritation and a twinge of humiliation surged through her, but she pushed them away. She had gone into this agreement with Malcolm knowing the consequences. She would live with them.

"I knew you were fire, lady. That you were a Valkyrie who would plunge me to the depths of your Valhalla."

"I have never been fire before, lord," she admitted quietly. "I am only so when you excite my body."

Malcolm's fingertips massaged her scalp to send relaxing warmth through her. "That is the way it should be, lady." He smiled. "You and I are going to create a magnificent son."

"Magnificent children," she murmured.

He did not answer. He drew her head onto his shoulder and covered their bodies with his tartan. Holding each other close, they lay quietly.

"Tell me about your parents, lord," Jarvia said.

He breathed deeply. "My mother, Muireall, is a Scottish princess. When she had seen the passing of ten-and-seven winters, she wed a Pict chieftain, Camshron—my father. A winter later she gave birth to my brother, and a winter after that she had me. I was only a few days old when the Northland sea raiders invaded our land. My father died defending our village. When the enemy overran it, my mother and her maid, each with a baby, tried to escape. The maid and my brother were killed. Holding me in her arms, my mother and another of her faithful servants escaped on Northland ponies they found in the forest. Under Muireall's guidance, they took refuge with Fergus, chief of Clan Duncan of the Northern Scots."

"You never knew your father or your brother?" Jarvia said.

"Nay."

Malcolm pushed the tartan aside and rose to dress.

But the truth was that at times he had the strange feeling

that he *did* know his brother, that his brother was not dead but alive and with him. He had actually felt that at times he could reach out to touch him and talk to him.

This strange conviction had haunted Malcolm ever since he could remember. Sometimes he felt it more strongly than others. When he became a warrior. When he defied Fergus and went against Highland custom by learning to read and write the *ogham*. When he killed his first boar. Always Malcolm had felt that someone shared in his victories, in his glory . . . and in his defeats and sorrow.

Only once when he was a small lad had he discussed these unusual feelings with his mother. Taking him by the hand, Muireall had led him into the forest to the rushing mountain stream. As he had talked, she had listened and understood. She had explained that the gods were speaking to him. Because he was a special child, she said, they had chosen him to be king of all Northern Scotland. It was his destiny to unite the Northern Highland tribes into one kingdom, to lead them on a new pathway—one of peace. Her words were proved true when he received his vision on becoming a warrior, when he received the torque of heirship to the kingdom of Northern Scotland.

Guided through the ritual by Feich, the Wise Woman, Malcolm had fasted for days and set himself apart from other young warriors. On the tenth night he finally received his dream. He started out as one warrior, then became two—although as the second one he was dressed in strange garb. As long as he was the double warrior, no one could defeat him. He stood side by side with himself, one of his forms wielding a sickle sword with the right hand, the other with the left. In his vision he vanquished all his enemies. The next morning when he awakened, he felt a strength flowing through him that he had not forgotten or doubted ever since. He knew the gods had chosen him, that in him ran the wisdom and the strength of two warriors. From that day forward Malcolm had determined to fulfill his destiny.

The day Fergus had fastened the golden torque about his neck, Malcolm had closed his eyes and seen another warrior, a huge, burly man—mayhap Camshron, his father—putting a silver torque about his neck. In this vision, he was once more holding a sickle sword in the right hand, not the left one.

He had asked Feich about his dreams, about his being both right- and left-handed, but she had told him that at the proper time all things would be revealed. So far, the proper time had not arrived. He still had not unraveled this mystery.

Breaking into his thoughts, Jarvia said, "You are fortunate, lord. You have your mother and your foster father."

He looked down to see her fully clothed sitting on the coverlet. "Aye, I am fortunate, lady."

"I have no family, not even a recollection of them. The closest to a family that I have ever had was Gerda. She has been with me since she was a wee babe who had not even seen the passing of a winter. I had seen only ten winters myself. We are like sisters." Jarvia was quiet for a moment before she added, "And for four winters I had Ein-her."

"How did you become the king's slave?"

"When my parents died in the plague, they owed a huge debt to Wyborn. I was only a baby, but as payment he took me for his slave. Five winters ago Ein-her bought my freedom and married me. He was like a father to me. I miss him very much."

Malcolm caught her in his arms and held her against his chest.

"Tell me about your mother," she said.

He laid his chin on the top of her head. "Although she has lived forty-and-eight winters, her hair is yet black and her eyes a vivid blue."

"Like yours," Jarvia said.

He laughed softly. "Some say so. They also say I am stubborn like her."

Jarvia lifted her head from his shoulder and looked up at him. "Do you think she will approve of me as your wife, lord?"

"Aye, lady, I do."

She smiled and nestled against him. After a while, he began to talk quietly, and Jarvia listened. He spoke again of his mother and of his and her life together in Fergus's village. Although Malcolm never said outright that he loved his mother, Jarvia knew he did. Everything he said bore witness. Jarvia also heard admiration and respect for the woman who had placed her life at risk to save him and have him fostered in the king's house.

During the earlier years of Malcolm's life, when he was living with Fergus and his first wife, Malcolm had been allowed to see his mother frequently. They walked in the forest; they hawked and hunted; they played games requiring intellectual skill. Several years after Malcolm's foster mother had died, Fergus married Muireall.

She insisted that Malcolm learn to read and write the *ogham*. Only by gaining knowledge, she asserted, could he become the king that the gods had ordained him to be. Disagreeing with Muireall on this issue, Fergus had, at first, refused to allow Malcolm to take instruction from a priest, but Malcolm had insisted.

At the time that Muireall had sought refuge in Fergus's village, the northern tribes of the Scots and Picts were enemies. And although Muireall was Scottish herself, she suffered greatly because she had married a Pict chieftain and borne him a son. She taught Malcolm to be proud of his ancestors and to ignore the taunting. Her guidance had given his life focus and direction.

Malcolm also loved and respected his foster father. In teaching Malcolm to be a warrior, Fergus had taught him the underlying concepts of the warrior's code. It was Fergus who instilled the idea in Malcolm that strength and glory were to be found in peace, and that war was the last resort of failed negotiations. The only major disagreement Malcolm and his foster father ever had was over Malcolm's education, but Fergus had acquiesced to his son's desires.

Malcolm talked at length about Fergus's dream of uniting the northern Scottish clans. While Fergus had brought them together in a loose confederation, he knew there was yet much to do. This, he told Malcolm, would be his task.

Finally Malcolm lapsed into silence.

Jarvia understood this man she was taking to be her husband much better now. While he respected and admired his parents, he was his own person. He valued the lessons they had taught him, the foundation they had given him, but he walked his own path now.

She also knew with certainty that willingly or unwillingly she would be walking that path with him. Later, as the evening shadows lengthened, Jarvia stirred.

"I must return," she said, "I would help Bertha with the cooking."

"I shall escort you."

He rose, held out a hand, and tugged her up. While Jarvia replaced the eating utensils in the basket and folded the coverlet, Malcolm strapped his weapons about his waist.

"I would have you with me when we dress the kill."

"Aye," she said.

"Also, Jarvia, I have reconsidered our agreement. Tonight I want you to return to your house to stay with me. I do not want us to spend any more time apart."

Jarvia stopped walking and faced him. "Lord, already you dishonor me by possessing my body when I am rightfully betrothed to another. You have proved to me that I am weak when it comes to passion. Please do not dishonor me further."

Twilight did nothing to soften the resolve in his expression. "I have spoken, lady. So be it."

So be it.

Chapter 14

◁~⌒⊙⊙⌒~▷

By the time Jarvia and Malcolm returned to her house, the village glowed with torchlight. Men and women laughed and talked as they cleaned and dressed the animals that had been slain in the hunt.

A horn sounded. Talking ceased; activity stilled. Everyone listened. The horn sounded a second time.

"A ship," Jarvia exclaimed. "A ship has arrived."

"A ship!" The cry went up throughout the village.

Those not dressing animals leaped to their feet and ran to grab torches. Lighting them, they rushed toward the harbor.

"Mayhap it is Lord Lang's ship," Jarvia whispered.

Malcolm dropped the basket and coverlet on Jarvia's porch and caught her hand. They joined the villagers who raced to the dock to await the ship. Some ran down a path cut into the side of the mountain; others waited at the quay. Men, women, and children, crowding around, held aloft their torches so that light danced on the water.

Jarvia's gaze skimmed past the dark silhouettes of cliffs that lined the craggy shoreline of the Southerland coast. Hoping Lord Lang's *langskip* had come, she strained to see. At first she saw only a yellow dot on the horizon, but it soon grew into a brilliant flare of light. Reflected in the glow of the ship's many torches was the blue-and-white hoisted dress sail. As the *langskip* drew closer, the dragon head on the prow dipped and rose gracefully with the swell of the loch. Round shields, alternating blue and white, hung in a row along the outside of the hull.

The villagers began to cheer and to wave their torches. The captain guided the ship around the quay.

"Is it Lord Lang's?" Malcolm asked.

"Aye," Jarvia replied. " 'Tis Lang's colors."

Malcolm caught her hand and squeezed it, the only indication that he was eagerly awaiting the lord's answer to their petition.

Aboard the ship activity increased. Sailors furled, tied, and stored the sail. The captain steered the ship against the wooden dock, landing with a gentle thud. Northland sailors shipped the oars, then unfastened their sea trunks.

A young man, large and magnificently dressed in a white shirt and blue trousers, disembarked from the dragonship. His blue mantle hung from his broad shoulders in thick swirls; his boots clicked as he walked across the wooden dock. Though richly clothed and an emissary of Lord Lang of Northland, the man's sword was strapped about his waist. He was a warrior.

"I am Ragnar, vassal to Lord Lang," he declared. "Take me to King Wyborn. I deliver a message from my lord."

"Lady, our waiting shall soon be over," Malcolm said.

Jarvia nodded. Her breath quickened.

Following the messenger, Jarvia and Malcolm hastened back to the village. By the time they entered the Great House, servants were rushing to prepare a great feast. Ragnar had delivered his message to Wyborn and was consuming a large tankard of ale. A grin stretching from ear to ear, Wyborn proclaimed the news: Lang had agreed to break the betrothal.

As Jarvia had expected, the Northland lord demanded a costly sum—far above that which she had speculated he would demand—for the rupture agreement.

Ragnar placed two large chests before the High Seat in Wyborn's Great House. After Jarvia had given all her possessions, Malcolm ordered his men to fill the two chests with valuables he had brought with him from Northern Scotland. Jarvia gazed in awe at the riches. Never had she seen so much wealth. Shields, swords, and lances gilded with copper, silver, and gold. Jewel encrusted dishes. An assortment of jewelry.

When the chests were filled and the lids fastened, Malcolm held out a sword to Lang's emissary. "This is a Highland Sword," he said, "crafted by the best smith in the Highlands. Each year the High King of Northern Scotland bestows this sword to the winner of the summer games. In the same spirit that the sword was given to me,

I give it to Lord Michael. Tell him it is a special gift with great magic."

Taking it, Ragnar said, "I shall do so, sire."

"And the stallion," Malcolm said. "He is a prize also. Take care of him."

"Aye," Ragnar said. "He will receive special attention. My Lord Michael loves ponies, sire, and will greatly appreciate such a fine gift."

Relief washed over Jarvia when Ragnar set sail for Northland the next day. To insure the safe return of such wealth, the lords of Southerland ordered escort ships, under the command of Madelhari the Trader, to sail with them. In high spirits, King Wyborn and his lady prepared for the wedding. Under normal circumstances Jarvia would have participated in three separate ceremonies: the adoption, the betrothal, and the wedding. Southerland law demanded that the adoption ceremony be separate, but Malcolm mac Duncan insisted on combining the betrothal and wedding into one. Yet he would adhere strictly to tradition for both ceremonies, so that he and Jarvia would be legally wed. Not wanting anything to hinder the wedding, the king and queen hastily agreed.

That same day King Wyborn and Queen Adelaide formally announced their intention to adopt Jarvia and Gerda as their daughters. Although Jarvia did not wish personally for the king and queen to become her parents, she knew they must in order for her to save Gerda and the babe, and to ensure the alliance between Southerland and Northern Scotland. As the law-giver she made sure custom was strictly adhered to.

Resentfully, Wyborn selected a three-year-old ox, had it slaughtered, and ordered a boot to be made from the hide of its right leg. Seven days later the adoption was celebrated with a feast. Wyborn and Adelaide set the boot in the middle of the hall in front of the High Seat. First Wyborn slipped his right foot into the boot then removed it. Jarvia did the same. When she removed her foot, Wyborn clasped her hand and raised it in the air.

"I, King Wyborn of Southerland," he shouted for all to hear, "declare that Jarvia is now my daughter."

The people cheered; the men clanged their weapons

together. Then the queen put her right foot into the boot to signify publicly that she accepted Jarvia as an equal member of the household. After Gerda was adopted in the same way, Jarvia breathed a sigh of relief and settled back to enjoy the feast.

Although betrothals and weddings were private in the sense that they did not involve officials, Malcolm mac Duncan made public the wedding announcement between him and Lady Jarvia. On the specified day in Lambs' Fold Moon, all the villagers gathered in the Great House for the combined ceremonies.

Jarvia, wearing her new dress and the jewels given to her by the king and his lady, entered the *skáli*. The king and queen, walking on either side of her, escorted her to the High Seat. Here they all awaited Malcolm.

Jarvia was increasingly apprehensive. She had bragged she had the wisdom to handle the warlord. While she was secure in her wisdom, she also knew her passion for him played her wisdom for a fool. How quickly he had shown her the fragility of her resistance when he began to excite her body and mate with her. How much more in control he would be when they returned to his kingdom, legally wed.

The entrance door opened. Malcolm mac Duncan and his best-man, Lachlann, entered the *stofa* to take their places opposite the king's High Seat. Queen Adelaide and Jarvia rose to fill their pitchers with imported wine. The queen served her husband, Jarvia the Highlander.

As soon as the first tankard had been drained, Malcolm rose and faced King Wyborn to begin the first phase of the combined betrothal and wedding ceremony. "Lord, do you promise to give to me your daughter, Princess Jarvia, to be my wedded wife?"

As the skald spoke the translation, the queen refilled the king's goblet with wine. He lifted it and shouted, "The gods bring luck! I betroth my daughter."

Jarvia refilled Malcolm's goblet. He raised it high.

"In the presence of the Council of Justice and the people of Southerland, Princess Jarvia and I plight our troth."

Before the translation ended, everyone drained their goblets. The people cheered. The men clanged their weapons together. The women slapped their hands on the tables.

Afterward all raised refilled tankards in salute to the betrothed couple.

"As a seal of our betrothal"—Malcolm tossed his goblet aside and reached for Jarvia.—"I now kiss my intended bride."

By the time Malcolm had uttered the words, he had taken Jarvia in his arms. The people needed no interpretation.

Before Malcolm's lips touched hers, he whispered triumphantly, "Now, lady, you are mine. Any time. Any place."

"I am to be your wife, not your possession."

"In the law, lady, there is no difference."

She did not answer, for he spoke the truth.

"Now, lady, I would kiss you and taste once more what is mine."

Malcolm's breath caressed her forehead. His mouth covered hers, moving gently and warmly, his tongue testing the seam of her closed lips. He exerted more pressure.

"Lady." He sighed, then added a tad irritably, "Must I—"

She laughed softly. "Nay, I will do it." She captured his mouth with hers.

Surprised, he pulled back. His lips curled. "Are you flirting with me?"

"I know not," she whispered. She clasped both sides of his face with her hands and brought his mouth to hers.

Now he laughed. "Aye, you are, lady, and I like it."

Their mouths touched; their heads slanted and they fit more closely together. He tasted of wine. His kiss, his embrace, reminded her of their last coupling by the mountain stream. It set her body to yearning for fulfillment once again.

At first their kiss was tentative and soft, but when Jarvia moved against him, he forced her mouth open. Jarvia arched her back to the gentle pressure of his big hand. Warmth spread across her breasts and sank into her belly, filling her entire body with a wonderful tingling.

Finally Malcolm broke the kiss, and his lips nipped hers, moving around her mouth, across her cheeks, and back to her lips.

The people cheered and clapped. Smiles creased their faces; their eyes gleamed.

"Would you play loose with me, lord?" she teased.

"Ah, lady, I would." His eyes twinkled. "You are playing loose with me."

Jarvia knew at that moment that Malcolm mac Duncan was the most handsome man she had ever seen. She laughed, suddenly realizing that laughter had never come so easily to her before. She moved out of his embrace, the delicate material of her long wedding tunic swishing about her ankles.

Malcolm caught her hand in his and pulled her back to him. The movement threw her cheek against his chest. Again he wrapped his arms around her. Next to her skin she felt the softness of his shirt and beneath that a body that had surely been forged with hammer and iron, by fire and heat. Only the beating of his heart reassured her that Malcolm mac Duncan was made of flesh and blood.

"I am glad, madam, that you were the one whom destiny decreed for my bride."

"Thank you, lord." She straightened her back and tilted her head so she could properly look into the warlord's face.

"I admire you, madam. I have heard the words of your bards who pay tribute to the law-speaker's strength of character, her poise, her steadfastness and equanimity in the face of calamity."

Lord Malcolm mac Duncan was calamity.

"And her stubbornness," Jarvia added. "Her spirit."

"Aye," Malcolm drawled with a smile. "Surely you have that. You are indeed a fine woman."

"Flattery, lord?"

"Nay, lady. I have only admiration for you. I am proud that such a woman will be the mother of my sons."

"What if Frey places only daughters in my womb, sire?" With great interest she awaited his answer.

"Mayhap you believe your god Frey has control over your womb, madam. I do not. I have decreed that you shall give me a son . . . and by the Blessed Mother you shall."

"You are conceited to think you can dictate to the gods."

But secretly she admitted that even his conceit exhilarated her.

"If being certain of myself, of what I want, is conceit, madam, then I am conceited."

He lowered his head and touched his mouth to the skin above the neckline of her dress. Her insides tightened; she trembled. The kiss he had given her earlier had not stirred her senses as much as did this gentle and warm brushing of his mouth on her collarbone.

As easily as if she were the tiniest flower blooming in the meadow, Malcolm scooped Jarvia into his arms. He walked the length and breadth of the *skáli*, showing her off to the crowd. People shouted, laughed, and clanged their weapons together. Music began to play. Villagers clapped their hands in rhythm and sang.

Finally he carried her back to the center of the *stofa*. Giving her a kiss on the forehead, he placed her on the settle. Once seated, Jarvia leaned back and laid an arm along the armrest of the straight-backed chair. With a sinking heart, she watched the barbarian as he stood beside the settle, his hand over hers.

Indeed, she did belong to this darkly handsome Highlander.

Lachlann rose and lifted his tankard in a salute. "Lords and ladies, people of Southerland," he said, the skald translating, "my lord, the Duncan, awaits King Wyborn's pleasure."

The king rose. "Lord Malcolm, will you signify that you have chosen my daughter and my legal heir, Princess Jarvia, to be your wedded wife?"

Malcolm lifted Jarvia's hand and rubbed the small white indentation where Ein-her's ring had been for the past five winters. Holding her hand in his, lightly stroking her third finger, Malcolm said for all to hear, "Lady, I shall slip my ring on your finger. This signifies that I have chosen you to be my wedded wife."

He held out his right hand.

"Take the ring off my finger."

Jarvia looked at the golden sickle ring his father had had crafted for him, then back up at him in surprise.

"Aye, madam," he said, "I would have you wear my ring. I want all to know that you belong to Malcolm mac Duncan . . . to him and him alone."

Jarvia slipped it off and handed it to him.

He slid it on her finger, the gold gleaming in the sunlight.

Malcolm raised her hand high and walked her up and down the aisle so that all could see the ring. They stopped many times to let the people peer at the exquisite design and craftsmanship, to rub it, and to know that it was an item of great value. To know how much the Highlander valued his bride.

"Now, people of Southerland," Malcolm shouted, "I give my bride her betrothal gift."

Amid cheers and salutes, Malcolm caught Jarvia's hand and led her out of the *stofa*, the people following to fill up the king's yard and to spill into the street. As they stood in the blaze of sunlight, a Highland warrior approached leading a pony. Murmurs of admiration rose from the crowd.

Malcolm waved a hand for silence. "This, lady, is your gift. One of the finest ponies in my herd."

Truly, the pony, about fourteen hands high, was one of the most magnificent Jarvia had ever seen, and she had seen many in her lifetime. The Southermen were known for their fine horsemanship.

"I chose her especially for you," Lord Malcolm said.

The pony was a rich, red gold, its coat polished to a high sheen, its sleek, powerful muscles well defined.

"She is beautiful," Jarvia breathed, gazing at the long, silky mane and tail, both a striking shade of silver.

"The color of your hair," Malcolm said.

Jarvia was not accustomed to seeing a flowing mane on a pony. The Southermen cut close the manes of their steeds so that they stood erect, the crescent shape giving a pronounced crest to the neck.

Malcolm drew her closer to the pony. "Come meet your mount, lady."

He caught the reins and gently rubbed his hand up and down the mare's face. He spoke softly and soothingly to her.

"What would you call her, lady?"

"I know not, lord. I am overwhelmed." She turned to him, tears in her eyes, "Thank you, lord. I have never received so wondrous a gift."

She threw her arms around him and kissed him soundly on the mouth, backing away before he could embrace her.

The people cheered.

Malcolm grinned and winked. "Lady, you were too quick, else I would have taken more from that kiss."

Jarvia knew that and blushed.

He touched the tip of his finger to her cheek. "You continue to surprise and delight me."

After telling his kindred men to stable the pony, Malcolm held out his right hand; Jarvia laid her left palm over it. He escorted her back into the king's house. When all were assembled and seated once more, Malcolm stood.

"I, Malcolm mac Duncan, chief of Clan Duncan of the kingdom of the Northern Scots, have completed all requirements of the betrothal. The kiss of union. The marriage ring. The bridal gift. Be there any who question my right to declare Princess Jarvia my lady-wife?"

He moved up and down the *stofa*, looking at the people, waiting for an answer. None spoke a word. He retraced his steps until he stood in front of the High Seat.

He held out his hand. "Princess Jarvia, join me."

She rose and went to him.

"Have you anything to say, lady, before this wedding is declared?"

"Aye, lord." She smiled at the king and his wife. "My father, Lord Wyborn, I have made a gift for you and my mother, Queen Adelaide."

The king and his wife exchanged glances as Jarvia returned to the table and picked up a square piece of wood about the size of a man's shield, with markings on it. She held it aloft for all to see. Wyborn and Adelaide paled. Both of them knew she was guaranteeing her freedom by sealing the king's alliance with Malcolm, in words. Her gesture let them know openly that she did not trust them.

They cowered from her.

Sweetly she spoke. "My father, my mother, I have placed the magic of the runes on this wooden marker and on a rune stone that I am erecting for all the world to bear witness. I shall have Lord Kirkja read the inscription to you and to those celebrating my wedding. They shall be witness to the words." Jarvia handed the piece of wood to Lord Kirkja.

"What does this mean?" Malcolm whispered.

"Words are magic sent to us by Odin, the wisest of

gods," Jarvia answered as Kirkja read the runes aloud. "I have put into writing the agreement made among King Wyborn, you, and me. Once the words are read aloud and witnessed, King Wyborn and Queen Adelaide are forever bound to hold them true. I have made the lord and lady promise they shall never disown me or Gerda, that we will be their daughters forever."

When the reading was over, Kirkja stepped back. Solemnly he said, "A rune stone engraved with these words shall be erected for all to see. On threat of death, my lord king, my lady queen, you are bound by these words."

Lord Wyborn sat so still and pale, Jarvia thought perhaps he had been turned into a statue.

" 'Tis a curse," the queen hissed, her small beady eyes glittering maliciously. "The woman has placed a curse on us."

"Nay," Kirkja said, "this is the magic of the runes as delivered to us by Odin in his great wisdom." Kirkja continued to stand in front of the High Seat. Finally he spoke. "Wyborn, what say you?"

"So be it," Wyborn muttered. Then he shouted, "Is there anyone else who would speak before this wedding is declared?"

Silence filled the *stofa*.

Wyborn lifted his goblet, ale sloshing over the side. "I declare Lord Malcolm and Princess Jarvia wed. What say you, Lord Malcolm?"

Taking a piece of the marriage cake baked from the first grain to insure the blessings of fertility, Malcolm turned to Jarvia. "My lady-wife."

He fed her a bite of the cake and gave her a swallow of wine from his goblet.

Wyborn shouted, "What say you, Princess Jarvia?"

She also took a piece of the marriage cake.

"My lord husband."

She fed Malcolm a bite of the cake and he took a sip of her wine.

"Let there be celebration," Wyborn declared.

The people cheered.

Female servants with large trays of food entered the *stofa*. Others carved meat from haunches cooking on the *langeldar*. Male servants rolled large *skapkers* of beer into the room. Women refilled their pitchers so they could serve the rejoicing crowd.

Malcolm and Jarvia returned to their settle. Once seated, Malcolm leaned over and whispered. "Lady, you are indeed crafty."

"What would you expect, lord, since *my father* is such a crafty man?" Jarvia teased, but Malcolm's eyes darkened. He studied her intently, as if searching for answers—answers to what, Jarvia could only wonder.

Making no comment, he gazed somberly at the revelry. One of his men, the one called Thomas, slipped through the crowd to stand beside Malcolm. The two spoke in low tones so that Jarvia could not hear.

After Thomas left, Malcolm sighed; his expression grew heavy. He finished off his goblet of wine. When Jarvia offered to refill it, he shook his head. He caught her hand in his and rose, bringing her also to her feet.

"My lord king," he said, "my warriors and I are grateful for your hospitality. I, Malcolm mac Duncan, am even more grateful for the bride with whom you have blessed me." Malcolm raised his tankard. "May we salute my bride, Princess Jarvia, and the birth of many strong sons."

Again shouts and cheers reverberated throughout the *stofa*.

When the toast was over, Malcolm said, "Now, my lord, my lady-wife and I bid you good-bye."

Shocked, unprepared for such a quick departure from the marriage feast, Jarvia stared at him. The translation sounded. The villagers smiled slyly.

"Before I go, my lord," Malcolm continued with a wave of his hand, "I have provided well for your entertainment." His warriors rolled four barrels into the room. "Scottish ale, King Wyborn, the like of which you have never tasted before and may never taste again."

More cheers filled the building.

"Thank you, Lord Malcolm," Wyborn said. His eyes bleary with drink, he leered at Jarvia. "I can understand why you are leaving the celebration early. I bid you good-morn and good pleasure, Lord Malcolm. Later, if you are able, we shall continue the wedding festivities."

"Not good-morn, my lord," Malcolm said. "Your skald must have misunderstood my intent. My lady-wife and I do not retire to her house. We bid you good-bye. We begin the journey to my kingdom this morn. Two moons have passed while I have been away from my kingdom, lord. I must return."

Must return. The words reverberated through Jarvia's mind. She turned to him. "Today?" she whispered in Gaelic.

"So soon?" Wyborn asked.

"Today," Malcolm replied aloud, though his face softened at his wife's fearful expression. "Urgent matters need my attention. Being a king, my lord, you understand, I am sure."

Wyborn nodded. "May the gods be with you."

Jarvia knew King Wyborn was eager to have the Highlanders on their way, out of his domain. He was also glad to be rid of her.

Malcolm swung Jarvia into his arms and walked down the aisle. The cheering villagers toasted them afresh with refilled tankards and threw the firstfruits of grain over them to bless their union and Jarvia's conception. The grain slid off them, but the ale drenched their hair and clothing.

"Lord," she cried, "we cannot leave now."

"We have no choice."

"We must bathe and change clothing. I cannot have our belongings packed and ready. You said nothing to me—"

"I spoke to Morag and Gerda," he answered. "They have completed the packing. We are ready to begin our journey."

"What about—" Jarvia sought an excuse to delay their departure. "What about our wedding feast?"

"Have no concern. We shall feast aplenty. I have sent word to my people. My mother, High Queen Muireall, is preparing us a marriage banquet that will outshine this one."

"Lord, are we leaving prior to our sleeping on the marriage bed?"

Malcolm grinned. "I shall miss the comfort of the marriage bed, but for a verity, lady, we would be doing little sleeping if we remained in Southerland." He pressed his lips to her forehead. "I promise you all the pleasure, even though we have no bed."

He pulled back and brushed grain from her face. Laughing, he said, "We have no need to pack food. We have enough grain on us to eat until we arrive at my village."

"Aye." She gave him a small smile and brushed an ale-damped lock of hair from his forehead. "Still, lord—"

"Nay, my lady-wife. Give me no more argument."

Jarvia, the matron who had seen twenty-and-five winters, the one who always nurtured others, felt bereft and alone. More than ever, she missed Ein-her. She stared at this stranger to whom she was now married, a man who had promised to carry her to bliss, who now promised to carry her far away from the only home she had ever known.

When they had mated, Jarvia's only thought had been to reach bliss. She had not considered what lay beyond. Now she did.

"I do what I must," Malcolm said.

Jarvia blinked back tears and nodded. "Aye, my lord."

"*Aye, my lord . . .*" He ended the words in a question.

"Aye, my lord husband."

Chapter 15

"Trousers!" Jarvia stood in the center of her house, her hands clamped on her hips. She looked disdainfully at the black garment Malcolm held out to her. "I have never worn them."

"You will now, lady."

"I prefer to wear my own clothes."

"And you may wear them when we arrive at my village, but you will be riding, lady, astraddle your pony. Trousers, not long tunics, are better suited to such a journey."

"I can manage in my own clothes," Jarvia insisted.

"Aye, but I want more, madam. We shall be moving at a fast pace. All Highlanders love their ponies and are accomplished riders. All of us—men and women—find trousers preferable for pony riding." Malcolm crammed the clothing into the crook of her arm.

"I may be married to a Highlander, but I am a woman of Southerland, not an accomplished pony rider." Jarvia held the clothing up and inspected it in the glow of sunlight through the smoke hole in the roof of the longhouse. "Ein-her would have divorced me, had he seen me wearing trousers."

"Ein-her is no longer your husband, madam," Malcolm snapped. "I am. And you will be wearing trousers quite frequently when we live in my village."

"I think not."

"Aye, you will prefer them after a hunt or two, and several days spent hawking," Malcolm said.

"You jest, lord?"

"Nay."

"In Southerland the men hunt, not the women," Jarvia explained. "Sometimes we hawk, if we've a mind to."

"Have you ever had a mind to?"

Jarvia stared a moment, then confessed, "To be honest, my lord husband, I have. I have often wished I could put on a helmet and ride off on a pony to hunt, or sail off in the longship, rather than remain home and worry."

"Then, madam, you are going to find life interesting in my land. I shall take great pleasure in teaching you how to hunt and to hawk."

"Thank you, lord."

"Now make haste and get dressed."

"Whose are these?" Jarvia held the pair of trousers up to her waist.

"They belong to Arthur, a Highland lad who is about your height and weight."

"Your bard?"

With a nod, Malcolm said, "They should fit fairly well. I had Morag alter them since you and Arthur are built differently."

Jarvia looked up to encounter the twinkle in her husband's eyes. Her breath caught in her throat, leaving her voice wispy when she said, "I think I shall be miserable wearing these."

"Nay, lady, I promise before the journey is over, you will thank me."

Jarvia went behind a partition over which was draped her shirt and stockings. Highland cuarans lay on the floor.

"A pair of Arthur's boots?" Jarvia asked.

"Aye," Malcolm answered.

Morag had entered the house in time to hear this last exchange. "I measured them to a pair of your boots," she added. "They are big, but the lining I inserted will make them fit snugly."

As Jarvia stripped, Morag packed her wedding finery. Malcolm directed the Highland warriors who moved in and out of the room loading the carts and beasts of burden outside.

"I am much too big to wear clothing like this," Jarvia grumbled.

" 'Tis doubtful," Morag muttered. "Now, if you looked like Queen Adelaide, I would agree, but you are tall and slender."

When Jarvia stepped from behind the partition, Morag looked her up and down.

"As I thought, you cut a fine figure in them," Morag said

and slipped a leathern girdle around Jarvia's waist, then attached it to her trousers and legging undergarments.

"You would think I look presentable whether I do or not," Jarvia said.

"You look more than presentable, madam," said Malcolm.

Jarvia looked up to see him standing in the open door. Wearing a yellow-and-red plaid mantle, another draped over his arm, he dwarfed the opening with his huge frame. The cool breeze did little to alleviate the fire he set to burning within Jarvia.

"For a verity, Arthur never did for the trousers what you are doing," he observed.

His crooked smile and teasing words sent pleasure through Jarvia.

"What am I doing for them, lord?" she dared to ask.

His blue eyes darkened until Jarvia felt they were hot enough to melt bog ore into iron. "Lady, I would like to show you."

Jarvia enjoyed knowing that the Highlander found her desirable.

In a husky voice, he said, "I like trousers on you much better than those layered dresses that you women wear. I can see your figure, madam, and know you are not shapeless."

"Acht!" Morag waved her hands and rolled her eyes. "Lord, you be jesting. Anyone with half an eye can tell by looking, even when my lady wears the dress of the Northland, that she is not shapeless."

Malcolm grinned. "Still, good woman, I enjoy seeing the lady Jarvia's backside filling out those trousers."

Morag chuckled with him. She lifted a cloak from the back of a chair and moved to Jarvia.

"Nay." Malcolm unfolded the mantle from his arm. "My lady-wife will wear my colors from now on. I have brought one of my tartans for her use."

He crossed the room to stand behind Jarvia. Quick movements settled the cloak over her shoulders. Moving in front of her, he straightened the material, drawing it together over one shoulder.

A mass of nerves, Jarvia stood, her eyes closed, and let Malcolm finish dressing her. When Ein-her had been alive, he had often thrown her cloak about her shoulders and fastened it, but he had not aroused in her the same feelings that Malcolm did. With Ein-her she felt like a treasured daughter. With Malcolm she felt like a woman—a needy woman.

"Madam, do you trust me to pin your cloak together?" Gentle amusement underscored his words.

Jarvia opened her eyes. "Aye."

He loomed over her, deftly securing the plaid mantle about her shoulders. He made her feel like a cherished and desired woman. This was a new feeling for her, one that even Ein-her had not been able to arouse in her.

As she had done to the Highlander that night so long ago, he ran his palm over the shoulders of the mantle to press out the wrinkles. "The colors of the Duncan look good on you, my lady-wife."

"Thank you," she murmured. "I shall wear them with pride."

"I know you will."

"Malcolm." A call came from outside.

"Make haste, my lady. We leave shortly."

Jarvia nodded and watched Malcolm as he strode out the door. Hardly had he stepped from the room than the full impact of his words hit her. Nervous, frightened, she began to pace the *stofa*. She ran her hands over the top of the tables; she paused in front of the loom.

This house, and everything in it, was hers.

She was leaving behind all that belonged to her, all that had been Jarvia of Wybornsbaer, wife to Ein-her.

Her palms were clammy, her legs shaky.

"The events of the day are tiring you, aren't they?" Morag said quietly. "I'll brew a cup of heather tea. That'll settle your nerves."

How like Morag to transfer her attention to the inconsequential when she was worried, Jarvia thought.

"I am leaving, Morag," she said. "Leaving, never to return. Leaving behind the only good life I have ever known."

"Aye, mistress, I know how you must be feeling. I too am leaving the land of my birth."

"Oh, Morag," Jarvia said, instantly contrite, "I was so caught up in my own problems, I gave no thought to you. I guess I thought that since you are a Highlander, you wanted to go."

"In a way I am glad to be leaving." Morag pulled her handkerchief from her girdle and dabbed her eyes. "I want to be with my people again, and for the most part, I dislike the Southerlanders. But . . ." She shrugged and sniffed back her tears. "This is the only home I have ever known."

"I am so sorry, Morag," Jarvia said.

Morag dismissed her oversight with a wave of the hand. "Acht! I'll get over it. 'Twill be all right for both of us, lady. Mayhap we'll find a new and better life."

"Mayhap," Jarvia murmured.

"Nay, not mayhap," Morag said. "For a verity we will."

"I am so frightened," Jarvia confessed. "I have had no time to get to know my husband before we travel to his land."

" 'Twill be all right, lady." Morag soothed and embraced Jarvia. They clung together.

Eventually Morag gently broke the embrace and said, "We'll have that cup of tea. Heather tea. 'Tis exactly what you be a-needing."

The old woman moved to a basket that yet remained on the table. Taking out a small jar, she opened it and poured golden brown liquid into a cup. She brought it to Jarvia.

"Drink this."

Gratefully Jarvia drank deeply of the tepid tea. Morag returned the jar to the basket and carried it to the door, handing it to one of the Highlanders who was assisting with the packing.

Malcolm and Lachlann entered the room.

"Have we any more to pack?" Malcolm asked.

"That is all that remains." Morag pointed to the chest where she had placed Jarvia's wedding dress.

"Where is Gerda?" Jarvia asked as she set her half-filled cup on the trestle table. She felt guilty for having been so caught up in her own concerns that she had not thought earlier about her friend.

"She's outside, lady," Lachlann answered. "Bundled up in one of the carts."

"She is all right?"

"Aye. She's excited and eager for the journey to begin."

Lachlann moved to the door. "Morag, if you are ready?"

"I am." She looked at Jarvia. "Mistress?"

"You may go," Jarvia said.

Servant and best-man exited the *stofa*, leaving Malcolm and Jarvia alone.

"You are having second thoughts?" Malcolm said.

"That does not matter. I made my decision."

"The journey is going to be hard."

Jarvia lifted her cup. "Heather tea. 'Tis Morag's cure for all ailments." She took a swallow.

"She is right about that, lady."

He took the cup from her unresisting fingers and lifted it to his own mouth, setting his lips on the same spot she had drunk from. A thrill of pleasure went through Jarvia.

She had mated with Malcolm to prove her virginity; she had married him to save Gerda and the baby. Both actions had tenuously joined them. But his drinking out of her cup seemed to fuse the bond.

In two swallows he drained the cup and returned it to the table. "We shall have to travel fast, resting only as required by the animals. You, my lady-wife, will have to be stouthearted as well as strong in body. I shall expect you to set a good example for Gerda and the servants you are taking with you."

"I understand my role. I have been a matron before, lord."

"Is there anything else you wish to take with you?"

Her gaze swept slowly over the house. Her home, her security, given to her by Ein-her. She was leaving, never to return, no matter what the outcome of her marriage to the Highlander.

"Nay, lord, I have all I wish to take with me." Again she bit back tears.

He reached out to capture one of her hands. "Lady, I regret that our marriage begins on such a note."

Jarvia said nothing.

" 'Twill be better once we arrive home."

Late afternoon sun glared down on the small cart that jostled along the mountain trail. They had been traveling all day, but it seemed much longer to Jarvia. Gerda had become violently ill shortly after they departed Wybornsbaer. Despite all Jarvia did to help her, she was not getting better. Jarvia pushed strands of limp hair out of Gerda's eyes and washed her face with a damp cloth.

"I did not know carrying a bairn could make me so ill." Gerda's face turned from white to ash-gray. Grabbing a side rail, she pulled herself up, leaned over, and retched.

"My lord," Jarvia called to Malcolm's broad back, "surely we can take some time to stop. Gerda is ill."

Malcolm continued to ride.

Gerda continued to retch.

Jarvia's fury grew . . . as did her frustration. All she had seen of her husband since they left Wybornsbaer was his back as he led the procession through the glens and over the mountains.

He had invited her to ride with him, and Jarvia wanted to. She loved her pony—whom she had named Moonbeam. But she had felt she should stay with Gerda. Malcolm had insisted that any of the women servants could serve Gerda, but Jarvia insisted that she must do it. After all, she had told her husband, she was the lady of the house, and it was her duty to care for the ill.

Malcolm had acquiesced, but Jarvia had known he was angry. His subsequent actions had proved it. He had not spoken to her all day. Exhausted and worried about Gerda, Jarvia had had enough of her husband's arrogance, of his childish behavior.

"Lord Malcolm!" She raised her voice and moved farther up in the cart.

Her husband did not turn, stop, or even slow his pace.

"My lord husband," she shouted angrily for all the world to hear, "I am speaking to you."

Malcolm tensed but still did not stop or turn around.

"Malcolm, do not ignore me!"

He halted the stallion. The entire company jolted to a sudden standstill. Jarvia lurched forward, then backward. Had she not been holding on to the railing, she would have fallen. Rigidly still, Malcolm looked straight ahead. His men awaited his response.

Without turning to his wife, Malcolm rode forward and spoke to Lachlann. Nodding, a grin on his face, the best-man looked toward Jarvia. Malcolm turned his pony and rode back. No storm had fury to compare with the anger darkly mirrored on Malcolm mac Duncan's face. Speaking not a word to Jarvia, he rode past her cart to the last one in the train. When he returned, he held a struggling Morag about the waist, pressed against his side. He deposited her feet-first in the cart.

"You are tired, my lady-wife." The words were dry and hard. His face was closed, his eyes slitted. "Morag will tend to Gerda. I would have you ride with me."

"I shall ride in the cart and take care of Gerda, lord. I shall be fine after we rest a while."

His hard gaze unsettled Jarvia.

"I presume, lord, that we are stopping for a moment."

"No, my lady, we are not. Morag will tend to Gerda. You will ride with me."

"Why is he angry, Jarvia?" Gerda asked. "What is he saying?"

Jarvia explained to Gerda, then added, "But do not worry. I will stay with you."

"He is your husband, Jarvia," Gerda said. "Go with him. I'm feeling better now, and Morag can stay with me."

Malcolm looked down at her. "Gerda is sick, Jarvia, but you will be, too, if you do not rest. Morag will tend to her, and you will come with me."

Jarvia pushed back in the cart. "Nay, lord—"

Malcolm wrapped his arm around her waist and jerked her from the cart. She screamed and flailed. He plunked her on his horse in front of him, and Jarvia was glad she was wearing trousers, else she would have been most embarrassed. All around them, the laughter of the Highland warriors rang in her ears.

"See to Gerda's needs," Malcolm ordered Morag.

"Aye, lord, I shall take good care of her." The servant's voice carried to Jarvia as the Highlander rode off with her.

To her husband, Jarvia said, "I suppose I am being punished."

"Do you think you deserve to be punished?"

"You are a hard man," Jarvia accused. "You have pushed us beyond our endurance. We have traveled all day without stopping for rest, and Gerda is in a delicate condition. She cannot—"

"You are in a delicate condition also, my lady-wife, although you are not carrying a bairn. You have waited on Gerda since we began our journey and are exhausted."

"Mayhap you are upset because you think I have been giving her more attention than I have given you?"

"As you told me, madam, 'tis your duty to take care of those who are infirm," he said. "Now cease your prattle. You have need of your strength."

Urging the stallion into a trot, Malcolm soon pulled away from the others. Jarvia felt the iron-cord strength of her husband against her back. At first she sat rigidly, looking straight ahead, pretending nothing was amiss, that she was not in such close proximity to him.

Much to her disappointment, he seemed not in the least disturbed by her nearness, or her attempt to ignore him. His arms circled her body, but he continued to guide the pony along the steep, narrow pathway.

Traveling fast, they soon lost the company far behind them. Since every step the pony took threw Jarvia against Malcolm's hard chest, she eventually tired of her struggle to keep her distance from him. Still, she would not allow herself to relax completely.

After they had ridden a distance, she heard the rush of water. The black picked its way up a sharp incline. Malcolm's arms tightened around her. She heard the steady beat of his heart and felt the even rhythm of his breathing.

"I wish, lady, that I had some heather tea to give you."

Despite her irritation, Jarvia laughed softly. "You sound like Morag. She thinks tea is the answer to every problem."

"Mayhap not to every one," Malcolm said, "but to most of them."

They rode farther.

" 'Tis said among our people that heather tea is good, but heather ale is miraculous. If I knew the secret recipe, I would brew you some of it. 'Tis said by the ancients that it is made of the purple heather and is magical. One swallow would revive you immediately."

"Why is the recipe secret?" Jarvia asked.

"According to the bards, for generations the recipe was guarded by one Pict family, passed down from father to son. When the Scots sailed across the seas and landed on the shores of Caledon—what we now call Scotland—they traded with the Picts for this delicious brew."

Lulled by her husband's voice and the easy gait of the stallion, Jarvia began to relax.

"The Scots offered great prizes for the recipe, but the Picts would not divulge it."

Jarvia chuckled. "I am glad to hear that some people defy the arrogant Scot Highlanders."

"But not for long, lady."

She heard the smile in his voice.

"One day the cunning Scots captured the guardians—the father and son—of the recipe."

"I should have known, lord. You Scots have a way of getting what you want, do you not?"

Her lids grew heavy.

"First the Scots bribed the guardians for the recipe. When they still could not get it, they tortured them. Finally the father said he would tell the secret if they would kill his son first, since he did not wish his only heir to see him dishonored. The Scots killed the son. Then the father refused to tell the secret."

Turning slightly to press a palm to his chest, Jarvia burrowed her cheek into his soft mantle and closed her eyes. She laughed softly. "So the Scots were foiled."

"Aye, my lady, but not for long."

She was tired . . . so tired. The sound of rushing water grew louder; the incline seemed steeper.

"The old man laughed and taunted the Scots, confessing that he would never tell them the secret. He had his son killed because he was young and had many years left to live and would not have readily given up this beautiful world of seabirds, high cliffs, and foaming sea."

Jarvia burrowed deeper into the strength that was Malcolm mac Duncan and listened to the peaceful gurgle of the mountain stream in the background.

"Furious, the Scots tossed the old man over the cliff. He died and now shares the secret of heather ale with the sea."

"And no one knows the secret for making heather ale?" she mumbled.

"We Scots created our own heather ale, my lady-wife, but we never recovered the secret of the magical brew that died that day with its Pictish guardians."

"Mayhap someday, lord, you will brew me some of the Scottish heather ale."

"Aye." He lowered his head, his chin resting on top of her head. His arm circled her body, his hand resting just under her breasts.

She felt warm and protected . . . secure.

Chapter 16

When Jarvia opened her eyes again, the stallion was standing still. She turned her face and gasped when she beheld the breathtaking sweep of a Highland glen. Green-topped mountains dipped and rose around them. Wildflowers were dots of brilliant colors: yellow, lavender, and red.

Leafy trees jutted up here and there, but for the most part the glen was flat, covered with low growth. The delicate hues of bracken and heather on either side of the pathway were broken by the mountain stream. The rushing water was the purest blue Jarvia had ever seen—the color of Malcolm's eyes.

"What do you think of this, lady?"

She would have pulled away from him, but his arm held her fast against him.

"I have not the words to describe it," she said. " 'Tis more than beautiful."

"Aye, 'tis the Highlands."

Jarvia continued to gaze about her. "Aye, it is."

" 'Tis said the Highlands is the home of the fiercest animal in the land, lady. The wildcat."

"I have no doubt," she murmured. She pressed her hand against his chest and gently stroked her own Highland wildcat. "You remind me of your country, sire."

"How so, lady?"

"This is a proud and spirited land, like the wildcat wild and untamed. As are you."

"I take that as a compliment."

"Aye."

"Thank you, my lady-wife." Both sat quietly for a moment, breathing in the clear, fresh air. "Highlanders are spirited people, madam, and we admire that trait in others."

Jarvia recognized his tone of voice. Now he would punish her for her harsh words to him that afternoon.

"I admire it in you," he continued, "but I will not have you shouting at me as you did today. I am the chief of Clan Duncan; my men must respect me, else they will not follow my orders. You, lady, will not be allowed to undermine my authority."

She quaked inside. She remembered the strength of the Highlander's hands when he had held her fast in the guest chambers of the king's house. His fingers had bitten painfully into her upper arms.

"I did not mean to undermine your authority, lord, but I will not have you ignore me."

Their eyes met and held, his commanding, hers defiant.

"I had good reason, lady."

"So did I, lord."

For an endless time he stared at her. Finally the corners of his mouth lifted. His powerful arms tightened around her.

She took courage. "Had you told me your reasons, sire, I would not . . . have . . . shouted." She lowered her face to nuzzle his chest once more. "I would promise never to do it again, but . . ."

Malcolm chuckled. She felt it as it rumbled from his chest; she heard the sweet, rusty sound as it washed over her.

"Knowing you, lady, I wager it would be a broken promise. One best not made."

"Aye," she answered breathlessly, leaning into him.

He felt her sigh as he hugged her close. It felt good to hold her, to banter with her.

His thoughts strayed to Thomas's report on Berowalt, King Wyborn's emissary to Northern Scotland. Malcolm was glad he had had the foresight to post mounted riders at measured intervals along the way from Northern Scotland to Southerland so they could quickly relay messages back and forth between the two kingdoms.

Malcolm had wondered why Wyborn's emissary had not reported Hilda's death, why Berowalt himself had not been in Southerland to greet Malcolm. This morning at the wedding feast, his question had been answered. Thomas had reported that Berowalt had purportedly been taken prisoner by Duncan clansmen, but had recently escaped his confinement and was on his way to Southerland.

Malcolm had been disturbed by the news. He knew his clansmen had not captured the Southerland warrior, and he feared the lies and rumors the man would report to his king. Rather than stay to refute whatever accusation Berowalt might make, possibly delaying his return home by several weeks, Malcolm had decided to return posthaste to Duncan territory and fight his diplomatic battles from there.

Malcolm felt a deep stirring of desire as Jarvia snuggled against him. For the moment he pushed aside his concerns about the kingdom, about the trouble Sybil and Angus were stirring up, the cattle raids, the lies. He would deal with them when he arrived home. Presently other things were more important, like Jarvia's warmth and femininity, her enticing womanly fragrance, her weight on his chest.

He had wanted her to ride beside him, to see her face as she first experienced the rugged grandeur of his country. Instead she had chosen to stay in the cart and nurse her friend. Although Malcolm knew Gerda was ill, and innocent, he wanted Jarvia with him. He wanted her to touch him, wanted it ferociously. No matter how short the time since they had last mated, it had been far too long.

Caring was easy for him. Needing was hard. He had discovered ages ago that as long as he needed nothing, he could not be hurt. His strength and his solitude resulted directly from that understanding. He could care, possibly he could love, but he refused to *need* to be loved.

Feeling the pressure of his arm around her, Jarvia looked up. He lowered his head and captured her lips in a long, sweet kiss.

"I apologize, lady, that so soon after your wedding we began our journey."

"The suddenness of our departure does not bother me," Jarvia answered. "I am worried about Gerda. She has been ill since we began, and you have allowed us no time to rest. The motion of the cart makes her retch, lord. If only we could have stopped long enough for her stomach to settle, then perhaps—"

"Lady, I could not stop. As I told Wyborn, trouble in my kingdom forces me to travel fast." He slid off the stallion, caught her by the waist, and brought her down beside him. Gazing across the stream into a distant copse of trees that ran up the incline of the next mountain, he said, "Before we left Wybornsbaer this morning, I sent two riders ahead. One was to scout for us; the other was to take word to my people that I am returning with my bride. My scout has not returned, and his delay concerns me."

Holding on to the pony's reins Malcolm caught Jarvia's hand in his. They walked to the stream, their boots crunching on the gravel that lined the rugged bank.

"Also, lady, since we left Wybornsbaer, we have been followed at a discreet distance."

"Aye," Jarvia said, "I heard your warriors talking about it, but they did not seem alarmed."

"Nay, I suspect they are Wyborn's men, seeing that we leave the kingdom directly. I shall worry only if they do not stop following us when we cross into Duncan territory. No matter. I have sent warriors back to keep a closer watch on them."

He turned full circle, looking in all directions.

"We shall camp here tonight."

"Just you and me, lord?" Jarvia asked.

He smiled. "The idea is tempting, but I told Lachlann where I was headed. He and the company will join us later."

Jarvia knelt at the stream's edge. Cupping her hands, she filled them with cold water and splashed it on her face. With damp hands she brushed strands of hair from her face. She tugged the shirt from her trousers and lifted the hem to dry her face. Malcolm led his stallion to a tree and tied the reins to a low-hanging branch.

"Wait here, Dhubh-righ," he said.

"Black King," Jarvia murmured. "He is indeed a beautiful pony, lord, and rightfully named."

"Aye," Malcolm said absently, and Jarvia knew his thoughts were elsewhere.

He pulled a leathern bag from the back of the horse and slung it over his shoulders. "I know a quiet place farther up that is sheltered, lady. If you wish, you can take a bath and change your clothing there."

Jarvia raised a brow.

He grinned and patted the bag on his shoulder. "I have a change of clothes for you here. We have time before the others join us."

"*My* clothes?" she said.

His grin widened, and Jarvia's heart skipped a beat. "More trousers that I had Morag alter for you. Also, lady, I gave her instructions to begin sewing shirts and trousers for your own, so that you would not have to wear borrowed clothes. That way you will always be in *your own clothes*."

Hands on her hips, Jarvia stared at him.

"Do you find the trousers so uncomfortable to wear?" he asked.

"Nay," Jarvia answered, "but I would have preferred to be consulted about my clothing before you ordered them sewn."

After a moment's consideration, he said, "Let us make a pact, lady." Jarvia nodded. "For the most part I shall let you select your clothing. If you wish to wear tunics for the remainder of the journey, simply tell Morag."

Jarvia slowly smiled. "I wish to wear the trousers, lord. I only want to have a little say in the matter."

Malcolm chuckled softly. "Lady, I have a feeling you are always going to have more than a little say in any matter."

Carefree and happy, they laughed together. Jarvia clasped the hand he held out and walked beside him to a sheltered curve in the stream. Glad for the warmth of the overhead sun, she unpinned her hair, stripped out of her soiled garments, and stepped into the cold water. After the initial shock, she sank below the surface to wet her entire body.

As she rose, she tipped back her head, letting water rush down her face and over her shoulders. The breeze touched her body. She shivered, but the chill felt good.

She opened her eyes to see Malcolm standing naked on the shore. Her exhaustion fled at the sight of him. His flesh was gilded bronze by the sun. His calves, thighs, and flanks were all dark, richly hewn in hard, sleek lines.

He was hers.

Deep down she felt a hot throbbing in her lower body. He had stirred this longing in her, had awakened her to desire. Once awakened, she could not deny her feelings.

Slowly he walked into the water toward her.

Slowly she walked toward him.

When she stood in front of him, she laid her hand against his cheek, the day's beard stubble an abrasive caress on her palm. "I am glad you brought me here, my lord husband."

"I am, too, my lady-wife."

He welcomed her touch; it was achingly sweet. She reached with her other hand to cup his face and guide it to hers.

"I would taste you," she murmured.

"Ah, lady," he breathed, "I would have you taste me."

Her mouth claimed his. Doing to him as he had done to her, she leisurely explored his mouth with gentle brush strokes of her lips, her tongue. She coaxed him to open to receive her. He did. With the drugging kiss, she asked for an even hotter invasion.

Melting beneath his heat, Jarvia wrapped her arms around him, holding safely to his shoulders, then brushing her palms down his muscular chest.

Though they had known each other intimately, Jarvia was still surprised by the contrasting textures that made up Malcolm, her Highland warrior. He was warm and soft, cold and hard. He was all sinew, an uncompromising clan chieftain. Rough and rugged, he took with authority and conquered by force. Now in his nakedness, all his glorious maleness confronted her. The warrior gave way to her lover. She felt a tremor of vulnerability.

Her hands caressed him, and he moaned against her mouth. The guttural cry incited a quivering response in her. Her breathing became labored; her heart thundered.

"My lord—"

"Malcolm," he whispered. He trapped one of her trembling hands against his bare chest until she felt sure her skin was seared.

"Malcolm" came her breathy cry.

"Shhh. We have little time. Don't talk. Just feel."

Jarvia did. She lost herself in the newly aroused sensations that Malcolm had introduced to her. Wonderful. Timeless. Hot and exciting.

Malcolm kissed her again and again. His hands gentled and soothed her, yet his mouth continued to plunder. His lips burned a trail down her throat and over her breasts.

She arched her back to offer more of her neck, her breasts. All of her wanted to be caressed by him. Throat. Chin. Mouth. She panted.

His hands slid up to cup her breasts; his thumbs rubbed her nipples until they hardened. His hands slid down, over her hips, the outside of her thighs. They trailed lightly over her stomach. Her muscles jerked. His fingers touched the juncture of her thighs.

"My Mal—"

His fingers slipped over the soft flesh, arousing a flood of expectation in her.

"I want to mate with you," he said.

She too wanted to mate. More, she wanted him to make *love* to her.

He nuzzled his face between her breasts. "Now, lady. Right this minute."

"Aye."

He raised his head slightly to see the breeze swirling her damp, unbound hair about her shoulders. Several strands tickled him. He caught them with his hand. They were like silvery moonlight—soft and silky, as elusive as night shadows.

Again she guided his mouth to hers. They stared at each other through passion-darkened eyes before their lips met in a fierce kiss.

She pulled her mouth slightly away, her lips brushing against his as she said, "Make love to me, my Highland warrior."

"Aye, my lady-wife."

He scooped her into his arms and moved to the shallows with her. Both fell back, cushioned by the lapping water. He kissed her mouth, her cheeks, her neck, working downward in a wet, sultry trail to the peak of one quivering breast.

His lips moved persuasively. She parted her thighs for him.

Since the beginning Malcolm had admired Jarvia's strength, her intelligence, her independence. All that was Jarvia of Southerland. During their mating he savored these qualities, drew them into himself.

But he had been surprised, to a degree humbled, by her gentleness. It touched him in places no one else had touched. He was not sure if that was good, or if he liked it, but he had to have her. He feared that her gentleness would cause him to need her. This must never happen. He must never succumb. Never!

As he entered her slowly, pleasure rippled through his body from the soles of his feet to the top of his head. She was tight and warm. Her silken depths received him graciously, closed around him greedily.

Gently but firmly, he pulled back a little and then moved into her all the way. Her legs tightened around him to draw him deeper still. He was enveloped in her warmth and softness.

A sudden urgency gripped him. He thrust into her again and again. Each time, she rose to meet him, straining with him.

She rose one last time against him. Supreme bliss claimed them, consumed them, held them for several shattering moments, before they were finally hurled into complete and utter satisfaction.

Chapter 17

Dusk settled over the glen, one of many Jarvia had
traveled through during the past four days. Yet each
time she saw a new glen, each time she witnessed another
sunset, she was awed by their beauty. The wind, growing
stronger, blew her clothes against her body. It brushed
against her cheeks, whispered in her ears. As she stood at
the edge of the cliff and gazed down at the river below, as
she listened to its rushing music, the magic of the Highlands
captured her. Willingly she gave herself up to its spell.

The air was crisp, and she pulled her red-and-yellow
plaid tartan closer about herself. Yet she basked in the
sweet aftermath of her recent mating with her husband. As
he had promised, their trip had not kept them from sleeping
together.

The fear she had experienced four days ago when she
had first embarked on this journey was subsiding. She had
received no pledge of love from the Highlander, no promises of tender feelings from him, but a peace and contentment she had never felt before permeated her entire being.

The wind tossed tendrils of hair about her face; they
teased her cheeks, the end of her nose. When she tucked
them behind her ears, she felt the long weight of her hair.
She smiled, thinking how much she enjoyed wearing her
hair long and loose, how much she enjoyed being free from
the marriage scarf, which Highland women did not wear.

She looked down at her hand, at the marriage ring
Malcolm had given to her. A wide gold band with its sickle
design signified that she was his wife. She liked that too.

Aye, she enjoyed many aspects of being married to the
barbarian. As she grew to know him better—oddly enough,
the more they mated, the more she learned about him—she
knew that the accusations Hilda had made against him could
not be true.

184

Ein-her had often praised Jarvia for being a good judge of character, and she was. She would never have had tender feelings for a man who was the beast Hilda had painted Malcolm to be, and she believed that Hilda had seen the man as she wanted to see him . . . or as she wanted others to see him.

For a verity, Malcolm was a lusty fellow. He admitted as much. But he was also a skilled lover, and he was never bestial.

He could well be called insatiable, Jarvia thought, but where her husband was concerned, she herself was insatiable.

Aye, she had tender feelings for him. With infinite patience and finesse, he had touched her secret places, her secret self, and brought her great joy. He had taught her she had nothing to fear from passion, and the knowledge had lessened many of her inhibitions. She was gradually falling in love with him.

Her only disappointment was that Malcolm mac Duncan did not feel the same about her. She wanted more than letching from him; she wanted to be more than the mother of his sons.

Jarvia looked up into the darkening sky and saw a cluster of three stars, graduated in size. They reminded her of a family—father, mother, and child. As she gazed at the twinkling night beauty, she vowed she would make Malcolm mac Duncan fall in love with her. She would do it by loving him so completely that his letching for her would turn into love.

"Princess Jarvia!"

Morag's call from the distance shattered the spell the Highlands had cast over Jarvia; it jarred her back to the present.

"Up here," she answered.

" 'Tis getting late, lady." The old woman said, huffing as she climbed the hill toward her mistress. "Time you were getting in bed. I would imagine that we'll be starting our journey early in the morn."

"I would suspect so. How is Gerda doing?"

"She's resting peacefully," Morag answered. "Which is more than I can say about Brian."

Malcolm's best-man had been attacked by a boar sow earlier in the day. He, Lachlann, and Ghaltair had been searching for a stray pony when they had inadvertently stumbled into the boar's lair. Startled, Brian's pony had thrown him, and he had become prey to the angry sow.

"His leg is badly wounded."

"For a verity, lady," Morag said, "that boar sow fairly tore into it. Do you think it will have to be amputated?"

" 'Tis bad," Jarvia answered, "but I think we can save it."

" 'Twould be no worse for him to lose it than to be unable to walk on it," Morag said.

"If I heal it, Brian will not be a cripple. That I promise."

Morag nodded. " 'Twill teach him to be more careful during farrow season. Any mother will protect her young, and the boar is one of the most vicious."

"Aye."

Quietly they stood, savoring the magical silence of the scene.

Eventually Jarvia asked, "What is my husband doing?"

"He's visiting with the Highland warriors who joined us earlier. He probably will be for hours to come." She took a step or two down the pathway. "We should be returning to camp. You know what his lordship said."

"Aye," Jarvia smiled lazily and turned the ring on her third finger. "I remember what *his lordship* said."

He had promised to take her to bliss many times before death. So far he had more than kept that promise. He had taken her to bliss and beyond. Again warm pleasure flowed through her as she remembered their last coming together.

But no matter how frequently they mated, she still hungered for his touch. Knowing he was yet in a meeting with his warriors, she was in no hurry to return to camp. She enjoyed being here by herself.

"You go ahead and prepare our bed. I shall be along." Jarvia breathed deeply of the pure, crisp air. "Also, please check on Brian for me. I left the containers of medicine out in case his bandages need changing."

"I'll take care of 'im," Morag said.

"If he is not better," Jarvia instructed, "let me know. I shall sit up with him. He is bound to be feverish tonight."

"If he's not feeling better, I'll sit with him myself. You need rest."

Jarvia called out her thanks and watched the servant disappear into the shadows. Wistfully she glanced up at the night sky once again and saw the three stars. Their stars, she thought. Hers and Malcolm's . . . and their firstborn child.

A few minutes later Jarvia heard a noise and turned, but she saw nothing. Probably a night critter, she thought, and began to move toward camp. At first she was in the open, bathed in moonlight. Then she entered a narrow passageway between high, jutting rocks that blocked out the moon.

She heard a crunch. A footfall? Bracing a palm against the left wall of rock, she stopped and listened. She heard the ping of pebbles sliding down a rocky incline. Then all was quiet.

She waited. She listened. She took another step, moving deeper into the darkness of the passageway. Two more steps. Three. She saw a sliver of moonlight. She walked faster. She was at the opening.

A hand clamped around her mouth; an arm encircled her body. Her scream was muffled. She tossed her head, but hard, callused fingers dug into her cheeks. Her assailant dragged her behind a cluster of rocks.

"Cease fighting, lady," ordered a low, rough voice.

Shocked, she ceased struggling. The hand eased from her mouth.

"Kirkja?" She could not see him, but she had recognized his voice. "Is that you?"

"Aye." He slid his hand completely away from her mouth but did not release her shoulder. "Please do not betray me."

"Why are you hiding?" Jarvia asked. "We are allies with the Northern Scots."

Kirkja remained behind her, the iron strength of his body pressed against hers.

"Perhaps," he said, and released her.

She turned to see him step back, the moonlight gleaming on his conical helmet. Dust coated his clothing from helmet to boots. Sighing, as if he carried the weight of the world on his shoulders, he stripped off his leathern gloves and slapped them against his trousers, then tucked them into his girdle. He took off his helmet and laid it on a nearby boulder.

He studied her as intently as she studied him. "You are wearing trousers, lady?"

"Aye," she answered. "They are comfortable for riding. My husband tells me that Highland women wear them when they go hunting and hawking."

Kirkja frowned and shook his head. " 'Tis an odd custom, lady."

"Which? The clothing or the hawking and hunting?"

"Both."

"I thought trousers for women was odd at first too, lord, but I do enjoy wearing them. They are much more comfortable." She smiled. "Surely you did not come here to chastise me for the clothes I wear."

"Nay, my warriors and I have been following the barbarian for some time."

"Aye, we knew we were being followed."

"We rode slowly, lady, because I was not sure what to do. You are already married to him. The damage has been done, and I can prove nothing."

"What are you talking about, Kirkja?" Jarvia asked. "Do not speak in riddles."

" 'Tis the barbarian," he blurted out. "He has deceived us."

"How?"

Kirkja's weathered face was creased with worry, his movements fraught with agitation. "The day after the barbarian departed from Wybornsbaer with you and Gerda, Berowalt arrived in the village."

Jarvia noticed that Kirkja called Malcolm "the barbarian". This was unusual for him. Ever respectful of the Highlander, Kirkja had never before referred to him in derogatory terms.

"Had Berowalt arrived prior to the barbarian's departure"—Kirkja curled his hand into a fist—"you would not have been forced to marry him. We would have seen the barbarian for the deceiver he is."

Kirkja's accusation pained Jarvia. "This is the second time you have spoken of my husband's deceit, lord. What do you think he has done to deserve such accusation and disrespect?"

"When the barbarian learned that Berowalt was on his way to Southerland to tell us about Hilda's death, he ordered him captured and imprisoned. He wanted to make sure we did not hear the true story of Hilda's death. But Berowalt managed to escape."

Jarvia's earlier contentment ebbed away with each word that Kirkja spoke. An awful taste filled her mouth.

"What does Berowalt say the true story about Hilda is?"

Kirkja shook his head. "The barbarian killed her."

"No!" Jarvia's legs refused to hold her up. She leaned against the nearest boulder.

"Hilda had learned that her husband—*your husband*—intended to betray the people of Southerland. Clan Duncan was already conspiring with some of the Picts to overthrow our colony. Hilda informed Berowalt of all that was taking place and sent him home with the news. After he was captured by Lord Malcolm's men, Hilda decided to warn us herself, but the barbarian found out. He captured her also, and in a raging fit he beat her until she died . . . and with her the child. That's why he brought back her ashes for the memorial ceremony. He wanted no one to see her body."

"No, Kirkja, I do not believe this!"

She looked at her hand, at her marriage ring. The man who had mated with her, who was teaching her the subtleties of love, could not . . . Jarvia mentally checked herself. She, not Malcolm mac Duncan, was the one who was thinking in terms of love. He had sworn from the beginning that he was teaching her to enjoy carnal pleasure. Carnal pleasure! That was all!

Still, she believed in him and would defend him. "Malcolm wants a son too much to have killed Hilda when she was with child."

"Berowalt bears the tidings." Kirkja's voice was soft. He stepped closer to her. "Will you believe Malcolm mac Duncan over me?"

"I believe you are telling me what you believe to be the truth, but I do not believe Malcolm . . ."

Nay, she could not believe it of him. For a verity, her tender feelings for him stood in the way, as did the knowledge that he wanted a son more than anything in the world. Also standing in the way was her judgment of character. Something deep within her wanted to believe—*did* believe—in Malcolm's innocence.

"Berowalt is one of my best warriors, Jarvia. He is an honorable man. He would not lie."

Jarvia had known when she left Wybornsbaer that her life would change, but she had never imagined it would change like this. The man whom she was beginning to love was accused of murdering Hilda and the unborn bairn. A man for whom she had the highest esteem and respect, Lord Kirkja, was the accuser. Her old friend would not levy such charges without just cause.

"According to what Berowalt heard, Malcolm wanted to be rid of her because she knew too much about his plans. She was a threat to him."

The man who made such tender love to her could not have tortured his wife, could not have killed his own unborn child. "But he returned to Southerland for another bride," Jarvia pointed out.

"Aye, that was part of his plan," Kirkja said. "He wanted someone who knew nothing about him or his schemes."

"No!" Jarvia shook her head. "I do not believe the news that Berowalt bears. It is lies, Kirkja. Lies! None of what you are saying makes sense to me."

"Berowalt brought word of another alliance," Kirkja said. "One formed to oppose the barbarian, one that seeks to make an alliance with us in order to end this treachery."

"One led by Sybil and her husband," Jarvia guessed.

Kirkja's eyes widened. "Aye. What do you know of them?"

Jarvia shrugged. "Only what I heard my husband say. No more than what you have said."

The old lord paused to think. Finally he said, "I have come to you in secret, Jarvia, to ask a favor of you. I know you did not marry the barbarian because you love him."

She said nothing.

"You did so to save Gerda and her babe." He peered into her face. "Did you not, lady?"

She only stared at him.

"Did you not, lady?" he insisted.

"Aye," she said, "that was the reason for the marriage, Kirkja." *At first.*

"Now, lady, I ask you to become my eyes and ears in Northern Scotland."

His request filled Jarvia with alarm. Her old friend, whom at one time she had thought was her only friend, wanted to use her. "Why me, Kirkja?"

"Because you know the magic of the runes and can send me messages that no one else can read. Because you are married to the prince of Northern Scotland and the chief of Clan Duncan. As his wife, you will be privy to confidential information that may be useful to your people." Kirkja pressed his case. "You are an intelligent woman, Jarvia. You will understand what is happening."

Jarvia was troubled by what she had heard about Malcolm, but she was not ready to believe it out of hand. Disloyalty to her husband did not come easily to her.

"I do not like what you ask me to do," she said. "I may not have married the Highlander out of love, but I do not wish to become an informant, possibly a traitor, within his household. I am his wife."

"I can understand your hesitation," Kirkja said, "and I would not ask if it were not important to the colony. Your people are depending on you. I must know who is conspiring with the Picts, Jarvia. Who of the Highlanders is to be trusted and who is not."

Wind whipped around Jarvia, and she tugged on the tartan her husband had given to her. She looked down at the red-and-yellow material, the colors of the Duncan. Malcolm had asked her to wear these colors with pride. Now Kirkja was asking her to hide behind these colors while she spied on her husband and reported what she saw back to Kirkja.

"What if all Berowalt has repeated to you is lies?" Jarvia asked. "What if Hilda did commit suicide?"

"If Malcolm forced her to take the poison," Kirkja said, "he is guilty of murder."

"What if Sybil and her husband—or someone else—are responsible for Hilda's death?"

"That is what I wish you to find out," Kirkja said.

"Did Wyborn send you to ask me?"

"Nay. He knows nothing of what I am doing."

"Is Wyborn already bargaining with Sybil and her husband?"

"I don't know."

Jarvia snorted bitterly. "You would have me spy on my husband and report back to you all I know, Kirkja, yet you will tell me nothing."

"I know not what Wyborn is going to do from one rising of the sun to another." He paced in front of her, finally stopping to plow his hand through his hair. "I must know the truth, and you are the only one who can help me."

Jarvia moved away from the old warrior. Weighing her options, considering Kirkja's request, she stared at the rushing water below, hearing it more than seeing it.

"What if the report Berowalt made is true?" Jarvia asked.

Kirkja did not reply.

She turned. "If my husband learned that I was an informant, my life would be in danger, sire, and the life of my babe, should I conceive."

"Aye." He looked miserable. "As I said before, you are resourceful and intelligent, more so than Hilda. It is obvious the barbarian has a letching for you. Use it to your advantage."

Conflicting loyalties tore at Jarvia. Everyone wanted to use her. She lowered her head to gaze at the river below. The sound of boots crunching over gravel alerted her that someone was coming. She and Kirkja turned at the same instant.

She raised a finger and touched her lips to silence the Southerland lord. Although they had been speaking in her native language, and as far as she knew the only people in camp who spoke it were Morag and the bard, she cautioned Kirkja to say no more.

Malcolm appeared in the glade. "I was worried, my lady. The hour grew late, and you had not yet returned to camp."

"I apologize for causing you worry," Jarvia replied. "I met Lord Kirkja, and we were talking. I took no notice of the time, my lord husband."

The Highlander and the Southerland warrior confronted each other.

"Lord Kirkja, I am surprised to see you."

With Jarvia interpreting, the two men conversed.

"Me perhaps, but not us . . . surely," Kirkja said. "You must have been aware that we were following you."

"That we were," Malcolm agreed. "But I am surprised to see you here, talking with my wife."

Although Malcolm spoke quietly, Jarvia saw the dangerous glitter in his blue eyes. As she spoke the translation, she tried to keep her voice calm.

"I beg your pardon, Lord Malcolm," Kirkja said. "I came directly to the river to give drink to my pony. I saw Lady Jarvia standing here, gazing down. I could not stop myself from coming to talk with her. Now that you have pointed it out, I realize that it was most improper. As you know, I have the fondness of a father for Lady Jarvia. I meant you no slight."

Malcolm's body radiated tension; his voice was hard. She did not doubt that Kirkja also felt his displeasure.

Jarvia had long since interpreted Kirkja's words before Malcolm said, "We take offense when custom is not adhered to."

"Again I offer my apology," Kirkja said.

Malcolm nodded. "I invite you and your warriors to spend the night in camp with us, Lord Kirkja."

"Thank you," the old warrior replied. "I accept."

The three of them returned to camp in silence, Malcolm and Kirkja walking together, Jarvia deliberately lagging behind. She considered what Kirkja had said about her husband, about the man with whom she was falling in love.

Aye, she was falling in love with Malcolm mac Duncan, and the thought frightened her. She had once bragged that no man had the power to make her take her own life; she was in control of her destiny. But if Malcolm had killed Hilda, he was the one who controlled destiny. How easily Jarvia could become his next victim . . . if what Berowalt had said was true.

By the time they reached the camp, Jarvia was thoroughly confused and agitated. Old fears had returned to haunt her.

She stopped at Brian's pallet where Morag was in attendance. As she had feared, Brian was feverish and sleeping fitfully.

Malcolm and Morag held torches close so that she could examine the wound on his leg. Using a cloth dipped in warm water, she cleansed it again. Then with her knife she slit open a carefully selected root herb and squeezed the white, jellylike pulp over the raw cut.

"It is bad," Malcolm said in a low voice.

"Aye." Earlier in the day, immediately after Ghaltair and Lachlann had returned to camp with Brian, Jarvia had slit his trouser leg. Now she spread the material aside, caught Malcolm's hand, and directed the torchlight lower.

"I have seen men lose limbs with wounds much less severe than this one," he said.

" 'Twas what I was a-telling her, lord," Morag said, bending closer. "Do you see any streaks in the flesh?"

"Nay," Jarvia said. She touched the warrior's thigh. "His body is burning up with fever, but so far I see no other signs to indicate the wound is festering."

"Will he be crippled if he keeps the leg?" Malcolm asked.

"Nay, lord. The sow tore well into the flesh, but she did not sever the muscle. Although his leg will be stiff and sore for a long while, and he will boast a horrible scar for the remainder of his life, he should make a full recovery."

She picked up a vial filled with a dark-colored liquid made from sorrel leaves. "Hold his shoulders up," she instructed Malcolm. "I want him to take several swallows of this potion to lower his fever and help him sleep."

Brian roused when Malcolm lifted him. He opened bleary, fever-reddened eyes. "What are you doing, my lady?" he slurred.

"Trying to mend you," she said, and laid the lip of the vial against his mouth. "Drink some of this."

He took a swallow, gagged, and jerked his head away. "By all that's holy!" He spewed out the rest of the draught. "If the wound doesn't kill me, lady, the cure surely will."

Jarvia laughed. "Best-man Brian, you are well on your way to recovery. Now, I have no more sorrel leaves, and"— she held up the half-filled vial—"only this much tincture remains. If you wish to rest in some comfort tonight, you will take two swallows of this and keep it down."

A spasm of pain caused him to wince. "I'll try, madam," he murmured.

When Brian once more lay sleeping on his pallet, Jarvia pulled his mantle over him. She looked up at Malcolm. "With your permission, lord, I shall stay the night with him."

"Let me, mistress," Morag said. "You're exhausted from having to take care of Gerda."

"Aye, lady, I agree with Morag," Malcolm said.

After Jarvia made certain she had prepared enough medicine to last the night, she gave Morag instructions and rose. Malcolm escorted her to their tent.

"I shall return shortly, lady," he said. "I would speak longer with Lord Kirkja."

Jarvia might have known that Malcolm would not forget her earlier conversation with the Southerland lord. A reckoning would indeed be forthcoming. "I shall come with you to interpret," she offered.

"There is no need," he replied. "I will get Arthur."

Summarily dismissed, she murmured, "Good night."

"I would speak with you when I return, lady."

She nodded and slipped into the shelter. Without lighting a lamp, she shed her clothes and donned her sleeping gown. Glad for the thickness of the pallet, she slid between the bed coverings. Again she was consumed with thoughts of Malcolm, of the black deed he was accused of committing, of what Kirkja had asked her to do.

She knew not where her loyalty lay.

Time passed. Activity in the camp died into quietness. The only light was that of the great fire, which a warrior tended. Jarvia dozed fitfully and was eventually awakened by the rustle of material as Malcolm pushed the opening aside and entered the tent. He knelt on the pallet.

"Are you asleep?" he asked.

"Nay." She heard the dull clink as he took off his weapon belts and laid them close beside the bed.

"Will we be leaving early in the morn, lord?"

"Nay," Malcolm said. "We shall rest part of the day."

"Did you check on Brian before coming to the tent?"

"Aye. He is still sleeping, and Morag said he is less fitful than before. I also checked on Gerda. She is sleeping soundly."

Malcolm pulled off his shirt, unlaced his cuarans, and slipped out of them. Jarvia lay quietly. She had been waiting for him to question her about her conversation with Kirkja. She would not make the inquisition easy for him.

"I suppose you and Lord Kirkja had a friendly chat," he said.

"Aye."

He took off his trousers and stretched out beside her. She had come to cherish sleeping with him. Being together in the intimacy of the pallet in their tent always brought an immediate rekindling of the fire that only Malcolm mac Duncan could light in her body. But now the report that Malcolm might have murdered Hilda and her unborn child came between them. Kirkja's request came between them.

She had to decide where her loyalties lay—with the people of Southerland or with her Highlander husband.

She turned on her side; so did he, cupping her back against his naked chest and loins.

"What tidings did Kirkja bring you?"

Innocent was the question, but double the meaning.

Not ready to answer the question, yet unable to lie, Jarvia turned in his embrace. Until she had decided what to do, she intended to keep her own council.

She ran her hand lightly up his thigh to his naked chest, pushing her finger through the thick pelt of black hair. Her mouth found his nipple; her tongue began a gentle assault.

"My lord husband," she murmured, "let us not discuss inconsequential matters."

Malcolm scooped her into his arms. "I agree, my wanton. Why should we waste good time talking when we can be enjoying carnal pleasures?"

Carnal pleasures! The words clamored in Jarvia's head until she thought surely she would scream. But she did not. Nor did she allow the hateful taunt to stop her from mating with the barbarian . . . from making love to the man she called husband.

Chapter 18

J arvia, dressed in her trousers and shirt and ready to resume the journey to Malcolm's village, stood beside the temporary pen Malcolm had erected to corral the ponies and pack animals. Thinking about all that had taken place during their encampment, she watched Moonbeam canter among the small herd.

"Good morn, lady, did you sleep well?"

Malcolm strode to the corral to stand beside her.

"Aye, lord." Jarvia colored. They had slept little.

She saw the devilish glint in his eyes and the twitch of his mouth. She had no doubt his thoughts were the same as hers.

"You have eaten sufficient to break fast?"

She nodded. He lifted a hand and lightly ran his gloved finger below each of her eyes.

"The skin is shadowed."

She met his searching gaze and once more wished she could stop the questions with the fire of their passion . . . the passion he had awakened in her, the one she shared so shamelessly with him.

"Mayhap you are yet tired?"

The words expressed concern, but she heard an undertone of suspicion, as if he knew something and was encouraging her to confess. Or did guilt make her imagine it?

"Nay, lord, I am more rested and content than I have ever known myself to be."

Malcolm hiked his brows. "Worried, mayhap, for Brian?"

Again she felt as if Malcolm suspected something.

"Nay, lord. When I changed his bandages at early morn, he was raging like a bull, ready to be up and about. He is limping and in a great deal of pain, but he denies it." She glanced over her shoulder to see Brian talking with Lachlann. "Speaking of your best-men, lord, I believe Lachlann has a tenderness for Gerda."

"He has orders to take care of her," Malcolm said.

He caught Jarvia's chin and gently turned her head so that she was forced to look into his eyes. He waited for the answer to his question, the question he did not have to repeat. She had not forgotten.

She had spent the night in his arms, letting passion blot out her problems, her doubts, letting it push into abeyance the moment when she must decide between Kirkja and her husband.

She had spent the morning considering her choices and wished she could take the easy way out. Malcolm had no way of knowing what Kirkja had told her, what he had asked her to do. Nothing compelled her to tell him. Nothing but her penchant for honesty and her desire for a true marriage between her and her husband. Nothing but a chance for them to have a future together.

Malcolm broke the silence that lay between them. "What concerns you, lady?"

Life had taught Jarvia that honesty, no matter how painful, was always the best solution to any problem. She had always tried to adhere to this policy and could not, would not, change now.

"Lord Kirkja informed me that Berowalt, our emissary to Northern Scotland, returned to Wybornsbaer the same day that we departed, sire."

"So Kirkja told me," Malcolm said, his face unreadable.

"He also said . . ."

Malcolm listened quietly as Jarvia repeated the gist of Kirkja's conversation with her. She omitted Kirkja's request that she become an informant for him.

When she concluded, Malcolm said, "You have laid at my feet accusations made by your people, lady. You ask for my side of the story now?" His eyes again scrutinized her face as he added, "I wonder if you are ready to hear it."

"Try me, lord."

"I have no alternative. But I fear my answer will not please you, lady."

All Jarvia's fears and doubts returned to loom larger than before.

"You were married to an old and impotent man, lady, one

who took refuge in the reading and the giving of law."

Jarvia bristled at his evaluation of Ein-her. "You speak as if that were a weakness, lord. It was not. My husband was a gentle man, one who lived by high ideals."

"I will not argue with you as to what your *first* husband was, madam, but your second and present husband is none of those things.

"Now you are married to a warrior who is motivated by the sheer necessity of survival, one who lives by the sword." Malcolm sighed heavily. "As I told you once before, rumor is generally built upon a foundation of truth. It is so in this case."

He turned and walked a few steps away. His back to her, he braced his palm against a tree and gazed into the distance. "I told the truth when I was in Southerland. I took Lady Hilda prisoner when I learned she was guilty of treachery, but I did not murder her or the child she bore. She took her own life and that of her bairn."

"Berowalt reported that she was beaten to death."

"She had been beaten, but it was not the beating that killed her." Malcolm turned to look at her, his countenance hard and unyielding.

"Did you beat her?"

His eyes narrowed. "What do you believe?"

"I believe you are innocent of both charges."

I could not love a man who beats innocent women or is a murderer.

"I am."

He closed the distance between them.

"I confess I wanted to kill her, but had I done so it would not have been by poison. I would have done it with my own hands." His voice was as cruel as his countenance. "I wanted to put them around her neck and choke her to death for the dishonor she had brought upon me and my family's name. I wanted to kill her because she had dealt treacherously with my house and kingdom, because she was trying to deny me my son."

Fear raced down Jarvia's spine.

"I am sorry you lost your child, lord."

"I am, too, lady. For that I will never forgive Hilda.

She had already conceived our child when she began collaborating with the renegade Scots. She developed a sudden love of hunting and hawking, and I was concerned because she was not taking care of herself. At times, it seemed that she was deliberately risking harm to the child."

He breathed deeply. "Little did I know that her hunting and hawking jaunts were a ruse. She was consorting with the enemy. Shortly afterwards she ran away and joined them. My clansmen and I searched until we found her." With one hand he gripped the trunk of a nearby sapling; the other hand was flexed into a fist. "She was big with my child, but was sleeping with my enemy. I truly wanted to kill her."

"What about him, lord?"

Malcolm looked at her.

"Did you kill *him*?"

"I would have," he confessed, "but Hilda would not tell me who he was. I swore before God that the day I found out, I would hunt the bastard down and kill him."

Malcolm's face was dark and smoldering. Jarvia had seen it this way only once before, when she had insulted his honor in front of the Council of Justice. She trembled in the face of such undisguised anger.

"As we rode back to the Great Hall, Hilda taunted me with her lover and promised that I would never have the child I desired. She kept telling me that she would get rid of it. I paid her no attention. I thought she was just trying to make me angry." Malcolm shook his head as if he still could not believe what had happened. "Because of her condition we traveled slowly, resting frequently. I had no idea she had taken the poison until she was already dying."

He closed his eyes; perspiration beaded on his upper lip. "Her death was painful, and there was nothing I could do but watch . . . watch her die. . . . She would not tell me who gave her the poison, but I recognized the vial as one of Sybil's. Hilda did confess that the berries were supposed to have made her only sick enough to kill the baby . . . not herself. Still, in the face of death, she laughed at me and refused to tell me the name of the man who led the conspirators."

"If it was Sybil, do you suppose she intended to kill Hilda?"

"At the time I did not believe so. Knowing that Sybil feared my having a child, an heir, I thought she had intended only to kill it. But in light of recent events, I have begun to think differently. Possibly Sybil is working with the renegades and Hilda knew about it. If so, Hilda would have posed a threat to Sybil."

"Giving Sybil a good reason to kill her," Jarvia added.

"Aye. If any of this is true, both of them betrayed me." Malcolm walked to where Jarvia stood. He cupped her neck and gently drew her closer. "I think little of people who betray me, lady."

Tall, broad, and formidable, his face expressing all his hellish fury, he stood before her. Her body trembled, and she wanted to run away.

"Berowalt was captured and locked up," Jarvia said. "He claims it was by your clansmen."

"I do not know who is responsible," Malcolm said, his hand gently massaging her neck and shoulder, "but I did not give the order. He was Southerland's emissary to our kingdom. I knew he was sending messages back to his people, and for the most part I knew what these messages were. At that time he posed no threat to my father or me. Now I am not so sure. But I shall investigate this matter further when I reach home." He released her and stepped back. "Now, lady, have all your questions been answered, all your doubts assuaged?"

"Since you are innocent, why did we leave Wybornsbaer in such a hurry?"

"Thomas and Ghaltair brought me news that there was great unrest in the kingdom and that Berowalt, supposedly taken prisoner by my clansmen, had recently escaped his confinement and was on his way to Southerland. I knew my clansmen were not responsible for his capture, and I feared no true thing that Berowalt would report to the king, but I did fear the lies and rumors that might follow. They could have eventually been proven false, but that would have caused me undue delay; it might have cost me my bride. I had no time to spare, lady, so I decided to return and fight my battles from home."

"Have you talked as openly to Kirkja as you have to me?"

He nodded. "I respect Lord Kirkja. In order for our peoples to live together in peace, we must tell the truth and trust each other."

Malcolm pushed a tendril of Jarvia's hair behind her ear. The heel of his hand rested on her cheek.

"What do you think, lady?"

Gazing into his fathomless eyes, Jarvia said, "I believed in you, lord, and I still believe you."

Jarvia turned her face into his palm.

"Take note, my lady-wife, your loyalty now belongs to Clan Duncan, to your husband the chief of Clan Duncan."

Though he spoke softly, his words threatened. Jarvia pulled away and looked up at him. "I said I would wear your colors with pride."

"I am not talking about clothing or pride." His voice, sword sharp, sliced through her. "I am talking about loyalty. I will not be betrayed by another bride, madam. I will not tolerate another traitor."

"You have asked me to believe you, to accept your word as truth," Jarvia said. "You must also believe in me."

He brought her face closer to his, but Jarvia tensed. It hurt that he would not give her the same trust that he demanded from her.

"Did Kirkja say anything else, lady, that would cause you concern? Anything you feel I should know?"

Unsure about her feelings, unsure about the truth, Jarvia felt it would be wise to say no more. "Nothing of import."

Malcolm stared at her deeply before saying, "I accept you are telling me the truth, lady."

"I am."

"Lord!" Kirkja's voice sounded from the distance.

Malcolm dropped his hand. He and Jarvia watched the Southerland warrior approach them.

"I wanted to thank you for the hospitality you have extended to me and my warriors, sire," Kirkja said.

Jarvia began the translation.

Still looking at Malcolm, Kirkja said to Jarvia, "Lady, I speak to you only. Remember all that I spoke to you last night. Please consider my request."

Flustered, Jarvia hesitated, then translated, "Lord Kirkja will remember all that you have done to ensure his comfort and safety while he is in your country. He thanks you."

Malcolm's eyes narrowed. Jarvia knew he had noticed her hesitation.

"Tell Lord Kirkja he is welcome," Malcolm replied. "I hope all his questions have been answered satisfactorily."

Jarvia translated for Kirkja, then said to Malcolm. "They have, lord. He wishes to take his leave."

"Granted." Malcolm inclined his head.

Kirkja turned to Jarvia. "Lady, I take my leave. I place you in the safekeeping of the gods."

"Thank you, lord. I bid you a safe journey."

"I shall eagerly await word from you. Remember, Lady Jarvia, Ein-her taught you the magic of the runes so that you could help your people. You are married to the barbarian, but you are a law-speaker for the people of Southerland."

Kirkja slipped on his helmet.

"What you say, Kirkja, is true in part. I am married to Malcolm mac Duncan, but I am no longer law-speaker for Southerland. I give my loyalty to my husband."

Kirkja smiled sadly. "So be it."

"I shall miss you, Kirkja," Jarvia called.

He mounted his pony and twined the reins through his gloved hands. "I shall miss you also."

As the Southerland warrior rode off, Malcolm said, "You are sad, lady?"

"A little, lord. Kirkja has always been a friend to me."

"One of these days, he will be a more powerful leader than Wyborn," Malcolm predicted. "Already he marshals his followers."

"Southerland will be fortunate if Kirkja is its king," Jarvia answered. "He is a wise man, a much better leader than Wyborn. The people will eagerly swear fealty to him."

"And you, lady—" Malcolm said.

The tone of his voice caused Jarvia to look up at him.

"To whom do you swear fealty?"

"You are my lord."

"That I am, lady. Never forget it."

"I shall not, lord, not because you threaten with words and a thunderous frown, but because I believe in you. I ask that you extend the same courtesy to me."

Looking directly into his stormy face, his ominous warning still chilling her, she drew in a deep breath as if for courage. "I had debated telling you this, lord, since it has no import to either you or me, but I shall. You may believe me if you wish. Because Kirkja fears what will happen to the people of Southerland, because he fears treachery from your—our—people, he asked me to become an informant. I told him I would not."

"Kirkja said nothing of this matter to me."

"Whether you believe me or not is your choice."

"I believe you."

"You do?"

"Aye, I know you speak the truth."

"You believe me." A wonderfully warm feeling spread through her.

He nodded, opened his mouth, and closed it again.

"Thank you, my lord husband, for trusting me."

"Jarvia . . ." He hesitated.

"Yes?"

"I also have a confession to make."

She waited.

"I speak your language," he said.

Cold shock dissipated the warmth. Jarvia gaped at him.

"I heard everything you and Kirkja said to each other."

"You have been eavesdropping on us . . . on me . . . ever since you walked into the village!" she exclaimed.

He looked discomfitted. "I . . . wanted to see if you would tell me what Kirkja said."

"Now I wish I had not!" she shouted. "Do you also write our language, lord? Is that how you knew what messages Berowalt was sending back to us? You intercepted and read them."

"Aye."

Anger made Jarvia tremble. Hot, consuming fury. "All

this time—" she spoke slowly, emphatically—"all this time, you have known what we were saying? Yet you never let me know."

"I had my reasons."

"You always have your reasons!" Again she shouted, not caring who heard, not caring that she lost her temper. "Always you try to trap people in lies and deceit. Well, my lord, one of these days you will hear some truth that will not be to your liking, and 'twill be your undoing. Do you trust no one?"

"Lady, I apologize. I also debated whether or not to make this confession, but I want your trust. I am giving you mine. Something I did not and will not do for Wyborn. It was to my advantage not to let anyone know I understand the language."

"But why could you not have told me?"

"Until now, my lady-wife, I was unsure of you also. You are a woman of Southerland."

"I am your wife."

"Aye, you are." Malcolm smiled gently. "Thank you for telling me what Kirkja asked of you, and thank you for your trust." He paused, then added, "Forgive me, lady, and accept my trust in you from now on."

Lord Lang sat on the High Seat of his *skáli* in Ulfsbaer, Northland. Ingrid, his sister, sat in the guests' settle, watching both her brother and the tall, gaunt stranger sent by Wyborn in Southerland who stood before them. As the man spoke, Ingrid listened, but her gaze rested on her brother. Lang was not reputed for his patience, and this visitor from across the seas was provoking his anger.

"As a result, my lord," Madelhari said with a flourish of his hand that swept open his mantle to reveal a wealth of gold, silver, and beaded chains about his neck, "I regret to say that your name has been dishonored."

Without moving, Lang stared at Wyborn's man. With a quietness that belied his strength and his anger, he asked, "Who brought this shame upon my name?"

" 'Tis a Highland barbarian called Malcolm mac Duncan."
Lang tensed.

"A Highlander, you say?" Ingrid asked.

"Aye, mistress. He wanted Lord Michael's betrothed, but evidently did not wish to pay the rupture endowment. We only recently learned that the ship carrying your emissary and the rupture endowment had no sooner sailed from our shores than the barbarian sent his warriors after it."

Ingrid shifted on the settle, reaching to adjust a cushion at her back. Lang was hiding his emotions, but she knew her brother well. Ever since his wife had died seven winters past, Ingrid had lived with him, serving as companion, hostess, and housekeeper. She knew the anger that roiled within him, the desire to avenge his and his son's names. Lang lived only for Michael.

The old lord brushed a hand through his hair, which was yet thick and black. He pulled on his beard, which was equally dark and thick. The likeness between Lang and Michael was uncanny. Ingrid's eyes misted as she thought of her nephew.

Lang focused on the Southerland colonist. "How did you learn of such treachery, Madelhari?"

"Your emissary, Ragnar, managed to escape the sea raiders, sire. Although he was critically wounded, he reached our village with the grim news. He was delirious, and it was many nights before he could tell us what had happened. He wanted to leave for Northland immediately, sire, but was in no condition to do so. King Wyborn promised to send a messenger to you."

Lang nodded.

"By the time Ragnar had recovered consciousness, the barbarian and his warriors had crossed safely into their own territory. My lord Wyborn would have taken matters into his own hands, but he thought it imprudent to do so without discussing the matter with you first."

Lang lifted his drinking horn. Ingrid rose and refilled it with imported wine.

"Above all things, sire, my lord Wyborn desires to have peace with you and your people," Madelhari said. "If you give word, he is prepared to make good the rupture endowment himself."

Lang snorted and slumped into his chair, staring morosely into the burning *langeldar*. He drained his drinking horn.

Ingrid refilled it again. He turned his dark and frightening gaze on Madelhari.

The visitor fidgeted. Not surprisingly, Ingrid thought. Messengers had been killed for delivering news that was less grim than this. The longer Lang wallowed in his anger and resentment, the more he would drink. Soon he would be inebriated. Ingrid loved her brother but did not want him to make an oath when he was drunk. Many a Northman had, much to their regret.

Finally Lang said, "Can Ragnar identify the man who led the attack on our ship?"

Madelhari nodded. "So he says, lord."

"How soon before he will be recovered enough to travel?"

"Another week, lord."

Lang nodded. "Return to Southerland, Madelhari. Tell Wyborn I thank him for his honor and integrity, but he cannot ensure the honor of another by paying the rupture endowment."

The lord doubled his hand into a fist and slammed it on the armrest of his High Seat.

"I shall not rest until this insult to my name and honor, to my son's name and honor, has been avenged."

Madelhari's stance became more relaxed. "My lord Wyborn believes that the Princess Jarvia and Malcolm mac Duncan conspired together, sire. Both are guilty of treachery."

"I find this hard to believe," Lang said. "Surely Ein-her would not have spoken to me about a betrothal between Jarvia and my son if she was capable of deceit."

"Ein-her was an old man, lord," Madelhari said, "easily deceived by a beautiful young woman. Wyborn spent long hours trying to dissuade him from buying the woman's freedom and marrying her."

Lang brushed his hand over his beard.

"What you must remember, lord"—Madelhari's voice was low and calm—"is that Princess Jarvia was a slave, and slaves are known to be deceitful. They will do anything to win their freedom."

"If she practiced deceit against me and my house, she shall be punished."

A thin smile crossed Madelhari's face. Lang motioned for him to be seated. A servant poured him a goblet of wine, and the men drank in silence.

Finally Lord Lang said, "If Highland barbarians have no regard for our territory in the seas, if they raid our ships, I shall show the same disregard for their territory. I shall march across their lands and raid their farmsteads and villages."

Lang's promise frightened Ingrid. She feared for his and Michael's lives if they sailed to the shores of the barbaric Highlands.

"Aye, lord." The smile on Madelhari's face widened.

" 'Twill not be the first time Northmen have stepped on the shores of the Highlands, nor the first time we have fought the Highlanders."

Madelhari lifted the tankard to his mouth and drained it. "Even so, lord, you must be careful of this particular Highland barbarian. We have word that he killed King Wyborn's only blood offspring."

Madelhari launched into the story of Malcolm's deceit, telling how he murdered Hilda and her unborn child in a fit of raging anger, how he convinced Wyborn to adopt not one but two women and to make them heirs forever through the reading of the runes and the erection of the rune stone.

When Madelhari had finished speaking, Lord Lang said, "Indeed, this man is as crafty as he is treacherous, an enemy to our people."

"If the man's story is true," Ingrid said softly.

Madelhari gave Ingrid a hard look. " 'Tis a verity, lord."

"If not," Lang said, "you know what we in Northland do to those who lie?"

Madelhari curtly bobbed his head. "Remember, lord, you are dealing with an uncivilized man, one who does not think like us. You must be—"

"Thank you for the warning," the lord said, "but my son and I are not afraid to fight for our honor. No man on the face of the earth is as fearsome as Michael Langssonn. Even berserkers quake at the thought of doing battle with him."

Biting back a grin, remembering Wyborn's mockery of Lang's son, Madelhari said slyly, "Word has it, sire, that your son is indeed a brave and honorable warrior, and that he is now a-viking."

"Aye, there is no finer warrior than my son," Lang said proudly. "Truly he is blessed with the strength of Thor and the wisdom of Odin."

"I understand, lord, that your son makes marks of the waterways upon which he sails." Madelhari would know if Wyborn had heard the truth about Lang's son.

The old lord nodded. "Aye, he is a rune master. Now he will use his magic to find a route through the waterways of the Highlands. Talk is finished. Revenge belongs to the household of Lang." He clapped his hands. "We eat."

Content that he had satisfactorily completed his errand, Madelhari remained the evening feasting with the lord, not leaving until the wee hours of the morning. Afterward, keeping to the shadows to make sure he was not followed, he made his way to the water's edge and waited. Soon another man joined him.

"Is that you, Madelhari?" asked the familiar voice.

"Aye."

A warrior moved out of the darkness and stood beside him.

Madelhari said softly, "I have a message I want you to take back to Wyborn, posthaste."

"You will not be returning with us?"

"Nay, Lord Lang wishes me to stay longer. For me to leave now would arouse suspicions we can ill afford." As he spoke Madelhari gazed at the longship, dipping and swaying at the dock. "Tell Lord Wyborn that the gods are with us. Our plan is going as arranged. As soon as Ragnar is recovered and Lord Michael has returned from a-viking, Lord Lang intends to seek revenge. Soon we will be rid of the Highlander without jeopardizing the peace agreement between our two people."

Chapter 19

The travelers stopped at midday by a small stream to rest and to drink. Jarvia examined Brian's wound and found it was healing nicely. When she rose, she saw Gerda asleep on a thick pallet beneath a shade tree. Later, astride Moonbeam, she rode away from the main group, seeking the shade of a separate copse of trees. She was weary of the journey and longed for the day when they would arrive at Malcolm's village. Pressing her hand above her eyes to shield them from the afternoon glare, she looked all around, then untied the water bag, lifted it to her lips, and drank deeply. Her parched lips and throat welcomed soothing liquid.

Looking across the way, she gazed at her husband. Although he rode with four other Highland warriors, she had noticed him immediately. No matter how he dressed, no matter whether he wore his helmet or not, he was like a dark fire that drew her to him. He dominated his surroundings with his height and powerful build. He dominated his people with his forceful, even ruthless personality.

A soft mewing caught her attention. She looked around but saw nothing that could be making the noise—no small animal or wounded bird. She retied the water skin to her saddle and guided Moonbeam forward.

The mewing sounded again.

She stopped. She strained to hear. The soft noise was coming from close to the ground. She squinted against the bright sunlight and scoured the earth around her.

She slid off the pony and tied the reins to the lowest branch of a nearby tree. Then standing still, she closed her eyes and listened, not daring to breath.

A cry? A whimper?

She was not sure what, but she knew where. Her hand on the hilt of her dirk, she moved cautiously toward a clump of bushes growing between two large boulders. Kneeling, she pushed one of the straggly plants aside . . . and saw a baby in dirty swaddling lying there. Jarvia dropped her dirk and fought through the prickly bushes to reach the infant.

When she laid her hand on the baby's stomach, she heard the low snarl and she saw the fanged grin of a wolf. Frightened, Jarvia left her hand where it was, but her heart raced erratically. Slowly, as her breathing became less ragged, she searched the area for signs of an altar or evidence that other sacrifices had been left nearby. She found none.

The wolf whimpered. The baby sniffled.

"Both of you are hurt," Jarvia said, "but you are no longer alone. I will take care of both of you." She spoke softly, soothingly, hoping that the sound of her voice would reassure the wolf. "I believe you love the baby," Jarvia said, "but you are going to have to trust me if you want her to live." She stared into soulful, golden brown eyes. "You do want her to live, do you not?"

The wolf whimpered and dropped its head, its muzzle resting on the baby. As if the wolf's whine were a call for help, it tugged at Jarvia's heart. She was still frightened, but she had to help the baby. If the wolf would let her, she would help it also.

"What is wrong?" She moved her hand slightly, slowly, and touched the animal's nose.

The wolf started, growled low, then its resistance wilted. Its thin body convulsed with a deep breath. Jarvia moved closer, cautiously. She saw that the wolf was a bitch and that it had been beaten so severely its fur was matted with blood. It gazed pensively at Jarvia.

"If you were a human, I would say that you were taking my measure," Jarvia murmured.

As Jarvia pushed the bushes aside, her gaze swept over the dying animal. She saw the ruffled fur at the wolf's neck, the raw and exposed flesh that suggested it had been shackled recently.

"You have been tamed," she said, her voice low and calm. "Mayhap you escaped to come find the baby? Or mayhap you were abandoned with the child."

Jarvia reached out to touch the raw flesh that circled the wolf's neck. "Or mayhap someone who loved the baby left you behind deliberately so that you could care for it. Whoever owned you kept you tied up." When Jarvia pulled back her hand, she saw the blood; she felt its stickiness. The wolf whined, and anger roiled through Jarvia. She hated the idea that any living thing had been chained up and abused.

The baby whimpered fretfully, and Jarvia reached for it. She knew she was taking a chance but she must. When she clasped it about the waist, the wolf growled; it opened its jaws, and clamped its teeth into Jarvia's flesh, trying to bite, but was too weak.

"Wolf," Jarvia said, "please trust me. I will take care of both of you. First, let me take care of the babe. Then I will doctor your wounds."

As if it understood, the bitch whimpered and removed its teeth. It laid its head on the ground beside the baby.

Bringing the child closer to herself, Jarvia quickly examined it to determine that it was only dirty and a little insect bitten. She pushed to her feet and moved to her and Malcolm's cart, grabbing a food pouch. The wolf tried to drag itself behind Jarvia, but could not move. Jarvia returned and was soon sitting on the ground, cradling the baby in the crook of one arm and feeding the wolf from the other hand.

Once the bitch was full, Jarvia opened a jug and gave the animal drink. She poured the rest of the water over the wolf's face, then over its bloody neck. All the while Jarvia talked to the animal softly and comfortingly. She ran her hand lightly over the wolf's ribs, down its stomach, and over its flanks. The beating had left long, raw gashes over the entire body. Jarvia brushed bloody and matted hair aside to examine the wounds. The baby let loose another yell, and Jarvia knew she must tend to her.

"Wolf, your hunger and thirst have been quenched," Jarvia said. "I will be back to doctor your wounds. Now I must take care of your little companion."

Jarvia walked back to the cart, and this time the wolf remained where it was without making an effort to follow. With one hand, she tugged bed covers together until she had created a thick pallet. The baby let out another lusty wail.

"There, wee one, do not cry."

Using her dirk, she cut the swaddling and stripped it from the infant.

"Ah, my little love, you are a beauty. Perfectly formed." To the wolf Jarvia called, "Your little mistress."

A damp cloth and gentle hands soon had the lass clean. Her soft mews turned into gusty cries. Laughing, Jarvia scooted into the cart. She rummaged through her chest looking for a leathern glove. When she found none, she opened one of Malcolm's trunks. After more rummaging, she found a glove and snipped off one of the fingers. After attaching it to a jar of goat's milk and honey, she began to feed the child.

"Ah, lassie," she cooed, holding the baby close to her bosom, "you do slurp loudly, but I understand. You are hungry and thirsty."

Jarvia gazed in adoration at the cherubic face with its bright blue eyes, framed by thick auburn lashes. She brushed the tufts of auburn hair on the baby's head. A little hand, much too thin, gripped Jarvia's finger tightly, tugging at her heart as well.

"I will take care of you, always. I promise."

"By all that's holy!" Morag exclaimed.

Jarvia jumped. She had had no idea the old servant was anywhere near the cart.

"My lady, where did you get *that*?"

Jarvia did not take her eyes from her precious find.

"Exactly what I would like to know, my lady-wife!"

Again Jarvia jumped. The leathern nipple slipped out of the baby's mouth, and she set up a howl. Morag reached for the baby, but Jarvia tightened her hold. The little girl was hers. The gods had decreed that she should find her and keep her. The baby cried louder.

Malcolm dismounted, hitched Dhubh-righ to the back of the cart, and glared at Jarvia. She sucked in her breath at the sight of him. He removed his helmet and set it on top of the back cart pole. The sun glinted off his sweat-dampened raven-black hair. His eyes, now darkly blue, narrowed under prominent black brows. His firm lips drew into a line of disapproval.

He raked his hand through his hair, and perspiration trickled down his temples and cheeks. It darkened his shirt on his chest and under his arms. But even perspiration and dirt only added to the masculine aura of this powerful and intensely sexual male. The hand resting on the hilt of his sword drew Jarvia's gaze downward to his slim hips and long legs. Tight trousers outlined his body so truly that her mouth went dry. Her heart stopped beating for a moment, then lurched into heavy, erratic pounding. Her entire body throbbed to the rhythm. She wished the babe she held to her breast were theirs—a child they had created together.

"Where did you get the babe, madam?"

Replacing the nipple in the infant's mouth, Jarvia slowly raised her head to look into her husband's fire-blue eyes. "I found her."

Malcolm reached out to touch the child. The wolf lunged at him.

"Hell's fire!" he shouted and jumped back. The wolf was so weak it fell to the ground at his feet "A wolf!" He jerked out his dirk.

Jarvia caught his wrist. "Nay, lord, she is nigh into death. She cannot hurt you."

Malcolm pulled loose and shouted, "What do you mean by endangering yourself like this, lady? Surely you know better than to behave so irresponsibly!"

The baby, losing the leathern nipple again, screamed, and Jarvia replaced it in her mouth. "Look at the poor bitch, lord, and tell me how I have endangered myself. The wolf is dying. The life has been nearly beaten out of her."

"Nature takes care of its own," Malcolm said.

"Mayhap nature does, sire, but this is not nature's doing," Jarvia snapped. " 'Tis man's. The wolf has been tamed, but has been shackled so tightly that her neck is injured. And she has been beaten. Look at the gashes along her body."

The bitch whined; Malcolm studied the animal. Keeping its head between its outstretched legs, the wolf shimmied up to him. With its nose it nuzzled the toes of his cuarans. He breathed in deeply.

"Both of them are females, lady?" he asked.

Jarvia nodded and laid the baby on the pallet. She pulled aside the clean linen into which she had wrapped her. "She is perfectly formed, sire."

Malcolm gazed at the child but made no offer to pick it up. "She is a scrawny-looking thing."

"She has been bitten by a few of the small critters." Jarvia brushed her fingers lightly down the child's cheek. "And she has done without food for a little while. Other than that, she is in good condition."

As if the bairn knew they were talking about her, she gurgled, kicked her legs, and flung her fists in the air.

"She was abandoned, lord," Jarvia said.

"Aye."

"I have examined her closely. She is a tiny child, but she is not sickly. Neither is she crippled or maimed in any way. I want to keep her."

"She was abandoned for a reason," Malcolm said.

"Probably because she was a girl."

"Mayhap she was a sacrifice to the old gods."

"Nay," Jarvia answered, "I think not. I found no sign of an altar or of other sacrifices. Someone—perhaps her mother—nestled her in the shade of the bushes."

"And the bitch?"

Jarvia shrugged. "Mayhap she and the babe belonged to the same people and both were abandoned, or—" She shrugged. "It makes no difference, lord. We have to save them both."

The teary softness of Jarvia's voice tugged at Malcolm's heart. "We can save the wolf while raising fewer questions than we can the baby," Malcolm pointed out. When Jarvia did not reply, he continued, "According to the Ancient Ones, rescuing an abandoned child will bring evil magic on the land and the people."

Jarvia picked up the baby and held her close to her bosom. "In our land, lord, we can rescue an abandoned child if we want to." She searched his face. "Surely, lord, you do not believe the old ways? You follow the Christ."

"There are many others to consider besides myself."

"You believe the custom of your Ancient Ones?"

"Lady, two moons ago, I would have said no and I would not have hesitated to rescue the child." Malcolm thrust his fingers through his hair. "But my father's kingdom is almost rent in two. Many of our people still adhere to the old ways. If we rescue her, they will believe we have brought evil upon them."

Jarvia grabbed his hand. Whipping off his glove, she pressed his palm to the babe's tummy. "She is a wee thing, lord. If we keep her, I will make sure that none suffer." She looked down at the child.

Malcolm sighed. "Show me where you found her, lady."

"You do not believe me?"

"I will see for myself. I shall certainly be questioned later."

Jarvia's eyes brightened.

Leading the way, she showed him where the baby had been hidden. He looked all around, even picked up a stick to poke in the bushes. He looked for caves and checked out all the small crevices in the cliff sides. Finally he threw the stick down and returned to Jarvia.

"Are you satisfied that there is no altar?" she asked.

"Aye."

"We will rescue the child?"

He nodded. "But you and I shall not keep her, lady."

"What!" she exclaimed.

He cupped her elbow in his hand and guided her back to the cart. "I will pay a peasant family to rear her."

Jarvia twisted away from him. "Nay, I will not allow that. I found her. She is my child."

"I have spoken, lady. I will send for Lachlann. He will know what to do with the babe." Looking into the distance, Malcolm saw the copper flash of his best-man's helmet. He waved.

"I will not part with the baby, lord," she insisted.

Jarvia's already pale face became a deathly white. He saw more than defiance and stubbornness in her expression. He saw fear deep in her eyes. For such a large woman, she looked delicate, vulnerable. Malcolm felt as if he had been winded by the blow of a cudgel. Staggered by the feeling, he watched tears slip down her cheeks.

"Mother of God!" he muttered.

He wrapped his arms around her and held her to him, pressing her cheek against his chest. To see those tears, to

know that he had caused them made him burn as if from
a knife wound. Jarvia was not a woman who cried easily.
Since he had known her, she had faced situations with either
amusement or disdain, but rarely with tears.

"My lady-wife," he said, "I find that I much prefer your
sharp tongue to this weeping."

Jarvia leaned against him.

"She is so helpless, lord, and I want her."

Malcolm sighed. "Ah, lady, you said there would come
a day when I would rue being married to you. Perhaps that
day has already arrived." He looked over his wife's shoulder at the old servant, who dawdled at the cart. "Morag, we
will keep the orphan. You will be in charge of her until we
reach the village. Then I shall turn her over to the ard-righ
for judgment."

Jarvia pulled back and looked up at him. "I want charge
of the baby; I don't want her to be an orphan."

Her green eyes glittered, and her chin had a stubborn
tilt to it. She was ready to fight . . . and fight she would,
Malcolm knew.

"Lady, you must learn to know when to stop pushing."

They gazed at each other, locked in silent battle, until
Malcolm smiled and reached out to tuck an errant curl
behind her ear. "Have you not enough to do with your
time, taking care of me and my needs, woman?"

Jarvia caught his hand, pressing his callused palm against
her cheek. "I have enough time to do both, lord." *And plenty
of space in my heart to love both of you.*

His fingers curled around her neck, firmly, gently. "If,
lady, I find myself vying for attention with that young one,
I shall regret my decision to let you foster her."

Laughing, her eyes yet sparkling with tears, Jarvia looked
intently into his eyes. Then they both looked down at the
bairn. She lay in the rounded nest of bed covers. Her hair
aflame in the afternoon sun, she laughed up at Malcolm
and caught both feet in her tiny hands.

"What shall we name her, lord?"

Malcolm looked in wonder at the woman whom he had
taken to wife. He had always thought her beautiful. Today
she glowed, soft and warm and motherly. He could imagine
her with his child . . . his son . . . at her breast. He could not

describe his wonder, his joy of the thought. How much more joyful would be the reality!

"Lady, is it not enough that I am allowing you to keep her?"

Jarvia shook her head and looked down at the babe. So tiny. So helpless.

"Then you choose the name." His voice was gruffer than he had intended. "I have no experience in the naming of children."

Just then, Ghaltair rode up and slid off his pony with fluid ease. "You wanted me?"

Malcolm frowned. "Nay, I was motioning to Lachlann."

Ghaltair saw the baby. He looked back at his chief. "Whose child is it?"

"An abandoned child," Malcolm explained.

Ghaltair walked over to Jarvia. "I'll do away with it for you."

"You will not!" Jarvia swung the baby away from him.

"Nay," Malcolm said. "Go find Lachlann, Ghaltair, and tell him to come here. I have need of him."

"Aye." Ghaltair looked disapprovingly at Jarvia. He took a step, his boot coming near the wolf. It snarled. Ghaltair jumped. He cursed and kicked the animal.

"Stop that!" Jarvia shouted.

His dirk drawn, Ghaltair spun around and regarded Jarvia with pure hatred. "Never shout at me like that again, woman!"

As weak as the bitch was, it rose on all fours, the hackles rising on its neck.

Malcolm grabbed Ghaltair's weapon hand and twisted until the warrior dropped his dirk to the ground. "Never speak to my wife with such disrespect again!" he thundered.

"I'll kill the bitch!" Ghaltair muttered.

"Which one are you speaking about?" Malcolm asked in a deceptively soft voice.

Ghaltair looked from Jarvia to the wolf bitch to the baby. Slowly his gaze returned to Malcolm. "The wolf. She needs to be killed. Anyone can tell by looking that she carries disease."

"Aye, that is true," Jarvia said. "She is suffering from a human with an ill mind."

"Mayhap, *madam*—the people who beat her were within their right. We have no way of knowing what the wolf did to them."

"Pick up your dirk," Malcolm said, "and rejoin the men at the front of the company. Send Lachlann back to me."

"Aye." Ghaltair spat the word as he knelt and retrieved his weapon.

"Ghaltair, you and I shall have a talk later," Malcolm said. "I find your behavior intolerable and unacceptable."

The young warrior's eyes narrowed; his lips thinned. His face set in hard, uncompromising lines, Malcolm returned the stare.

Jarvia shivered. Holding the baby tightly to her chest, she watched Ghaltair turn, mount his pony, and gallop away. "He is a hard man, my lord."

"A bitter lad is closer to the truth, lady," he answered, "but I cannot allow him such liberties. If a warrior cannot control himself, he is no better than the animals about him."

"Ghaltair has much anger and hostility locked within him."

"Aye," Malcolm agreed. "But I promise, lady, he will not bother you or yours again. That you can count on."

Lachlann rode up shortly. "I didn't see you wave to me," he explained, "but Ghaltair told me about the baby. Do you want me to take care of her for you and the lady?"

"Nay, my lady is going to keep her."

Lachlann slipped off his helmet, and as Malcolm had done earlier, ran his fingers through his sweat-moistened locks. Surprised, he scowled at his chief. "I know you're angry with Ghaltair, but he is right. You canna keep the bairn." His brogue thickened; his voice rose. When Malcolm held up a silencing hand, Lachlann grabbed him by the arm and pulled him aside. "Think, mon. There is already much unrest among the clans. The Ancient Ones teach us that bad luck comes to the kingdom and to the person who rescues the child . . . especially a child that has been sacrificed to the gods. We don't know but what she wasn't meant as a sacrifice."

"I searched for an altar and found none," Malcolm answered.

"That doesn't mean there wasn't one."

"I have spoken." Malcolm looked at his wife. Holding the child in her arms, she bent her head and cooed softly.

"You have not spoken well!" Lachlann exclaimed. "Ever since this woman has come into your life, your rod has stayed hard while your head has gone soft. You're daft, mon. Daft!"

"Say not another word," Malcolm warned, "else I will trim you down to size, friend or no."

"You may trim me down," Lachlann said scathingly, "but Jarvia is doing some trimming of her own, my friend. Your rescue of this child will provide the dissenters with the weapon they need to prove that you and Fergus are not good for the land. If a few bad things happen, Malcolm, they'll call it black magic and blame you."

"We will make sure nothing happens," Malcolm said.

"Malcolm, this is no game that you're playing," Lachlann warned. "During the time of the Old Ones, when human sacrifices were frequently made, intervention was a crime paid for with death. Even today, some of our people believe the gods will punish us unless they receive their sacrifices of appeasement."

"I will say this only once more, Lachlann. I searched for an altar and for signs of other oblations, but found none. Also, I remind you, my father is a Christian."

"But he is ard-righ of the kingdom of Northern Scotland," Lachlann pointed out. "He has spent his entire life working to unite the northern Scottish clans, and even now the bonds are tenuous. He has always walked a careful line between the old and new ways. What you are doing, Malcolm, might destroy not only what your father has worked for but also what you have worked for."

"We shall have to see that it does not."

"Lord," Jarvia said.

Malcolm's gaze returned to his wife and the baby. Beside Jarvia stood Morag holding a basin of fresh water.

"The ceremony, lord," Jarvia prompted.

"You would make this sacrifice for this woman?" Lachlann demanded. "For this sickly child?"

"I would."

Lachlann shook his head in disbelief.

"You will witness my fostering of this child," Malcolm told his best-man.

"By all that is holy!" Lachlann swore. "You canna be naming the child!"

"Of course we are," Jarvia said. "You know full well, we cannot foster her unless her new father bestows a name upon her."

Lachlann rounded on Jarvia. "Do you know, madam, that rescuing an abandoned child—"

Malcolm caught Lachlann's upper arm, his fingers biting into the sinewy flesh. "Cease," he ordered, his cold, hard voice for Lachlann's ears only. "I have made my choice. I shall live with the consequences."

Lachlann glared at Malcolm, then clamped his helmet back on his head. "So be it."

Malcolm, followed by the scowling warrior, walked over to where Jarvia stood.

"Hold the babe," Jarvia said to Malcolm. When he made no effort to reach for her, Jarvia caught his hand and positioned his arms. She laid the baby in them. "She is easy to hold."

Malcolm had wielded weapons of war with ease and precision. He had caressed women with equal skill. But he had never held a babe. She was so tiny—her buttocks fit easily into one palm. Her eyes were blue, the color of a Highland loch. Her hair—little tufts of it on her head—was deepest red. It blazed like fire in the sunlight.

Brian rode up to join them. He stared in surprise at Malcolm. "Well, well, Duncan Chief, what do we have here?" Malcolm scowled, and Brian laughed. "A babe becomes you, Malcolm."

"A name, lady," Malcolm demanded impatiently. "You are the one who wants the child. What do you wish to call her?"

"She is a special bairn. Let us give her a special name."

Brian dismounted and limped over to Malcolm's side. "A name," he murmured in disbelief. "You are naming the babe, Malcolm?"

"Aye, Brian," Jarvia answered.

Malcolm's scowl deepened.

"Catriona," Morag suggested.

Lachlann stood to the right of his chief, Brian on the left. Morag stepped closer to Malcolm and held out the basin.

Clearly dazed, Brian said, "You're going to baptize her?"

"Aye, Brian," Malcolm snapped. He dipped his fingers into the water and sprinkled it over the baby's head.

"As witnessed by Lachlann mac Niall and Brian mac Lagan, both best-men of Clan Duncan, from this day henceforth you are Catriona." Malcolm glared at his two best-men, as if daring them to refute his words. "And you belong to Malcolm mac Duncan, chief of Clan Duncan, Prince of Northern Scotland and his wife, Princess Jarvia of Southerland."

Morag tossed the water away and replaced the basin in the cart. Jarvia began to rummage through one of the trunks.

"Lady, would you relieve me of the child," Malcolm barked.

"One moment, sire." Jarvia pulled out several pieces of linen. "I want to dress her for the journey."

Catriona gurgled, and Malcolm drew her closer to his chest. He kissed her forehead, unable to believe she was so soft and sweet. Then he felt a wetness flow through his hands, down his shirt and trousers, splattering on his cuarans. The babe laughed and crammed her fists into her mouth.

Brian and Lachlann guffawed. Not even Malcolm's glare stopped them.

"Lady . . ." Malcolm spoke ominously.

"I will be finished in an eye's blink, lord," Jarvia said, her back to him.

He heard the snip and click of scissors.

"This child wets."

Jarvia jumped off the cart.

"Aye, lord, she was born with that ability."

"On me, lady."

Jarvia laughed.

"You find this funny, madam?"

"*I* do, Malcolm," Brian admitted gleefully. "I do indeed."

Scissors in one hand, pieces of white linen in the other, Jarvia shook her head, her silver hair glinting in the sunlight. "I do not laugh in a harsh way, lord. I find you endearing."

"*Endearing.*" Lachlann snorted. "I shall remember the word when we arrive at the village and you present this child to the ard-righ."

"Ah, Lachlann, me friend," Brian said, "I have a feeling life is indeed changing for the Duncan."

"Aye, and for us, too," Lachlann grumbled.

"Put Catriona here, my lord husband," Jarvia instructed. "Together we will put on her diapering."

"I shall put her down," Malcolm said, "but I shall not diaper her, madam."

Gently Malcolm lay the baby on the bed covers and watched as Jarvia wiped her body with a damp cloth, then patted her dry with a soft white powder.

"This will keep her from getting the diapering rash," she explained as she handed Catriona to Morag to hold.

As Jarvia rummaged for a cloth with which to diaper the babe, Morag said, "It looks as if she has been swaddled for a long time, mistress. Leave her unclothed for a little while. Let her enjoy the sunshine and fresh air. I shall watch her."

"Aye," Jarvia said, and turned to Malcolm. "Now, lord, I shall tend to the wolf. Will you hand down my medicine chest?"

"My lady," Malcolm said, "have you always had a penchant for rescuing lost souls?"

"Aye."

Despite his grumbling, Malcolm helped Jarvia with the wolf. He moved the animal so that Jarvia could clean the wounds and apply ointment. When she finished spreading salve on the last wound, he rose.

"We are done, lady. It is past time for us to be on our way."

Jarvia gathered her vials together and returned them to the chest. "The bitch is weak, lord."

"Stronger now than she was before."

"I would like to take her with me also. If we leave her here, she is likely to die."

Malcolm brushed twigs and dirt from his trousers. "My lady-wife, you are indeed a generous woman, with a kind heart and soul, but we are not going to rescue every unfortunate animal we find between Southerland and my village. One, we have no room, and two, I have no inclination to do so."

"Only one wolf," Jarvia said.

"That, lady, may be one too many."

"If we leave her, sire, she will die," Jarvia repeated.

"Are you proposing that we foster the wolf also, lady?" He raised a brow, but Jarvia saw the twinkle in his eyes.

She smiled and nodded. Malcolm looked down at the same time that the wolf whimpered and nuzzled Jarvia's hand.

"Lady, your generous heart will probably be my undoing. I can see that this is going to be a recurring scene in our marriage." Still, he returned her smile.

Thomas rode up and joined them. "What is causing the delay, Malcolm?"

"A baby," Morag announced and held out Catriona. "Lord Malcolm and Princess Jarvia have fostered her."

Surprised, Thomas could only stare from the child to Malcolm and back again.

"Thomas," Malcolm said dryly, "you arrived in time to help us with the rescue."

The outrider looked dubiously at the squirming babe. "I am not a married man, Malcolm. I know nothing about taking care of infants."

"I am not talking about the babe," Malcolm said softly. "I am speaking of the wolf."

"The wolf?"

"Aye." Malcolm heaved Jarvia's medicine chest into the cart. "My lady-wife wishes to rescue the dying wolf bitch also."

Thomas, Brian, and Lachlann stared unsympathetically at the wolf.

"Who's to say she won't turn on us?" Brian asked.

Jarvia rubbed her patient's head. "I say she will not."

"Well, lady"—Brian moved back as she rose and walked over to the cart—"I declare that life has not been the same since the Duncan wed you."

"That is a fact, lady," Malcolm agreed.

Brian grinned. "We had expected change, but not the kind that you have brought to us."

"But 'tis good," Thomas added. "I especially like to see the Duncan changing."

"Thomas, lad," Malcolm said, "you had better guard your tongue. I have not forgotten the trouncing you gave me last even when we played the board game."

" 'Twas a sweet victory, Malcolm," Thomas confessed.

"Aye, I am sure it was," Malcolm retorted. "How many pieces of jewelry did I lose to you?"

"Three," Thomas replied.

"Ah, Malcolm," Brian teased, "it does my soul good to see you behaving like the rest of us mere mortals."

"It may do your soul good, best-man, but it is doing no good to my treasure coffers."

Thomas, Brian, and Lachlann laughed. At first Malcolm glowered at them, but finally he joined in.

"Aye, Thomas, 'twas sweet when you trounced Malcolm last even," Brian agreed. "That's the first time you've beaten him."

"And the last," Malcolm declared.

Thomas and Jarvia exchanged a knowing glance, but far be it from either one to confess that she—an accomplished player taught by Ein-her—had studied Malcolm as he played. Once she had figured out his basic strategy, she had given Thomas some winning tips. For Thomas, victory had indeed been sweet!

Malcolm's warriors picked up the wolf gently—despite their complaints—and laid it in back of the cart.

"Now, Morag," Jarvia said, "I shall clothe the baby."

"Then we shall be off," Malcolm announced. "Best-men, see that the company is ready to move."

The moment of levity behind them, the wolf rescued, the three men returned their attention to the business at hand. They nodded, mounted their horses, and rode away.

"As soon as you have clothed the baby, lady," Malcolm said, "I shall expect you to join me." Before she said a word, he added, "We will keep the baby and the wolf, but you *will* continue to ride with me. No more arguments, lady."

"I shall take good care of her, lady," Morag promised adding, "and the wolf, also." She pulled Jarvia aside to whisper, " 'Tis only right as the chief's wife that you ride with him. His people will expect it of you."

Jarvia looked at Malcolm, at the baby, then back at him. Reluctantly she nodded. "Aye, lord, I shall ride with you."

"Good," Malcolm snapped, and looked down at his soiled clothes. "Now, I will see to washing myself."

"I will get your clean clothes," Jarvia said, hastening to comply.

Taking the baby, Morag returned to her cart. Malcolm strode toward the stream to wash and change. When he returned, he slung his wet clothes over the cart railing. He was untying Dhubh-righ's reins when he noticed the set of gloves lying on the cart floor. He picked them up.

"My gloves! What are they doing out?" He gaped at the mutilated glove. "Madam, what happened?"

Jarvia wiped her hands down the side of her trousers. "I—I cut off one of the fingers, lord. I needed to make the babe—"

"You cut up my ceremonial gloves!" His face darkened, and he glared at her from beneath hooded lids.

Jarvia gulped. All items of clothing were valuable, but ceremonial garments were singular. Blessed, they carried the special magic of the gods. In cutting Malcolm's she had destroyed his good magic, the power that the garment provided for him.

"I—I did not know they were ceremonial gloves, lord. I was only thinking about the child."

"Lady, you will instruct your servant to make the child its own belongings posthaste."

"Aye." Jarvia again licked her dry lips. She laid her hand on Malcolm's arm. "My lord, Morag has much magic in her sewing, and she worships the same god as you. I could have her make you another pair of ceremonial gloves."

Malcolm glowered.

"We will use the leather that you gave to me in Wybornsbaer, sire. Truly the gods—your god—blessed the hunt with brave and worthy kills. Morag can make you new ceremonial gloves from the leather. They will have great magic in them."

Malcolm continued to stare at Jarvia.

"Lord, your god blessed your trip to Southerland altogether. You are most blessed to have me for your wife, and if I bear you no sons, you have Gerda."

"The gloves were special, madam," he said. "My mother, not a servant, sewed them for me."

"I am a good seamstress also. I, your wife *and your servant*, will sew you new gloves and embroider them with magic emblems. I promise to put great power in them. Good magic, lord. Maybe not as good as your mother's, but good."

Long, agonizing seconds passed. A smile eased across his face; then he chuckled, the soft sound burgeoning into deep, rumbling laughter. In surprise and wonder Jarvia watched him; she smiled, then laughed with him.

Finally he wiped the corners of his eyes. "Sew me another pair of gloves, madam. I am sure they will have more magic than my last ones." He stepped closer to her. "Remember the pact we made about your wearing trousers?" When she nodded, he said, "Let us now make another pact, lady." Again she nodded. "Promise me that if you are bent on destroying some of my property, you will allow me to have a *little say* in the matter."

"Aye, lord."

He stood so close she could see the lines of his skin, feel the warmth of his breath. She smelled the hot, earthy scents of sweat, sun, leather, and the man. They drew her to him.

She laid her face on his chest and pushed his shirt aside to feel the hot flesh of his chest beneath her palm. "Thank you for allowing me to keep the child, lord. And the wolf."

Her tongue followed the heated path of her hand over him. Shuddering, Malcolm laced his fingers through her hair and tilted her head back. His mouth closed over hers.

Surrounded by his strength and power, by his hunger, Jarvia responded fully to his kiss. She was his. He knew it; so did she. She opened her mouth to him, ready to give as little or as much as he wanted to take. She loved him. Aye, she did. Her loving was taking her beyond the emotional boundaries she had known before.

The kiss was long and hot and demanding. His urgency made him rough, yet Jarvia did not mind because her own need was equally urgent. His hands slipped down her back, cupping her buttocks. He pulled her closer to his hardness.

As always when they came together, so did heat and desire, wrapping around them, honey-sweet and mindless.

"Lady," he whispered, dragging his mouth along her throat, behind her ears. His breath, touching her warmly, was as evocative as the moist hotness of his mouth. "We must cease this or I shall have you in the bushes."

"I think I would welcome even the bushes, lord, if you were to carry me to bliss again." Lost in the emotion that only Malcolm could arouse in her, Jarvia clung to him. "I am beginning to understand letching. 'Tis a most delightful emotion, is it not?"

Malcolm slowly pulled his hands up her back and straightened. He was still embracing her, but his grip had slackened.

"I am glad you are teaching me the art of it," she continued softly. "I do enjoy our carnal pleasure."

Breathing deeply, she snuggled closer to him, refusing to let him pull away. She drew him into her embrace and laid her cheek against his chest. She listened to the steady, rugged beat of his heart.

"Lord," she murmured, "can all Highlanders give their women such pleasure?"

Malcolm's hands banded around her upper arms and he jerked her away from him. The movement was so sudden that her head lolled back. Swearing softly, he glared at her.

"I know not, I care not, what other Highlanders do, madam," he said. "Know that I am the only Highlander who can do it for you."

Jarvia cried out softly as his grip on her arms tightened.

"You are mine, lady. Mine alone. Do not make the mistake of seeking comfort in the arms of another, madam."

The joy of the previous moments gone, Jarvia stared into his stark face. "I meant nothing by my words, lord," she said softly. "I only wanted you to know that I appreciate your teaching me how to letch, that I truly enjoy it. I am not Hilda, lord. Not like her in any way."

Malcolm released her and she stepped back.

She wanted to tell the Highlander that she had a tenderness for him, that she cared, but he was a man who gave only passion, who wanted to receive only passion. She had promised earlier that she would not try to extract a promise from him as long as he was unwilling to give it.

She raised her hand to her cheek, the sunlight glinting on her marriage band, reminding her that theirs was a marriage by contract. She had initiated the agreement and would keep her part of it to the letter, and in doing so she would protect her heart as best she could.

In an effort to convince him of her loyalty, she said, "I made a marriage agreement with you, lord, and I shall honor it. No matter what!"

Her words did not soothe him. His face grew more thunderous. His eyes were blue flames of fury.

"Aye, lady, you will!"

Chapter 20

$\sim\!\!\text{O}\text{O}\!\!\sim$

As the journey continued Jarvia lost track of time. The closer they came to Malcolm's village, the more time he spent with his warriors. Even his nights were spent planning and organizing. For the most part, he slept outside the tent on his tartan. When Jarvia questioned him about it, he said he did not wish to disturb her sleep.

She missed him, wanted him with her, but knew he was first a king and a warrior, then a husband. Always he would put duty ahead of her. That was the way of the warrior. This was the way of a marriage based on convenience, not love. To have Malcolm at all, Jarvia must share him.

She turned her affections to Catriona, keeping the baby with her as much as she could when they traveled, feeding and playing with her when they stopped to rest. As the wolf—whom Jarvia called Magda—gained strength, it pushed its way into Jarvia's affection, and into Jarvia's tent at day's end. It also earned the grudging respect of everyone who traveled with the company. On several occasions Ghaltair tried to become friendly with Magda, but the wolf did not like him. It always raised its hackles and growled at him. He even apologized to Jarvia for his rudeness. She accepted the apology, but she did not accept his overtures of friendship. She did not trust a man who mistreated children and animals.

During the long nights that Malcolm spent away from Jarvia, she brought the child to her tent and slept with her. As long as Jarvia had Catriona . . . and the wolf . . . she was not alone.

One grueling afternoon, Malcolm halted the company and ordered them to stop for the night . . . for the last time. The village lay half a day's ride over the next rise. Everyone was weary, but anticipation lightened the mood of the camp.

Several warriors set up tents; some hunted; others gathered wood for the fire. By twilight the hunters returned to dress their kill. Jarvia, Morag, and Gerda prepared the evening meal—a succulent feast of deer meat with vegetables that had been supplied from storage bins in Wybornsbaer.

The warriors truly relaxed for the first time since they had begun the journey; they played board games, laughed, and talked boisterously. Malcolm sat with his men, not joining in the games and rarely participating in the gaiety. For the most part, he leaned back, propping himself on an elbow, and observed.

"Arthur," Jarvia said, sitting down beside the youth, "why are you so glum?"

"I broke the reed to my pipes," he answered, "and I have no replacement. My extra reeds were destroyed."

"How?" Jarvia asked.

"It looks as if they have been chewed to bits."

"Probably that wolf bitch," Ghaltair called out.

Jarvia looked over to see the warrior sitting on the ground near the fire.

"Magda does not destroy other people's possessions," Jarvia said.

"I'm not blaming Magda," Ghaltair said. " 'Tis Arthur's fault. He is a laggard, not a careful lad. On several occasions he has not done his work well."

Jarvia had not known Ghaltair when the journey began, but since she and Malcolm had rescued Catriona and Magda, she had developed a strong disliking for him. He preyed on other people's faults. To Jarvia, this suggested there was a weakness in him. She trusted Magda's instincts, and the wolf did not like Ghaltair.

"Ghaltair is right," Arthur said. "I have been a laggard. Even if the wolf did chew the reeds, 'twas my fault for not watching after them better. Malcolm is sorely angry at me."

Jarvia glanced at her husband, who was staring morosely at her and Arthur. "I do not think he is as angry as you think."

"More, lady. He fairly shouted at me when he learned that I will not be able to play the Duncans' song when we enter the village."

"Is it that important?" Jarvia asked.

"*That important!*" Arthur straightened up. "Aye, 'tis that important!"

"Jamie will be able to blow the lur," Jarvia said in an effort to cheer him up. "And there's the drummer."

"Aye," he said past gritted teeth. "Jamie will blow his lur, and the drummer will drum, but 'tis the pipes that announces the arrival of the Duncan. No self-respecting chief goes without his piper." The boy hit his chest with his fingers. " 'Tis I who should be piping."

"Let me see your pipes," Jarvia said. "Mayhap together you and I can repair your reed."

Arthur's face brightened. "Do you think so, lady?"

"Which one is broken?" Jarvia countered.

" 'Tis the *siunnsear.*"

Arthur hurried into his tent and returned with his pipes. As Jarvia inspected the instrument, the lad talked about it as if it were his lady-love. *Feadan. Ribhead. Siunnsear. Mal. Dos.* The terms began to run together in Jarvia's mind.

"You really love your pipes, do you not?" she said.

"Aye, mistress, that I do." Arthur's eyes shone brightly. "I can fair make the pipes talk. My father taught me, and his father played before him."

He watched as Jarvia carefully held the pipes and studied the damaged reed.

"We shall be able to mend this, Arthur, so that you can play the Duncan's song. I have some extra reeds in my medicine chest."

"Don't tell me, lady," Ghaltair broke in sarcastically, "that you have a miracle for the pipes in your medicine chest."

Jarvia looked in his direction. "Aye, Ghaltair, my medicine chest is filled with miracles of one sort or another. To have miracles, you only have to believe in them."

"Do you use reeds as medicine?" Arthur asked.

"Nay, I use them so that patients who cannot swallow from a tankard can suck liquid through them. I also fill reeds with medicine and, closing off one end with my thumb, I use them to measure out drops. That is how I put tinctures into sore eyes." As Jarvia talked, she ran her hand over the fringed tartan that covered the sheepskin air bag. Her fingers caught in a tear. "Would you like me to mend this?"

"Aye, my lady."

With a snort Ghaltair rose and walked away from the company. Jarvia was glad. As she worked on the pipes, she and Arthur continued their conversation.

Many times during the evening, Jarvia found Malcolm's dark, brooding gaze on her and a look in his eyes that told her he was hungry for her, as hungry for her as she was for him. Anticipating their night together, she made plans for Morag to keep Catriona. At Jarvia's earliest convenience she went to the stream and bathed. After she dried off, she splashed fresh herbal water over herself and donned a clean long tunic.

As she returned through the camp, she stopped in front of Malcolm and gazed down at him. She felt his eyes on her as she slowly walked the distance to their tent. Before she entered, she turned and again looked at him. He rose.

"Malcolm!" An outrider galloped into camp and nimbly slipped off his pony.

Never taking his eyes of Jarvia, brushing past the scout, Malcolm said, "I will hear your news in the morning."

" 'Tis most urgent," the youth said.

"On the morrow," Malcolm insisted, and continued toward his tent.

" 'Tis a message from your ard-righ."

Malcolm stopped. He sighed. Jarvia knew what his choice must be.

"Go to sleep, wife."

Her disappointment was so acute that she felt sure her heart would burst, that she would go mad with yearning for this man's touch.

"May I expect you shortly, lord?" she called.

"Rest, lady. You need it," he said, not unkindly and with an almost grudging reluctance. "I do not know when I shall be to bed."

Malcolm retraced his steps and draped an arm around the young scout's back. He led him to the center of the camp, where, talking in low voices, the Highlanders huddled around the fire.

Numb, hardly aware of what was going on around her, Jarvia entered the tent and lay on the pallet so that she could see through the parted opening. She fought sleep for as long as she could in the hope that her husband would eventually come to bed. But at last she accepted that he was not coming.

She made her way to Morag's tent to get Catriona. Despite the servant's whispered protests, despite knowing she might disturb the baby, she gripped the basket. She would have her child—the child that the gods had given to her—with her this night.

When she reentered her tent, she curled up on the bed and snuggled Catriona into the curve of her stomach. The soft, warm baby lying next to her brought comfort and peace. Magda, giving both Jarvia and Catriona a good-night lick, lay down at Jarvia's back.

"You are mine," Jarvia whispered. "The gods gave you to me, and no one is going to take you away."

Catriona breathed in deeply, her little body quivered, and she rubbed her closed eyes with her fists.

"You will not be deserted again, love, nor will you be a slave like me. I shall always protect you."

Jarvia caught one of the tiny hands and soon the little fingers were gripping Jarvia's. She loved the tight clasp of the delicate hands.

"I am an orphan," Jarvia murmured, her lids growing heavy, "but you, Catriona, will not be. That, love, is a promise."

Jarvia slept.

"Lady."

From beautiful dreams, Jarvia heard someone call her name. She felt the warmth of sunshine on her face.

"Lady."

She stirred and lifted sleep-laden lids to see Morag bending over her. Magda still lay to her back, alert and watchful.

"Make haste and dress," the old servant instructed. "Today we ride into Malcolm's village."

"Where is he?" Jarvia sat up and rubbed her eyes.

"Preparing for the journey."

Jarvia looked at his untouched side of the pallet. Her disappointment from the previous evening returned full force. "He was up all night."

Morag nodded. "I have your clothes here." She handed Jarvia a red silk blouse and black trousers that she had been sewing for her since they had begun the journey.

Jarvia took them. "I need to feed Catriona."

"I shall let Gerda do that," Morag answered. "His lord-ship said we must hurry, and I let you sleep as long as I could."

Jarvia lay Catriona in her basket and handed it to the servant. Magda trotted out behind Morag. Jarvia rose and began to dress. Remembering her discussion with Malcolm in regards to her clothing, she smiled. She loved the feel of the soft cloth against her body and was especially proud that she now had her own cuarans, which fit her feet without the aid of a thick inner lining. Malcolm had taken her with him when he asked Thomas to fit her foot and sew the boots for her. He had even sat by while Jarvia discussed their design with the warrior.

Shortly Morag and Magda returned to the tent. Magda lay down on the pallet, and Morag helped Jarvia finish dressing. After Morag brushed Jarvia's hair until it shone, she clasped the tartan about her shoulders.

"There, madam." Morag stepped back. "I am glad that you finally have a shirt and trousers of your own to wear." She brushed her palms across Jarvia's shoulders and down her back. "You are a fine figure of a woman. You'll do his lordship proud as you ride into the village. He will arrive for your shortly."

"He is coming for me himself?"

"So he said." Morag caught Jarvia's hands in hers and squeezed them tightly, reassuringly. "Are you nervous?"

"Aye," Jarvia said, "a little."

"There's no need to be."

"I married the barbarian to save Gerda and her baby," Jarvia said. "At the time I gave no thought to many of the consequences. Since we began the journey, I have had time to think. I was reared in the king's household as a slave. I know nothing about being a chieftain's wife, certainly not about being a princess."

"You have a fine head on your shoulders, mistress,"

Morag assured her, reaching up to catch Jarvia's face in both hands. "You will learn quickly. Even if I say so myself, ma'am, you will make a good chieftain's wife. Already you are a good princess."

"Thank you," she murmured, and forced herself to smile. "I wish I were as certain as you are."

Morag gave her cheek a pat and stepped back. "Don't worry. All will be well."

"I shall go see Catriona."

Leaving the tent, Magda at her heels, Jarvia crossed the camp to find Gerda sitting on the back edge of the cart holding the baby.

"Oh, Jarvia." Gerda smiled brightly. "She's such a sweet little thing."

Jarvia took the baby in her arms and held her tightly. Catriona was hers, hers to love. As long as she had the baby she would not be alone among strangers.

"I shall soon have a baby of my own, Jarvia."

"Aye." She nuzzled the baby, but Catriona would have only so much loving. Her tummy filled, she was ready to play.

Later Lachlann, leading Moonbeam, walked up to Jarvia. "Make haste, lady, your husband awaits you."

Jarvia gazed across the way to see Malcolm at the head of the column. The sun burnished his black hair; the breeze blew it wildly from his face. His black shirt and trousers emphasized his muscular physique, his handsome features, and reminded her of that night, seemingly so long ago, when he appeared in Wybornsbaer to inform the king and queen about Hilda's death. That night he had been wearing the same black trousers and shirt. Today he was as handsome—perhaps even more so—but he was not nearly as dark and brooding. He tossed his tartan about one shoulder and clasped it. He accepted his helmet from one of his men. Impatiently he looked about him. Aye, Jarvia thought, he was ready to depart.

She gave Catriona a last kiss before handing her to Morag. After she slipped on her gloves, she allowed the best-man to help her mount. Taking the reins, he led Moonbeam to the front of the company, where Jarvia joined Malcolm. Magda trotted beside Moonbeam.

With Malcolm on his black stallion, she on her golden red mare, they stood side by side. "Today, lady, we arrive at my village," Malcolm said.

"Aye, lord."

"Are you eager to arrive at your new home?"

"Yes, lord," she answered, "but I am also apprehensive."

He caught one of her hands in his. "Do not be. I am with you."

"Aye, that gives me strength."

He released her hand, raised his left one, and brought it forward. The company began to move. Jarvia held her head high and sat a little straighter as she gazed at the banner man riding directly ahead of them. Like all Highland warriors, he rode the pony as if he had been born to it, his shoulders squared, his face forward. As he had been the first time Jarvia had seen him, he was dressed in the red slash-sleeved vest that fitted over the short yellow tunic. In his left hand he held aloft the iron standard that carried the Duncan's colors. On either side of the banner man rode two more warriors, dressed in the same colorful garb. Jamie carried the lur; Arthur held the pipes.

At early morn, they began their journey; by midday they had crossed the valley. On the rising hill ahead of them—not more than half an hour's ride, Malcolm said— Jarvia saw the village. Even from that distance it was a grand sight. Large fields, neatly tended and divided by low stone fences, surrounded the entire village, which was protected by a deep ditch, two retractable bridges, and wooden palisades. Malcolm's village was much larger than Wybornsbaer, and much more colorful. Red-and-yellow banners placed intermittently around the walls snapped in the wind.

Already people from distant parts of the kingdom had begun to gather for the marriage ceremony. Tents and pavilions of all sizes, shapes, and colors—the colors always reflecting the clan or family house—had been erected on the grounds surrounding the village. Temporary wooden enclosures corralled horses and oxen. Old men sat and talked in small groups; the older women cooked while the younger ones prepared their goods for bartering. Children played.

In a meadow between two stands of trees, warriors practiced their martial skills. Two wrestled; a third refereed. A few—the more fortunate ones, Malcolm pointed out—thrust special spears at a stuffed, leathern bag suspended by a rope from a tall tree branch. Many more practiced swordplay; even more threw a different kind of spear at stationary targets. The majority practiced archery. Jarvia imagined they were all caught up in a festive spirit.

"That is where we are going to live?" she asked.

"Aye, the village of the Duncan," Malcolm said. "Many of our people prefer to live on farms away from the settlement, but they always seek refuge there when we are attacked." He pointed to a mountain in the distance. "Beinn Malcolm."

Malcolm's mountain. Pride underscored his words.

Jarvia turned to gaze into her husband's smiling face. He made her feel as if she were the only person who existed in the world. One smile and a few words from him made her share his joy at being home.

Although he was dressed entirely in black, with the exception of his tartan, which bloused loosely about one shoulder, he was not the brooding warrior she often knew. Excitement softened his harsh features.

"Now it shall be your home."

"If your people accept me." Jarvia answered softly.

"They will accept you, lady."

In the distance behind Malcolm, Jarvia saw Ghaltair checking one of the carts. He looked up at the same time, and their gazes locked. Again she glimpsed hostility on his countenance and knew that it was directed toward her. She had once mentioned it to Malcolm, but he had shrugged it aside. She had not mentioned it again.

"You are beautiful, Jarvia," she heard him say.

"You think your people will accept me, my lord, because you say I am beautiful?"

They laughed together.

"They will appreciate your beauty," he said, "but they will accept you as my wife because you are intelligent and wise, and because you are a leader."

Jarvia felt his gaze move over every feature of her face before it slid down to the red silk blouse and black trousers.

His eyes darkened to smoky blue, and Jarvia did not have to wonder at his thoughts. The soft material of the blouse clung to her breasts, revealing their fullness. The trousers, of a courser, nattier material, fitted snugly over her hips and thighs.

"I feel a fire in my belly every time I look at you," he confessed in a husky voice that sent ripples of pleasure through her.

"If you feel this way, lord, why have you not come to our tent for the past few nights?"

So passionately inflamed were his eyes, his words, that Jarvia lowered her lashes. Still she could not stop her body from responding.

"I have stayed away because when I am around you, I think only of you, of your passion and fire. I had to have my wits about me. A king is no good to his people if he is a prisoner of passion, dictated to by his rod."

Jarvia's breasts tightened as longing curled through her to reside in her lower stomach. She ached for her husband's possession; she yearned to claim him as only a man and woman can do in mating.

"Look at me, lady," Malcolm said. "I would know your thoughts."

Jarvia let him see the answering hunger in her eyes. Laughing joyously, he caught her hand and squeezed.

"Lady, you are a delight to me."

"May I always be, lord."

The laughter faded but not the smile on his lips. His eyes grew somber. "Aye," he said slowly, "may you always be."

Still clasping her hand, he turned his attention to their triumphant entrance into his village.

"Ho, Jamie," he called, "sound the lur. Let the people know that the Duncan is home."

Thrice Jamie blew, the coarse blare echoing across the valley. In the distance they heard the answering lur sound three times. Cheering, waving branches in the air, people stood on the rampart that framed the village entrance. Others poured through the opened gate onto the retractable bridge that spanned the huge ring-ditch.

"Ho, Malcolm," Thomas called, his wrinkled face

wreathed in a smile. " 'Tis good to be home again, among friends."

"Aye."

"And among pretty Scottish lasses," Ghaltair added.

The men laughed and sat a little straighter on their ponies. Even the animals sensed a change; their gait was a little brisker, and they swished their tails.

"I should have a new son or daughter," Brian called out.

"Probably a lass," another teased. "How many lasses do you and Sorcha have now, Brian, me boy?"

"Three, but I don't mind another."

"Nor would I if she looks like her mother," Ghaltair said.

"Well, I grant I'm more muscular and hairy than the lady-wife"—Brian held out one brawny arm—"but I'm not so hard to look upon."

His words were greeted with hearty laughter.

"But for all that, a lot is to be said for having lasses."

"And what would that be?" Thomas asked.

"The lady-love and I have to keep working at having laddies!"

Their laughter was infectious, and Jarvia enjoyed it. Although nervous, she too anticipated greeting their families. She was eager to meet Malcolm's mother and father.

Although they were still several miles from the village, Malcolm ordered Arthur to begin playing the pipes.

The piper, who was also the bard, began to blow on the pipes. The wailing sound was not as unpleasant to Jarvia as it had been the first time she had heard it. This was her husband's pipe tune. Everyone would know that Malcolm mac Duncan was returning victoriously from the . . . hunt.

Aye, he had his prey—his Southerland bride.

As Malcolm's warriors shouted the war cry, chill bumps covered Jarvia's body, and she shivered. She clutched Malcolm's hand tightly.

"Frightened?" he asked.

"A little anxious. The sound of your pipes and war cry does nothing to help."

Malcolm grinned. "Mayhap the war cry of Clan Duncan will always send a twinge of fear up your spine, lady, but you will come to love the music of the pipes. 'Tis the sound of the Highlands."

"Ah, I love that sound." Morag said with a sigh.

"It is one I can live without," Gerda replied, clamping her hands tightly over her ears. "I have never heard the like in my life."

Morag laughed. "Get used to it. You shall be hearing it aplenty from now on."

Morag smiled as she sat on the seat of the cart, jostling from side to side. Tears smarted in her eyes. For the first time in many years she was entering a village governed by her people. She would be surrounded by those who spoke the same language, who shared the same beliefs. She was home.

And so was her mistress.

Looking at Jarvia and Malcolm, she smiled. They were indeed a sight. Riding together at the head of the column, both were dressed in their finest regalia, befitting a clan chieftain and prince of Northern Scotland and his bride.

Jarvia's hair, pulled back by decorated combs, hung in long waves down her back and glimmered in the morning sunlight. Morag was proud of the shirt and trousers she had made for her mistress, at Malcolm's request. Aye, Morag thought, he had taken a real fancy to his lady-wife, else he would not have fostered the child that now lay sleeping in a veiled basket at Morag's side.

Catriona stirred. She smacked her lips and tucked her chin into her chest, resting a fist against her cheek. Cooing softly, Morag pushed the veil aside and adjusted the neck-line of the baby's dress, which she'd made from remnants of material left from Jarvia's new shirt.

Sitting on the other side of the baby basket, Gerda peered into the distance. "Lachlann has been kind to us," she said.

"Aye," Morag replied, reverting back to Norse. "He is a good man." After a pause, she said, "I think perhaps he is a little kinder to *us* because he is interested in you."

Gerda's eyes rounded, and her cheeks turned a delicate shade of pink. "You jest, Morag!"

"Nay, I have seen the way he looks at you."

As Morag spoke, Lachlann turned on his pony and gazed back at them.

"Aye, he has a fondness for you," the old woman concluded.

Sighing, Gerda squirmed again and made a face as she found no comfortable position.

"We will soon be at the village," Morag said softly, "and you won't have to be a-sitting on these hard seats any longer."

Gerda nodded. She flexed her shoulders and laid her hands on her stomach. "I am growing bigger."

"Aye, that's the way it is with childbearing."

"I am glad I have my freedom," Gerda said, "but I wonder about Sven."

"I'm sure you do."

"Even though he was better as a smith than a warrior, he was kind in his own way."

"I'm sure," Morag agreed. "Do you still have a tenderness for him?"

Gerda lowered her head and played with the fringe on her shawl. "I had a tenderness for him . . . or I thought I did. I slept with him because he was going to buy my freedom and marry me." She looked at the older woman, her heart troubled. "The farther we get away from Southerland, the less I think about Sven."

Morag laid a hand over Gerda's. "Do not worry. Sometimes we mistake the tenderness of gratitude for that of love. Do you now find yourself attracted to Lachlann?"

"Aye," Gerda murmured, "but I doubt he would be interested in a woman who carries another man's child."

"I think, Gerda, my child, that our Lachlann does find you attractive—whether you are big with child or not. Else he would not be scowling so when he is away from you, and he wouldn't be dancing attendance on our cart all the time," Morag said. "Even so, there is nothing you or anyone else can do until Jarvia becomes pregnant."

Gerda smiled.

"I am hoping we will hear some good news fairly soon," Morag said. "Then Lord Malcolm will see that you are properly wed. Mayhap to Lachlann."

"Do you think so?"

"Lachlann is his best friend, and you are Jarvia's dearest friend. I think perhaps one or both of them could be persuaded to betroth you to Lachlann if he should ask for you."

The idea pleased Gerda, and she smiled as she saw Lachlann riding toward them. "He is handsome, Morag," she said. "Indeed, much handsomer than Lord Malcolm."

When he reached the cart, he said in Gaelic, "My lady Gerda, are you doing all right?"

Having learned this phrase from Lachlann, Gerda nodded.

" 'Tis time we reached the village," Morag said. "She's a mite miserable."

"Aye," Lachlann said, his gaze moving over Gerda's swollen abdomen, then back up to her face. He smiled. "Her hair is the color of autumn leaves."

Morag turned to look at Gerda. "Aye, 'tis at that," she murmured.

"What did he say?" Gerda asked.

When Morag translated, Gerda blushed.

Lachlann laughed.

"Shouldn't you be returning to the front?" Morag asked. "We shall be entering the village soon."

"Nay, I shall ride beside you, good woman," he said. "Not many men are blessed to ride beside two beautiful women."

"Acht!" Morag laughed and repeated his words for Gerda, who smiled shyly at him.

"Malcolm and Princess Jarvia are indeed a handsome couple, are they not?" Lachlann said.

"Aye," Morag murmured.

"I will be glad to see them blessed with a child."

"And I'm sure they will be happy also," Morag said.

"I hope it's soon," Lachlann added. "Very soon."

Chapter 21

"**L**ady, what is of such interest that you continually look over your shoulder?" Malcolm demanded.

"I worry about Catriona riding at the back of the company. We stir up so much dust."

"You put a dust veil over the basket, so let the matter rest." He spoke sharply. "You know full well that I cannot allow the child to ride with us, on this day of all days."

Jarvia looked straight ahead, but Malcolm saw the glint of tears on her lashes.

"Lady, you push me sorely," he said softly. "And your tears do touch me. Where you are concerned, I sometimes behave like a callow youth and leave reason behind. I cannot, *will not*, do so this time."

"Could we not let the cart ride directly behind us, lord?"

He shook his head. "I bring home a second bride from Southerland, one whom all my people are not convinced I need. I must overcome their fears and prejudices. I must also find out who among us is creating trouble between our people and the Picts, who is destroying the peace alliances I am trying to build. All this I reckoned on. But now, thanks to your loving nature, lady, I have even more to contend with. Now I am also bringing into the village an injured wolf, which is fast recovering, and I have only your word that it is tamed."

"Of that I am sure," Jarvia answered.

"Strange as it may sound, lady, I am not as worried about explaining the presence of the wolf as I am the child."

"Yours is a strange people, lord, who see less value in a child than an animal."

"Aye, but many think this way, lady."

Jarvia nodded, and Malcolm saw she was afraid. He wanted to hold her, to press her face against his chest and chase those fears away. Letching for this woman was indeed turning him into a milkmaid. He had thought that mating with her would sate his longing, that in time he would become bored with her. Not so far!

With each passing day Malcolm wanted Jarvia more than before. His wanting was so intense that it angered him. He had withdrawn from her in an effort to end his letching, but abstinence had only intensified his desire for her.

Still, he told himself, the letching would eventually end. It always did. It must. The gods had chosen him to be a king. As a chosen one, he owed his entire life to the welfare of his people. To this end he made plans; he worked to bring about his dreams and ambitions. He could let nothing—no one—stand in his way.

"Malcolm, your father will not make us take Catriona back, will he?" Jarvia asked.

"I have accepted Catriona into my household . . . for better or for worse, lady," he answered. "I shall speak in her defense before the ard-righ."

"I shall speak for her if you prefer," Jarvia said.

He snorted. "That, lady, would be my undoing. I am the master and well capable of speaking for myself. Now, turn your head forward and straighten your shoulders. When we ride into my village, I will be presenting a wife for my people to see."

"Do you present your wife proudly, lord?"

Her eyes were the green of heather and bracken in the springtime. Her hair shone like moonglow. Every time he looked at her, he saw her anew . . . and she was more beautiful than before.

"My lady-wife, I present you most proudly."

A tremulous smile touched her lips. "Thank you, my lord husband."

"I am here to protect you." He smiled. "Now, hush, and look forward."

Her lips curled into a delightful . . . and tempting . . . smile. "Aye, my lord husband."

A warm pleasure swelled through him. He felt kindly toward her.

A few minutes later, Jarvia noticed a large hill in the distance that was crisscrossed and encircled by pathways from top to bottom. The closer they came, the more curious she grew.

"What is that, lord?" she asked.

" 'Tis called Labyrinth Hill. Running through it is a tunnel called the Chamber of Fire. 'Twas used as a place of ancient worship."

"The pathways are clearly marked." Jarvia held her hands over her eyes to cut the glare. "They appear to be still in use."

"Aye, people still make annual pilgrimages," he answered. "At the top of the hill is a pool of clear fountain water, which Highlanders consider to be holy. They take offerings to Our Lady of the Lake, who is said to visit the pool once a year, at mid-summer. The few who have seen the lady claim to have received a miracle from her.

"There are stone-paved chambers in the interior of the hill," Malcolm added, "but pilgrims no longer use them. Although it takes longer to make their climb, they use the exterior pathways."

"You describe it as a holy hill, lord, but just looking at it sends bumps of fear up my back. I would have to want a miracle desperately to climb it," Jarvia confessed. "It frightens me."

"Aye, 'tis to be feared," Malcolm said. "During ancient days trials of ordeal were performed there. The stone-paved chamber tunnels form a ring around the hillside. One part of the chamber was filled with fire, the other with rushing springwater. Those facing the ordeal were forced to run from one end of the tunnel to the other. Old folk say if the fire did not kill you, the water would."

"But, those who escaped proved their innocence," Jarvia guessed.

"Tradition tells us that none have ever lived through such a trial," Malcolm said. "I have witnessed only two trials by fire personally, and neither person survived."

She gasped. "You still use it!"

"We did until Fergus became ard-righ. He prohibited it."

Relieved, Jarvia murmured, "Good." Still, as if some supernatural force had control of her eyes, she could not pull her gaze away from the hillside. Again she shivered.

Malcolm caught her hand in his and squeezed. "Do not be alarmed, lady. All the pilgrimages now are peaceful ones. People carry their votive offerings to Our Lady and return from their journey with tales of joy and gladness."

Grateful for the warmth and strength of his hand, for his caring, Jarvia returned his smile.

"Mayhap one day, lady, you and I shall make a trip to the holy lake."

"Mayhap." Jarvia knew this was a trip she would dread rather than anticipate.

Shortly after midday, they arrived at the large meadow that surrounded the village; they swung off the pathway onto a deeply rutted road. Cries of celebration sounded all around them. The song of the Duncans swelling in the air, Malcolm and the company crossed the main bridge into the walled enclosure. From all sides cheering people pressed in on them, their adulation and happiness adding to the festive air. The people waved brightly colored banners and lush green tree branches. Young and old alike threw bracken and heather on the road in front of the returning chief and his company.

Greetings echoed around them. The children, laughing and shouting, threw cereal grain over them. The village women ran alongside the ponies, touching Malcolm's and Jarvia's cuarans and the pony trappings. The old men brandished their weapons.

Concerned about Catriona and Magda, whom she had ordered to ride in the cart with Morag, Jarvia looked back over her shoulder, but the villagers had crowded so close that she could not immediately locate the cart. As she and Malcolm moved slowly forward, she continued to search behind her. Then she saw Lachlann ride through the village gate. Next came the cart. Morag and Gerda were both beaming with happiness, albeit for different reasons, Jarvia surmised. Between them lay the baby's basket . . . and Magda. Her head held high, the wolf gazed about her.

"Look, Malcolm," a woman called.

Jarvia turned to see a villager hold up her tiny infant.

"He was born while you were gone."

"*He!*" Malcolm exclaimed.

The woman nodded.

Malcolm stopped the pony and leaned down to touch the baby's forehead. "A boy!"

"Aye." Her face glowed. "Finally a boy."

Malcolm pulled aside the baby's covering. "Ah, Sorcha, God be praised. He looks like you and not Brian. We worried about the babe."

The woman laughed again.

"Sorcha!" Brian called. He galloped past Malcolm. "Is that you, love?"

" 'Tis me, Brian." Turning from Malcolm, the woman ran to the burly warrior, who slid off his pony, no sign of a limp in his walk today. "And our son."

Brian clasped his wife by the waist and lifted her and the baby into the air. "Lads, did you hear? I'm the father of a boy."

"Well then, Brian," Thomas called out, "you won't have to be a-trying for any more children."

"Ah, mon, I wouldn't be a-saying that," Brian replied. "I surely wouldn't." Into large, muscled arms he cradled the baby and pushed back the covering. He smiled and crooned softly. Jarvia watched him with a tender heart.

He turned his head to gaze at his wife. "But I would have loved the babe as much if it were a girl."

Sorcha's eyes sparkled and she nodded her head. "I know."

Jarvia felt as if she had been caught eavesdropping. Quickly she averted her head. For all Malcolm's kindness, she wished the cord of love that bound Sorcha and Brian bound her and Malcolm.

"Here, lady." Jarred from her thoughts, she looked down to see a child handing her a bouquet of flowers. She accepted them with thanks. More flowers and talismans were thrust at her, more blessings pronounced. Happily she accepted them all. Unlike Wyborn's subjects, Malcolm's loved him, and they seemed to love her.

"My lady—"

Jarvia felt someone tugging on her trouser leg. She looked down at an elderly woman who stood beside her pony.

"I picked these for you today." She held up a bouquet of flowers. "Welcome to Clan Duncan."

The blue eyes were aged, but vivid and alert. She touched her hand to the toe of Jarvia's shoe and murmured a prayer.

"God bless you, ma'am," she said.

"Thank you," Jarvia replied, tears in her eyes. "Who are you?"

"I'm Feich, the Wise Woman and the midwife. If you have need of me, I live on the other side of the village."

"Do you think I am going to have need of you soon, midwife?"

"In time," the woman answered.

When Malcolm saw Feich, a smile gentled his features. "Good day, my old friend."

"Good morn to you, Malcolm." She moved around the ponies so that she could walk beside him. " 'Tis good to have you home."

" 'Tis good to be home."

She laid a hand, twisted and knotted with arthritis, on his thigh. "The muddy waters are stirring, my son. Trouble is on the way."

Malcolm laid a gloved hand over hers. "Aye, I have felt the stirring."

"Big trouble." Feich pulled her shawl over her head and walked away. "I must go now. I have work to do."

Jarvia watched the old woman until she was swallowed up by the crowd. When she glanced back at Malcolm, he too was staring after her.

"She is the one you told me about?"

He nodded. "She delivered me and has been with me my entire life. She is one of the few people whom I trust implicitly."

His brow furrowed, Malcolm lapsed into silence. People continued to press in on them, handing them charms and potions, blessing them in the names of the new god and the old ones.

Eventually Malcolm asked, "What do you think of your home, lady?"

" 'Tis beautiful," Jarvia answered. "The buildings are magnificent. I have never seen their like before."

Nor had she ever seen such streets and walkways. All were paved and curbed with stone, the ponies' hooves clopping on them as they pranced through the village. The main street led directly to the Great Hall; other streets and pathways connected the many buildings.

At the end of the street and to the right she saw a huge semi-circular wooden platform that rose into the air. "What is that?" she asked.

"Outdoor seating," Malcolm answered. "The Grand Rostrum. Each row of seats is elevated a step above the last, so that all who sit on it can see without any distractions."

"It is wondrous," she breathed. She pointed toward a small semicircular booth at the base of the seating platform. A bright cloth formed a canopy above the woven wicker structure. From it the Grand Rostrum fanned out, each tier becoming broader. "Is that for the speaker?"

He nodded.

Behind it stretched a tourney field. Jarvia had seen many such fields in Southerland. She looked at the houses, the larger ones residences, the smaller ones outhouses. Food stores. Privies. Bathhouses. Workshops. Servants' houses. Animal sheds. Kennels. Stables. Pens filled with sundry animals—horses, cattle, goats, sheep, pigs, and chickens—ran along the outside wall of the village.

Large vegetable gardens surrounded the outbuildings. They were neatly laid out and divided with stone fencing, just like the larger fields outside the village. To the right of the Great Hall were five smelting furnaces, not too different from those in Southerland. Beside them were piles of charcoal, bog ore, and wood. Bog ore was burned with charcoal in these big clay ovens to form iron. Close by was a large hut. Judging by the anvils, wrought iron rods, hammers, tongs, and bellows she saw scattered about, Jarvia assumed this was where the blacksmith worked.

On the left, farther down the street, was a large storage hut. The large doors stood open, and Jarvia saw several carts, plows, and other vehicles packed inside.

On they rode, the people still moving beside them.

Malcolm pointed to a large rectangular building with a thatched roof. "The Small Hall," he said.

Surprised, Jarvia could only stare. The Small Hall was larger and grander than Wyborn's Great House.

"This houses my personal warriors," he announced.

"And their families?" Jarvia asked.

"Nay. When the men marry, they move to their own farmsteads. This is for the single warriors who have no families. Over here are the guest houses. Each has two rooms." He waved his hand to include four large structures that flanked the Small Hall. Again Jarvia was surprised by the luxury of the village. Each of these buildings was larger than her home, and the two rooms of each provided privacy, an extravagance afforded only by Wyborn's home in Southerland.

"Two of our major festivals in the Highlands are held in the spring and autumn. Because so many people gather at the ard-righ's village for the celebration, they bring their own pavilions. But if only a few of us are visiting, all our villages have guest houses like these."

"Truly, your village is beautiful, lord," Jarvia murmured. "I have never seen so many grand structures in one place before." As she continued to look, she saw a large tent-shaped building, its thatched roof spiking into the air. "What is that?"

"The weaving hut," he said. "It is large enough for many looms."

"My lord husband, does this mean that there are no looms in the homes?" she questioned.

"Nay. If you wish, you may have one for your personal use," he replied. "The women use these communal looms to produce material that we barter. They donate so many hours a week to weave on these looms. Any trade items we receive in return belongs to the people and go to the clan storehouse. What individuals make and trade for is theirs."

"You take care of your own," Jarvia said.

"Aye." He pointed. "And that, lady, is my—is *our*—home."

Jarvia gazed in awe at the huge, imposing rectangular building ahead of them.

"The Great Hall," Malcolm said proudly.

"It is built differently from Wyborn's Great House," Jarvia said, "which has only the two front entrances. Yours has doors on all sides. And the smaller openings higher up on the wall, what are they?"

"Windows," he explained. "They allow light and fresh air into the building."

"But in cold or rainy weather I would imagine they can be troublesome," she said.

"When it rains, we roll leather flaps down over the windows. Wooden shutters cover them when it's cold."

" 'Tis wondrous, lord," Jarvia murmured. "I have seen nothing like this in all my life."

Malcolm described the construction of the house, and Jarvia listened with interest. Finally he stopped Dhubh-righ and pointed to a large domed clay oven. "This is our kiln, lady." He waved again to indicate additional large thatch-roofed buildings. "Our barn. Mill. Kennels. Stables. And a smaller house for the chickens."

"Truly, you are a wealthy man, lord."

"Aye, my people and I have been blessed," Malcolm answered. "Fergus has been a good and wise king, teaching us to give freely to the land for all that it gives to us."

A woven wattle fence, as high as Jarvia's waist, surrounded Malcolm's estate, including all the outbuildings, the guest houses, and the Small and Great Hall. An old man, his wrinkled face creased in a large smile, opened the gate for them. They rode through.

"Welcome home, my lord—" He looked at Jarvia. "And you, too, my lady."

" 'Tis good to be home, Cleit," Malcolm said. "Greet your new mistress, Princess Jarvia."

"Welcome to Duncan territory, Princess Jarvia," Cleit said. "We've been looking forward to your homecoming."

"Thank you, Cleit," Jarvia said, a warm glow filling her.

She looked up to see a mature, dignified couple walk onto the porch of the Great Hall and stand beneath the canopy of red-and-yellow plaid.

"My mother and father," he said.

"Aye, lord, I knew from your description of them."

The queen was beautiful. Afternoon sunlight gave an ethereal softness to her face, which was framed by delicate veils a lighter shade of blue than the long tunic she wore. Although the king, standing at her side, was much older, he was yet a formidable figure. His beard and thick hair, cut shorter than Malcolm's, were pure white. Both contrasted dramatically with the midnight blue mantle he wore.

Malcolm and Jarvia stopped their ponies in front of the house, and Malcolm dismounted. He walked around his pony, caught Jarvia by the waist, and swung her to the ground. Jarvia was so nervous, her hands were clammy. At this moment she could not see the king and queen, but she felt their gazes on her.

"Welcome home, my son," the queen said, her voice deep and melodious. "We have missed you these two moons that you have been gone."

"Greetings, my mother Ard-banrigh Muireall," Malcolm said. An arm around Jarvia's shoulders, he guided her forward.

Jarvia would have recognized Malcolm's mother anywhere. Tall and majestic, she had black hair and blue eyes . . . like Malcolm's. But her eyes had a lingering sadness that suggested she had endured many hardships.

Malcolm hugged his mother, then pulled away and turned to Fergus. "My father."

Fergus was not as tall and muscular as Malcolm, but he was still a large man. He opened his arms and hugged Malcolm tightly. "Thanks be to God, you are home, Malcolm."

"Aye, Fergus, thanks be to God."

"Much has happened since you have been gone."

"Aye, so I have heard." Malcolm's brows drew together in a frown. "When Ghaltair arrived in Southerland he told me that you collapsed."

"I shall have to talk to your man," Fergus said. " 'Tis nothing to be concerned about, and I told him not to worry you with it."

"I respect you as ard-righ, my father, but you are not to discipline my men," Malcolm answered. "They know what is of concern to me and what is not. They also know that anything that pertains to you and my mother is of utmost importance to me. I would kill the man who keeps news of your health from me. Now I would know what happened."

"I was exhausted after having sat in a council meeting all day and most of the night. They argued and argued, neither side willing to compromise. I simply passed out. I am better now." He stepped back and smiled kindly at Jarvia. "Now, introduce us to your wife."

"Aye," Muireall agreed.

Malcolm drew Jarvia into the family circle. "Father, Mother, this is Princess Jarvia of Southerland, my lady-wife."

"Hello, my dear." Muireall reached out to clasp Jarvia's hands in hers. As Jarvia gazed into her mother-in-law's eyes, she thought how like Malcolm's they were. Muireall made Jarvia feel as if she were the only person in the world at that moment. "Welcome to our family."

"Thank you."

"I know we cannot take your family's place, but my lord husband and I should like to be your friends."

"She has no family that she knows about," Malcolm said. "Both parents died in a plague when she was a baby. As payment for a debt, Wyborn made her his slave. Her first husband bought her freedom."

Sympathy softened Muireall's eyes. "Then, Jarvia, I should like to be more than your friend. Mayhap one day you will look upon me as your mother."

"Aye," Jarvia said, "I would like that."

Muireall hugged Jarvia, then stepped back. "Malcolm sent word to us that you were tall like me, and you are." The queen tilted her head slightly to one side and studied Jarvia. "He also said you were beautiful. You are that also."

"Thank you." Jarvia felt her cheeks flush with pleasure.

"Jarvia"—Fergus took her hands in his—"I join with my wife in welcoming you to Northern Scotland. We're pleased to have you in our family."

"Thank you, my lord."

Malcolm looked around. "Where is Sybil? I thought surely she would be here to greet us."

"Her servants are setting up her pavilion outside the village palisade," Fergus answered, "but she and Angus have not arrived yet."

"Ah, yes," Malcolm said dryly. "She is wearing Angus's colors now. I was surprised to hear of their marriage."

Fergus frowned. "The haste with which they married displeased me. Angus had not gone through a proper mourning period for Lily." The king shook his head " 'Twas indecent."

"Enough gossip." The queen looped her arm around Fergus's. "I congratulate you, my son, on your choice of wife."

"Aye, and I also," the king agreed.

"I'm sure she is eager to be settled in her new home," Muireall added.

"That I am," Jarvia answered. "I have lived in temporary shelters long enough, my queen mother."

Malcolm turned and shouted, "Cleit, begin unpacking the carts."

Immediately several lads scurried from the house. In a low voice Cleit issued orders.

Malcolm, his arm still draped around Jarvia's shoulders, guided her onto the porch of the Great Hall. He smiled at the young woman who stood in the opened doorway.

"Lucy," he said, "your mistress, Princess Jarvia."

The girl curtsied. "Mistress."

"My lady-wife and I are tired," Malcolm continued. "We would have a good meal and rest." She nodded and withdrew; he turned to his parents. "Would you join us?"

"Nay," Fergus said. "We shall return to the guest house. After you have rested, come see me, and we will talk."

"Mistress—" Morag shouted.

Jarvia looked around to see a cart lumbering to a halt in front of the Great House. Lachlann, sliding off his pony, assisted the old servant down before turning his attention to Gerda.

The handle of the baby's basket looped over her arm, the baby crying loudly, Morag walked stiffly to Jarvia's side. Magda followed briskly. "I think she is hungry, as well as tired of riding."

Muireall and Fergus cast puzzled glances at Jarvia and her maid.

"Of course she is." Jarvia pulled the dust veil aside and poked through the covers. "Hello, my darling," she murmured as she lifted Catriona from her bed.

"I knew you had been married before," the queen said, "but no one told me you had a baby."

Quickly Malcolm said, "Catriona is *our* baby."

The queen looked shocked.

"We found her," Malcolm added.

"Found her," the queen echoed.

"She had been abandoned," Jarvia explained. "Malcolm and I rescued and adopted her."

"May God have mercy on us," Fergus mumbled.

"Aye," Malcolm answered. "She is neither sickly nor deformed, and I searched for signs of an altar or of other sacrifices. I found none."

"Did you find her near a grove or by a stream of water?" the king asked.

Malcolm nodded. "But if either had been used as an altar, my father, there would have been signs."

"Aye," Muireall agreed.

Fergus nodded, but did not look convinced.

" 'Tis time for Catriona's feeding, my lord husband," Jarvia said. "I shall take her inside."

Malcolm nodded. "I will visit out here a while longer with my father."

"Will you see to Magda?"

"The wolf has seen to herself, lady."

Muireall looked down at the huge animal who sat at Jarvia's side. "This is your pet?"

"We have a wolf," Malcolm answered, "but we are not sure she is a pet. If my lady-wife has her way, the bitch will become a member of our household."

Jarvia smiled at her husband; his parents laughed softly. Holding Catriona against her breast, Jarvia described Magda's discovery to her mother-in-law as they entered the Great Hall, Morag and Magda coming after them.

When Jarvia had completed her story, Muireall said, "You may have your wolf. Personally I'll keep dogs as my house pets."

Jarvia gasped in awe at her surroundings. Magda trotted around the room, investigating the corners and sniffing the furnishings. Well lighted because all the windows were open, the interior was lovelier and more luxurious than the exterior. A fire burned brightly in the rectangular, stone-curbed fire pit, but the early summer breeze blowing through the room dispelled much of the heat. Trestle tables and benches, chairs and small stools were situated around the room.

At the far end was another door—it led into the kitchen, Jarvia surmised—and a large stone dais that dominated the room. The two High Seats were ornately carved and inset with jewels and metals. Many tapestries hung about the room, but an exceptionally large and colorful one hung on the wall behind the dais.

Catriona let out a lusty cry as Jarvia reached the High Seat. Magda raced back and settled down only when she was satisfied that Catriona was not hurt. Sitting down, Jarvia pushed the blankets aside and lifted out the baby. "Hush, little one," she murmured. "Mama is going to feed you."

"I'll go to the kitchen and get her milk ready," Morag offered.

"If you wish, Jarvia," Muireall said when the servant walked off, "we'll get Catriona a wet nurse."

Jarvia smiled and nodded. Magda lay down at her mistress's feet. "I think she would like that better, and it would be healthier for her." She paused, then asked, "I wouldn't have to give Catriona to the wet nurse to keep, would I?"

"Nay," Muireall answered. "Isabel and her husband, Lug, have been married for little over two winters. Her child is scarcely older than Catriona. Since Malcolm has many guest houses close to the Great Hall, Isabel and Lug could live in one of them until Catriona is weaned." When Jarvia nodded, Muireall clapped her hands and called, "Lucy."

The young woman rushed up to the queen.

"Send for Isabel," Muireall instructed. "Tell her I want her to become the wet nurse for Catriona."

Lucy looked puzzled.

"For my . . . granddaughter," Muireall added.

Wiping her hands on the huge apron that covered the front of her dress, Lucy nodded, then hastened to do the queen's bidding.

Morag returned to the Great Hall from the kitchen. "Here's the bottle," she said.

Catriona took the nipple with greedy determination. Muireall stood over Jarvia and watched.

"While you're feeding her, mistress," Morag said, "I shall unpack your belongings."

"Aye."

The old woman, following servants who had carried Jarvia's trunks into the Great Hall, made her way to the sleeping chamber at the far end.

"Catriona is a beautiful child," Muireall said.

Jarvia brushed a lock of hair from the baby's forehead. "Lachlann was angry because we rescued and adopted her."

"He was thinking about the old law," Muireall said, her eyes clouding. "Something we must do frequently, since there is a great deal of unrest in the kingdom."

"Is the discontent over the worshiping of the new god?" Jarvia asked.

"Only indirectly," Muireall answered. "Ultimately it is over power and who is going to wield it. There is a faction of warriors who claim that Fergus and Malcolm are cowards because they believe in the new god and his laws of peace. They are calling for a return to the old ways and to the glory of war." Muireall sighed. "But enough of this. Now that Malcolm has returned, I am sure he can quell the unrest."

Catriona cupped the bottle with both hands and slurped in contentment.

"Do you think the people will resent our having saved the child?" Jarvia asked, her fears returning.

"They may," Muireall said, "but based on what Malcolm has said, the ard-righ will grant Catriona asylum."

"Can the king's decision be contested?"

"Aye, if enough people are unhappy about it, they can petition their clan chief to appeal it to the Council of the Chiefs." Muireall laid a reassuring hand on Jarvia's shoulder. "Do not worry," she said. "Malcolm will protect the babe."

"I love her," Jarvia said. "I could not leave her behind, my queen."

"Nay, you could not," Muireall agreed. Her voice softened. "Nor would I have. I know many people abandon their children when they cannot take care of them, but I could not do that." She was quiet for a moment, then added, "Why is it that the women who want children do not have them and those who do not want them have so many?"

The question demanded no answer, so Jarvia made none. She moved her hand, her gold sickle wedding band glinting in the sunlight that streamed through the smoke hole.

Muireall said softly, "You wear Malcolm's ring."

"Aye."

"His father had that ring designed and crafted long before I gave birth." She smiled, her expression becoming nostalgic. "When we married, he declared I would give birth to no less than two sons. He would give each a special ring with great magic."

"Are you sorry I am wearing it?" Jarvia asked.

Muireall shook her head. "Nay, it fits your finger well, as if it were made for it. I am glad Malcolm gave it to you. He outgrew it many years ago, but he continued to wear it on his smallest finger."

Muireall rose and moved to one of the opened windows, framed on both sides by wall tapestries. Looking outside, she ran her hands over the decorative fringe at the bottom. Under Cleit's supervision, servants continued to bring in Jarvia's household goods, and Morag directed the placement and unpacking of them.

Muireall said, "My husband—Malcolm's father, Camshron—planned to give each of his sons a ring on the day each became a warrior and to have a new one crafted every three or four winters." She held her hand over her mouth. Her lashes sparkled with unshed tears. "But Northland sea raiders killed him and our eldest son before this came to pass."

"I am sorry," Jarvia said.

Muireall wiped her eyes. "I apologize. I don't mean to blither like a dolt."

Holding the baby to her shoulder, Jarvia joined her mother-in-law at the window. "I understand that you loved your husband and son and still grieve their deaths."

"Aye," Muireall murmured, "I believe you do understand."

Catriona gave a loud burp, let out a feisty yelp, and began to flail her arms. Muireall and Jarvia laughed. Stretched out in front of the High Seat, her head lying on the floor between her paws, Magda opened one eye.

"She needs a bath," Jarvia said.

"My lady," Fergus called from the door, "it is past time for us to take our leave."

"Aye." Muireall's gaze slid from Jarvia to the baby. "If you don't mind, Jarvia, I would like to take Catriona with me. I shall bathe and keep her until you send for her."

Gently Jarvia placed the infant into the queen's outstretched arms. "She's a good baby," she said.

"And I'll be a good grandmother," Muireall promised.

Chapter 22

olding his helmet under one arm, Malcolm stood in the open doorway as Muireall brushed past him with Catriona in her arms. Her blue eyes twinkling with devilment, she smiled at her son. "I shall leave you and your lady to rest, my son."

Magda had risen and was standing beside Jarvia, who was caressing the crown of the wolf's head with her fingers.

"Thank you." Malcolm looked at Jarvia, who remained by the High Seat in a spill of afternoon sunlight. "Both of us are weary, madam."

Muireall laughed softly. "Aye, my son, I have suffered such weariness before."

Malcolm's rumbling laughter joined with his mother's. Jarvia's cheeks flushed bright red. "I am sure you have, madam," he said. "Now be off with you."

Malcolm laid his helmet on a table. As he moved toward Jarvia, he shucked off his gloves and draped them over the arm of the High Seat. At her mistress's command, Magda lay back down in front of the High Seat.

When Malcolm stood before Jarvia, he caught each of her shoulders in a firm grip and looked deeply into her expressive green eyes. He had never become accustomed to their beauty; always he was startled anew by them.

"Well, lady, what do you think of your new home?"

"It is lovely, lord," she said. The breeze fluttered tendrils of hair about her face. Malcolm reached out to brush a curl from her cheek and ran the tip of his finger over one of her brows.

"What do you think of the many chambers?" he asked.

"I have been convincing the servants that Magda will not hurt them, and I have been tending to Catriona. I have not had time to look at them," she answered.

"Not even your sleeping chamber?" he asked.

"Nay," she whispered.

"Then, lady, it is time to do so."

"Just to look, lord?"

Malcolm laughed softly. "Ah, lady, you do set me afire with your flirtation. Never change."

"Time changes all people," she answered.

"Aye." He felt a momentary catch of sadness. "That it does, madam."

Malcolm recognized that his feelings for Jarvia were different from those he had for other women. But past experience had taught him that, even so, his tender feelings would inevitably alter. With time his desire would wane. He feared it would be so with Jarvia, and he did not want that to happen. She had brought something new and fresh into his life; he wanted to keep it.

"Change is not necessarily bad," Jarvia said. " 'Tis merely a fact of life."

Smiling at her, accepting the joy of the moment, Malcolm brushed his heavy thoughts aside. "Aye, madam, it is." He caught her hand in his. " 'Tis past time for you to make a tour of your domain, lady."

He started to lead her toward the sleeping chamber, but Jarvia tugged his hand.

"To the kitchen, sire," she said, her green eyes sparkling. "Since matrons spend most of their time there, I should inspect it first."

"My lady-wife, in this household the matron will spend most of her time in the sleeping chamber." He tugged her to follow him.

Leaving Magda to sleep in bored disregard for their teasing, Malcolm and Jarvia walked the length of the Great Hall to their private sleeping chamber.

"Oh, lord," Jarvia breathed when Malcolm had closed the door behind them, "it is beautiful."

The bed was elevated on four legs with a large, ornate headboard; the footboard was similarly decorated, though it was smaller and lower. An embroidered coverlet was spread over a thick mattress, and two large head cushions rested against the headboard. A chest had been set at the foot of the bed.

Fresh bracken covered the floor as it did in the main room, its clean fragrance scenting the room. A trestle table beneath the window had been polished to a high sheen, as had the two chairs on either side of it.

"A window. We have a window in our sleeping chamber." Jarvia sighed and ran across the room to look outside. Malcolm followed to stand behind her. "Your mountain," she said.

A breeze wafted through the window. Jarvia smelled the freshness of the outdoors. She felt as if she were inhaling the warmth and brilliance of the sun itself.

She turned in his arms. "Oh, my lord husband, this is indeed the most wondrous and beautiful house I have ever seen. And I have my very own window. I do not have to go out of the house to see the sunshine and to feel its warmth on my face. Every morning I can look out and see beauty all around me."

"My lady"—he kissed her on the forehead—"you give beauty to this room."

"My lord," Cleit called from outside the door. "The master of the hounds is here to see you. He said it is a matter of some urgency."

Malcolm sighed. "Tell him the lady and I shall be there." He looked down at Jarvia with resignation. "Keeper Beattie would not have come had his visit not been important. I need to see him."

Although she was disappointed, Jarvia said, "Of course, my lord. You are the clan chief."

They returned to the Great Hall to see a large, portly man standing in front of the dais. With him were two boys.

"Good day, Keeper Beattie," Malcolm said.

"Good day, my lord, my lady."

Jarvia greeted the visitor.

"How are the hounds doing?" Malcolm asked.

"Fine, sire. They are ready for the chase. They have been a-sniffing those foxes for too long."

"Aye, I would imagine."

"Foxes?" Jarvia asked.

"Aye," Malcolm replied. "We always end our summer tourney with a fox chase. Close to time for the chase, we capture the necessary number of foxes and pen them."

"Master of the chase told me that one of 'em died," the keeper said. "The silver one."

"Aye, but my men are already searching for a replacement. We shall have the proper number by the time the chase begins on the day after the morrow." Malcolm smiled. "Now, Keeper Beattie, what is your reason for being here?"

"These two boys, sire." He laid a hand on the larger boy's shoulder. "This is John." His other hand settled on the smaller boy. "This is Ronan. The boys' parents were killed in one of the Pict cattle raids. My wife and I took them in."

"That is good, keeper," Malcolm said.

"I wanted you to know that the boys are earning their food and lodging by tending to the kennels and the hounds. They help my wife with the garden, and she makes them clothes. But, sire—" Keeper Beattie stopped to draw in a deep breath. "The wife and I would like to adopt the lads. And for that, we need your permission."

"Are you boys happy living with Keeper Beattie and his wife?"

"Aye," both boys said.

"They're fine lads, lord. Someday they will be strong warriors."

"You have begun their training?"

The keeper nodded.

"You may adopt them, keeper," Malcolm said, "and I shall give you a monthly stipend to help pay for their expenses. At the appropriate time send them to Brian. He will foster the boys."

John and Ronan looked at Keeper Beattie and beamed.

"My lady-wife," Malcolm said, "do you think perhaps we can find Keeper Beattie and the boys a reward?"

"Aye, lord," Jarvia answered. "How about some apples and figs? I can also make them a wonderful sweet paste out of figs to spread on their hot bread in the morning."

The boys nodded eagerly.

"And some beautiful cloth and furs for Keeper Beattie and his wife."

"Thank you, my lady," the keeper said. "The wife and I do appreciate your generosity. Now, lord, we bid you good day."

"I shall send Cleit over with the goods later in the day," Malcolm promised.

"Thank you, sire."

Jarvia and Malcolm walked their guests to the door and stood on the porch as the keeper and two boys departed.

Hearing Lachlann shout Malcolm's name, they turned to see him standing on the porch of the Small Hall.

"Forbes and Baird have arrived," Lachlann called. "They've challenged you and me."

"You have your hands full," Malcolm called back.

Two more warriors—men whom Jarvia did not recognize—emerged from the building to stand beside Lachlann.

"They've even laid a wager," Lachlann added.

Malcolm laughed. "Forbes, I thought when I trounced you last time you would not challenge me again."

"I have to admit you got the best of me," the older of the two men called out, "but now I have one of my younger kinsmen to help me out. The two of us"—he pointed to the other man—"we're the best in Clan Kinsey. We'll take on you and Lachlann. If the two of you win, you can have that dirk of mine that you've always wanted. Lachlann can have the hunting lance."

"Save your strength and energy for the contests on the morrow," Malcolm said.

Forbes threw back his head and guffawed. " 'Tis the first time, Malcolm, that you have refused a challenge. Do I perceive that you are getting weak and cowardly in your old age?"

Malcolm laughed also. "Just wiser, Forbes."

"Malcolm," Lachlann said, "think of me if not yourself."

Malcolm looked down at Jarvia, then back at the three warriors.

"Think about it," Lachlann encouraged. "The dirk you've always wanted, Malcolm. It won't take us long to get it, then you can return to your lady."

"What kind of contest is he talking about?" Jarvia asked.

"Arm wrestling," Malcolm answered.

"Tomorrow you will have the same contest?" she asked.

"On the morrow all warriors who wish to will compete against each other in selected jousting games," he explained.

Laughter rang out in the Small Hall.

"I want Forbes's hunting lance, Malcolm," Lachlann said.

"His boar lance?" Malcolm asked.

"Aye."

"Far be it from me to keep it from you."

"You are going to join the warriors?" Jarvia asked.

"Aye," Malcolm replied.

He guided Jarvia into the Great Hall. She blinked as her eyes grew accustomed to the darker interior.

"I will not be gone long," Malcolm promised. "Forbes's lance is one of the best in the kingdom. Lachlann will do well to have it."

"And you will do well to have the dirk?" Irritation boiled within Jarvia.

"Aye, lady, I want Forbes's dirk."

"More than me?"

Malcolm's eyes narrowed, and his features hardened, but when he spoke, his voice was soft. "There is no choice to be made, lady. I have only to choose in which order I take each."

Malcolm spoke the truth, but the words hurt, nonetheless. Always when Jarvia believed that he almost loved her, he reverted to become the cold, harsh Highland warrior. Still, at the moment, she wanted him. Her whole body ached for his possession.

Any amount of time that Malcolm spent away from her would be long, she thought. It irritated her that he would leave her to go play games with the men. She would willingly come second to his duties as chief, but she would not play second to his gaming. She would have him make time for her. He might never love her, but sometimes she must come first.

This was such a moment, when she felt a great yearning that only he could fulfill.

She laid a hand on his lower arm and moved closer to him. "I thought we were going to rest, lord."

"We are, lady, in due time."

"Good." She caught his hands in hers and kissed him. At first his lips were closed, but as she tempted him, his mouth softened and molded to hers.

They had mated many times during their short marriage, but Jarvia had never felt the confidence to take charge, to totally give herself up to the passion flowing through her. She had not been sure enough of her skill or her appeal. But now, standing in their house, it seemed wonderfully right to tempt her lover, the man who had introduced her to passion.

He had carried her to bliss. Why could she not do the same for him?

"My lady-wife, what are you doing?" he asked, his lips moving against hers as he spoke.

"Well you know, lord. *In due time* has arrived."

Their hands still entwined, he kicked the door shut and leaned against it. She kissed him again, this time taking her time as her lips and tongue seduced him. When at last they pulled away, his breathing was irregular, his eyes glazed with hunger.

Jarvia pressed close to him and began to rub against him.

"Lady, I must . . ." He inhaled deeply. "Go."

"Aye, my lord, you will . . . in due time."

Through their layers of clothes she felt his corded muscles. She pulled his shirt from his trousers and ran her hands beneath it to touch warm, pulsating flesh. She prolonged the exploration to make it thorough and tormenting. She shoved up the material and lowered her head to brush kisses over his chest. When she sucked on his nipple, he arched against her.

In a thick, husky voice he said, "Lady, do you think to arouse me so that I cannot leave you without mating with you?"

"Aye." She continued her investigation with a growing sense of power and urgency.

"Madam, you are a tempt—"

His words were cut short when Jarvia eased her hand beneath his leathern girdle into his trousers and touched the sensitive skin below. She moved her hand lower, and felt his body responding to her touch. He sucked in his breath.

"What say you, lord?"

"This."

Malcolm caught her face in his hands. His mouth slanted across hers as his fingers splayed in her hair. Still she did not relinquish control, did not let him become the aggressor. She had initiated this; she would complete it. She moved her lips, opened them, and slipped her tongue between his lips. With newfound confidence, she willingly lost herself to passion. She would go beyond desire to show her love to Malcolm.

To her surprise, her physical discovery of Malcolm led to an inner discovery of herself. She had always prided herself on being in control, of using extreme caution in making her decisions, in weighing all options before choosing. For this man she threw it all aside to be wild and wanton. She wanted her husband with a desire that transcended all else.

"I give myself to you, lady."

"Lady?" she murmured.

"Jarvia."

Mindless with desire, Malcolm relinquished himself to the fire that Jarvia set to burning in him. He was not sure he knew this wanton creature he held in his arms, but he would have her.

Such a short time she had been with him, yet already she knew exactly where to touch him, how to caress him, to arouse his passions to fever pitch. In their bedchamber, *she* mastered him. Yet even so, he reveled in her power as a woman, trusting her to use that power to pleasure, not enslave, him.

Her taste had always been wonderful; now it was darker and riper, fully matured. Her body was like the great fire as he cupped her buttocks with both hands and pressed her to him. With her lips, her hands, she reminded him of what he had missed, of what he had denied both of them for the past few nights.

Jarvia delighted in her prowess as a woman. Her touch— *her touch*—made him weak, desperate with longing. *She* brought this wild barbarian to his knees. The knowledge filled her with heady exhilaration. She pressed her lips to the racing pulse point on his neck. She lay her cheek against his chest. A shudder ran through his body.

"Jarvia," he moaned.

"Malcolm."

Her hands slipped from his trousers. They brushed up his chest to lock around his neck. His mouth moved across her cheek, to her throat, her ear.

"I would have you now, lord."

"I surrender."

She nibbled on his lower lip.

"Willingly," he muttered.

Her lips brushed one corner of his mouth.

"Gladly, my lady-wife."

She lifted her head slightly to move her mouth.

"Now, Jarvia."

His mouth slanted across hers in desperation. She caught his head in her hands, communicating her own urgency.

"Now, Malcolm."

He swept her into his arms and carried her to their sleeping chamber. A sharp command from Malcolm sent Magda scurrying off the bed and out of the room.

Stripping off their clothing, lying on the grand bed, they greedily sought, demanded, took. Her body sleek with perspiration, Jarvia was close to bliss. Opening her legs to Malcolm, she guided his hardness into herself. The moment she received him, they were locked into an urgent rhythm, driving each other to further heights.

Higher, higher they climbed. They reached the pinnacle.

Both gasped as fulfillment shuddered through them. Clinging to each other, they floated slowly back to earth.

Exhausted, replete, Malcolm held Jarvia until she fell asleep. He rose, pulled a cover over her, and quietly dressed, then walked to a table across the room and pulled a flower from the vase. Returning to the bed, he laid it on her pillow and bent to kiss her.

"Until I return, my lady-wife."

Jarvia stirred, briefly opened her eyes, and smiled. She lifted a hand, and the coverlet fell below her breasts.

"My lady-lover," Malcolm whispered.

Jarvia brushed a finger lightly down his cheek. "I give you permission to go now, lord."

"Thank you, lady." He went to the door.

"Lord—"

He stopped and turned.

"You had better return home with that dirk."

He chuckled softly. "Aye, my lady-wife, I shall."

Iridescent rays of the setting sun splayed through the window of the guest house. Muireall sat in a chair, looking down at the basket where Catriona slept. The queen leaned over and straightened the coverlets. She brushed the tips of her fingers through the fiery red tufts of hair on Catriona's head. Fergus stood behind his wife, his hands on her shoulders.

"She's a beautiful child," Muireall said.

"Aye, but I fear she is going to bring us trouble," he replied.

"Perhaps not." Muireall leaned back against her husband and laid a hand over his. "Malcolm made sure there was no altar or signs of sacrifices."

"Aye." Fergus squeezed her shoulder. "Still, I worry. He found her beside a grove and a stream, lady."

"But it may not be an ancient place of sacrifice, my lord."

"True, but the fact that it *could* be will lend truth to the argument against the child."

Sighing, Fergus strode to the window and gazed out.

Concerned, Muireall looked at him. "Does your chest hurt again, my lord?"

" 'Tis tight," he confessed, "but not painful."

"I fear for your life."

Fergus smiled at her. "Do not, my wife. 'Tis not time for me to cross over yet. I still have work to do here. There is much to settle . . . even to understand."

"Such as?" Muireall questioned.

"When you and Jarvia were inside feeding the lass," Fergus said, "Malcolm and I talked. He told me that Berowalt, Wyborn's emissary to our kingdom, was taken and held prisoner. The man escaped and returned to his people with the tale that Malcolm had murdered Hilda and their unborn child, and that in order to keep the Southerlanders from learning the truth about Hilda's death, members of Clan Duncan had captured and tortured him."

"Malcolm's people would not have done that!" the queen exclaimed. "That would undermine his own efforts to reach a peaceful agreement with them."

"Someone did," Fergus said.

"Surely not any of our people!"

"I would think not, but Malcolm believes so. Had Hilda lived, we might have learned more about a possible rebellion among the Northern Scots. As it is, we must wait and see."

"Hail, my lord Ard-righ Fergus," a young man called from the doorway.

"Who goes?" Fergus answered.

"Jamie mac Niall of Clan Duncan."

"Enter," Fergus answered.

The lad entered the room. "Lord Malcolm and the warriors invite you to join them in the Small Hall. They have laid wagers and are contesting, sire."

Muireall smiled. "Join them, Fergus. 'Twill do you good. Today they are acting like lads, and sooner or later they will need you to settle a dispute between them."

Fergus laughed with his wife. "Jamie, tell Malcolm that I shall join him shortly." After the boy left, Fergus asked the queen, "Will you go with me?"

"Nay, I am weary. I shall stay here to be with the child."

"If you did not have the child, you would go with me?"

"Aye," she answered, "I would. Are you jealous?"

"A little, lady. I have grown accustomed to having your undivided attention." He paused. "I could stay with you."

She shook her head. "Nay, I am expecting Isabel. I shall talk to her about being Catriona's wet nurse. You would be bored with our women's talk, lord. Besides, I want Jarvia and Malcolm to have time together. I told Morag to tell her mistress that I would keep the child until she comes for her much later."

" 'Twas wise of you," he said.

"The people need to be around Jarvia so they can learn to like and trust her," Muireall said.

" 'Twill be difficult for many of them after what Hilda did to us. And Malcolm's rescue of the babe, at Jarvia's request, isn't going to endear her to our people's hearts. The master of the chase reported today that the silver fox died."

Muireall looked at him in surprise.

"You know some people will interpret the death as a bad omen," he said, "a sign that the gods are unhappy."

Muireall nodded. "Mayhap we can catch another fox before the chase."

"Mayhap," Fergus answered. "Malcolm has already sent his best hunters after one." Fergus gazed somberly at his wife, who continued to straighten coverlets in the basket that did not need straightening. "You are taking the child to heart, madam."

Muireall nodded and brushed her fingertips over Catriona's head. "You are going to grant her asylum, are you not?"

"Aye, I shall. But if enough people contest my decision, Malcolm will be forced to bring it before the Council of the Chiefs for a final judgment. They could demand that he take her back to her place of abandonment."

"I am painfully aware of that possibility, lord."

Long after Fergus had left, Muireall sat watching Catriona sleep. It had been so long since the few short weeks during which she had cared for her own babies. Renewed loneliness and despair at the loss of her older son swept over her; she had learned to live with the feeling, had kept it hidden in the secret coffers of her heart, but it had faded only a little in the past thirty years.

Muireall had meant it when she told Jarvia she would have rescued Catriona if she had found her. And she would have done so whether or not she also found an altar or evidence of sacrifices. No one would have stopped her.

A maid entered the room, banked the central fire, and lit several lamps. When she left, Muireall stood, hugged her arms to her chest, and paced around the room. She was well acquainted with how it felt to abandon a helpless babe.

Long ago she had been forced to contemplate abandoning one of her children, but fate in the guise of Northland sea raiders had taken the choice out of her hands. By killing one son, her eldest child, they had saved the younger's life.

Only one person in Northern Scotland, Feich, knew that Muireall had given birth to twin sons. Feich and Muireall had lived with this secret for the past thirty years.

Whether they followed the Christ or the Ancient Ones, the people of the Highlands believed that multiple births signified that the mother had conceived one child from the devil. The youngest child—or if it were a boy and girl, the girl—was sacrificed to the gods because he or she was believed to be the evil one. Had Northland sea raiders not attacked the village, killing both Muireall's husband and the eldest twin, tradition would have demanded the sacrifice of the youngest, Malcolm, to the gods.

Muireall had been honest with Malcolm in telling him about his older brother, but she had not told him he was a twin. Nor would she ever tell him. Even when, as a small lad, Malcolm had often said he felt as if a special person shared his life, Muireall had not confessed the secret of his birth.

Malcolm himself was special—a man Muireall believed was ordained by the gods to unite the various tribes of the Northern Highlands. Wanting him to entertain no doubt about his destiny, she refused to burden him with the past.

Aye, his being a twin was a secret she would carry to her grave.

Making her vows afresh did not diminish Muireall's fears, which returned to haunt her anew. For the first time in years she was drawn back into the past. She thought of Camshron, her beloved husband, who was so like Malcolm in his youth and vitality. She never doubted that he, not the devil, had given her the two sons she had carried in her womb. Even as newborns, they had looked like their father. Always she would recall the moment Camshron had first held the eldest, not yet knowing he had a second identical son.

"My lady-wife," he had said, "never have I beheld such a perfect baby."

He swung around to show the child to his younger brother. "Geoffrey, what do you think of the future king?"

Muireall had often thought Geoffrey was jealous of Camshron, and when he had looked at the baby, her suspicions had been confirmed. Because Geoffrey's head was bowed, Camshron could not see his face, but from the bed where she lay, Muireall could. On his countenance she could see his hatred for the baby.

" 'Tis scrawny-looking to me," he said.

The lusty wail of the second child rang out. Water splashed. Feet shuffled.

Surprised, Camshron looked at Muireall, then toward the darkened corner. The midwife moved out of the shadows, where she had been washing the twin, into the firelight.

"Your other son, lord," Feich said. "As beautiful and as perfectly formed."

"Twins!" Camshron whispered.

"Of the devil!" Geoffrey exclaimed, horrified, backing away in fright.

"Nay." Feich shook her head. "Both of these babies are your sons, sire, and both are chosen by the gods, each destined to be a ruler of people."

"The woman lies!" Geoffrey backed farther away from Camshron and the child. "I never wanted you to marry the Scottish princess, Camshron. She believes in a strange religion and would have us turn from the old ways. She is of the devil, Camshron, an evil woman."

"Nay, lord!" Although she was weak, Muireall pushed up in the bed. "I am not evil, lord. I did nothing wrong. Remember the vision I received after I conceived."

Camshron, still holding the eldest child, approached the midwife and looked at the younger lad. "Aye," he said slowly, "I remember, lady."

"An angel appeared to me, lord, as I bathed in the sacred stream. He prophesied that you and I would have two sons, each destined for greatness."

"Aye, lady." Camshron sighed heavily.

"Do not listen to the woman, Camshron," Geoffrey said. "Do away with her and the children, else you will bring the wrath of the gods down upon us."

"My lord," Feich said, "the lady speaks the truth. Even if you try, you cannot kill the lads. They are marked by the gods."

"Marked?" Camshron said.

"Move closer to the fire, and I'll show you," she ordered. When both of them moved into the firelight, Feich pointed to a small brown spot on the eldest son's right knee. She held out the youngest son and pointed to his left knee. "The same kind of mark, lord."

" 'Tis a cursed mark," Geoffrey spat out. "The devil has claimed them, Camshron. As surely as you allow one of them to live, your kingdom is in jeopardy. You must kill Muireall and the twins."

"Nay," Camshron said. "I cannot, Geoffrey."

"As a king, you must," he insisted. "A king is king only because he is chosen by the gods, and as such you must put your people's welfare first. You must destroy the evil— Muireall and the twins."

In the end the religious leaders had convinced Camshron that he must sacrifice one of the twins, but he had procrastinated. Geoffrey's words seemed to have been prophetic. Evil in the form of Northland sea raiders descended on the village. Camshron and the eldest twin were killed. Knowing the people would always believe she had brought the wrath of the gods down upon them, Muireall and Feich had taken Malcolm and escaped on Northland ponies they found tethered in the nearby forest.

Even when a Northland sea raider came suddenly upon them, Muireall did not lose courage. Startled and frightened, she held her baby close to her bosom and stared at the warrior. He stared back at her. Then he turned and walked away, allowing Muireall and Feich to flee without harm. From that day on, Feich had been devoted to Malcolm.

Catriona's soft cries brought Muireall out of her thoughts. She knelt beside the basket. She was holding Catriona against her breast when a call came from outside.

"Hail, Ard-banrigh Muireall."

"Who goes?" Muireall called.

"Isabel."

"Enter," said Muireall, and she turned her full attention to the present.

Chapter 23

Jarvia opened her eyes to the soft glow of firelight coming from the doorway. At first she thought she was home in her bed, then she saw Magda lying on the coverlet and she remembered. She was at Beinn Malcolm, in her husband's village, in her new home. Hearing a noise in another chamber she scooted off the bed. She located her trousers and shirt on the floor where she had discarded them earlier and dressed quickly.

Heat suffused her face as she remembered the frenzied lovemaking between her and Malcolm, and that she had initiated it. For a verity, she had become quite brazen when it came to mating with Malcolm. Today she had shed the last of her inhibitions.

Sitting on the low stool, she put on her cuarans and went to the curtained entrance. She heard the light thud as Magda jumped off the bed and joined her. Brushing aside the colorful linen, Jarvia stepped through the door into the Great Hall. The fire still burned brightly in the fire pit, and cauldron lamps cast a soft, golden glow.

She and Magda walked past the fire pit to the dais. "Morag," she called.

"Yes, mistress." The old woman appeared in the back doorway that led to the kitchen. Wiping her hands on her apron, she entered the Great Hall.

"You should have awakened me sooner."

"Malcolm said to let you rest, that you were exhausted from your journey."

"Aye, I was." Indeed she had been gloriously exhausted from the journey . . . the last journey she and Malcolm had taken to bliss.

"Where is Malcolm?" she asked. "Still at the Small Hall?"

Morag nodded.

276

"Gerda?"

"She has retired to one of the guest houses," Morag answered. "Lord Malcolm is allowing the two of us to live together."

"And Catriona? Does the queen still have her?"

"Aye. She's quite taken with the wee thing."

"Perhaps I should go get her."

"The ard-banrigh said she would bring her over later. She thought perhaps you would like to celebrate tonight with Malcolm."

"In the Small Hall?" Jarvia asked. "Aye, I would. Prepare a bath for me."

Jarvia returned to the sleeping chamber, opened one of her trunks, and began to sort through her clothing. Not finding what she wanted, she opened another trunk . . . and another.

"Which tunic are you looking for?" Morag asked as she entered the chamber.

"The white one trimmed in green floss."

"Let me find it for you, mistress," Morag offered. "Since I packed your clothing, I know where everything is." Quickly Morag unstrapped a large trunk, lifted the lid, and pulled out two small caskets, which she handed to Jarvia. "Cosmetic colorings for your face, and your combs and hairbrushes."

Jarvia set the two boxes down on the trestle table. While she recombed her hair, Morag opened another trunk. By the time Jarvia completed her bath, smooth lumps of ironing glass were heating on the fire, and a long, narrow whalebone ironing board had been set up on the table.

Soon Jarvia, attired in fresh, newly pressed clothes, was walking the moonlit pathway to the Small Hall, from which she could hear boisterous laughing and singing. As she entered she saw Fergus and Malcolm seated in the High Seats beneath a huge canopy of red-and-yellow plaid. All around the room were hung different clan banners. Warriors, each wearing his individual clan colors, celebrated the coming marriage of their prince.

Malcolm had also bathed and changed clothes. Resplendently dressed in midnight blue trousers and a lighter blue shirt, his tartan glimmering brightly in the firelight, as did the gold brooch pinned over his right shoulder, he looked to Jarvia like the sun god himself.

Jarvia wore a long white tunic and diaphanous green veils. Her only jewelry was the marriage ring Malcolm had given her. Holding herself erectly, she squared her shoulders and tilted her chin a little higher, hoping the sweep of curls that Morag had styled on her crown would not fall down. The lacy veils that wrapped her head and framed her face swept down her back to form a train. She walked down the aisle toward the High Seat.

Malcolm was brandishing a dirk in the air.

"That had better be the dirk you took from Forbes, my lord husband," Jarvia said, raising her voice to be heard over the noise.

"Aye, my lady-wife, it is." He rose and stepped off the stone dais toward her, extending his hand.

She warmed to the adoration in his eyes.

"You are beautiful, madam," he said for her ears alone.

"You are handsome, lord."

"Hail, my father, Ard-righ Fergus!" called a deep, sultry female voice.

Malcolm stiffened even before he saw the woman who spoke. Revelry ceased. Silence fell over the hall. Slowly Jarvia turned to see a woman standing in the open door.

"Sybil," Fergus said, rising. "I'm glad you have arrived, my daughter. I was concerned about you and Angus."

One of the most beautiful women Jarvia had ever seen moved through the crowd toward her father. Her brown eyes, framed by heavily blackened lashes, glittered coldly. Her hair, a deep and fiery red, was pulled away from her face and hung down her back in a long braid. Tall and willowy, she wore a golden brown shirt that was the same color as her eyes, and dark brown trousers. Her clothing outlined her full breasts and gently curved hips.

"Angus and I had some trouble in Kinsey territory," Sybil said. "Picts raided our cattle."

All around the Small Hall, the warriors came to their feet, glowering their disapproval of the Picts.

"We gave chase," Sybil continued, "but they escaped. We did, however, manage to get our cattle back."

"I would to God that you had caught the miserable curs." A warrior whom Jarvia didn't recognize slammed the point of his dirk into the tabletop. " 'Tis time we taught the Picts that we Scots are not the cowards they think us."

"Aye," others shouted.

" 'Tis a subject Angus and I intend to bring up at the council meeting," Sybil said, her gaze going to Malcolm. "Good even, fosterling."

"Sybil," Malcolm said.

"I stopped by the guest house before I came to the Small Hall." She moved closer to Malcolm, her herbal scent wafting to Jarvia. "I saw *your child*, my brother, the one called Catriona."

"Aye."

"Muireall said the babe was abandoned and that you rescued her."

"Aye."

"In a grove near a running stream," Sybil continued.

Jarvia opened her mouth to speak, but Malcolm caught her arm and squeezed. The bite of his fingers into her flesh did not hurt nearly as much as Sybil's insinuations that the child was going to bring evil on the land.

"Did my mother also tell you that I searched the area for an altar, and for evidence of other sacrifices to the Ancient Ones, and found none?"

"She said as much, but sometimes, Malcolm, people do not construct a visible altar when they make sacrifice. You would have been wise to have left the child."

Jarvia tensed. Sybil's persistence in declaring that Catriona was evil, the sweet odor of her herbal essence, and the heat in the room, all stifled Jarvia. She did not consider herself a violent woman, but at the moment she was so angry at Malcolm's foster sister that she wanted to physically lash out at her.

"The babe would have died if we had not rescued her," Malcolm said.

"Better she die than—" Sybil paused and looked around the hall. She wanted to shout to the world that Malcolm had taken her birthright from her and that she was going to get it back, but she must bide her time. She would speak soft words, to placate the warriors and guarantee their loyalty to *her* cause. "Better she die, Malcolm, than our land and people suffer. You know the teachings of the Ancient Ones. If the king is crippled or diseased, he cripples and diseases his kingdom."

"I am not king," Malcolm said, "and neither am I crippled or diseased. Nor is the child. So I can bring none of this to the land."

"The land belongs to all of us," Sybil said, rallying cries of agreement from all around them. "Each of us has a responsibility to it. In rescuing an abandoned child, you ask for the vengeance of the gods. This punishment will not be meted out to you alone, but to all of us."

Throughout the Small Hall warriors grunted and nodded in agreement.

"Why didn't you consider your people when you made this decision, Malcolm?" Sybil's gaze settled on the gold torque around Malcolm's neck. "Did you forget that you have been elected by the chiefs of the clans of Northern Scotland to become king when my father dies? Do you so quickly forget that you wear the symbol of our people's trust in your leadership?"

"I have forgotten nothing," Malcolm answered.

Sybil looked at Jarvia. "Mayhap you can think of none other than your Southerland bride. I cannot imagine way. She's rather homely."

Jarvia breathed in deeply, once again inhaling the heavy sweetness of Sybil's herbal essence. She spoke in Gaelic. "You have me at a disadvantage, madam. I do not know you."

Shocked to find that Jarvia spoke their language, Sybil gaped.

"Princess Jarvia"—Malcolm put his hand around his wife's waist—"may I present my foster sister, Princess Sybil."

"But only recently treated as a *sister*," Sybil said.

"I can imagine," Jarvia said dryly. "You are a beautiful woman, my lady. I can understand any man's infatuation with you."

Sybil's laughter was without humor. "You are delightful, Jarvia. Much different from Hilda. She had no spark or fire and did not speak our language when she arrived here."

"I have a servant who spoke Gaelic and taught the language to me."

"Hilda was my friend," Sybil said. "Mayhap you and I shall be friends also."

"Nay, madam," Jarvia answered, "I am most selective about those whom I call friend."

They stared at each other until Sybil shrugged and moved to the nearest trestle table. She picked up a tankard and held it out for a serving woman to fill with ale. Then she raised it.

"To the chase, lads, and to the Highland sword."

"Hear! Hear!" resounded all over the room as the warriors waved their tankards in the air, sloshing ale over the sides.

Jarvia looked at Malcolm for an explanation.

"The Highland sword is a special sword that the ard-righ has crafted each year for the summer games. He presents it to the warrior who wins the fox chase." He pointed to Lachlann. "He wears one. Even from here you can see how beautifully designed and made it is."

"Aye."

"It is not only well crafted as a weapon, but also beautiful and magical. Designs run down both sides of the blade. All chieftains want to win it."

"Lachlann is so vain," Sybil said, "he even had his helmet crafted by the same smith so that it matches his sword."

"He has a right to be proud," Malcolm answered, taking umbrage at Sybil's belittling of his best-man, one of Northern Scotland's most valiant warriors. "Not many can boast of having captured alive the silver fox in the annual chase."

"Who is permitted to ride in the chase?" Jarvia asked.

"The clan chieftains, their wives, honored guests, and selected best-men," Malcolm answered.

"Any of them are permitted to kill the prey?"

"Nay, my lady-wife," Malcolm said. "This is simply a chase, not a hunt. No one is allowed to kill the foxes. Our goal is to capture and bring them back alive. All year we trap foxes, so that we have a red fox to represent each clan. We also capture a silver one. As Sybil explained, the warrior who catches the silver fox wins the chase. When the game is over, the foxes that have been captured are returned to the wild."

"The silver one also?"

"Aye, it too."

"You must have a large collection of swords, lord," Jarvia said, "if you have won the chase for many summers."

"Nay, lady, I do not hoard them. I have only my sword, Fire of Retribution. The other swords I have given to warriors of valor who have not the means of getting themselves a worthy weapon."

"How touching!" Sybil smirked.

"Is this also why you helped Lachlann get the boar lance by gambling?" Jarvia asked.

Malcolm smiled. "Aye, 'tis one of the best boar lances in the Highlands, and Forbes was foolish enough to wager it."

"Forbes?" Sybil shouted. "Forbes of Clan Kinsey! One of *my* clansmen wagered his boar lance?"

Malcolm grinned. "Lachlann won it from him, madam."

"No wonder your warriors are the best armed in the kingdom," Sybil yelled, a dark scowl on her face. "It is because you take advantage of warriors of other clans."

"Nay, foster sister." Malcolm laughed aloud. "We simply take advantage of their foolishness and turn it to our gain."

Sybil turned to Jarvia. "Mayhap Malcolm has contrived to win you a weapon from one of my men which you can use in the fox chase the day after the morrow."

"My lady will not be joining us," Malcolm said.

Sybil regarded him askance.

"Since Southerland women do not join their men in the hunt," Malcolm explained, "my lady does not have the necessary skills for the chase."

"Such a shame that she is unskilled," Sybil said mockingly.

"Aye," many of the warriors agreed.

"Catching the foxes and bringing them back alive is far more dangerous than killing them," Malcolm pointed out. "I shall give my wife instruction throughout the year. Next summer she will participate in the chase."

"If she is still here," Sybil said.

"I shall be here, madam," Jarvia replied, refusing to be intimidated.

"Our women are strong," Sybil said, "especially those of us who are wives of chieftains and kings. We are taught from childhood to be hunters."

"Aye," a new masculine voice shouted. "My lady-wife is one of the best hunters in the kingdom."

Sybil spun around. "Angus!"

A broad smile on his face, Lachlann rose and moved toward the newcomer standing in the doorway. "Angus, 'tis good to see you. We have missed you this eve. Already we have had many contests."

A dark man with thick brows and deep-set eyes, the red-and-green plaid of his tartan accenting his darkness, he was no older than Malcolm, but his face was more weathered. His long hair, a deep shade of lumber brown, was pulled back from his face and tied with a thong at the nape of his neck.

"Ho, Angus," Malcolm said. " 'Tis good to see you again. May I congratulate you on your recent marriage to my foster sister."

Still scowling, Angus curtly inclined his head. " 'Tis good that you decided to return to the kingdom, Malcolm, but we have no time for these silly war games. We have to guard against not only other animals but also the Picts getting our cattle. They are venturing deeply within the kingdom. Because they have branded the Northern Scots cowards, they raid with impunity, taking both our cattle and our ponies."

"So Sybil has been telling us," Malcolm said.

" 'Tis time we did something to stop this humiliation," Angus bellowed, his hand curling into a fist. "We are fools to pass the time of day by jousting and chasing foxes."

"In any case, our fox chase may not be as interesting this year as it has been in the past, Angus," Sybil said. "If I understand the master of the chase correctly, the silver fox died yesterday.

" 'Tis strange that the silver fox died," Sybil said slyly. "I cannot remember this ever happening before."

" 'Tis the curse," an aged warrior muttered. "The Ancient Ones are angry that your Southerland bride rescued the orphan."

"Nay, 'tis not the curse, Tindell," Malcolm answered. "According to the master of the chase, the fox was ill for a while. I have sent my warriors to search for another one."

"But you have not found one yet," Tindell said. "I still say it's the curse of the child upon us."

"Aye," came the shouts of several warriors. "Mayhap we are already accursed."

Tindell rose and shouted, "Fergus, have you granted asylum to the orphan?"

"Aye, Tindell," Fergus answered. "I found no reason not to grant it."

"I say the matter should be brought before the Council of Chiefs," Tindell said. "It concerns all of us, and I say it is a cursed affair."

A chorus of ayes filled the room.

"All we have to do to know that the gods are turning their wrath on us is to see the Pict warriors stealing our cattle," Angus said. "We should be hunting and killing these men who take what is ours."

"Aye." Tindell waved his long sword in the air. " 'Tis past time."

Fergus held up his hands. "Warriors of Northern Scotland, according to the powers granted the ard-righ, I made the decision to grant the orphan asylum. If you feel the matter should come before the Council of the Chiefs, you know what to do. Until then, the matter is settled."

"Until then." Sybil spat the words.

Fergus cast her a scathing glance. "Now, let us enjoy our coming together for the Scottish marriage ceremony of my foster son." He walked to stand behind Malcolm and Angus. Putting a hand on the back of each warrior, he said, "Let us put our anger and hostility aside and make good magic for the competition tomorrow."

Lonnie, chief of Clan Galway, rose to speak. "How can we make good magic if the gods are not smiling on us? I say we must settle this now."

"Nay, Lonnie." Fergus stared unflinchingly at the huge warrior. "We shall bring the matter before the council only if a majority of the chiefs petition to do so. I, ard-righ of the kingdom of Northern Scotland, have spoken. So be it."

For a moment Jarvia was not sure what was going to happen. The warriors, scowls on their faces, seemed disinclined to heed the king's counsel. They began to move slowly through the room, each coming to his lord's side.

Angus raised his arm, brandishing his battle-ax. "Fergus is right. The ard-righ has spoken. So be it." He paused. "Mayhap, my friends and fellow warriors, it is time for us to consider a new ard-righ."

Nods and grunts of agreement sounded throughout the Small Hall.

"Until such time," Fergus said, "I am ard-righ and my word stands. Wine," he ordered, and clapped his hands. "Bring in the imported wine."

Young men rolled in several barrels.

"Time to celebrate!" Fergus shouted.

Ayes rang throughout the room, and for a moment the tension seemed to ebb away. The celebration began once more. Jarvia, staying close to Malcolm, sat in a smaller chair beside him, watching him arm wrestle with Ghaltair. Angus stood over them.

"Ah, Ghaltair," Sybil called out, "you have gotten the best of Malcolm two out of four times." She stepped closer to the young warrior. "Mayhap you are on your way to a clan chieftainship."

"Aye, lady, 'tis a fact, I am."

Malcolm's face was tense, his muscles flexed. "The young pup will have to win three out of five before he gets the best of me, Sybil, and he is not warrior enough yet to do that." Malcolm gave a grunt, a heave, and flattened Ghaltair's hand against the table. "My game, Ghaltair."

"Aye, your game," the young warrior conceded. "But one of these days, Malcolm, it shall be mine." Ghaltair rose and smiled at his chief. "On the day after the morrow, I promise that the silver fox shall be mine."

"If the gods permit us to have a silver fox," Sybil softly interjected.

"The gods permit," Malcolm said.

"Aye, the gods permit," Ghaltair repeated. "By command of my chief, lady. I am on my way now to chase one of these elusive creatures. If I'm fortunate enough to capture one, I shall be fortunate enough to do so at the chase."

"Ah, lad," Thomas drawled as he joined them, "be careful with your boasts. Brian is the one who will find the silver fox now. You'll be lucky indeed to grab one of the red ones. In the chase Malcolm has lost the silver fox only thrice since he became a warrior, twice to Lachlann and once to Brian."

"There is always a first time, best-man," Sybil said.

Lachlann pushed his way past the men who circled Malcolm and Ghaltair, and sat across from his lord. " 'Tis time to lighten the mood. Let me show everyone the man who has gotten the best of, and can still get the best of, the Duncan."

Malcolm grinned at his friend. Jarvia relaxed and leaned back in the chair. Holding her tankard in both hands, she sipped her wine and watched the men arm wrestle. Her husband lost three out of the five throws, and she felt he did it deliberately to lessen the tension. Then she saw Sybil moving toward the High Seat.

When the princess stood beside Jarvia, she said, "You wear Malcolm's ring."

Jarvia sat her tankard on the chair arm and looked down at her marriage ring.

"I had thought it would be mine," Sybil said. "It should have been."

"But it is not."

"To Malcolm's loss," Sybil retorted, and both women stared at Malcolm. "I loved him, as I have loved and will never love another man."

Evilly beautiful, Sybil's features were cold and harsh. Her eyes, shadowed with hostility and malevolence, caught and held Jarvia's gaze; they mesmerized, not letting go.

"I would have made Malcolm a much better consort. I have been taught from childhood to be a king's wife. How can you be his wife and help him govern his people when you do not understand his customs or his people? How can a woman who was once a slave understand honor and royal obligation?"

"I was once a slave, but now I am Malcolm's wife, my lady, and I shall do him proud."

"Aye, such as on the chase."

" 'Tis only a game of skill," Jarvia said.

"But the chase is a prelude to the hunt, madam. It is a test of a warrior's mettle. How do we know you have mettle if you do not prove yourself?"

All along Jarvia had sometimes doubted she could be a proper consort for her husband, but she had kept telling herself that her love for him would be enough, that giving him a child would be enough. But Sybil's taunts played on her imagined shortcomings.

"I shall prove my mettle," Jarvia answered quietly, "in my own way, madam."

Sybil smiled sardonically. "That will not do, lady. You must prove your mettle the Highland way. If you do not, you shall not be accepted—whether you bear Malcolm a child or not."

"And you, madam, are going to do everything within your power to see that I am discredited, are you not?"

"Aye, that I am."

After Sybil moved away, Jarvia was again inundated with thoughts of insecurity and inadequacy. She spied her husband as he and several other men threw their dirks at a wall target. Tired of the games and of Sybil's taunts and insults, Jarvia rose and joined her husband.

"Lord, with your permission I shall retire," she said. "The day has caught up with me, and I am weary."

"I understand, lady." Malcolm looked around, then said, "However, I had wanted to introduce you to Celdun."

"Who is he, lord?"

"Chief of the third largest clan in Northern Scotland and one of my staunchest supporters." As much to himself as to her, he murmured, "I wanted to talk to him about Berowalt and the raids by the Picts. Lachlann," Malcolm called out.

Jarvia spotted the best-man seated at one of the trestle tables in front of a gaming board.

He looked up. "Ho, Malcolm?"

"Have you heard anything from Celdun?"

His game figure curled in his raised hand, Lachlann leaned back. "Nay, I haven't. Is anything wrong?"

Malcolm shook his head. "I wanted to introduce him to Princess Jarvia before she retired for the night."

Nodding, Lachlann returned his attention to the game.

"I shall make the introductions later, my wife." Malcolm leaned over to kiss her on the forehead. "Have sweet dreams."

"Thank you, lord." Disappointed because she truly wanted Malcolm to leave with her, she turned and left the hall.

Chapter 24

Grateful for the cool evening breeze, Jarvia did not walk straight back to the Great Hall. As if she were guided by a supernatural force, she headed in the opposite direction and did not stop until she stood in front of a small hut set well apart from the other buildings.

"You have need of me, mistress?" a female voice asked.

Startled, Jarvia turned to see the old woman—the Wise Woman—moving out of the shadows. "I . . . do . . . not know," Jarvia replied. "I was not aware I was coming to your house."

Feich smiled. "Come inside. We'll share a cup."

"Of heather tea, perchance?"

"You'll see."

Jarvia followed Feich through the door into the one-room hut. Embers glowed in the central fire pit. Fragrant herbs burned in a shallow dish; pale light flickered from a small lamp.

"Sit over there, lady." Feich waved toward the table. "I'll be with you in a little while."

As Jarvia sat on the bench, the old woman knelt beside the fire and plunged a dipper into a large cauldron of bubbling liquid. After she had filled a cup, she straightened and moved to the table, where she sat across from Jarvia.

Jarvia studied the drink Feich had set in front of her. "This does not look like Morag's heather tea," she noted.

" 'Tisn't. 'Tis a potion brewed especially for you."

"You knew I was coming?" Jarvia looked into the Wise Woman's wrinkled face.

"Aye, 'tis an herbal potion that will help you conceive a child. And I give you this charm to protect you against evil."

Jarvia looked down at a long cord made of three lengths of colored floss braided together. Knotted into the cord at regular intervals were different colored feathers.

"Hang this where only you can see it," the old woman instructed. "As I said, 'twill protect you against evil magic."

Feich picked up the cord and tied the ends together to form a circle. Then she passed it through the lamp flame and through the herbal smoke. As she sprinkled it with salt and water, she chanted, "In the names of the goddesses and the god . . . by air, earth, fire, and water, I . . ."

Staring at the charm, Jarvia listened to the old woman. When the incantation was over, the blessing performed, Feich told Jarvia to drink the potion.

"Many will consider you past your childbearing years," Feich said, handing the feather charm to Jarvia, "but you will give Malcolm the child he needs."

"A child," Jarvia mused. "That is not good enough for Malcolm. He wants a son. Is your magic not strong enough to guarantee a son?"

"My magic is strong," Feich said, "so strong that I guarantee you will produce the child Malcolm needs to complete his goal as king of the Highlanders." The old woman cackled. " 'Twould be like the gods to give him a daughter. No matter, my lady." Feich laid a hand over Jarvia's. "Malcolm will love his children and will be a good father to them."

"I have never doubted that," Jarvia answered. She looked at the arthritic hand lying on hers. She gazed at the feathers fluttering in the evening breeze. "Will my husband ever come to love me, old woman?"

Feich removed her hand. After a long pause, she said, "He will always honor you as his wife."

Hurt by the answer, Jarvia pulled her hand away. "I am talking about love, not honor or faithfulness or anything else. I want to know that I am first in his heart."

"A good king, one chosen by the gods, does not have that freedom," the old woman answered kindly. "Always his people and his kingdom must come first."

"Aye." Jarvia sighed. "He told me as much."

His thoughts troubled, Malcolm left the Small Hall with his father. A breeze blew, ruffling his hair and stirring the hem of his tartan about his legs.

"I have been concerned about all that is happening in the kingdom, my father. Hilda's perfidy and death. The raids by the Picts. And tonight I saw many of the clan chiefs who had been loyal to us shifting their allegiance to Angus."

"Aye," Fergus murmured.

"And Celdun was not even present. No one has heard from him since he left his village." Malcolm reached up to rub the back of his neck. "I am worried about my old friend. It is not like him to be late without sending word."

"Troublesome times are upon us, my son," Fergus said, continuing the onrunning dialogue he had had with Malcolm all evening, "and like you, I fear that those whom we had counted as loyal followers and friends may desert us. I see the tenuous union among the clans falling apart. I fear that all we have accomplished may be short-lived."

"Because Angus and Sybil are manipulating events to suit their own purposes."

"Their followers are growing by the day," Fergus agreed. "Many want to return to the old ways. Did you see the number of chiefs who supported Sybil when she lashed out against you for having rescued the child? Aye, my son, there are a great number, our friends included, who believe we should bring the matter before the council."

Fergus paused and took in several deep breaths. He pressed a hand to his chest.

Concerned, Malcolm caught him by the shoulders. "Are you having pains?"

Lowering his hand and straightening, Fergus shook his head. "I'm tired," he answered, "and I get winded easily."

"The burden of your kingdom is weighing heavily on your shoulders."

"Aye, to some extent it is," Fergus confessed. "What weighs on it most heavily, my son, is this conflict between you and Sybil. 'Twas evident tonight." Fergus began walking again, although a little slower this time. "Both of you are my children, she born of my loins and my heart, you of my heart. I cannot bear to see you fighting as you are."

The two men walked a ways before Malcolm said, "I would that it could be different, my father. I do not deliberately hurt you where Sybil is concerned, but I cannot agree with her."

"My son, you have to try to work with Sybil. I cannot watch all my life's work destroyed because of two strong-willed leaders."

"Do you wish me to go against the teachings of the Christ?" Malcolm asked. "To return to the old ways?"

"Nay, I am not asking that you recant all that you believe. But there is a middle ground on which you and Sybil can walk. You can blend the two together and create a better world for your people. Remember, Malcolm, the pressure to return to the Ancient Ones comes not only from Sybil. It comes from other chieftains as well. They want to declare war on the Picts. Certainly the Pictish cattle raids justify retaliation by the warrior's code."

"Aye, and I promise, if the Picts are indeed responsible for the raids, I will be the first to seek retribution." Malcolm halted his steps and turned to look into his father's moonlit face. "But we cannot attack them, my father, until we know for sure they are guilty."

"Do you doubt the word of your own people? Do you have a stronger alliance to the people of your birth father than you do to mine?"

"Nay, my father. 'Tis true I am half Scot, half Pict, but I am fully your fostered son. My allegiance belongs to Clan Duncan and to the Kingdom of Northern Scotland. Ever since I became a warrior and received my vision, I have dedicated my life to my people and their welfare. All decisions are based on this, my father."

"That is good," Fergus said.

They resumed walking, and neither spoke until they stood in front of the guest house. Fergus laid a hand on Malcolm's shoulder. "Good night, my son. I hope the morrow will bring better tidings than this day."

Long after Fergus had entered the hut and closed the door, Malcolm stood on the pathway staring at the distant mountain. At times he saw the flicker of fireflies and smiled. He remembered the nights when he and Angus had played together as children, chasing the illusive creatures.

He proceeded on to the Great Hall. His hand curled around the handle, but he did not open the door. Voices from the past called to him, and once again he looked at the surrounding hills. As surely as they had beckoned to

him when he was a lad, they called to him tonight. When
he was a child, he had not known what they were saying; he
still did not know. He had always sensed they were trying
to tell him a secret.

He headed away from the village, becoming more
immersed in the past. As he had done so often, he
wondered what his life would have been like if his
father and older brother had lived. Would the people in
the kingdom of his birth father have turned on him as the
people of his adopted kingdom seemed to be doing?

All his life Malcolm had been lonely for something . . .
for someone. Perhaps it was the father he never knew or the
brother he lost, or both. Although Jarvia had brought great
happiness and contentment into his life, Malcolm knew
that something was still lacking. Would he never find that
portion of him that was missing?

Returning from Feich's hut, Jarvia was on her way to get
Catriona when she saw Malcolm walking down the main
street. At first she thought perhaps he had come looking
for her. She waved, but he passed by without looking in
her direction. She called out to him; still he did not stop
walking. She ran behind him, but was so far from him that
she could not catch up. By the time she crossed the bridge
at the edge of the village, Malcolm was out of sight.

Thinking he would return shortly, she waited at the village gate for a long while. She even walked toward the hill
several times and found the worn pathway. A part of her
wanted to follow him; another urged her to return to the
Great Hall.

Eventually she gave in to her desire to go after him.
Straining to see in the moonglow, she cautiously made her
way up the worn pathway. Higher and higher she climbed.
Winded by the time she reached the summit, she stopped.
In the distance she saw a light. She moved toward it.
Finally she stood hidden in a cluster of bushes, staring at
her husband and Sybil.

Mesmerized, Malcolm stood outside the entrance and
gazed into the cave where he and Angus had played as
children. Only now it was not full of toy swords and shields.

It was filled with tables and stools, the furniture arranged around a huge central fire pit. A large cauldron suspended from a metal hook dangled above the dancing flames. Its vapor spiraled into the air. Flagons and vials decorated the tables, all filled with dark, murky liquids. Dishes of smoldering herbs sat on the tables. Flaming candles, of all sizes, shapes, and colors, flickered throughout the cave.

Dressed in a flowing tunic, Sybil, stood in front of the huge fire. Her auburn hair hung loose down her back. Her hands uplifted, she chanted softly.

Malcolm could only stare at her. He had always thought she was beautiful; he thought no differently tonight. Firelight filtered through the thin material of her tunic to reveal her nude body beneath.

The chant became a song. She picked up a musical instrument, made of leather stretched over a round frame with rows of small metal medallions strung on wires around the edge. As she danced, the seductive sway of her hips, the melancholy pings of the vibrating disks, touched cords of memory in Malcolm. He understood Sybil, knew her motives, perceived the evil that ran deep in her, yet still he was drawn to her.

He always had been. She spun around, her dress and hair twirling about her body. Her arms above her head, her breasts swaying as she breathed deeply, she smiled at him.

"I've been expecting you." Her husky voice wrapped around him, drawing him closer. She was darkly beautiful and seductive. "I wondered how long it would take you to get my message."

"I received no message, else I would have been here sooner." In keeping with his promise to his father, Malcolm fully intended to talk with Sybil and to effect a compromise. He feared for his father's life should the union of the Scot clans dissolve.

"Aye, you did, my love." She ran her tongue around her berry-red lips. "Else you would not be here at all."

She moved toward him. He moved toward her. The closer he came to the cave, the stronger was the scent of the burning herbs, the stronger was the fragrance of the herbal water she always wore. She reached out and ran a finger over the gold brooch at his shoulder.

"I am glad you came," she said.

"I am, too," Malcolm answered. "I have been wanting to talk with you all evening . . . alone."

Sybil laughed. "You have me alone, my lusty warrior. What would you say to me?"

Lost in memories, Malcolm stared into her face. How could she be so beautiful, yet so malevolent?

"Do you remember this cave, Malcolm?"

"Aye." How could he forget?

"This is where we first made love."

Jarvia could not hear what they were saying without moving closer. But she would go no closer. She was not sure why. Perhaps she feared that Malcolm did indeed prefer Sybil to her. She only knew her heart was breaking. She had to be away from them.

Full of churning emotions—hurt, anger, disappointment, and humiliation—Jarvia retraced her steps. She would not remain there to see what happened between her husband and the woman who had been his mistress at one time . . . mayhap would be again.

"How dare you come up here to try to convince me to change my mind!" Sybil shouted, her face contorted in anger. "You are here because I summoned you, not because you choose to be. Never doubt the strength of my powers."

"I do not doubt them," Malcolm answered, "but I also respect the strength of *my* powers."

"They are not as great as mine," Sybil claimed. "Did my father suffer pains in his chest a short while ago?"

Cold fear settled around Malcolm. "Perhaps," he said.

Sybil laughed. "Aye, he did. I left the Small Hall early and came up here to *our* cave, Malcolm." She moved to one of the trestle tables and ran her fingers around the outer edges of the musical instrument, the ping of the metal disks ringing through the night air. "Make love to me, Malcolm. Let it be like old times for us."

She reached out to touch him, but he dodged away from her. "Nay, Sybil, both of us are married."

"But for each of us, it is a marriage of convenience. I married to be a chief's wife, you for a son."

"Nonetheless, each of us has spoken vows."

"You shall never have a marriage based on love, Malcolm. I will not allow you to love another woman. Nor will you have a child of your own loins. You shall die seedless."

"Is that why you killed Hilda?"

"She killed herself," Sybil answered. "She didn't want to carry your child. I told her how many berries to eat in order to get rid of it. She ate too many."

"And Berowalt, Sybil? What do you know about his capture?"

"King Wyborn's emissary?" She shrugged her shoulders. "I know nothing but what I have heard, and that is that you had your clansmen capture him so that he would not take word back to Southerland that you had killed Hilda."

"You know that is not true."

"Do I?" She smiled.

"Feich has seen the stirring of the waters," Malcolm said. "Do you know what she means?"

"Aye." Sybil picked up a flagon and poured some of the liquid into a small cup. "The clans of the Northern Scots are deserting the new way, Malcolm. We are returning to the old gods, to the old way of life with its glory and honor. Men you had counted as loyal friends and supporters are joining Angus and me."

Malcolm closed the distance between them. "You claim that your first interest is the welfare of the people, but you use religion, Sybil, to control and to gain power, not to worship any god, either the new one or the old ones."

"Tell that to Angus and to those who are following me." She laughed softly. "See if they will believe you."

"You and Angus," Malcolm said. "I would not have thought of the two of you together. Lily was too young to have died so tragically."

"Was she?" Sybil said. "She was a stupid woman who was in the way."

Sybil went to the fire, slipped the gourd dipper into the boiling mixture in the cauldron, and stirred. She said nothing, but she did not have to. Malcolm understood perfectly what she was telling him. He could remember the curses of those who served the Ancient Ones. The stirring of black waters. The unexpected deaths of perfectly healthy people.

"My father is ill also," Sybil said, "and the more he opposes me and my followers, the worse it shall become."

"Leave Fergus out of this," Malcolm shouted. "For the love of God, Sybil, the man is your father!"

"Fergus is a man, Malcolm, like any other." She spoke coldly. "I have given him the opportunity to join forces with me, but he prefers to listen to you and to that Christian fool of a high priest, Rudie."

"For a verity Fergus listens to the counsel of the high priest," Malcolm agreed, "but the ard-righ also seeks out the counsel of all his chiefs. You are angry because he makes his own decisions."

"I am angry because he makes the *wrong* decisions," Sybil said.

"Only because they are not your choices."

"I found someone to help me." Sybil gloated. "Angus. Someone the people respect and to whom they will listen."

She laid the dipper aside and stood once more. She smiled, a sinister curving of the lips. An eerie feeling crawled over Malcolm. The evil that emanated from this woman was frightening. He knew Sybil would let nothing stand in the way of getting what she wanted. The evening breeze teased the soft material of her tunic, molding it against her full breasts and rounded hips. Strands of auburn hair blew across her face.

"I told you long ago, Malcolm, that I shall be the ard-banrigh of the kingdom, and I shall be. I asked you to join with me, but you refused."

She moved to where he stood and pressed herself against him, flattening her palms on his chest. "Before it is too late, Malcolm, renounce your belief in the new god. Return to the old ways with me, and let us share the glory of the kingdom of the Northern Scots."

Malcolm grabbed both of her hands and slung her away. She fell to her knees in front of the fire.

"You want me, Malcolm," she taunted. "Your body is hard now with thoughts of making love to me." Like an adder, she slithered toward him.

"You're an evil woman, Sybil, but you are not more powerful than the followers of the new god. You are a follower of the darkness, but the new ways have brought light. Light that casts away the darkness of your spells and breaks your magic."

Sybil leaned back, stretching out her legs and bracing her weight on her palms, thrusting her breasts forward. She laughed. "Say that if you wish, Malcolm, but you do not believe it. Even now you should begin to worry about the lives of your foster father, your mother . . . your wife . . . and that orphan you rescued. She will be your downfall. I shall stir up the people even more, so that they demand you return her to the place of abandonment. Even now she may be ill."

Malcolm turned and began to walk down the pathway toward the village.

"The muddy waters are stirred, Malcolm. Death hangs over Clan Duncan!"

Jarvia had gotten lost as she made her way down the mountain, and it had taken her a long time to return to the Great Hall. When she opened the door and entered the main room, she saw Morag sitting in a chair on the far side of the room. The old woman was embroidering. Magda uncurled from one of the darkened corners and padded over to her mistress.

"I expected to find you in bed," Jarvia said.

Morag knotted off her floss and laid the frame aside. "Catriona has been a little irritable since the queen brought her home."

Jarvia hurried to kneel beside the child's basket. Magda stood next to her, nuzzling into the covers with her nose. The pale light of the lone lamp flickered over Catriona. "Do you think she is sick, Morag?"

"Quite possibly her tummy is upset. She suckled from her wet nurse's breasts for the first time tonight."

In desperation Jarvia looked into Morag's face. "What will I do if she gets sick?"

"Are you worried about how the villagers will accept the news?"

"Nay," Jarvia said, "I am worried about the baby. I love her."

"She will be fine. Give her time to make the adjustment."

"She was having no problem on the goat's milk that you prepared for her. Mayhap we should go back to it."

"Isabel's milk is probably best for her," Morag said. "Let us not worry unduly. If it's all right with you, mistress, I'll take her to my hut tonight."

"No," Jarvia said. "I want her here with me."

" 'Twill be best," Morag said gently, "if no one knows about her sickness, madam. Already the people of the village are astir because you and Lord Malcolm saved the babe. If certain people find out that she is ailing, they could demand that Lord Malcolm return her to the place of abandonment."

"Thank you for your concern, Morag, but she will stay with me. She is my daughter, and I shall take care of her."

"Shall I stay here in the Great House with you?" Morag asked.

"I would appreciate that."

"Let the baby sleep close to me," Morag said. "If she wakens, I'll get you."

"Nay, I will keep her with me." Jarvia caught the handles of the basket and carefully lifted it so as not to awaken the baby. "If I need you, I will call."

As she had done so frequently on the journey from Southerland, she went to bed with only her child and her wolf. But she did not go immediately to sleep. She worried about Catriona; she wondered about Malcolm.

In the wee hours of early morn Jarvia awakened from a fitful slumber. The fire had turned to embers. Magda had curled around Catriona's sleeping basket. In the glowing haze Malcolm was undressing. When he was clad only in trousers and cuarans, he banked the fire, then sat down at the table to pour himself a tankard of wine. Holding it in both hands, he leaned forward and stared into the flames.

The starkness of his expression touched a cord deep within Jarvia, but it was not enough to put out the flames of anger that yet lapped within her.

"So, my lord husband, you decided to return home."

Clad in her night shift, she slipped out of bed.

"You sound shrewish, madam."

"Nay, lord, I am angry."

He glanced over to see Catriona's sleeping basket. "Why is the child sleeping with us?"

"Tonight she suckled at the breasts of her wet nurse for the first time. She has been fussy."

"Christ and Him crucified!" Malcolm swore. Sybil's words returned to haunt him. Again he felt the cold, clutching tendons of fear wrap around him and squeeze. "Let us pray that she does not become ill. Already the people are worried about our having rescued her."

"Aye, several of the clan chiefs demanded that Fergus bring the issue before the council for judgment," Jarvia said. "Do you think he will?"

"I know not, lady. My father is worried about the unrest in the land."

"I will not let them have Catriona," Jarvia said. "She is mine. The gods gave her to me."

Malcolm leaned back in the chair and sighed. "The way most people look at it, my lady-wife, you stole her from the gods."

"Not so! The gods are far stronger than mere mortals. If they had not wanted me to have her, they would have stopped me. Furthermore," she added, "what god wants a girl sacrifice? She is of no value."

"Do you blaspheme?" Malcolm asked with a ghost of a smile.

"If telling the truth is blasphemous, then I am guilty."

"You have convinced me." Malcolm chuckled, but Jarvia did not laugh in return. "But I am not the one we have to be concerned about. 'Tis the entire Council of the Chiefs."

Jarvia moved closer to Malcolm. "I shall not let them take the child from me." She breathed in deeply, and suddenly realized she was inhaling the herbal essence that Sybil wore. She jerked back.

"I saw you leaving the village," she said.

"Aye."

"I called, but you did not answer."

"I did not hear you. I assume from the tone of your voice, lady, that you know where I went."

"Aye."

He took a sip of wine and lowered the goblet.

"But you ran away too soon to know what happened," he guessed.

"Oh, I know," Jarvia accused. "I saw what was happening. And no matter, *my lord husband*, that this is a political marriage, it is a marriage. You have no right to be with Sybil."

Slowly Malcolm rose from the chair. "You, *my lady-wife*, had better never speak to me in this tone again. I, and I alone, determine what I have a right to do. In the running of this clan I make the decisions. Do you understand me?"

Angrily he glared at her. He felt guilty because he did not love Jarvia; he only letched for her. He felt an even deeper emotion, mayhap humiliation or anger or both, because his body had responded to Sybil. He had not given in to his desires, but he had wanted her. It bothered him that she still had this power over him.

"I hear you, Malcolm mac Duncan, but you must hear me too." Jarvia burned with anger. "I will not tolerate being treated like this. Until we have fulfilled to the letter the terms of our marriage contract, you will honor it. I will not tolerate another woman in your life or in your bed."

Malcolm's hand curled tightly around the goblet. "You presume to tell me what I can or cannot do?"

"As long as I am honoring our agreement, so will you. Once I have presented you with your child—"

"My son."

"Your child, then and only then can you change our relationship. And, my *lord husband*, I have already laid down the rules for that also."

Malcolm tossed the goblet to the floor and strode over to where she stood. They glared at each other.

"I told you once, Jarvia, that until we married I would let you set some rules. Now we are married, and I am master. You will do what I say, when I say it."

Malcolm's experience with Sybil earlier had left him shaken, but he would not confess this to Jarvia. To do so would be to admit a weakness. As chief of Clan Duncan, as the heir to the ard-righ, he could have no weaknesses. Malcolm never doubted his prowess as a warrior, but he had begun to doubt his strength to say no to the old ways, the old spells. He had witnessed his father's pain; he now witnessed the baby's illness.

"I have promised to wear your colors with pride, lord," Jarvia said, drawing herself to her full height, "and I shall. I am a woman of my word. But I expect the same consideration from you. I will have it."

Malcolm bent and picked up his goblet. Silence was thick and heavy in the room.

"Surely, my lord," Jarvia said, "she has not blinded you to the truth. She is an evil woman who wants to destroy you, and in doing so she will destroy anyone or anything that gets in her way. You yourself told me what she did to Hilda."

"I admit she is a dangerous enemy."

"Then why, lord? Why would you go to her?" Jarvia hugged herself. "Oh, do not answer that. I know why you went to her. She is a beautiful and desirable woman. But . . ." Her words trailed off.

Malcolm set the glass on the table. Softly he said, "Sybil is all you have described, my lady-wife, and more. She is an addiction."

Jarvia's lips trembled, but she forced the tears back and turned from him. She would not let him see her cry.

"But I did not go to her for the reasons that you think."

"No?"

"I went to her because my father asked me to. I wanted to talk with her, lady. Talk. Nothing more." She heard the splash of wine as Malcolm refilled his goblet.

"Do you believe me?" he asked.

"Aye," she said in a low voice.

"Then turn around and look at me."

She did. Again they stared at each other.

"I have not slept with another woman since I met you," he said. "I shall not. I, too, honor my word."

Jarvia was pleased with his confession, but with all her heart she wanted it to be a confession of love, not one of honor.

"Tonight, lady, I saw warriors whom I had not seen in several moons, warriors whom I had reckoned were loyal to me, to my ideals and dreams, shift their allegiance to Sybil. I promised my father that I would work with her to effect a peaceful compromise, but that is not to be."

He lifted the goblet to his mouth and took several swallows of wine. "Much mischief has been practiced while I have been away, and I fear that Sybil is the source of it."

"Truth always wins out," Jarvia said.

Malcolm gave her a sad smile. "I wish I had your ability to believe in the best. Somehow I have often been a part of the darker side of life. I have more faith in it than in the good."

"Sybil cannot, *will* not, win against you," Jarvia said. "Whatever your faults—and you have them, lord—deceit and lying are not among them. You are good, not evil."

Malcolm's face softened. "Lady, all of us have the capacity for deceit and lying, and most will commit such sins if the right circumstances present themselves."

"You are a champion," Jarvia reminded him.

"A champion is but a man with an exaggerated reputation. Championship is a worrisome and difficult garment to wear."

"But the people need their champions," Jarvia insisted.

"So they do." He paused then said, "I am concerned because one of my staunchest supporters, Chief Celdun of Clan Donal, has not yet arrived for the marriage celebration." He took another sip of wine. "Mayhap he has changed his allegiance also."

"Nay, lord," Jarvia said, "surely not."

Malcolm returned to his chair and sat down, staring morosely into the fire.

"This has been a long day, lord," Jarvia said quietly. "Things will look better when you awaken on the morrow."

"I hope so, lady."

"Have you eaten?"

"Nay."

"I shall get you something from the kitchen."

Lacing his fingers through hers, he tugged her onto his lap. "Greedy as I sound, lady, I have an insatiable hunger for what is right here. I want you, only you."

He caught her face in one hand and raised it. His lips covered hers in a deep, hungry kiss. Holding her in both arms, he rose and moved to the bed, laying her down. As she watched, he stripped out of his cuarans and trousers, and was soon stretched out naked beside her.

His hands moved over her body, desperately, hotly. "God help me, Jarvia," he whispered raggedly, "but I need you. I do not want to, but I do."

Harsh but wonderful sounded the confession. Jarvia knew it was the warrior-king who spoke, inwardly battling with the man whom she called husband and lover. She gave herself to the beauty of the moment. Always before Malcolm had confessed only to wanting her. Now, a part of him admitted he needed her . . . and she needed him.

For the first time since they had mated, Jarvia felt as if Malcolm was allowing himself to enter into her world, into her passion, her need. The moment was one of the most exhilarating she had ever experienced.

By the time both were sated and Malcolm slept, glowing embers once more illuminated the sleeping chamber. Jarvia held her husband in her arms. She prayed that this night, through giving comfort and solace as well as passion, she had opened the doors of his heart. She prayed that soon she would be in his heart as he was already in hers.

Chapter 25

J arvia, sitting beside Malcolm and his parents on a raised and canopied platform at the end of the tourney field, saw Gerda weaving her way through the crowd. Finally she reached Jarvia.

Bending low and whispering for only Jarvia to hear, she said, "Catriona is fretting, and the wet nurse refuses to feed her. She fears the wrath of the Ancient Ones. Because of her, the other servants are getting nervous."

Jarvia sighed. "I shall be there shortly."

Malcolm leaned closer to Jarvia and asked softly, "Is something wrong, lady?"

Jarvia repeated Gerda's message.

"Christ's blood!" Malcolm swore under his breath and curled his hand into a fist.

Sybil, sitting on the other side of her parents, leaned back. "Is something amiss, my brother?"

"Nay, Sybil. Return your attention to the games."

Sybil's mocking laughter caused Jarvia to shiver.

Malcolm said to his wife, "Attend to the matter, lady."

"Aye, lord." She rose.

"You are leaving, Jarvia?" Muireall asked.

Jarvia nodded. "I must oversee preparations for the banquet tonight, my queen mother."

"Do you want me to help you?"

"Nay, please enjoy the gaming," Jarvia said, and added with a smile, "I would like to show my husband how proficient I am as a house manager."

"That is well and good, my dear, but I think the wiser move would be to prove yourself indispensable."

"That, my lady queen, is indeed what I shall do."

The queen's soft laughter followed Jarvia as she hurried to the Great Hall, where she found Isabel slumped on one of the benches. Morag, holding the fretful child in

305

her arms, sat near the open window. Magda lay at her feet. Lucy and Cleit paced nervously on either side of the hearth.

"My lady," Cleit said, "I am so glad to see you. The baby is getting worse."

"She is no worse," Morag interjected. "Just more fretful."

"And Isabel—" Cleit continued.

"I'm not going to feed her anymore." Isabel planted her hands on her hips and glared defiantly at Jarvia. "You should have left her where you found her. She may bring the plague of the gods on all of us."

"Hush your prattling, woman," Jarvia ordered. She took Catriona from Morag and held her close to her breasts. "If a plague comes on you, 'twill be your own doing, not Catriona's. The child is simply getting accustomed to a change in milk."

Jarvia turned to Morag. "What are her symptoms?"

"Her bowels are firming."

"Then what is the problem?"

"She is accursed," Isabel said. "She frets continually."

"Has your baby never cried?" Jarvia asked. "Has it never suffered with runny bowels?"

"Aye, but my child was not abandoned," Isabel answered. "Nay, madam, I shan't be a-feeding that babe with the same paps that I feed my own. I will not risk hurting my own child."

"Catriona is not accursed," Jarvia declared. "Consider what she has endured. All of us are under pressure. Morag, you and Isabel are glum. Lucy and Cleit, you pace nervously. No one wants to feed Catriona."

Morag laughed. "You are shouting, and Catriona is crying."

"Aye." Jarvia lowered her voice. "So I am. Isabel, if Catriona should stop her fretting, will you agree to feed her?"

"Nay."

"What if her bowels get firmer?"

Cleit moved closer to Isabel. "Go ahead, lass," he said. "You know the Duncan would not have brought the child home if she was accursed."

"Nay." She shook her head vigorously. "I am afeared."

"Leave then," Jarvia said. "I shall find someone else to nurse her."

" 'Twill be a miracle if you do, mistress," Isabel said. "Word has spread throughout the village about the accursedness of the abandoned child."

"Be gone!" Jarvia ordered. "If I hear tell of you spreading one word of evil about this child, I shall make sure you are duly punished. I have heard that in some countries people who spread malicious gossip can have their tongues cut out."

Isabel's eyes rounded, and she cupped the lower part of her face with her hand. "We have no such custom here," she said, her voice muffled.

"Do not be so sure," Jarvia said. "I am married to the chief of the clan, and I am an important and persuasive person. Mayhap, Isabel of the sacred paps, I can persuade my husband to order such a punishment."

Fearfully, Isabel backed up to the door and slipped outside.

Jarvia turned her attention to Catriona. "Gerda, get a piece of rhubarb root from my medicine chest and set it to boiling." As Jarvia strode toward the sleeping chamber, Magda right beside her, she yelled instructions for the boiling of the root over her shoulder. "Do not leave it for any reason."

"Aye," Gerda answered.

"Cleit, Lucy," Jarvia ordered, "the two of you see to the preparations for the banquet. Morag, we shall return to the old way of feeding Catriona. It seemed to be working much better."

By the time Gerda brought the herbal beverage to the sleeping chamber, Jarvia had quieted the baby and changed her soiled diaper. Catriona lay in the middle of the bed, kicking her legs.

Gerda pinched her nose. "Ah, Jarvia, for such a little one, Catriona creates a big stink."

"But her bowels are much firmer," Jarvia answered. She took the container and a spoon and sat down on the bed beside the baby. "And after a dose of this she will feel better."

"You are not going to have Isabel's tongue cut out, are you?" Gerda asked.

"Nay." Jarvia sighed and wiped dribbles of medicine from Catriona's chin. "I do not even know that such a custom exists anywhere."

Gerda moved closer to her friend and laid a hand on her shoulder. "You are frightened?"

"Aye."

" 'Twill be all right."

A bottle of milk in hand, Morag entered the sleeping chamber. "Shall I feed her?" she asked.

"Nay, I will," Jarvia answered. "The two of you help with the banquet preparations. I want nothing else to go wrong."

By the time Malcolm entered the Great Hall, Catriona was sleeping peacefully in her basket. Morag and several young girls were at the doors setting up the basin racks, tall poles with wrought iron circlets where basins of water could be set and towels could be hung.

Farther up the room, the High Table was set, a beautiful linen cloth that Jarvia had herself embroidered draped over it. Behind it were six chairs, all of them polished to a high sheen. On the table in front of each chair was a silver goblet, a platter, and a spoon.

Women servants sat in a corner around a table trimming lamps; men and boys set up trestle tables and benches down the length of the hall. Several girls, directed by Lucy, covered these with white table linens. More followed with the table settings. These included hand-carved and jewel-decorated wooden tankards, bowls, and spoons.

The odor of cooking food permeated the entire building.

A serving woman entered from the kitchen, a small cauldron in one hand, a spoon in the other. "This is the special sauce you wanted for the beef, mistress. Would you like to sample it?"

"Aye." Jarvia dipped the spoon into the thick gravy and touched the tip of the spoon to her lips. "Add a little more garlic and a tad of mustard. Did you make the mustard paste?"

The woman nodded.

"What about the boar's head with brawn pudding?"

"Doing well, as is the squirrel stew. The fruit tarts are tasty. Also, mistress, according to your instructions, the shellfish have been scented with jasmine, rosemary, and marigold."

"Good. Have Lucy check on the honey cakes."

When the servant departed, Jarvia looked around the room, trying to collect her thoughts and decide what she should do next. She had the feeling that she was being stared at. She turned to see Malcolm leaning against the door.

"My lord husband," she said, "I did not see you enter."

"Nay, lady, you have been busy." He walked toward her. "Is all going well?"

" 'Tis now," Jarvia answered. "Are you ready for your bath, lord?"

"Aye." He stripped off his gloves and mantle.

Jarvia clapped her hands. "Catriona is much better, but I fear Isabel has spread word through the village about her illness."

" 'Tis something we shall deal with if it arises."

"I think the proper phrase would be *when it arises*, lord." Jarvia moved to the High Table, where she moved the goblets, first to the right, then to the left, and finally back to their original positions. "I doubt those who advocate returning to the old ways will pass this opportunity to advance their point." Jarvia clapped her hands again, shouting, "Cleit, see that Lord Malcolm's tub is filled with water."

"Aye," the old man called.

Three bailers, all young lads, rushed out of the kitchen, carrying cauldrons of hot water; three more followed with pails of cold water. After them came two more boys, one carrying a bowl of soft soap made from mutton fat, wood ash, and soda, others carrying scented herbs and flowers.

"Are you going to bathe now, lady?" Malcolm asked.

"Nay, lord. I have more to do before everything will be ready for tonight. I have arranged for your parents and Sybil and Angus to join us at the High Table."

Malcolm nodded. "Also have Cleit set up two smaller tables and chairs in front of the dais. We may have unexpected guests tonight, and I will want them to have an honored position."

"Lucy," Jarvia called out, "get more platters for two extra tables."

Lucy's head bobbed around the kitchen door frame. "We have no more, lady."

Jarvia felt as if the weight of the world rested on her shoulders. Sybil had taunted her about proving her mettle, and she knew that tonight was her first big test. Everything must proceed smoothly; the food must be delectable and plentiful; the wine must flow freely all evening. A cool breeze blew through the building, and Jarvia was grateful for the open windows. At least the Great Hall would be cool.

"Look through my large chest of cooking utensils," Jarvia instructed. "I brought some beautiful hand-carved bowls with me. They should do well on these tables. Also, get Morag to search for my colored linens. They should add a touch of elegance and make these tables special."

"Aye, mistress. What about spoons and goblets?"

"You will find plenty of spoons," Jarvia said. "As far as the goblets, look for the jewel-inset drinking horns with gold filigree holders. Use them."

"Aye." Lucy bounded away.

While Malcolm took his bath, Jarvia continued supervising the meal. In part she kept herself busy because it allowed her little time to think about her troubles. She also did so because—as her mother-in-law had pointed out—she wanted to prove herself indispensable to her husband. True, Malcolm had made love to her last night after he had gone to see Sybil, had even told her that he needed her, but he had not admitted to more than letching for her. Needing someone was different from wanting someone, and wanting was different from loving.

At one time Jarvia had thought letching would be enough for her. When she had discovered it was not, she had entertained the hope that she could make Malcolm fall in love with her because she loved him. But she had given up that hope. Loving someone did not guarantee a return of that feeling.

Jarvia went to the large cauldron on the fire in the

kitchen. Many foods cooked in the huge kettle. She pulled out a large leather pouch, untied the thong, and tasted the pudding. It was not done. She tied off the bag and dropped it back into the boiling water. She checked on the container with the seven chickens. They were cooking nicely.

A spit had been erected over a smaller fire, where a lad using an old, wet archery target as a fire screen, tended roasting pigs. Attached to the frame beneath the meat was a long pan to catch the drippings.

Jarvia pinched off a piece of bread from one of the freshly baked loaves piled on the table. She dipped it into the hot liquid, then tasted it.

" 'Tis flavorful," she said.

"Aye, 'tis," the lad answered.

Jarvia raised a brow.

"To be sure, my lady," the boy quickly explained, "I've been tasting it all along to make sure it was properly seasoned."

Jarvia grinned. "To be sure." She pinched off another section of bread and daubed it in the pan. As she munched, she said, "Be sure to put many bowls of drippings on the table. I want everyone to have more than enough for sopping their bread."

"Aye, mistress," the lad answered, slowly turning the spit.

She took several steps, stopped, and turned back. "And, Keenan—"

"Aye?" He looked up.

"I shall depend on you to taste the drippings and occasionally the meat to make sure it is flavored properly."

Keenan grinned and bobbed his head. "Aye, mistress."

Satisfied that all was going well, Jarvia dropped her cooking towel over the pole rack by the kitchen door and returned to the Great Hall. Brushing perspiration-moistened tendrils of hair from her neck, she went to stand in front of one of the open windows. She closed her eyes and enjoyed the cool breeze.

The lur sounded. Then a second and a third time.

"Honored guests," Lucy yelled and ran to the door.

Malcolm, freshly attired, emerged from the sleeping chamber fastening the neck button of his shirt.

"Were you expecting someone in particular?" Jarvia asked.

"Celdun," he answered.

He and Jarvia stepped onto the porch and watched the company of warriors ride up the main street.

"Your friend?" she asked.

He shook his head. "Nay, 'tis not Celdun's colors. 'Tis Pict warriors."

Malcolm strode off the porch onto the pathway. He stopped when he reached the small gate that led to the inner yard of the Great Hall and held up a hand.

"Hail, Chief Fibh of Clan Ogilbinn of the Northern Picts."

The Pict warrior, a young man no older than Malcolm, pulled his pony to a stop. He answered in Gaelic. "Hail, Malcolm of Clan Duncan."

"You honor us with your presence. Welcome to my village and to the celebration of my marriage."

"I received your marker," Fibh replied, and Malcolm nodded. "I congratulate you on your marriage." He removed his helmet and brushed his gloved hand through his black hair. "Thank you for inviting us to share in your celebration and in the fox chase. To show how honored we are, we have brought you a special gift." He waved his hand, and two of his warriors dismounted.

Jarvia watched as they brought forth a wooden cage and set it in front of Malcolm.

"A silver fox," Fibh announced proudly.

Jarvia smiled and sighed her relief. One of her troubles was over. Now Sybil could no longer blame her for the lack of a prize fox.

"We caught him for you," the Pict warrior continued. "Now, Malcolm of Clan Duncan, 'twill be up to you to catch him for yourself if you intend to win the Highland sword."

"Thank you," Malcolm answered, and exchanged a knowing glance with Jarvia. "I am honored. Now my people will know that the gods are smiling on us." Malcolm put his arm around Jarvia's shoulder and drew her closer to him. "Chief Fibh, I want you to meet my wife, Princess Jarvia."

"Princess Jarvia," Fibh said.

"Chief Fibh," Jarvia said, and curtsied. "Welcome to our

home. Please enter and share our blessings with us."

Fibh nodded. "Where are my warriors to go?"

"To the Small Hall until we gather for the banquet later this evening," Malcolm answered, then called to one of the stable boys who had gathered at the gate. "Robbie, run to the Small Hall and tell Lachlann I wish to see him."

By the time Robbie returned with Lachlann, the Picts's ponies had been led to the stables.

"See to the comfort of Fibh's warriors," Malcolm instructed his best-man, "and notify my father, the ard-righ, that we have honored guests at the Great Hall."

"Aye."

"I am worried about these cattle raids, Malcolm," Fibh said. "Since I received your *ogham* marker, I have kept my eyes and ears open. I have seen and heard nothing from my people."

"But there is a traitor among us," Malcolm said.

Jarvia thought surely the gods were smiling on her. Catriona was greatly improved, and the feast was progressing beautifully. She had heard nothing but compliments on the foods she served, and the honored guests were indeed pleased when she presented them with the jewel-inset drinking horn and gold-filigree holders as gifts.

Sybil, sitting at the High Table with her parents, foster brother, and husband, glared throughout the banquet. She ate little, but drank plenty. Her goblet was never empty. Apprehensively, Jarvia kept her eyes on her. She did not doubt that Sybil would attempt to ruin the celebration; she only wondered *when*.

"The boar's head with brawn pudding is succulent," Chief Fibh declared. "Thank you for honoring me with such a worthy meal."

" 'Twas a worthy kill," Malcolm answered.

"By worthy warriors," Sybil added.

Jarvia tensed.

"Unlike many warriors whom we hear about," Sybil said, "our warriors hunt worthy kills."

Fibh laid his haunch of meat on his plate, wiped his hands on the cloth that hung from his neck, and rose. "Do I detect a deeper meaning to your words, *lady*?"

"Nay, *lord.*" Sybil also rose, braced her weight on the palms of her hands, and leaned forward to glare down at the Pict chieftain. "There is only one meaning, Fibh of the Picts. You and your warriors are not honorable."

"*Sybil!*" Fergus and Malcolm shouted in unison.

Fibh jerked the cloth from his neck and tossed it to the table. "You have insulted our honor, lady."

"My lord Fibh," Fergus said, "I apologize for my daughter's behavior."

"An apology does not retract the insult," Fibh declared.

"No apology is needed when truth is spoken," Sybil declared.

"Sybil," Fergus shouted, "cease speaking at once. You are placing the entire kingdom in jeopardy." The ard-righ turned to Angus. "Chief Angus, remove your wife immediately and see that she does not participate in any of the marriage festivities. Also you will give ten choice cows to Chief Fibh to pay for the insult your wife has cast upon him."

"My lady-wife and I shall leave the Great Hall," Angus stated, "but we shall not pay ten cattle to the Pict chief. Not when they have blatantly disregarded the peace treaties they negotiated with us and have raided deep within our territories. Not when they have killed defenseless women and children."

"My people are innocent of these charges," Fibh said. "We have honored our agreement with your people."

Fergus, breathing deeply, pressed a hand to his chest.

"Angus," he said, "take Sybil away."

"I shall leave, my father," she said, "but only because I refuse to be in the same building with dishonorable warriors." Sybil walked around the High Table, off the dais, and over to the Pict chief. "This is what I think of you." And she spit in his face.

Throughout the hall, warriors shifted toward their clan chiefs, hands resting on their weapons.

"Those who wish to return to the glory of the old ways," Sybil said, "follow me."

"Chiefs of the kingdom of Northern Scotland," Malcolm shouted, "you cannot walk out with Sybil and Angus without heaping dishonor upon yourself, by dishonoring your vows before God and to the other clan chiefs. Before you decide whether to follow Sybil and Angus, let us have a meeting of the Council of the Chiefs and discuss our problems. Let us see if we can resolve them without dishonor and bloodshed."

"Aye," Lonnie of Clan Galway shouted. "I want to return to the glory of the old ways, but I will not follow Sybil and Angus without meeting with the council first."

Slowly, reluctantly, the majority of the warriors agreed.

"We shall meet on the morrow after the chase," Fergus declared.

"Nay," Lonnie cried. "Not after the chase, my lord king, before the chase. This matter must be put to rest before we continue the celebration, before we sanction Malcolm's marriage with the Southerlander."

Ayes chorused through the Great Hall.

"My lords—" Fergus began, but Tindell interrupted.

"Chiefs of Northern Scotland, shall we have a show of hands over whether to hold the council meeting before the fox chase?"

All through the room clan chiefs raised their hands.

"So be it," Fergus said.

"My lady-wife and I take our leave," Angus announced.

"Halt," Tindell called out. "Ard-righ Fergus, all this day I have heard many people complain bitterly about your having given asylum to the orphan called Catriona. By show of hands, I would like to know the number of chiefs who would like to appeal your decision to the Council of Chiefs."

Fergus nodded. Hands rose all over the Great Hall.

"Count them aloud, Tindell," Fergus ordered. "If it be a majority, we shall concede to your request."

When Tindell had completed his count, he said, "We have a majority, my lord king. This subject shall be addressed by the Council of the Chiefs."

"So be it."

"We take our leave now, ard-righ," Angus said.

Fergus nodded again. As they walked out, he said, "My lord Chief Fibh, as a sign of my sincere regret for this unfortunate scene, I give to you ten head of my choice cattle and three of my best hounds."

Fibh nodded his acceptance. "I appreciate your generosity, Ard-righ Fergus."

Swaying forward slightly and bracing his hands on the table, Fergus took several deep breaths. "Chief Fibh, we would be honored if you and your warriors would join us . . ." He paused, again breathing with effort. "If you would join us for the . . . chase." Fergus clutched at his heart and slowly collapsed to the floor.

"Father!" Malcolm shouted, and rushed to the crumpled figure.

"Fergus!" Muireall, her face ashen, also fell to her knees beside the ard-righ.

Jarvia slipped past both Malcolm and Muireall. "Give him some fresh air," she ordered. After she examined him, she said, "Carry him to the sleeping chamber. I will care for him in there."

"Nay," Muireall said. "Take him to the guest house, where we are staying."

" 'Tis the curse," Tindell shouted, as people parted to let four of Malcolm's best-men carry Fergus out of the Great Hall. "The orphan has brought the curse of the Ancient Ones upon us."

"Malcolm has brought this trouble upon us by rescuing the orphan," the Galway chief shouted. "We are accursed until we take her back to her place of abandonment."

"Father!" Sybil ran into the Great Hall. Malcolm caught her, but Sybil twisted free.

"If my father dies," she shouted, "I shall hold you responsible, Malcolm mac Duncan. *I shall demand the death judgment from the Council of Chiefs!*"

Jarvia arrived at the guest house right behind Malcolm and his best-men. No sooner had they laid Fergus on the bed than Jarvia began unpacking her medicines and giving orders to the servants.

They banked the fire in the central hearth and suspended from the ceiling beam a large cauldron, which they filled with water. Among the vials and flagons arranged on a nearby table was a mortar and pestle. Painstakingly Jarvia measured her herbs and roots and ground them. On small wrought iron racks laid across the fire pit she prepared salves and pastes. These she spread over Fergus's chest, covering them with hot, wet cloths. She boiled herbs and roots and concocted potions.

Having arrived soon after Jarvia, Feich knelt beside the bed and chanted her magical spells. She hung talismans around the room. Muireall, having lit candles and placed them next to a wooden cross on the chest next to Fergus's bed, prayed for her husband. Malcolm paced back and forth, then finally left during the wee hours of the morning to quiet a ruckus that had erupted in the Great Hall among the chieftains.

Jarvia sat on the bed next to the king and coaxed several swallows of an herbal potion down his throat. When she had done all she knew to do, she left the house. Feich joined her.

Leaning against the exterior wall, Jarvia gazed toward the Great Hall. Through the open windows, she could see Malcolm standing in front of the High Table, talking quietly to the chieftains who were sitting before him. All seemed calm, but Jarvia knew tension ran high; it was tightly drawn like a bowstring. Anything could set it off.

"Is Fergus going to die?" she asked the old woman.

"Maybe not. Come with me."

"I need to check on Catriona," Jarvia said. How long ago it seemed since Fergus had collapsed. As she collected her medicine chest and supplies from the sleeping chamber in the Great Hall, Jarvia remembered that she had instructed Morag to keep Catriona with her for the night.

"Where is she?" Feich asked.

"With Morag."

"She is safe. Leave her. Now, mistress, if we are to save Malcolm we must save the king."

With no further argument, Jarvia followed the old woman out of the village. When they reached a clearing on the side of the mountain, Feich sat down and removed her shoes.

"Do the same," she ordered. When Jarvia was standing in her bare feet, Feich said, "Close your eyes."

Jarvia did as she was told.

"Breathe deeply," Feich said, dropping her voice. "One. Two. Three." She continued to count, getting slower and slower.

When Jarvia was completely relaxed, she heard Feich say, "You feel energy, the life force, pulsing through your body."

"Aye," Jarvia murmured.

"Visualize a white light filling your body. It will enter the top of your head and slowly move down, out your feet and up again, circling your body."

Jarvia nodded.

"This is the light of healing. Now direct the energy down, through the soles of your feet into the earth below."

When Jarvia was completely calm, Feich instructed her to lie down on the ground with her eyes closed, her legs apart, her arms outstretched in line with her shoulders. Her palms lay flat on the ground, and her head was pointed toward the east.

She breathed deeply, and again following the Wise Woman's instructions, she sensed the energy of the earth. She breathed deeply; she listened. Finally she felt it pulsing; she heard the deep, sonorous throb of Nature. She allowed herself to flow with the beat. She breathed and merged into the white light.

"Repeat after me," Feich ordered.

Jarvia did. "Mother Earth, I know not the names of the gods of the Scots, but they know you, as I know you. You have given life to all of us. Please let your life-giving energy flow through me. Let my light be stronger than the darkness of Sybil's magic."

"When you feel as if you are being absorbed by the energy of the earth, imagine that you can see Fergus," Feich said. "Picture him clearly lying beside you in the same exact position."

"Aye."

"Now direct the light into him," Feich said.

Jarvia tried again . . . and again.

"I cannot," she cried. "I keep losing him."

"Try again," Feich commanded. "Concentrate. Breathe deeply and relax." Softly the old woman talked. "Sybil is stirring the waters, my child, but you are stronger than she is. You are the one the gods have ordained to be Malcolm's wife, to be the mother of the child."

Jarvia felt the sting of tears.

"Relax," Feich said, her voice low and soothing. "Visualize the healing light as it flows through you into Fergus."

Breathing deeply, feeling the coolness of the night about her, Jarvia imagined the energy flowing through her. She remembered how pale Fergus had looked lying in the bed. She visualized Malcolm lifting his father in his arms and bringing him to the meadow. He laid him down beside Jarvia, then looked at her and smiled.

"My lady-wife," he said, "I have confidence in you."

Then . . . and only then . . . Jarvia imagined the radiant flow of golden light leaving her body and entering Fergus's.

"I did it!" she cried. "I did it, Feich. I see the white light—the healing energy—entering his body."

"Aye. What else do you see?"

"I see Fergus smiling at Muireall." *I see Malcolm smiling at me.*

Slowly Jarvia let the energy leave her body. She lay in the meadow, gazing up at the star-studded sky.

" 'Tis time for us to return," Feich said.

"Is Fergus healed?"

"If he wishes to be."

The women put their shoes on and made their way back to the village. When they entered the king's house, Malcolm stood at the door to the sleeping chamber.

"Where have you been?" he asked, his face drawn with worry.

"She has been taking care of your father," Feich replied curtly. "How is he?"

"He regained consciousness, but he is yet weak," Malcolm answered.

"All of you leave me," Feich said. "I shall stay the night with him."

"I shall stay with you," Jarvia said.

The old woman shook her head. "Nay, lass, 'tis something that I must do alone."

"Please," Jarvia said.

Moving to her side, Malcolm laid an arm across her shoulders. "Come," he said. "Feich knows what she is doing. It is time for you to be abed."

She nodded. Her exhaustion catching up with her, she wilted against him. "Sorry," she mumbled. "I did not know how tired I was."

Malcolm swept her into his arms and carried her out of the guest house, across the village to the Great Hall. When he reached their sleeping chamber, Magda rose and sniffed them. Satisfied, she returned to her pallet in the corner. Malcolm laid Jarvia on the bed and stretched out beside her. Her silver hair, glimmering delicately in the firelight, flowed over the bed cushion.

"Thank you," she murmured.

He brushed tendrils of hair from her face. "Go to sleep, lady."

"What about Catriona?"

"She is sleeping soundly in Morag's hut, and Sorcha has agreed to suckle her."

"Sorcha is not afraid of the Ancient Ones?"

"Nay. She wanted me to tell you that she is grateful for your having saved Brian's leg. You gave life to her husband; she will give it to our child."

Although Jarvia felt as if she were drained of energy, she pushed up on the bed.

Malcolm shoved her back down. "What are you doing?"

"I have something for you," she said, and sat up again.

"It can wait."

"Nay, 'tis something I want you to have now." She slid off the bed and went to a storage chest. Opening it, she withdrew a pair of gloves. "These are yours."

He took them.

"New ceremonial gloves," she said. "I fashioned them from the skins of the animals you slew while we were yet in Southerland. They are blessed and have great magic, both mine and yours. I was going to give them to you as a gift during our Scottish marriage ceremony, but I want you to have them now."

Malcolm brushed his thumb over the soft leather. He turned them over, studying them. As neat and beautiful as the tight stitches that held the leather together was the decorative embroidery in orange and yellow floss—a flaming torch. He looked at her.

"For my lord of fire," she said, and brushed her hands through her hair. "They will bring you luck during the chase and during the hearing before the Council of the Chiefs."

Few times in his life could Malcolm remember having been humbled. He felt so now. "Thank you, my lady-wife." Laying the gloves on the bed, he rose and took her in his arms.

"Malcolm, all will go well before the council, will it not?"

"Aye."

"I did not wish to bring harm to you and your people."

"You did not, my lady-wife. This is an instance when life gave us no choice. Now we face the consequences of what we did proudly and with a clear conscience."

"I have spoken the words in judgment many times," Jarvia confessed, "but right now, I do not like the way '*proudly*' and '*with a clear conscience*' sit on my shoulders." She felt the warm bite of tears. "I know our marriage was based on convenience, lord, but I . . . I have come to love you."

He looked at her for a long time before he said, "My lady, I have a tender feeling for you, and I wish I could say that I love you, but I do not, cannot, profess love."

Jarvia laid her hand gently over his mouth. "Nay, lord, do not apologize. One cannot offer what one does not feel."

"Love, lady, is an emotion that has eluded me all these years." With his thumb he wiped her tears away.

"Mayhap you have eluded it, lord."

"Mayhap." He kissed her lightly on the forehead. "I do promise, lady, that you will not lose me or the baby. I am your protector and shall remain so. I have a plan to save Catriona if the council should decree that she must be returned to the place of abandonment."

"What about you, Malcolm?" The tears spilled down her cheeks. "Sybil is not going to rest until you are out of the way. Have you a plan for yourself?"

He spoke in a soft and soothing voice. "I have no intention of dying soon, lady. I have many promises yet to keep, many desires to fulfill, many more trips to take to bliss . . . with you." He smiled so tenderly at her that Jarvia felt as if she would melt. "Now, my lady-wife, will you get in bed and rest?"

A smile trembled on her lips. "Aye."

Chapter 26

❧

Clouds gathered in the night sky, completely closing out the moon and stars. Standing on the side of the mountain outside the cave above Malcolm's village, Sybil gazed down at the tents and pavilions that had been erected all around the palisades. Among all the temporary dwellings, hers stood out; it was by far the grandest. Even in the firelight she could distinguish her colors.

She heard a noise in the bushes behind her.

"I expected you sooner, Ghaltair," she said.

She now wore a leathern loincloth and a short tunic that scarcely covered her breasts. A leathern girdle circled her waist, and dangling from it was a long gold chain. Knowing Ghaltair followed, she walked to the back of the cave. When they stood in a small room, he took off his helmet. Candles set in niches in the walls cast a golden glow. She poured two goblets of wine.

"Is all well?" she asked.

"Aye, the trap is set. On his way to Malcolm's village Celdun will intercept the message stick that will convict Malcolm, just as you planned."

"One way or another, Malcolm will be disgraced and die."

"We do have a problem," he said. "The old outrider has become suspicious of me."

Taking a swallow of wine, Sybil raised a brow.

"He overheard me setting up the plan to have Celdun intercept the message stick. I suspect he has been following me."

"You are not as careful as you ought to be, Ghaltair," Sybil muttered. "Your carelessness irritates me."

She brought him a goblet of wine. "You know what you will have to do?" When he nodded, she said, "Then do it, and leave no evidence behind. Let no one know you are the culprit."

"Aye." He gazed into her dark, sultry eyes. Even lamplight could not diminish their beauty, their promise of pleasure. As always when he looked at her, his body responded. Even now he could see her gaze moving to the crotch of his trousers. She reveled in her power to arouse him, as did he. Yet it angered and humiliated him to know that she had this effect on all men.

"Where is Angus?" he asked.

"Are you still angry that I married him?"

"There was no need," he grumbled. "Why couldn't you have waited just a little while longer?"

She moved closer to him.

"I almost did not come," he said.

"But you did."

Always he did.

"While I was out riding tonight, I saw Berowalt and his retinue headed for the village," Ghaltair said.

"I expected he would return."

"Malcolm is already investigating Berowalt's report of his capture and torture. It will not be long before he knows for sure that his clansmen are not guilty of the crime."

"And that I am." Sybil's husky laughter filled the cave. "He can guess all he wants to, but he cannot prove anything." She dipped her finger into her wine and ran it over Ghaltair's lips. "Are you afraid, my love?"

Ghaltair trembled with need for her. "How can you call me your love," he exclaimed, "when you married Angus, when you tried to get Malcolm to make love to you?"

"So you were eavesdropping earlier the other evening, my young one. You were supposed to be hunting the silver fox." Again Sybil laughed. "Because I killed the other one. It does look like bad magic is following Malcolm, and 'twill not be long before others tire of it."

"Malcolm's wife was watching also," Ghaltair said, goading Sybil.

"Good," she drawled. "She is going to be more difficult to control than Hilda was."

"Aye, she is a different kind of woman." Ghaltair quaffed down the contents of his goblet. "You will not convince Princess Jarvia of Malcolm's evil, as you did Hilda. You will not persuade her to get rid of her child, should she conceive, or to end her own life."

"Do not lay all the blame for Hilda's corruption on me, my love. You were there to encourage Hilda, were you not?"

Ghaltair did not answer.

"I take it you have forged no friendship with Jarvia."

"Nay." He spat out the word, burning with humiliation when he remembered how she had dared shout at him, dared give him an order.

Sybil laid her hand on his arm. "You are tense, love. Are you thinking about the time she rescued the child and the wolf?"

"She shouted at me," he said between clenched teeth. "She, a woman of Southerland, once a slave, shouted an order at me, and Malcolm defended her."

"He humiliated you in front of the entire company," Sybil said, goading him.

"Nay, 'tis not Malcolm's way, but when he took me aside to talk to me, to tell me he would kill me if I acted so disrespectfully to his wife again, everyone knew what was happening. Everyone began dancing attendance on *Princess Jarvia*. Especially Brian."

"I thought Brian would be out of our way by now. You did promise me, Ghaltair."

"He would have been, but Jarvia saved him."

Ghaltair ran his finger around the rim of his wine goblet. " 'Twas not hard getting Brian to search for the pony in the area where the boar farrowed, and once she charged, there was so much confusion I had no problem unseating Brian from the pony."

"No one can point a finger of blame at you?" Sybil asked.

"Nay, 'twas only Brian, Lachlann, and I. Brian's pony stumbled, and Lachlann rode to the side and in front of him. I was behind on the other side of Brian. I kicked his foot to unbalance him. Later he thought the pony had pushed him against a nearby tree. By the time Lachlann and I fended off the boar, Brian's leg was badly wounded. I had not counted on the Southerlander having such a knowledge of herbs and medicine, Sybil."

"Did you not have the vial of powder that I gave you?" she asked.

"Aye, and when neither Lachlann nor Brian was looking, I was able to sprinkle some of the poison on the open wound. Later I was able to put some on one of his bandages. But after that either Jarvia or that old woman servant of hers stayed with Brian." He shrugged. "In this case, Sybil, Jarvia's magic seems to be stronger than yours. Brian sings her praises because his wound has healed and he has no limp."

"Never say that woman's magic is stronger than mine!" Sybil shrieked. " 'Tis your fault! You did not perform your tasks well." Deep in thought, Sybil paced around the cave. "I hate Jarvia of Southerland!"

Her anger and jealousy of Jarvia filled Ghaltair with a certain amount of satisfaction. "She is going to be a thorn in our side," he said.

"Then we shall have to remove her, Ghaltair."

"Aye." He picked up the wine jug from the trestle table. As he refilled his goblet, he looked at the huge and numerous chests stacked against the cave wall and smiled.

With a smile Sybil followed his gaze, then lifted her goblet. "To a job well done, love."

Ghaltair threw back his head and laughed. "Ah, 'twas that, wasn't it, Sybil. We took great pride in being sea raiders. We left only one alive to tell the tale."

"That Malcolm mac Duncan stole back the rupture endowment from Lord Lang. He will always believe Lachlann is the man he saw."

"Aye." Again Ghaltair laughed, the memory of his raid rushing through him with the same power it had the day he and his men had attacked Lang's ship. "We made sure the Northlanders heard us use Malcolm's and Lachlann's names several times."

Sybil moved closer to the stash of goods and ran her fingers over a copper-and-jewel-inlaid helmet. She moved her hand to an ornate long sword—also decorated in copper and jewels—lying next to it. Ghaltair followed to stand behind her.

"An exact replica of Lachlann's helmet and his Highland sword," he boasted. "I wore both myself along with a tartan bearing the Duncan's colors. And it was I who wounded Lang's emissary—a man called Ragnar. I made sure he would recognize the helmet, the sword, and Malcolm's colors, should he ever see them again."

"No one will ever suspect us," Sybil said. "Not even my *dearly beloved husband*. Soon Lord Lang will sail into the Highlands and demand revenge. He will kill both Malcolm and Lachlann." Sybil's hand curled tightly around her goblet. "I live for the day when I shall rule over all of Northern Scotland."

"Until then, Sybil," Ghaltair said, "we should be more careful about our meetings. You are now married to Angus, and I would not have Malcolm learn that I am—"

"We shall have to meet," she said softly. "You have things I want, Ghaltair, that I must have." She dropped her goblet to the floor. The wine puddled before it seeped slowly into the hardened dirt. She moved closer to him, took his own goblet from him and tossed it away. She began to unfasten his weapon belt.

Ghaltair caught her hands to stop her. She laughed and pulled away; he let her. Always his body played traitor where Sybil was concerned. She laid the weapons aside. "Not now, love. You have no worry. No one will come."

A faint smile played about her mouth as she pulled his tunic from his trousers and pushed it over his head. With a rustle it fell to the ground.

"You are so handsome." Her eyes darkened with passion; her hands roved hotly over him. "I cannot live without you."

Even now, knowing what kind of woman she was, Ghaltair ached for her; his body responded quickly, fully.

It was all he could do to keep from ripping the short, sleeveless tunic and loincloth from her body. Her smooth skin, baked to a golden bronze by the sun, was oiled and sleek. He knew how glorious it would be without clothing to mar its flawless perfection. How it would glisten in the lamplight. How it would taste.

But she always wanted to be the aggressor. He allowed her that because she gave him exquisite pleasure. Never in his life had he tasted anything so delectable as Sybil. The ache in his groin intensified.

Her hair was pulled tightly back from her head, held by a leathern thong at the nape of her neck. Long gold earrings dangled from her ears. Matching armbands circled her forearms and wrists. Dangling from the leathern girdle about her waist was a long gold chain.

"What about Angus?" he asked, knowing his husky voice betrayed his passion for her.

"What about Angus?"

He heard the smile in her voice.

Ghaltair wondered how long it would be before Sybil tired of him and looked for another lover, before she worshiped another warrior's body, teaching him the many and varied secrets of passion. Jealousy, and a fear of losing her, gripped him.

"Do you say words like this to him also?"

"Be content with what I say to you," she said.

Her hands traveled from his stomach up to his chest, rubbing across his nipples as they went. They stopped, and she scored his nipple with her fingernail. Desire streaked from his chest straight to his groin. His manhood strained against his tight trousers.

She leaned closer to him. Her lips touched the gold medallion hanging on the chain about his neck. Then she kissed the skin below the chain on either side of the medallion. She slid her hands to his girdle, her fingers slipping beneath it.

"Have you ever played these kinds of games with Angus?" he asked.

"Angus has never played games in his life. He has always been true to the code of the warrior." A nasty smile twisted Sybil's lips. "That is why he is so important to us and our cause." She pressed her lips softly against Ghaltair's and whispered, "Now let us cease talking, my love. I want you. And you want me. Now."

Again she scored his nipple with her long fingernail, then touched the tip of her tongue to the flat nubbin. Ghaltair's face constricted with passion. He was about to lose control, and that is what Sybil wanted.

"You, Ghaltair, are young and beautiful, and your life is just beginning." She dipped her hand in scented oil and brushed it over his smooth chest. "Look at you gleam in the lamplight."

No woman worshiped a man's body as Sybil did.

"I am so glad you have no hair to mar its beauty."

She rubbed his chest with both hands; she encircled his body, pulling him close, and ran her hands up and down his spine. Each movement sent her hands deeper into the back of his trousers, her oiled fingers slipping easily over his buttocks, between them. Her breasts, covered in soft leather, rubbed against his chest.

"As I have taught you the secrets of your body and mine," she crooned, "I shall teach you about life. I have always loved younger men."

She dropped to her knees, her mouth brushing down the smooth contours of his chest and stomach to the leathern girdle about his waist. Sybil rubbed her cheek against the leather, over the gold buckles. She tilted back her head, her red hair pooling about her legs and feet. With the tip of her tongue she traced the outline of her lips.

Putting her arms around him, cupping his buttocks, she drew him closer to her. She pressed her cheek against his thigh and felt his hardness.

"I want you." She ran a hand over his other leg.

Still kneeling in front of him, she unbuckled his girdle and pulled it aside. She caught the waistband of his trousers and pulled them down to reveal his turgid arousal. She leaned back to gaze at him.

"Your endowment is magnificent," she murmured.

"Sybil—" he groaned. "We should not be doing this. What if someone should—"

"No one will," Sybil repeated.

"All the lies we told, Sybil, all the deceptions," Ghaltair murmured. "Lying to Angus and murdering his wife, turning him against his best friend, stealing cattle from our own people and killing them in the process."

Ghaltair stopped talking and shook his head.

"Angus will not live much longer," Sybil said. "I promise you. Since he has declared me his best-man, I will rule after he is gone. You and I, Ghaltair, can be married. You will be chief of Clan Kinsey. Be patient. One day you shall be chief of Clan Duncan, then ard-righ."

She touched his engorged member.

"Now, my love, I shall show you pleasure such as you have never experienced . . . not even with me."

*   *   *

Malcolm stood in front of the open window and watched the storm clouds swirl against the graying morning sky. His foster father slept on the bed, his mother on a pallet on the floor beside him. Feich sat in a corner surrounded by her amulets and talismans. All over the room lamps and candles flickered. The bed creaked, and Malcolm turned.

"Is it still night?" Fergus asked.

Malcolm stepped closer to the bed. "Nay, it is only dark because the sky is overcast. We are going to have a spring storm."

As if to accent his words, a flash of lightning streaked across the skies, and thunder cracked.

"Where is your mother?"

"Asleep on the floor beside you."

"Awake now, my lord." Muireall sat up and brushed the hair from her face. "How are you feeling?"

Fergus inhaled deeply. "I'm tired, my lady. Extremely tired." He closed his eyes and lay still for a few minutes. "Fibh . . . Malcolm, did you correct the insult to him?"

"Aye. I gave him ten of my choice cows, five oxen, and three Highland ponies."

Fergus smiled weakly. "That was an expensive insult."

"Aye."

Muireall sat on the bed beside her husband. Reaching into the basin on the nearby chest, she wrung out a cloth and gently wiped his face.

"The council meeting," Fergus said. "I must get ready."

"Nay," both Muireall and Malcolm said together.

"Until such time as I am removed from my office," Fergus said, his voice strong with purpose, "I am ard-righ of the kingdom of Northern Scotland. I will preside over the meeting."

"My lord," Muireall said, her voice teary, "if you are not careful, you will not be presiding over anything. Your body is weak; it can only endure so much."

"Mother is right, Fergus," Malcolm put in.

"I must preside," Fergus said. "Tensions are too high. Sybil and Angus have agitated our chieftains until they are on the bank of rebellion."

"The chiefs are worried and think returning to the old

ways will bring stability back to their lives, but they are not fools," Malcolm said. "They will listen to reason, Father."

"You hope." Fergus sighed. He grabbed the washcloth from Muireall's hand and tossed it to the floor. "I want to rise from this bed and get dressed."

"Fergus," Muireall pleaded, "please do—"

"You may help me, lady," he said, "or get out of my way."

Muireall rose. "I shall help you, husband."

Slowly Fergus shoved up in the bed and sat for a few minutes as he marshaled his strength. "My son, have you dressed for the meeting?"

"Nay."

"It is time you did so." Fergus swung his legs to the floor and rose unsteadily. Both Malcolm and Muireall stood poised to catch him if he fell. Without help he regained his balance. "Are you ready to answer any charges that will be brought against you?"

"Aye."

"Then be on your way," Fergus ordered. He turned to the old woman who huddled in the corner. "Feich, thank you for your incantations and magical spells, but it is time you were gone. I have much to do."

Malcolm crossed the room and lowered his hand to the old woman. She laid her palm in his and let him help her to her feet.

"Aye," she said, " 'tis time, Fergus."

Malcolm led her from the room. When they opened the front door of the guest house, they were greeted by a gust of wind. Feich stepped onto the small porch, held a gnarled hand above her eyes, and peered at the storm's blackness.

"We are going to have a genuine tempest today," she announced. "The turbulence is in keeping with the attitude of the village." She stepped away from Malcolm and headed toward her house. "But once it is over, the world will be cleaner . . . and better."

"Good day, Feich," Malcolm called to the retreating figure.

"Good day, Malcolm. The gods are with you and your lady."

Worried about his father's health and the fate of the kingdom if Fergus should not be able to rule, Malcolm slowly
walked to the Great House, but he did not immediately
enter. He circled to the back and leaned against the corral
fencing. He heard footfalls. It was a man, he could tell, but
he did not turn.

"Good day, Malcolm," Lachlann said.

"Good day."

"At early morn Chief Fibh chose his oxen, cattle, and
ponies. Soon afterwards he and his warriors departed."

"I heard them," Malcolm replied. "With so much unrest
and open hostility, Fibh was wise to leave."

"Sybil and Angus have spent the night agitating the
chiefs. She is trying to convince them that whether her
father lives or dies, his condition is your fault. She is
pressing for your death, Malcolm."

"I am not so easily killed," Malcolm answered. "And I
am not worried about myself. I am accustomed to facing
death, am resolved to accept it honorably at my appointed
time. But I fear for Jarvia's safety. She is a brave woman,
but she is not accustomed to our land or our ways. Without
me she will be alone."

Malcolm turned to his best-man, to his best friend.

"I failed in my duty to her," he said. "She is my wife,
and my first duty is to protect her."

"You made a grave mistake in allowing her to rescue the
child," Lachlann agreed.

"Nay, I do not regret having saved the child, but I should
have put the welfare of my people above my wife's soft
heart. I should have insisted that we give the baby to a
peasant family to raise as their own. As heir to the throne
of Northern Scotland, I had no right to foster the child.
My irresponsibility contributed to the growing unrest in the
kingdom."

"Do not be so hard on yourself, Malcolm. A man has
tender feelings for the woman he loves, and makes soft
judgments where she is concerned."

Tender feelings. Woman he loves. Soft judgments. Phrases
Malcolm would not have thought could apply to him. He
had prided himself on remaining emotionally detached. He
enjoyed carnal pleasures, but had never allowed his heart

to be won. Until now. Until Jarvia. And indulging her by allowing her to keep the child might now cost her all that she held dear.

About that time a stable lad led the ponies out of the stables and loosed them in the corral. Malcolm put his fingers to his mouth and whistled. Dhubh-righ pricked his ears forward and trotted over to his master.

He nuzzled Malcolm's shirt, searching for a treat.

"If the council should decree death for my actions, I have the right to make a death request of them, one they cannot refuse by law."

"Aye."

Malcolm rubbed the stallion's forehead and fed him grass.

"I shall ask them to grant Jarvia sanctuary and to see that all terms of our marriage contract are honored."

Lachlann nodded.

"But that is not enough. There will be those who want my wife dead." Malcolm turned to Lachlann. "I ask that you become Jarvia's champion, her protector. There are those who will protest, but in front of the council I will also give Gerda to you as wife."

Lachlann's face brightened.

"I did not guess amiss, my friend?" Malcolm asked.

"Nay, I have tender thoughts for Gerda."

"And her child?"

"Aye, I shall adopt the child."

Malcolm nodded. "Jarvia is Gerda's legal sister, so then, my friend, it becomes your obligation to protect her . . . as well as Gerda."

"I will," Lachlann promised.

"To the death." Blue eyes burned into golden brown ones.

Quick came Lachlann's pledge. "To my death."

"I ask an ever greater favor of you. Take care of the child."

"Catriona?"

"Aye, I have baptized her and given her my name. She is my ward, my fostered child. It is my duty to protect her. With me out of the way, many will see her as a threat. Like Jarvia's, her life will be in danger."

"If judgment goes against you," Lachlann said, "the

child will be returned to the place where we found her."

"Nay, I will save the child."

The lur sounded.

"The meeting of the chiefs will begin soon," Lachlann said.

"Aye, 'tis time for me to dress."

"I wish you well, my chief. My friend."

The two men looked at each other for a long time. The lur sounded a second time. They embraced tightly, then without a word, Lachlann turned and walked away. Malcolm stood for a moment longer, staring out across the meadow beyond the corral.

He closed his eyes and leaned his head against a post. All he could see was a woman with forest green eyes and silver hair. He was surrounded by her laughter and her goodness. He wanted her. Aye, with every fiber in his body. More, he wanted to protect and to cherish her, to take care of her.

In memory he saw her holding the baby, Catriona, to her bosom. The same warmth and wonder he had felt whenever he saw her suffused his body. Jarvia had looked so soft and motherly. Even now Malcolm could not describe his wonder, his joy at the images.

No price was too high to pay for his wife's and his baby's lives. He must convince the council to spare Jarvia and Catriona.

"Malcolm."

He imagined Jarvia calling his name.

"My lord husband."

She *was* speaking. He turned to see her coming toward him, clad in a long and flowing yellow tunic, the pleated kind worn by Southerland women. Her silver hair, glimmering in the morning light, flowed over her shoulders and down her back. Her green eyes sparkled. Her rosy lips smiled.

"You did not waken me," she chided.

"Nay, I wanted you to rest."

The light filtered through the sheer material to silhouette her figure and remind Malcolm of her sweetness and goodness.

"How is your father?"

"Weak, but better," Malcolm replied, then told her what Fergus was planning to do.

"Do not worry," Jarvia told him. "He is a strong man."

She reached him and laid a hand on his chest. Warmth turned to fire and burned Malcolm to the core of his being, resurrecting all those sensations that only Jarvia could evoke.

"Did you plan to attend the council meeting without me, lord?"

"It might be better if you were not there to hear their accusations."

"That is not to be," Jarvia said. "We must face them together, lord."

She leaned forward to press her breasts against him as her lips lightly touched his. He folded his arms around her and crushed her to him.

"My lord husband, I cannot get enough of the taste of you."

"Ah, my lady-wife, I fear my hunger for you can never be assuaged."

She locked her arms around his neck.

"The letching." Jarvia strewed kisses over his face. "It is not soon to run its course."

"Lady, letching is like the small stream that comes only with the rain and dries up quickly."

The wind blew strongly, enveloping them in his tartan and her tunic skirt.

"What I feel for you is like the sea that surrounds all the kingdoms of this land," she said. "It will never run dry. Yea, it flows deep and rich."

Their mouths touched, each giving, each taking equally. Passion flared between them, but neither had the desire to mate. They hungered only to hold each other, to know the warmth of their embrace, the security of their shared desires.

Malcolm pulled his mouth from hers and buried his face in the sweet curve of her neck and shoulder. He inhaled her fragrance.

"Strawberry water," he murmured.

"Aye." Tilting her head, she gazed into his face. Her eyes sparkled like green jewels. "I have sunken low, my lord husband. I will do almost anything to keep you in my bed." *To bring you into my heart.*

Malcolm's arms tightened around her. "My sweet, sweet Jarvia. I feel the same about you. If this is letching, I letch for you. If it is caring, I care."

Her face pressed against his chest, she mumbled, "If it is loving, my lord, I love you."

"Aye, my lady-wife."

For a moment the sparkle in her eyes dimmed, then the shadow passed.

He pulled away. "I must give instructions to my best-men. I shall return to the hall shortly."

"Where will the meeting convene?"

"Normally at the Grand Rostrum," Malcolm answered, his gaze going to the darkened sky. "But with the coming storm, we shall meet in the Great Hall."

"I shall be ready," Jarvia said. She gave Malcolm a quick kiss and hurried to the Great Hall.

Jarvia stood by the cradle set near the High Seat of the Great Hall and looked at the sleeping babe. How contented Catriona had been since she had begun suckling from Sorcha's breasts. Mayhap this was the only child she and Malcolm would ever have. She recalled her words to Malcolm the night he had asked her to be his second wife, when she had sworn never to bear him a son.

Mayhap the gods had heard her and would make true her words. Many times during their brief marriage, she had repented of the hasty promise. Feich had said she would conceive Malcolm's child, but what if she did not? The thought frightened as well as saddened her.

Morag took Catriona with her, Magda following. Jarvia went to find Malcolm. She could not bear to be away from him, not for even a second.

She found him in the bathhouse, sitting in a tub of water. She knelt beside him.

"If I remember correctly, my husband, you said that bathing and rubbing your body would be part of my wifely duties."

"Hmm, so I did."

She loved it when his voice dropped to that low, husky timbre. He touched the tip of her breast with his wet finger. She sucked in a breath. The thin fabric soaked up the water

to become transparent and adhere to her like another layer
of flesh. Her nipple puckered and thrust out. The soap slid
from her hand into the water. She began to search for it.

"I would not be remiss in my wifely duties," she murmured. Her hand closed around his manhood.

He caught her head and guided her lips to his. "I would
not have you be remiss."

He was out of the water.

She was out of her clothes.

They lay naked on the wooden bench, their bodies wet
and shining from the steam that filled the room. His mouth
was heavy and full, his skin flushed. Passion glittered in his
blue eyes. Jarvia wondered how she had ever thought them
cold and hard. His gaze was like liquid fire.

Malcolm reached out to crush her hair in his hands. Jarvia
kissed his chest. He groaned, and she felt the quiver of
his flesh beneath her mouth. Her lips made their way to
one nipple. She rubbed her tongue over it. Malcolm made
an inarticulate sound, and his fingers clenched even more
tightly in her hair, tugging at her scalp. Jarvia felt the prick
of pain, but it was sweet and heady. It made the taste of his
flesh against her tongue even more enjoyable.

"The first time I saw you, you stirred my blood. I thought
it only letching." He kissed her hard, passionately. "Now
you stir my heart, and I know it is loving."

"Oh, Malcolm!"

He kissed her again, as deeply, as richly.

"I love you, Jarvia."

Springs of joy bubbled within her. Jarvia thought surely she would drown from sheer pleasure. She could only
repeat, "Oh, Malcolm."

She kissed his mouth, his cheeks, his entire face.

She laughed. They laughed together.

No moment in Jarvia's life had been so sweet, so perfectly wonderful.

They held each other close.

He loved her. She loved him.

"You love me," she whispered over and over.

"I love you," he repeated, somehow sensing that she
needed to hear the words again. "And this morn, my lady-
wife, I am taking you in love."

Once more he played with her breast until she was arching up to him, lost in passion, caught in the delirium of happiness brought about by his confession. Malcolm lowered his head and took her nipple into his mouth. Jarvia gasped as delight so exquisite it was almost pain flooded through her body.

He loved her.

Malcolm sucked her breast, his tongue circling and lashing the nipple. His mouth widened hungrily, and he suckled hard and deep.

He loved her.

Everything would be all right.

Jarvia almost sobbed aloud as desire seared through her and set up a throbbing between her legs. Even this intensified, and she moved restlessly, seeking fulfillment.

Although they had made love recently, he felt like a starved man released upon a banquet. He could not get enough of her, of touching, tasting, loving. His mouth moved to her other breast and began to caress it. He murmured her name against her skin, his hand seeking out and finding her femininity. She was ready for him. Excited, he slid his fingers into the hot, wet place between her thighs.

Jarvia moved against his touch. She stretched out a hand to caress his manhood, to clasp it gently and give him the same pleasure he was giving her. Malcolm groaned and rolled over, pulling Jarvia beneath him.

Her legs fell open. He slid into her and began to thrust. Jarvia matched his movements. Their rhythm sent their sensations burning out of control. They moved together in a desperate frenzy. Pushing. Demanding. Taking. Giving . . . until at last the passion burst deep within them, pulsating through their bodies in a final wild and enervating fulfillment.

Jarvia wrapped her arms tightly around him. Malcolm shuddered as his seed poured into her, as she lovingly received it. Gasping for air, he collapsed against her, drained of all energy and afloat in a haze of spent passion. Jarvia buried her face in his shoulder and held on to him.

It was a long time before Malcolm rolled onto his side, his hand still resting on Jarvia's stomach. His other arm pillowed his head. He smiled at her, lazy, exhausted, and utterly content. He leaned over and lightly kissed her shoulder.

"I would that I were carrying our child," she murmured. "A son who looks like you."

"Or a daughter who looks like you."

Jarvia raised up on an elbow. "A daughter?"

"Aye, *after* we have a son. I would be remiss in my kingly duties, lady, if I did not provide a future chief."

Jarvia smiled and ran her finger over his lips. "That is your only reason for wanting children, sire?"

He captured her fingers with his teeth. "Nay, my love, I would have a daughter with forest green in her eyes and moonbeams in her hair. I would have my wife's daughter to love and to cherish."

They laughed, but as they looked into each other's eyes, the laughter faded with the sheer joy of being. He lowered his head, his lips barely touching hers.

"I love you, Jarvia," he whispered raggedly. "I love you."

Jarvia's heart swelled with happiness. He was such a hard, even stern, man so much of the time. She had seen him unbending, sharp, and unrelenting. It made his gentle confession and tender touch even more special.

"Malcolm"—her words were a heartrending groan—"I am so afraid. We have just now found each other. I cannot bear to lose you."

"That first night that we talked, that night in Southerland in my sleeping chamber, I told you that birth and death are the cycle of life. For some it is a longer circle than for others. We do not know when our life has run its full course."

"If I should lose you," she said, "I will not have even a part of you. We have Catriona, but I have not a child of our loins, a child of the land."

She began to cry, the dry racking sobs of someone for whom tears did not come easily.

"Long ago I said I would never give you a baby," she sobbed. "But I did not mean it. I think perhaps the gods may punish me. Mayhap, my lord, I shall not conceive your child."

"Nay," he whispered. "The gods are not so petty, love."

She wrapped her arms around him and leaned her head against his chest and cried out all her frustrations and confusions. Soothingly Malcolm's hand traveled over her head and back while the other held her tightly to him. He curled around her protectively, resting his cheek against her hair.

"I promised you a baby," he said, "and I shall give you one."

"You promised me a son." She hiccuped.

Malcolm chuckled. "Perhaps I was being a bit arrogant and presumptuous, lady-love. Shall we settle for a child of either kind?"

"Oh, yes," she breathed. "But how?"

"By making love," he told her.

Puzzled, Jarvia pulled away. "We have been doing that."

"Nay. We have mated. Not until today have we made love."

Jarvia smiled. "No more letching?"

He pulled a face and looked studious. "As long as I love you, cannot I also letch for you?"

Jarvia lifted her face, and Malcolm buried his mouth against hers. They kissed passionately, their tongues hot and seeking. This time when they made love, it was sweet and slow. They took time to explore, to taste, to satisfy their curiosity and to arouse their passions to the fullest. At last they reached the blazing peak of fulfillment together and came softly floating down to rest on the shores of bliss.

"Now, lady-love, let us go fight off the wolves that howl at our door."

Chapter 27

T he storm broke. Rain pelted relentlessly down on the Great Hall. Malcolm and Jarvia stood on one side of the High Table, gazing at the man who stood below the dais in front of them. Magda sat beside Jarvia, her golden brown eyes fixed on the stranger.

"Lord Malcolm," Berowalt said, "thank you for receiving me at such an early hour."

"We are pleased to receive any of King Wyborn's emissaries at any hour of the day," Malcolm answered, then said to Cleit, "Please see that Berowalt's retinue is housed in the Small Hall."

The old man nodded and took the wet mantle that Berowalt handed to him. As Cleit left the main hall, the Southerland warrior shucked off his gloves and waved his hands to indicate all the chests that had been set down around him. "Princess Jarvia, I bring you and your husband wedding gifts from your family and friends in Southerland."

"Please return to Southerland with the message that my husband and I thank our family and friends," Jarvia said.

"Aye," Malcolm agreed. "We are glad that you will be here to join us for the Scottish celebration of our marriage."

"I am also, lord," Berowalt said, "but I must confess that I am here in regards to other diplomatic matters also. To those regarding the relationship between our two kingdoms."

"Aye," Malcolm said, "I have been anticipating this visit."

"May I speak privately with you, lord?" Berowalt asked.

"You may talk freely in front of my wife," Malcolm replied.

The Southerland warrior inclined his head slightly in acknowledgment. Quietly servants slipped in and out of the room, setting the High Table for the morning meal.

"As you know," Berowalt said, stepping closer to the hearth, "the rumor has spread rapidly through your kingdom and ours that you murdered your first wife, Hilda."

Malcolm crossed his arms over his chest. "As you know, that is nothing more than rumor."

"My king *accepts* that it is rumor, sire." Berowalt waited a moment before adding, "But I was captured and held prisoner when I attempted to return to Southerland with the report of Princess Hilda's death."

"Aye, I heard," Malcolm said.

"I was held by warriors of Clan Duncan, sire. Your clan. It would appear that you did not wish me to arrive in Southerland with the news of the princess's death before you reached there and negotiated for your second wife."

"My clansmen did not hold you prisoner," Malcolm said. "I cannot prove this, nor do I know who did take you prisoner. But I am investigating the incident, Berowalt. You may report this to your king. When I have learned the answer, you will be the first to know. You may also talk privately with Princess Jarvia and with Gerda. Ask them any questions that you will to satisfy your curiosity that they are being treated well."

"Thank you, lord," Berowalt said. "I shall do just that."

"The morning meal is prepared," Lucy announced.

Jarvia turned to Berowalt. "Have you broken fast?"

"Nay, lady, I have been traveling quickly in hopes of arriving in time for your wedding ceremony."

"Please join my husband and me for the morning meal," Jarvia invited.

"I will."

As servants entered with trays of food, Berowalt took a place at the High Table beside Malcolm. Lucy poured their tankards full of milk and spooned hot oatmeal into the bowls.

"I also have other grave news to bring to you, Lord Malcolm."

Wondering if the situation could become any graver, Malcolm lifted a brow.

"On its return to Northland, Lord Lang's ship was attacked by Highland sea raiders." Berowalt seasoned his oatmeal with several spoonfuls of the heated meat drippings that

Lucy handed him. "The rupture endowment was stolen, and all of Lang's warriors save one were killed."

Malcolm leaned back.

"Highland sea raiders?" Jarvia repeated.

"Aye, Ragnar, Lang's emissary, escaped to return to Southerland with the story."

"Can he identify any of these Highland sea raiders?" Malcolm asked, stirring honey and milk into his oatmeal.

"Aye. Lord Kirkja wants you to know that one of our traders, Madelhari"—the Southerlander looked at Jarvia, who nodded that she knew him—"reported Lord Lang of Northland has vowed to sail to the shores of Northern Scotland to avenge his honor. He has taken a blood oath to kill you, Chief Malcolm of Clan Duncan."

"Me!" Malcolm exclaimed. "I know nothing about the stolen rupture endowment. Am I the only Highlander whom Lord Lang can think to blame?"

Jarvia laid her spoon down and lowered her hands to her lap. Her heart had never been so heavy.

"You are the only one he has cause to blame," Berowalt said.

"If it were Scottish Highlanders who attacked his ship," Malcolm said, "they could have been from any of several kingdoms."

"Ragnar reports that one of the raiders was a man whom he recognized as one of your clansmen."

"One of my men," Malcolm repeated in disbelief.

"Aye, lord. Ragnar said he would recognize him if he ever saw him again. This Highland raider boasted that you, Malcolm mac Duncan of Clan Duncan, had taken Lord Michael's bride without paying the rupture endowment. He gloated in your dishonoring the Northland warrior."

" 'Tis a lie," Malcolm muttered. "Why would I jeopardize the future of my kingdom with such a dastardly act?"

"I know not, lord," Berowalt said. "In telling you this, I am only following orders given to me by Lord Kirkja."

"Aye, so you are," Malcolm said.

After they finished their morning meal, Malcolm walked Berowalt to one of the spare guest houses and saw him comfortably settled. When he returned to the Great Hall, he joined Jarvia in their sleeping chamber.

She took his wet tartan and hung it near the fire to dry. "You are worried, lord?"

"Aye."

"About Michael's coming to seek revenge?"

"Not so much about that, lady, as about who in my kingdom is a traitor." Malcolm gazed out the window at the storm. Black clouds swirled; thunder boomed; talons of lightning clawed the dark sky.

The wind howled. It roared. It slapped ruthlessly against a blue-and-white sail—the colors of the House of the Wolf. It whipped the turbulent sea against the *langskip*.

Braced for the storm, her mantle flying about her, Ingrid stood on the *lypting* and gazed at the ship's captain, her nephew, her brother's only son, his heir. Michael Langssonn was indeed his father's son, a warrior and champion of high repute.

Strongly chiseled features defined a ruggedly handsome face that was clean-shaven. About his neck he wore a silver torque from which hung a large, thick Thor's hammer. But he did not need the neckband to herald his nobility. His aristocratic bearing did it for him.

He governed with quiet authority, honed battle skills, and a smooth, deceptively strong body. His tall stature and confident stance made strong men tremble, weak men faint. No one made the mistake twice of thinking his quiet demeanor and intellectual interests were signs of weakness.

Sitting on the deck of the *langskip* with Michael was his huge silver-gray wolf, its wet coat glistening like diamonds. Michael had found the wolf when it was a pup. He had named the animal Ulf and raised it as a pet. Ulf had sworn allegiance to Michael and to him only. No one dared touch Michael in the presence of the brute.

Ingrid leaned closer to her brother, who stood next to his son. Although Lang was a tall, burly man himself, his son was taller and more formidable.

"My brother, you should thank the gods for giving you such a worthy son."

Lang nodded. The spray of the ocean touched his skin and clung in droplets to his beard. "I do, sister. Every day I send a special prayer to Thor."

Ingrid returned her gaze to her nephew, a man who defied custom by not wearing a beard, who recorded descriptions of strange lands and inhabitants, and drew representative pictures of the routes he had traveled. He did not care that people laughed behind his back, for none dared laugh in his face. He gloried in his education and in his ability to read and write the runes, in his ability to speak and to write in several languages.

He also gloried in his physical prowess. As a child he had been unusually gifted, with strength and wisdom that surpassed those of most children his age. To his father's joy, Michael had always excelled in whatever he did, games and contests of the mind, of endurance and agility, of might. Early in life Michael had had his vision—truly an extraordinary one—and had become a warrior.

His vision had been so memorable that he had quickly excelled over others his own age. He had become such an outstanding warrior and sailor that Lang had grudgingly tolerated his more unusual pursuits.

The ship lurched. Ingrid stumbled and would have fallen, but Michael reached out and caught her.

"Careful, Aunt, or you will be one with the water." His deep, rich voice carried above the clamor.

Oddly enough Ingrid felt that Michael could subdue even the elements if he so chose.

The wind shrieked through the rigging. The *langskip* dipped, then crested with the swelling waves. It refused to surrender its sovereignty to the savage sea.

As arrogant and confident as the ship, Michael braced his feet, clad in knee-high boots, against the *lypting* and crossed his arms over his thick, broad chest. His silver-blue eyes beneath black brows stared into the thunderous clouds and mountainous waves. The wind played against his black hair that had escaped the ornate silver helmet he wore; it billowed the blue mantle, straining the cloth against the silver broach that secured it about his broad shoulders. The furor of the storm whipped salt spume into his face and against his oiled leather trousers and white shirt.

"We could not ask for better weather to try our ship," Lang said.

"Aye, my father," Michael answered. "If it endures this,

it will take me to the Highlands and bring me back to
Northland in victory, our honor restored. 'Twill not be long
before Ragnar will be completely recovered and ready to
sail with me."

"As soon as he has fully recuperated, Ragnar will be
going," Lang answered, "but not you, my son. This is *my*
battle, not yours."

Lang's announcement relieved the anxiety Ingrid had felt
since Wyborn's emissary, Madelhari, had announced that
Malcolm mac Duncan, the Highland warlord, had stolen the
rupture endowment from Lang and violently and needlessly
murdered all Lang's warriors.

Michael laid an arm about his father's shoulders. "Nay,
my father. This is my battle. Your blood is my blood, your
name my name. Your dishonor is mine."

Lang rubbed his beard. "I am the one who betrothed you
by proxy to a woman you had never heard of, much less
knew. A betrothal of which you were unaware."

"That matters not, Father. She was my betrothed, and the
betrothal was dishonorably ruptured, bringing shame on the
House of the Wolf. I will not rest until I have been avenged.
I swear by the gods on this day."

Michael pulled his sword from its sheath. Holding the hilt
with both hands, he raised it high into the air, the long, thick
blade gleaming silver in the eerie, storm-gray light.

"Thor, god of thunder and lightning, and keeper of the
Oaths, hear me this day. I swear I shall kill this treacherous Highland warlord for bringing shame on my father's
house."

Thunder clapped so loudly that Ingrid felt the ship vibrate
beneath her. Lightning streaked across the darkened sky and
appeared to enter the tip of the sword and fill Michael with
its brightness, its deadly current. Rain fell in a thick curtain,
and through it, Ingrid saw her nephew. Truly, he was rightly
named.

Elemental, virulent, avenging, Michael Langssonn was
indeed the Lord of Thunder, the son of Lang Thorssonn.

The sound of the lur died and was replaced by the wail
of the bagpipes as Arthur played the song of Clan Duncan.
Malcolm's warriors, sitting at tables lining the Great Hall,

rose and clashed their spears repeatedly against their round, studded shields, until the clamor reverberated throughout the building.

Whereas before Jarvia had thought it only noise, today it was music. It inspired her. Wearing a white tunic and veils presented to her by the queen, Jarvia held herself erect. As she had done last night, the only jewelry she wore was the marriage ring Malcolm had given to her.

Glad that both Catriona and Magda were at Morag's hut with the old servant, Jarvia squared her shoulders and tilted her chin a little higher. Today, of all days, she must look regal, and Morag had assured her that she did. Her hair was swept atop her head in a braided coil, and her face was framed by delicate veils.

"Malcolm mac Duncan," the herald announced. "Princess Jarvia of Wybornsbaer of Southerland."

Proudly Jarvia walked down the length of the hall beside her husband toward the High Seats, where the king and queen were seated. Sybil and Angus sat to the left of Fergus and Muireall; two empty chairs had been reserved to their right. For her and Malcolm, Jarvia thought. She made herself smile at Sybil as they passed her.

Below the dais, chairs fanned out in a semicircle. In these sat the seven clan chieftains of the kingdom of Northern Scotland, and each chief's successor, his chosen best-man. Noticeably absent were Celdun of Clan Donal and his successor. Again Malcolm wondered where his friend was; he worried that he had received no message from him.

Jarvia turned her attention to the queen. Draped over her shoulders was a flowing white robe trimmed in fur of the same color. Beneath it, she wore a long tunic of a soft blue fabric. Delicate silk veiled her head and neck; a gold chain cinched her waist. She smiled at Jarvia.

Jarvia smiled back. Then she glanced over at Ard-righ Fergus, Sovereign King of the kingdom of Northern Scotland. He was a little pale, but otherwise he showed no effects of his illness. He wore white robes—denoting truth and purity, Malcolm had explained to her. Strapped to his side was the great Sword of Justice. In his right hand he held a long white wand topped with a large quartz crystal.

Both Jarvia and Malcolm bowed low to the ard-righ and ard-banrigh.

"Sovereign Lord Fergus, my mother the queen," Malcolm murmured.

The ard-righ lightly tapped Malcolm and Jarvia with his scepter. "Chief Malcolm of Clan Duncan. Princess Jarvia," he acknowledged. "Rise."

Both straightened. Fergus waved them to be seated.

"Chief Malcolm, Princess Jarvia, you have been summoned before the Council of the Chiefs." Fergus motioned to a young man. "Speak the charges."

The lad moved to stand before the dais, facing the king and queen and the chieftains. In a loud and clear voice, he said, "Chief Malcolm, the Council of Chiefs is concerned about your lack of loyalty to the kingdom. With the reluctant consent of the council, you went to the kingdom of Southerland to marry a native daughter of Lord Wyborn. Instead, you married a woman whom King Wyborn adopted. On the trip home with your bride, you rescued an abandoned child. According to our ancient law code, this is a crime punishable by death. What say you?"

The boy's words echoed throughout the Great Hall.

"Chief Malcolm," the ard-righ said, "answer the charges."

Malcolm, resplendently dressed in midnight blue trousers and a red shirt, rose and walked to stand below the dais in front of the chieftains and the king. "Chiefs of the Northern Scots, first I shall address my marriage to Princess Jarvia of Wybornsbaer of Southerland. I did travel to Southerland to marry a blood relation to Lord Wyborn. The council was skeptical of my marrying a second woman from Southerland. Wyborn had no blood kin living in his land. The closest lived in Northland. Had I married one of these women, her loyalty would not have been to Southerland or to her new home-by-marriage."

Malcolm paused, his gaze moving from one chief to the next, as he allowed them time to understand his words.

"According to Southerland law, an adopted child is reckoned a native child. King Wyborn and his wife adopted Princess Jarvia; thus she became their native child."

He walked slowly around the semicircle of chairs. "I assumed this would be met with your approval because we have a similar custom in our land."

Long strides carried Malcolm to the hearth in the center of the room. From one of the aisle posts, he unhinged a torch and extinguished it. With the charred end, he drew a circle and divided it into five equal parts. "The Old Ones say blood kinship is represented by two of these divisions." He blacked two of the wedge shapes. "Fostered kin is represented by the other three. This means they are more important than blood kin, does it not?"

He replaced the torch on the post.

"Who would speak?"

One of the chiefs rose.

"Luthe, speak," Fergus said.

"How do we know the Southerlanders will regard this woman as their blood kin and honor their agreements with us?"

"Princess Jarvia reads and writes the *futhark*, the letters of her people," Malcolm answered. "These runes have great magic and are eternal if they are written into a stone. Princess Jarvia had the contract between her and King Wyborn carved into a stone monument, which was erected in Southerland. My best-man, Lachlann, and several of my trusted warriors, among them Ghaltair and Thomas, can testify to this. Lord Kirkja in Southerland guarantees this rune stone monument."

Luthe nodded. "I am satisfied."

"Will anyone else speak?" Fergus asked. When no one stood, he said, "Address the second charge, Chief Malcolm."

Jarvia began to take heart. Malcolm was an eloquent speaker. She observed that the chiefs seemed satisfied with his answer. Not so Sybil. Jarvia glanced at the queen, and they exchanged a hopeful smile.

"My lords, chiefs of the clans of the Northern Scots," Malcolm said, "I did rescue and foster an abandoned child. Catriona is now a member of my household, under my protection."

An older chief rose. Fergus recognized him.

"Why did you go against our customs?" He peered at Malcolm from beneath shaggy, white brows.

"I went against the customs of the Old Ones," Malcolm said, "but I did not go against the teachings of the Christ."

Malcolm waved his hand toward the High Seat of the king. He looked at Rudie, the Christian high priest of Northern Scotland, who stood to the side of, and slightly behind, the ard-righ. In response to Malcolm's invitation to officiate at the wedding ceremony, Rudie had arrived in the village early that morning. As an old friend of Fergus and Muireall, he was staying with them. Having been on a religious retreat to the mountains for the past few months, he had not been aware of the discontent among the chieftains.

"High Priest," Malcolm said, "explain the teaching of the Christ concerning human sacrifice and the saving of lost souls."

Rudie, a large man dressed in dun-colored shirt and trousers, stepped forward. He was one of the few men of the Highlands who boasted a beard. His black mantle swaying around him, he raked a large hand through his thinning brown hair.

"The Christ teaches that he was the only human sacrifice we should offer to God."

"According to our new religion," Malcolm said, "the Christ is almighty, and we need no other gods. What about the Christ searching for those who are lost?"

"Although the Christ has ninety-nine sheep in his fold," the priest said, "he searches for the lost one."

Luthe spoke again. "I care not about sheep in the Christ's story. I am concerned about us and our sheep, our cattle, our families. The ancient gods are many, the Christ only one. Can he save us from the punishment of the many? I say not! We shall have pestilence of some kind."

"Nay," Malcolm said. "Did you not hear the good father? God is stronger than all the ancient gods and will reward us for saving lost souls. This babe was lost. My lady and I shall be rewarded for having saved her. And as our cup of blessing runs over, it spills onto the land and the people. We shall have many blessings, Luthe."

The people in the Great Hall were so quiet that the clip of Malcolm's cuarans could be heard as he moved in front of each council member.

"My lady and I fulfill the laws of the land because we bring healing to the people. We replace war with peace, fear with faith, and grief with happiness."

Angus rose. "My sovereign king, I would speak."

Fergus inclined his head.

"We have only Malcolm's word that he and his lady bring all this good to our land. I am skeptical of these promises. Those of us who have been here have witnessed the evil that has befallen us since the orphan was rescued."

"Aye!" cried several of the chiefs.

"Although I do not share your fears," Malcolm said, "I understand them. I honor the Christian god, but I also accept that many of you still worship the Ancient Ones. If it pleases the council, I shall make a sacrifice to the ancient gods that is greater in value than the orphan."

Surprise and interest registered on the faces of the council members.

"Why are you doing this?" Sybil demanded.

Malcolm touched the torque at his neck. "Because of my people and my land."

"What is the sacrifice?" Fergus asked.

"I offer twenty-five choice oxen, ten milking cows, five Highland ponies," Malcolm said, "and my chosen stallion."

Jarvia gasped; the chiefs gaped.

"My son," Fergus exclaimed, "have you—"

"According to our laws," Malcolm said, "this is a payment of far greater value than an orphaned girl. Yea, greater even than a male child. A sacrifice of which the ancient deities would approve and accept." Malcolm turned to his father. "My sovereign king, I have spoken. I leave the judgment to the wisdom of the chiefs."

In a low voice, Fergus said, "Chiefs of the kingdom, discuss the matter amongst yourselves so that you can render judgment."

As Malcolm strode to his seat, the lad who had recited the charges moved to place a huge cauldron in front of the High Seat of the ard-righ. From a pouch he passed out two stones to each chief.

Fergus stood. "The black stone for guilty. The white stone for innocence."

Jarvia leaned close to Malcolm and whispered, "You were eloquent. I did not expect you to sacrifice so much for the child."

"I have fostered her," he said. "She is my responsibility."

"And you love her."

Malcolm clasped her hand in his and pressed it against his thigh.

Jarvia asked, "Do you think they will accept the sacrifice for Catriona's life?"

"I do not know. I have said and done all I can."

One by one, the chiefs rose and stepped up to the cauldron. The ping of stones hitting the bottom of the container reverberated through the building. Jarvia sat on the edge of her chair. With clammy hands she brushed the veils from her face. Her heartbeat accelerated as she prayed for the number of white rocks to exceed the black ones. When each chief had returned to his chair, the last remained standing. He cast his vote but stayed by the cauldron.

"Ard-righ Fergus," he said, "our vote is ready to be counted."

"Do so, Tindell."

The warrior turned over the cauldron and separated the stones into two piles. Jarvia felt as if she were strung tighter than a bowstring. The black pile looked larger. Tindell moved so that Jarvia could not see. She held her breath and watched as Tindell counted. At first the black stones outnumbered the light ones. Then the pile of lighter stones grew.

Tindell rose. "By vote, the council accepts the sacrifice of the oxen, cattle, and the stallion for the orphan."

Jarvia gasped for joy.

The doors of the Great Hall were flung open. A gust of wind sprayed rain over those sitting closest to the entrance. A huge warrior, dressed in a long-sleeved shirt, leather vest, and trousers, strode into the building looking as wild and untamed as the Highland wilderness. Behind him strode Lachlann, Ghaltair, and Brian, their faces drawn and dark.

"Celdun!" Fergus exclaimed.

"Hail, Ard-righ Fergus," Chief Celdun said.

"We have been worried about you," Fergus said. "We're glad you arrived in time for the celebration."

Celdun looked at Malcolm. "In time to reveal a traitor among us."

Malcolm studied the countenances of his best-men before he looked at the clan chief. "Who would this traitor be?" he asked.

Celdun's chest heaved as he sighed deeply.

"Who, Celdun?" Malcolm demanded softly.

As if the words were being dragged out of his soul, Celdun said, "The evidence points to you, my friend."

Jarvia froze. Once more she felt the agonizing suffocation of fear constrict her heart. She looked up to see the queen's white and frightened face. Dumbstruck, Fergus only stared. Even Angus's expression registered surprise. Only Sybil smiled.

Chapter 28

W ind rushed through an open window. It blew a light
spray of rain against Jarvia and stirred her veils,
the material brushing her face softly.

Celdun waved a hand, and one of his warriors entered
the Great Hall carrying a tartan-wrapped bundle over his
shoulder. Vass, one of Malcolm's young outriders, entered
with him. The Donal clansman laid his burden at the base of
the dais. Brian motioned for the outrider to stand near him.
Celdun jerked the mantle back to reveal Thomas's lifeless
form. Malcolm's countenance hardened.

Celdun pointed to the dead man. "He is the master of
your outriders."

Malcolm nodded. "Aye, 'tis Thomas."

"I found this on him." The Donal chief waved a wooden
ogham marker.

"Let Malcolm read it for us," Fergus instructed.

Malcolm took the message stick, his gaze moving swiftly
over the marks.

"Read it aloud," Fergus commanded.

As Malcolm continued to look at the marker, Jarvia knew
the message boded no good.

"My lord," Sybil said softly, "since Celdun has said that
the message stick condemns Malcolm as a traitor, perhaps
we should allow someone else to read it."

Malcolm gave Sybil a scathing look. "I am neither a
traitor nor a liar."

"We have only your word for that, fosterling."

"His word has always proven good, lady," Celdun said.

"Aye," Fergus answered. "Nevertheless someone else
should read the marker."

"Read it, Ghaltair," Brian said.

"Ghaltair is the master of my ponies, Sybil," Malcolm
said sarcastically. "Do you mind if he reads the marker?"

She shook her head.

Ghaltair took the marker from Malcolm. "I don't have to read it. I did so when we found it," he said. " 'Tis a message addressed to Chief Fibh of the Picts from Malcolm mac Duncan. It directs Fibh to kill Angus and Sybil."

Shouts of outrage and anger resounded. Bedlam broke out in the Great Hall as warriors leaped to their feet and argued among themselves; others rushed to stand with their chiefs.

"All of you sit down and be quiet!" Fergus ordered, his voice carrying easily above the clamor. "I'll have no more outbursts like that."

Slowly the men returned to their places.

"My name is on the marker, but I did not send the message," Malcolm said. " 'Tis true that both Angus and Sybil have questioned my right to lead, but I have made no attempt to kill either of them."

"He would be well served by their deaths," Tindell said. "At the moment Angus has more support among us than any other chief. If we were to have an election for another ard-righ, 'tis likely Angus would be our choice."

"Aye," Lonnie of Clan Galway said, "Malcolm does have reason to kill them."

"He knew we have been talking about electing a new king and a new heir to the High Seat," Luthe added.

"I said the evidence points to Malcolm," Celdun roared. "I did not say it was him. I know the lad. I have fought by his side many times. As have you, Tindell, and you, Luthe." Celdun went to stand next to Malcolm. "No matter how much he may want the High Seat, he would not commit murder for it. I believe in Malcolm, and I for one would not elect Angus to be our ard-righ."

"Aye," Brian added, "all Celdun presented is a marker with a written directive to kill Angus and Sybil. Anyone could have written it."

Jarvia rose. "My lords, anyone who can read and write your letters could have made these marks and signed Malcolm's name to it." She pointed to Ghaltair. "Even he could have done it."

Ghaltair regarded her with open hostility. "Except I have nothing to gain by doing so, lady."

"I am not speaking of motive at the moment, Ghaltair," Jarvia said. "I am merely pointing out that the message stick does not prove Malcolm's guilt."

"He is the one who would stand to gain if Angus and Sybil were dead," Tindell said.

Fergus waved his scepter. "All of you be seated. Celdun, tell us what happened."

"Our cattle have been disappearing," Celdun said. "In fact, a raid kept me from leaving my village early. Then I received a report that raiders were spotted on the opposite side of my territory. We investigated and found strange pony tracks and a Pictish dagger. Several warriors and I set out to discover the identity of our visitor. We followed his tracks and met Lachlann and Brian on the way. They were following the same tracks."

"As was Ghaltair when we met him," Brian said.

Fergus looked at Malcolm's warriors. All three nodded.

Lachlann, his helmet beneath his arm, stepped forward. "Brian and I had been hunting the silver fox for the chase when we noticed the tracks. We thought from the hoof markings that the pony belonged to Thomas. Since it appeared that the pony was limping, we thought Thomas might be in trouble."

"We . . . er . . . we wondered why he would be headed in that direction," Brian said. "We were worried about him because he had been acting strangely since Chief Fibh and his warriors had arrived in the village, so we started following his trail. That's when we ran into Celdun and joined him."

"We followed Thomas's tracks for a long distance," Celdun said. "Eventually we saw him meeting with Nabhin, Chief Fibh's best-man. Evidently we made a noise that alerted them to our presence. Both men tried to escape. The Pict succeeded in getting away, but Thomas's pony stumbled and fell. When we reached Thomas, we saw that he had broken his neck and was dead. A short distance from his body we found the marker."

"Thomas's death is our sorrow in more than one way," Malcolm said. "He was an honorable warrior, the master of my outriders, and is guilty of no perfidy. I regret that he cannot speak in his own behalf and that we cannot question him to find out why he was carrying this message stick and meeting with Nabhin."

"We know why," Angus shouted. "He was carrying out your orders, delivering a message to your Pict friend."

Ignoring Angus, Malcolm turned to Celdun. "You have another of my outriders with you."

"Aye. After we picked up Thomas's body, we back-tracked and found the lad waiting beyond the point where we first picked up Thomas's trail."

Malcolm turned to Vass, who twisted his cap in his hands. "Tell us what happened, lad."

"Thomas and me, we rode out late last night. Thomas said something was wrong, and he meant to find out what it was. He believed others besides us were carrying messages back and forth to the Picts. We were following a trail. I don't know whose it was because Thomas didn't say. Then we heard riders coming. Thomas hid me and the spare ponies, and told me not to come out for any reason. Then he rode away, and I didn't see him again."

"Can you identify the man you supposedly heard Thomas talking with?" Angus asked.

Vass shook his head.

"Would you recognize his voice if you heard it again?"

He thought for a moment. "They were speaking low."

"But perhaps you could," Malcolm suggested.

"Aye, perhaps."

"Leave the lad alone. He can add nothing," Angus said.

"If we knew who this man was," Malcolm pointed out, "we could question him and learn more about what happened."

"But we can't," Angus argued. "The boy said they spoke too low for him to hear."

Their arguments continued. Tempers rose; insults were exchanged. Nothing was resolved.

Finally Luthe said, "We cannot prove that you are guilty of this perfidy, Malcolm, but a cloud of suspicion hangs over your head. As Ghaltair said, he had no motive in writing and sending such a marker. You do."

"Perhaps, Luthe, Malcolm can prove his innocence," Sybil drawled. "There is a way to prove his innocence beyond a shadow of a doubt."

The Great Hall fell silent; no one moved. All awaited Sybil's next words.

"Let the gods decide," she said. "Trial by ordeal in the Chamber of Fire."

"Christ and Him crucified!" Fergus exclaimed.

"Our Blessed Mother have mercy," Muireall murmured, and pressed her cross against her breast.

Trial by ordeal. Chamber of Fire. Jarvia nearly collapsed in her chair.

"Nay!" Fergus rose. "I will have no trial by ordeal. I have outlawed the use of the Chamber of Fire. I have listened carefully and find no evidence strong enough to convince me that my foster son, the heir to the High Seat of the kingdom of Northern Scotland, is in conspiracy with the Picts or that he attempted to murder Angus or Sybil. He is innocent."

Tindell lumbered to the center aisle. "Fergus, as much as I detest the idea of a trial by ordeal, I must say that I am not sure of Malcolm's innocence." The old warrior struggled to speak. "I want to believe him, but so much has happened. He is part Pict. 'Twould be easy for him—" He broke off and shrugged.

"Mayhap, Ard-righ," Lonnie said, "we should have a show of hands. Then we could better determine what course of action we should take."

"Nay," Fergus said. "I have spoken."

"My father," Malcolm said, "several of your chiefs have voiced their doubts. I would have a show of hands."

Fergus stared at Malcolm a long while before he sighed and nodded. "Those chiefs and their designated best-men who want Malcolm to submit to the ordeal, raise your hands."

Slowly hands were raised all over the building. Out of the fourteen chiefs and their designated best-men, six voted for the ordeal, seven voted against, Malcolm abstained.

"My father," Malcolm said, "enough doubt has been voiced that I will submit to the ordeal."

"No!" Muireall and Jarvia cried in unison.

"I will not allow this. The vote is clearly in your favor," Fergus said, the wind blowing his robes about his body to reveal the Sword of Justice.

"The vote is in my favor," Malcolm agreed, "but I have not won their confidence. If I am to be heir to the High Seat, I must have it. I shall submit."

"No!" Jarvia rushed to Malcolm's side.

"Return to your seat, my lady-wife," he commanded. She started to shake her head until she saw his expression harden. Her heart breaking within her, she slowly backed away and sat down. She gripped the edge of the chair with both hands, fearful that if she did not she would fall off.

"Malcolm," Fergus said, "please reconsider."

"I am not guilty, my father, but I accept the challenge. I agree to submit to the trial by ordeal after my marriage ceremony."

"Nay," Angus shouted. "We cannot allow this marriage to be solemnized through Scottish rites until Malcolm's innocence is proved. If a child should be born, blessed by custom and God, it would have a birthright."

"Aye," Luthe said, "what Angus says is true."

"I agree to your terms, Angus."

"On the morrow then," Angus shouted.

"Nay," Fergus said. "The Chamber of Fire cannot be made ready by the morrow. Since it has not been used in years, we need time to prepare it."

"How long?" Angus asked.

"On the second day after the morrow."

"So be it."

As the council members and warriors filed out of the Great Hall, Jarvia stood at her husband's side, her arm wrapped around him. Fergus and Muireall still sat in the High Seats. Brian, having taken Vass into the kitchen, where Lucy and Cleit could feed him, returned to sit down at one of the tables. Lachlann braced a hand against the aisle post and gazed out the window.

Unable to believe what had happened, Jarvia held on to Malcolm tightly, blinking back tears. He brushed his hands up and down her back. She heard him sigh deeply and knew he was worried.

Fergus slowly rose from the High Seat and stepped off the dais. His face was as pale as the robe he wore, his walk slow and feeble. "My son," he said, "if you will excuse me,

I shall retire to my quarters. I am weary."

Jarvia pulled away from Malcolm.

"Aye," Malcolm said, "I understand. I shall visit you later. First, I must take care of clan business."

Fergus nodded. "I wish you well, my son."

"So do I," Muireall added, her eyes misty with tears. She laid her hand on his upper arm. "I don't know when I've been more frightened for you than I am right now."

Malcolm kissed her on the forehead. "I would tell you not to worry," he said, "but since that is impossible, I shall tell you to direct your worries into prayers."

"I will," Muireall promised. "I shall light candles for you tonight. Remember, my son, the gods have chosen you. They will not fail you when you walk through the death chamber."

Fergus put his arm around his wife's shoulder and guided her to the door.

Muireall turned. "Son, please be careful. Celdun spoke the truth when he said there is a traitor among us. This traitor is trying to kill you."

After his parents left, Malcolm knelt beside his outrider's body.

"It does not seem possible that Thomas is dead," Brian said.

Malcolm shook his head. "Lachlann, take the body to the family. Tell them that he died proudly and in the line of duty. As the chief, I shall officiate at the burial."

Lachlann squatted beside Malcolm and began to adjust the tartan so that it covered Thomas's body more fully. Something thudded to the floor. Lachlann dug through the bracken and found a small round amulet on a chain.

"What is it?" Malcolm asked.

"Thomas's talisman," Lachlann answered, paying scant attention. He handed the talisman to Malcolm. "The chain is broken."

"Have my smith repair the chain so that he can be buried wearing it," Malcolm said.

Brian reached for the piece of jewelry. Dangling it from the chain, he studied the disk more closely, "Nay, Lachlann, 'tis not Thomas's. 'Tis the medallion Ghaltair wears. The one that belonged to his father."

Both Malcolm and Lachlann stood.

"Remember?" Brian said. "He showed it to us that night in Southerland when we were staying in Princess Jarvia's house."

"Aye, I remember." Lachlann looked at Malcolm. "Do you?"

"Aye. But what would Thomas be doing with it?"

"I don't know," Brian said. "Ghaltair was never without it. 'Twas his good luck talisman. I shall keep it for him. He probably dropped it when we picked up Thomas's body."

"Aye," Lachlann said.

Then both men looked at each other.

"What is wrong?" Malcolm asked.

"Ghaltair did not help us," Lachlann said. "In fact, he did not join us until we were almost upon Thomas and the Pict. When we went to Thomas, Ghaltair stayed on his pony and held the reins for the rest of us. 'Twas Brian and me who wrapped Thomas in his tartan and put him over the pony."

Brian pursed his lips. "So we're back to the question, why would Thomas have Ghaltair's talisman?"

"Mayhap Thomas pulled it from the man who killed him," Malcolm said.

"Nay," both said.

"Lachlann and I saw Thomas with the Pict," Brian said. "We saw him fall off his horse while Ghaltair was with us."

"Mayhap Thomas had been killed earlier and his body laid in the bushes where you found him," Malcolm suggested. "Were you close enough to be sure it was Thomas? Or did you see a man dressed in Thomas's clothes, wearing his tartan, and riding his pony?"

"What are you saying, Malcolm?" Brian asked.

"Think about what Vass told us. Someone whom the lad cannot identify rode up and spoke with Thomas. Later, leaving Vass hidden with the extra pony, Thomas rode off and was killed. Presumably his neck was broken when he fell off his pony."

"Aye," Brian murmured.

"You and Lachlann said that you recognized the hoof

marks as those of Thomas's pony, and you said the animal was crippled."

Brian snapped his fingers. "Thomas would not have been riding a crippled pony, not when he has an extra one."

"I suspect Thomas did not meet with a Pict at all. He knew the man who met him. Thomas was killed shortly after he rode off with him. Probably, during the tussle, the pony stumbled and broke its leg."

"Ghaltair," Lachlann said.

"He can read and write the *ogham*," Brian said.

After a pause, Lachlann spoke. "But we cannot prove any of this, Malcolm, and what Ghaltair said earlier is true. He has no reason to want Angus and Sybil dead."

"No reason that we know of," Malcolm corrected. "But we do know for sure that his good luck talisman was on Thomas."

With interest Jarvia had been listening to the discussion. But as quickly as her hopes soared, they now plummeted. "What are you going to do?" she asked.

"I need to think about it," Malcolm said.

"While you are thinking, my lord," she replied, "I shall tend to Thomas's pony."

"His leg is broken, lady," Lachlann replied. "He cannot be helped."

Gently Malcolm added, "My lady-wife, you may have been able to save Brian's leg, but I doubt you can save the pony."

"Once a pony's leg is broken, it cannot be repaired," Brian said, and smiled. "Not even with a miracle from your physician's chest."

"My lord," Jarvia said, "I can try to repair it. The old woman who taught me about medicine also taught me that sometimes when a bone is broken, it can be bound with hard, straight pieces of wood so that it can mend."

Malcolm smiled at her. "My lady, will you forever be rescuing the unfortunate?"

"I am a good physician, lord, as you are a good chief. And 'tis the unfortunate who are in need of rescuing."

"Cleit," Malcolm called out, "get Lady Jarvia's physician's chest and meet us in the stable. Also tell the lads to hitch a cart for me. Lachlann will need it to carry

Thomas's body back to his family. My lady and I shall join you shortly."

Cleit nodded.

Malcolm walked over to the window and gazed at Labyrinth Hill. "We cannot let Vass out of our sight. Whoever met Thomas will soon know, if he does not already, that the lad was with him."

"And Vass's life will be in danger," Brian said. "Where shall we hide him?"

"For the moment right here," Malcolm answered. "Post guards. Then meet me at the stables."

Leaving Vass in the kitchen, Brian left. Lachlann, lifting Thomas's body and slinging it across his shoulder, followed Malcolm and Jarvia to the stables. Lachlann laid Thomas on a bed of straw in a cart and made sure the tartan covered his body.

Ghaltair emerged from the corral into the stables. "Do you want me to take Thomas's body to his family?" he asked.

"Nay," Malcolm answered. "Lachlann will do it."

Ghaltair went to the cart, moved a portion of the mantle aside, and looked at Thomas's face. "I am going to miss him," he said.

"Aye, all of us are," Malcolm replied. "He was a good man."

"My lord," Jarvia said, "I shall leave you to your business."

"I will go with you," Malcolm said, and turned to follow her into the stables.

As Malcolm passed Lachlann, he gave a slight nod.

"If you don't mind," the best-man said, "I shall look on too, lady. I love to watch you perform miracles."

When they were inside, Malcolm motioned for Jarvia to join Cleit at the other end. He and Lachlann stayed at the door and watched Ghaltair. He pushed the tartan fully aside and began a frantic search of Thomas's body.

Malcolm, followed by Lachlann, joined him. "Looking for this?" He held out the medallion.

Wide-eyed, Ghaltair stared at them. Finally he said, "Aye. I—er—I let Thomas wear it."

"Your father's good luck talisman?" Lachlann said. "I

think not. Remember what Thomas said the night we were in Princess Jarvia's home in Southerland? *No man can borrow another man's luck. He must seek his own.* Surely Thomas would not have worn another man's talisman."

"You have some explaining to do," Malcolm said.

With a stricken look Ghaltair tried to bolt, but Malcolm and Lachlann caught his arms and held him fast. "You don't have enough evidence to prove I had anything to do with Thomas's death," Ghaltair said. "Besides, I didn't have a reason to murder him. I don't have a reason for wanting Sybil and Angus murdered either." Ghaltair threw back his head and laughed. "You may hold me captive and have my medallion, but *you* will die, Malcolm."

"Who are your accomplices, Ghaltair?" Malcolm asked. " 'Twill go better for you if you tell us willingly."

Ghaltair spit on Malcolm's boot. "That is what I will tell you."

Malcolm quickly bound Ghaltair and had Lachlann lock him in a shed behind the Great Hall. Then Malcolm instructed one of his men to take Thomas's body to his family for burial.

Later Brian and Lachlann stood on either side of Malcolm beside the corral. Malcolm held the chain, letting the medallion spin.

"Ghaltair is right," he said. "We need more evidence."

"Mayhap we can get a confession out of him," Lachlann said.

"Nay," Malcolm answered, "that still would not be enough to convince all the chiefs."

Leaning forward, Brian crossed his arms over the top railing and gazed at the ponies. "What if Ghaltair escaped, Malcolm? Mayhap he would lead us to his hideaway."

Malcolm nodded. "Not a bad idea, Brian. But 'twould be better if we could catch Ghaltair trying to silence Vass. Only the man who had something to hide would do that."

Both Brian and Lachlann turned to look at their chief.

"Ghaltair heard Vass give testimony today. All we have to do is make sure Ghaltair overhears a conversation in which we tell him that Vass has given the matter a great deal of thought and believes he could recognize the voice if he heard the man speak again. On the morrow, we will call together all the men who were in the council meeting today and have Vass listen to them talk. Also we shall let Ghaltair overhear where we have Vass for safekeeping."

Brian nodded. "That should unsettle Ghaltair enough so that if he escaped he would go hunting for Vass."

"I think Ghaltair is crafty enough to escape," Lachlann said, grinning.

"Aye." Brian grinned also.

"You shall stay here, Brian, and protect Vass," Malcolm said. "Lachlann and I shall go to one of the mountain huts, where we shall pretend to have Vass. We shall also take Lonnie, Tindell, and Celdun."

"Tindell?" Lachlann said. "Why him?"

"We need a warrior who opposes us to witness Ghaltair's perfidy," Malcolm answered. "But no one else is to know."

"You believe others are involved?"

"Aye. Sybil. Ghaltair is not intelligent enough to have planned and carried out such a plot on his own. Nor does he have the patience. Sybil does."

The best-men nodded.

"Now, to set our plan into action."

The next day, two riders met in thick underbrush close to an outcropping of rocks. Sybil, wearing trousers and a shirt, glared at Ghaltair, who had just escaped his captors.

"I told you not to be so careless," she grated. "You have jeopardized years of work."

"Thomas was getting suspicious. He was following my trail. He knew that I had been sending messages to the Picts also. I had to kill him, Sybil. I had no choice."

"Nay." She sighed and looked around, not wanting to be seen with him. " 'Twas a shame you let him tear the medallion from your neck, but as you told Malcolm, that is not proof that you had anything to do with the killing."

"Malcolm wanted to know who else was involved, but I told them nothing."

Sybil nodded. " 'Twill be best if you move all the goods out of the cave."

"My men are already doing that."

"You ordered them moved without my prior approval!" Sybil exclaimed angrily. "Where are you taking them?"

Ghaltair grinned. "To a place for safekeeping. I shall show you later."

"You should take refuge somewhere else for a while until we get Malcolm out of the way."

"I shall do that, but first I must get Vass. He might identify my voice."

"Leave the boy alone, Ghaltair," Sybil said. "No one is going to listen to him anyway."

"You have no cause for worry, Sybil, but I do. If they listen to the boy, it's my hide."

While Brian and Lachlann followed their master's orders, Malcolm spent precious time with Jarvia. Locked away in the privacy of their sleeping chamber that night, they swore their love to each other. Later, when Malcolm was sleeping, Jarvia slipped out of bed, her heart too heavy for sleep. As she paced outside, she looked for the cluster of stars she had once seen. Vainly she searched. They were not to be found.

An omen, she thought. The gods had spoken to her.

Rough hands settled gently on her shoulders. Malcolm stood behind her. She had not heard him approach, still did not see him, but she knew his touch. He tugged her against his chest. He was so strong; she felt so secure.

"What are you doing out here?"

"I was thinking." Her eyes filled with tears, she continued to gaze up at the heavens.

Malcolm turned her around so that she was looking into his moonlit features.

"I have brought you much sorrow," she whispered.

"Much happiness," he insisted.

She traced the outline of his thick brows. "Because of me you are doomed to the Chamber of Fire. You are going to lose all that you have worked for."

"At one time, my love," he murmured, "my kingdom was all that mattered to me. Not so anymore. You are the most important thing in my life."

He hugged her tightly, almost painfully. She did not mind. The pain pierced the numbness that enshrouded her. The pain was love; it bound the cords of her heart and soul with his.

"But I will prove my innocence."

"Aye, you must. When are you leaving to take Vass to the mountains?"

"Soon."

He buried his face in the curve of her neck and shoulder. His breath warmed her skin, soothed her frayed nerves.

"I may not give you a son," she whispered. *Even if I do, you may not live to see him born.*

They looked into each other's eyes again. His face was chiseled in silver; his eyes gleamed like blue-white iron. Yet Jarvia was not frightened of him as she once had been. She knew now that his strength was gentle, that his gentleness was strength.

"I care not that you give me a child at all," he answered. "I care only that you have given me a completeness that I lacked before. You brought contentment to my life. Peace. Happiness. A wholeness, my lady, that none other ever gave or can ever give me."

Jarvia laid her palms against his chest. How she loved to feel his muscles beneath her hands. His warmth. His confidence. His being. She felt the steady beating of his heart, and knew they were the drumbeats of life. Such a strong and purposeful life. She allowed all that was Malcolm mac Duncan to flow into and through her.

She forced herself to smile at him. "You are destined by the gods to be a king, and a king you must be."

"Destiny chose you to be my bride."

Jarvia laughed softly in spite of herself. "Many would say, my lord, that it was your letching, not destiny, that chose me."

Malcolm smiled. "Do you think destiny has never letched?"

Again he clasped Jarvia close to him.

"Deep within yourself," she said, "you knew there was the chance I was beyond my childbearing years. That is why you had Wyborn adopt Gerda. As you once told me, lord, 'tis your duty to give your people a son."

Malcolm tensed. "Say no more, lady. I know your thoughts before you speak them. I do not wish to be married to the child. Long ago I told you I was a man with a man's sexual appetite. Only a woman"—he clasped her by the shoulders

and pushed her away so that he could look into her face—
"only you, Jarvia of Southerland, can satisfy my needs and
desires. Now that I have you, I shall not let you go."

Jarvia raised her head; he lowered his. They kissed long
and deeply. Their bodies had become one long ago. Now
their souls merged as well. They had moved beyond passion
to love.

Night settled over the village. Malcolm and Lachlann had
ridden out early in the morning. Not having received any
word from them, Jarvia was worried. The Great Hall was
silent. The fire in the central hearth burned low, as did the
lamps set out on tables. The servants moved quietly about as
they cleaned up. Jarvia sat in her sleeping chamber, watching Sorcha feed Catriona. Magda lay beside her mistress.

"Malcolm can take care of himself," Sorcha said. "He is
the best warrior in the kingdom."

"Aye," Jarvia replied. She rose and went to the window.
Even in the dusk of early evening, she could see Labyrinth
Hill rising above the wooden palisades of the village. " 'Tis
not a fair trial by ordeal. 'Tis a death trap."

"Aye," Sorcha agreed.

"But if anyone can come out alive, it will be Malcolm."

"Aye."

"If he finds Ghaltair," Jarvia said, "he may not have to
go through with it."

"Mistress," Lucy called from the doorway, "Princess
Sybil is here to see you."

"Tell her I am busy."

"I can see how busy you are." Sybil pushed past Lucy and
strode into the room. Her hair hung in a single braid down
her back, and she was once more dressed in shirt, trousers,
and boots. "What I have to say to you will not wait."

Growling low, Magda rose at Jarvia's side.

Sybil looked down at the suckling babe. "I saw Malcolm
and Lachlann ride out early today," she said. "They took
the young outrider Vass with them."

"Aye."

"I have heard that the boy thinks he can recognize the
voice of the man who supposedly called to Thomas and
possibly killed him," Sybil said.

Jarvia did not answer.

"Malcolm and Lachlann pretend that they fear for the boy's life so they are hiding him in the mountains," Sybil added.

"They aren't pretending," Sorcha said. "They are frightened. I think it wise of them to hide him."

Sybil smiled. "You know, Jarvia, Malcolm *will* go through the Chamber of Fire on the morrow. Nothing will save him. According to folktales, no one has ever proved his innocence by coming out of the ordeal alive."

"Malcolm will," Jarvia said.

"Nay, Malcolm won't." Sybil stared into Jarvia's face. "Malcolm is going to die, that I promise you."

"Whether he goes through the Chamber of Fire or not?"

"If you are wise, you will take the baby and leave."

Jarvia raised a brow. "Desert my husband?"

"If you want to save the baby and yourself, you had better leave now," Sybil said. "I shall give you safe escort to the borders of our kingdom."

Jarvia could only imagine how safely Sybil would escort her.

"If you wait until after Malcolm has died in the Chamber of Fire, I'm sure the council will be persuaded to kill both you and the baby."

"Malcolm has already paid the price for the baby."

"Aye, but the gods do not always accept our sacrifices. When they do not, their wrath is worse than before. I think the council can be persuaded to change its mind."

"Are you saying the council *shall* be persuaded to change its mind—by you?" Jarvia asked.

"Aye." Sybil laughed softly and reached down to touch Catriona's head. "Such a sweet child. Surely you would not want something to happen to her."

"Get your hand off her!" Jarvia ordered.

"My, my! You are touchy where the orphan is concerned."

"I said get your hand off my child!"

Sybil did not move.

Jarvia strode across the room, shouting as she walked. "Get out of my house and do not come back."

Sybil stepped away from Sorcha and moved to stand

in front of Jarvia. "Never speak to me in that tone of voice again." She raised her hands and pushed against Jarvia's chest.

Snarling, Magda leaped between the two women. Sybil slapped at the wolf bitch. Her hackles raised, her mouth creased in a fanged grin, the wolf clamped her teeth on Sybil's hand. Yelling and shrieking, Sybil kicked out and struggled violently with the animal. She howled with pain and tried to free her mangled hand.

"Magda," Jarvia commanded, and the wolf released Sybil and sat down on her haunches.

Sybil slapped Jarvia's cheek. The sound echoed through the room. Growling, Magda leaped again, this time knocking Sybil down. She screamed as she fell, and with a sickening thud the back of her head hit a wrought iron rack next to the fire pit.

Sybil's groan became a low moan. Her body twitched and then abruptly grew still. Fear rushed through Jarvia. Her heart pounded. She knelt beside Sybil's body and laid her hand across Sybil's chest but felt no heartbeat; she put her hand beneath Sybil's nose. She was not breathing. Jarvia caught her by the shoulders and shook her.

"Sybil," she called. "Speak to me!"

Holding the baby in her arms, Sorcha knelt beside Jarvia. "Is she all right?"

Dazed, Jarvia touched the back of Sybil's head and felt a warm wetness. She stared at her bloody fingers. "She is dead," Jarvia said. "Sybil is dead."

Chapter 29

"Dead!" Angus bellowed, and pointed a finger at Jarvia.

Fergus sat slumped in the High Seat of the Great Hall. His face, already weathered by age and responsibility, reflected his grief at the death of his daughter.

"Last evening, Council of Chiefs of Northern Scotland," Angus continued, "this woman—*this woman*—killed my wife."

"Nay!" Brian rose, looking glum. "Princess Jarvia did not kill Sybil. Your wife fell and hit her head on the wrought iron cooking rack over the fire pit. 'Twas an accident."

Fergus gazed blankly into space; Muireall stood beside him, her hand on his shoulder. Father Rudie stood at his side.

"It would not have happened," Angus said, "if the Southerlander had not rescued the wolf bitch and the child."

Standing in the spill of early morning sunlight in the center of the Great Hall before the ard-righ and the chiefs of the clans, Jarvia said nothing. She had already argued her case, but few had listened to her. Few wanted to believe her. They were caught up in Angus's emotional outrage, and it was easy for them to believe that Jarvia was the cause of their misery and could be disposed of. Her death would reverse the bad magic . . . so they reasoned.

Outside the Great Hall, the people assembled. Their protests had begun as a low rumble; now they were deafening cries for her banishment from the village.

"What price would you have Princess Jarvia pay for having taken your wife's life?" Luthe asked.

"I demand her death."

"Nay!" Brian strode angrily across the room. Someone hurled a rock through an open window. Brian dodged it and moved to stand in front of the chiefs. "You have heard the lady speak. She did not kill Sybil, as Angus charges."

"But she is guilty all the same," Luthe said. "As Angus has said, if she had not rescued the child and the wolf, Sybil would not be dead today. Lady Jarvia has brought the shadow of death to our land. In the short time she has been here, two people have died."

"Sybil is dead because she threatened Princess Jarvia," Brian argued. "Because she was hitting her."

Outside the people yelled, "Cast her out! She has brought the curse of the Ancient Ones on us!"

"Nevertheless, Sybil is dead," Luthe argued. "Ard-righ Fergus, I ask that we take a vote."

"Chiefs of the clans of Northern Scotland," Brian said, "we are missing four of our council members. Malcolm. Celdun. Tindell. Lonnie. Let us wait until they return to address this matter."

More cries of "Send the Southerlander away!" sounded throughout the village.

"Aye," Fergus said, "we must not be hasty."

"My lord high king," Luthe said, "we have not been decisive and look what it has brought to us. Our land is ravaged with death and destruction. We must rid ourselves of this evil."

"Aye!" others agreed.

"Let us vote."

"My lords," Brian said, "are you forgetting the alliance we have with Wyborn of Southerland?"

"We have no need of an alliance with the Southerlanders," Angus said. " 'Twas Malcolm's desire alone that pushed for that. A selfish desire, one unworthy of a Highlander."

"Not so," Brian answered.

Tempers flared again. Angry ultimatums reverberated. Threats resounded. Compromise was denied.

Jarvia stood silent, her heart pounding as each of the chiefs cast his vote by dropping a black or white stone into the cauldron. They did not have to be counted for her to know the black ones outnumbered the white ones.

"My lord high king," she said, after the tally was announced, "I would address the council for a last time."

His face drawn, his hand pressed against his chest, Fergus nodded. Outside the people hissed and booed so loudly that

Jarvia could not be heard. They picked up stones and began to hurl them through the windows. Brian jerked his tartan from his shoulders and wrapped it protectively around her. He drew her close to him, turning his body so that he took the brunt of the missiles.

Fergus rose and shouted, "Cease! Let the woman speak."

When the furor had died down, Jarvia stepped forward. "Lords of the clans of Northern Scotland, I am not the cause of your troubles. But if you think I am, then you have no cause to make Malcolm endure a trial by ordeal."

The chiefs regarded her in surprise.

She walked over to Sorcha and took the baby from her. "My lady high queen, your son gave a sacrifice to the ancient gods of your land for this babe. I ask that you take her and raise her as your granddaughter."

Tears sparking in her eyes, Muireall accepted Catriona. "I shall do as you wish," she said.

"In my land a person who is to be executed is granted a death petition, one that cannot be denied." Jarvia turned to Fergus. "Do I have that right under your laws, my lord king?"

"Aye."

"Since you believe I am the cause of the evil that has come upon your land, I ask that you allow me, rather than Malcolm, to suffer the Chamber of Fire on Labyrinth Hill."

No one spoke; they all stared openmouthed at Jarvia.

"Malcolm is not to be blamed for any of my actions. I am the one who rescued the child and the wolf. I am the one you blame for Sybil's death. If I go through the labyrinth, I may possibly do away with the evil you perceive to be in your land."

"Nay, lady," Brian pleaded. "I canna let you do this. Malcolm will not stand for it. He loves you. Think of him."

"I am," she answered, turning to Fergus. "The chamber has already been prepared for Malcolm's ordeal on the morrow, has it not?"

Fergus gave a weary nod.

"Then I see nothing to stop me."

"Nothing," Angus shouted. "Highlanders, I say it is time that we began to act like warriors and reclaim the glory that

Fergus and Malcolm have long denied us. This is the first step in our return."

"Aye!" Angus's supporters rose to their feet and brandished their long swords.

"If the Southerlander wants to endure the Chamber of Fire, chiefs, I say let her."

More ayes rang out through the building.

"The chamber is prepared! Light the fire!" Luthe shouted.

"Warriors of the kingdom of Northern Scotland," Angus cried, "I call for the election of a new king."

Those who supported Angus slapped their hands on the tables. Those against him yelled their opposition.

Brian strode over to one of his clansmen. His voice low and urgent, he commanded, "Ride as fast as you can and get Malcolm. Tell him to come quick if he wants to save his lady-wife."

Nodding, the warrior hurried out of the Great Hall.

When the noise died down, Angus said, "We shall meet within seven days as specified by law. Each of you is responsible for seeing that the summons reaches all the people in your territory." He turned to those who supported Fergus and Malcolm. "Do not try to interfere with or thwart this election in any way," he warned.

His voice weak, Fergus said, "I shall admonish them to abide by the law, Angus. Until the election, I am the ard-righ." Fergus glanced at the chiefs sitting below the dais. "The summons must be repeated word by word to the head of each house. If possible you must repeat the message to the person who will carry it to the next house. At no time, except in truly impossible weather, must it stop traveling. If no one is home when the bearer arrives at a house, cut notches to denote how many days are left before the meeting. The head of every family, unless he is ill, must attend the meeting or pay a fine."

"Now," Angus shouted, "to the Chamber of Fire!"

A cloud of black smoke billowed out of the opening to the Chamber of Fire. Dressed in her black trousers and red shirt, Jarvia stood outside. Beside her were Morag and Gerda, their eyes red and swollen from crying. Morag promised Jarvia that she would take care of Gerda.

Magda sat on her haunches beside her mistress. Many of the villagers, those who did not believe Jarvia was cursed, had made the journey to the mouth of the tunnel with her. But even they did not press around her as they had done the day she and Malcolm had ridden into the village. They hung back, their faces long.

The only noise Jarvia heard was the wind blowing through the bushes and the tall grass. The sun shone above, but hanging heavy over everyone was the dark smoke cloud.

Feich hobbled to the front of the crowd. "Here," she said, handing Jarvia a leathern thong on which she had braided several feathers. "Wear this," she commanded. "It has good magic."

"Thank you," Jarvia murmured. She bent her head while Feich tied the talisman around her neck.

Then the old woman surprised her. She took her into her arms and hugged her tightly. "The gods be with you, my daughter." Feich pulled back and gazed into Jarvia's face. "You can conquer the fire. But your desire to succeed must be greater than any fear of failure."

Jarvia nodded.

"Lady." Someone tugged on Jarvia's shirtsleeve. She turned to see Keeper Beattie's two wards. Ronan swatted hair off his forehead with one hand and held the other out to her, palm up. "These are magical rocks. We climbed Labyrinth Hill with Keeper Beattie and his wife and got them out of the lake. They're blessed by Our Lady, ma'am."

"Select one of the stones for me," Jarvia said, "and keep the rest for you and your new family."

"Will the magic of one be enough?" John asked doubtfully.

"Aye," Jarvia answered. " 'Tis blessed by Our Lady, and she is a strong woman."

Ronan studied the stones thoughtfully and finally chose one. "This isn't the prettiest," he said, "but it's the biggest. I think it will have more magic than the others."

"Thank you, John and Ronan," Jarvia said.

In the distance she saw Arthur climbing the hill, his pipes in his arms. Then she felt someone else touch her shoulder. She turned to see her mother-in-law. Holding Catriona in her arms, Muireall pushed closer.

"I wish you did not have to do this." Tears ran down her cheeks. "Malcolm would stop it if he were here, and I don't know what will happen when he learns—"

"Nay, my mother," Jarvia said, "do not think sad thoughts. Believe that you will see me when I emerge from the chamber."

"Aye." Muireall wiped her tears with her hand. "And I promise I shall take care of Catriona for you as if she were my own child."

Jarvia took the baby and cuddled her once more, hugging her so tightly that Catriona squealed out. Jarvia gave a teary laugh and returned the baby to her grandmother.

"Tell Malcolm, my lady, that I love him."

Muireall could only nod.

Sorcha and Brian stepped forward. Teary-eyed, Sorcha hugged Jarvia first, then Brian did.

"My lady," he said, "have you a miracle in that physician's chest of yours?"

"Nay, Brian, not this time." *This time there were no miracles.*

"Then, lady, we shall produce a miracle for you," Brian said. "I have sent for Malcolm. He should be here any minute now."

"You should not have done that," Jarvia admonished.

"Aye, madam, I should. Malcolm left me here in his stead. I was to protect you, and I have not done so."

"Nay, best-man," Jarvia said. "Tell my husband that I chose to enter the chamber. He is the one ordained to be the leader of his people, not I. Also tell him that I know for a fact that I do not carry his babe within my body."

"Lady, Malcolm loves you whether you have his babe or not," Brian said.

"Aye," Sorcha agreed.

Jarvia smiled.

"Shall I keep the wolf?" Brian asked.

"Aye," Jarvia said. "You helped me rescue her. 'Tis only right that you should keep her."

"My lady Jarvia," Arthur called out, shouldering his way through the people. He handed her a reed and, smiling shyly, held out his pipes. " 'Tis the one you mended with your magical physician's chest. I took off this reed, lady, because it is also magical. I used it when I practiced your song. Take the reed with you. I promise it will save your life."

"Thank you, Arthur," she said, and wondered what she was going to do with all the talismans and amulets she was receiving.

As if in answer to her question, Feich unbound the leathern pouch that hung about her waist and tied it around Jarvia's. She took Jarvia's collection and dropped it into the container.

"You're going to need all of these," the old woman said.

"Princess Jarvia," a woman called. Out of breath, Keeper Beattie's wife ran up the hill; her portly husband followed. "I have made you a mantle," she cried. "One truly fit for the chief's wife."

As soon as the older couple was close enough, Keeper Beattie unfurled the garment and placed it over Jarvia's shoulders. Although it was heavy and large, it billowed in the morning wind.

Keeper Beattie clipped it at her shoulders with a gold pin. " 'Tis a brooch that belonged to my mother," he said. "She was a good woman, lady, and a strong one."

Jarvia thanked and hugged each of them.

Feich tugged the mantle. "When you enter the chamber," she said to Jarvia, "search for the small spring of water."

Puzzled, Jarvia stared at her.

"It is there," the old woman insisted, "but it is hidden and few know of it. Search for it. Do you hear me?"

Jarvia nodded.

"Wet yourself thoroughly." The seer stared into Jarvia's eyes, then said as if she were speaking to a child, "Wet yourself from the top of your head to the bottom of your feet, including the mantle."

Again Jarvia nodded.

"Good," Feich muttered. "You will save yourself."

She turned and walked away.

Then Jarvia heard the blast of the lur and looked down the hill to see Fergus leading the procession of clan chiefs—those who had remained in the village. At his side walked the Christian high priest Rudie. The ard-righ wore his white robes and carried his scepter. Around his waist was strapped the girdle that carried the Sword of Justice.

Jarvia smiled bitterly and wondered if justice was ever truly served.

The villagers stepped aside to make a pathway. Arthur pushed forward and climbed to the top of the tunnel opening. He positioned his pipes in his arms and settled his mouth around the mouthpiece. The lur sounded a second time, and the drum began to roll.

As if death were a person, Jarvia felt it envelop her. She gazed at the land around her, a land that she had come to love in so short a time. She looked at the people. All of them had grown dear to her. Yet this land and this people were demanding her life.

Lucy and Cleit waved to her. She waved back. She saw John and Ronan standing in front of Keeper Beattie and his wife. Morag held Gerda circled in her arms. Brian had one arm around Sorcha's shoulder, the other hand clasped around Magda's leash. Muireall, her back erect, her head held high, stood off by herself. Feich held a circlet of rounded beads in her hands. She rubbed each one, murmured a prayer, and moved to the next one. Her eyes were closed, her head raised to heaven.

Jarvia heard a man call her name; her gaze scanned the crowd until she saw Berowalt, pushing and shoving to reach her.

"My lady," he said, "I wish I could say the tidings of this would bring sorrow to your adopted father Wyborn, king of Southerland."

" 'Twill only make him sad because I have not yet produced an heir for the Highlander," Jarvia replied.

"Lord Kirkja will be most upset, lady, because he cares for you. I fear this does not bode well for relations between our two kingdoms."

"Please, Berowalt," Jarvia implored, "do not return with a negative message. Lord Malcolm can marry Gerda. She will produce him the son he needs to guarantee unity among our people. Let there be no talk of war between us. Tell Kirkja that I did what I considered best for both Southerland and Northern Scotland. He will understand."

"Aye, lady." Berowalt bowed and stepped back, leaving her alone.

The wind blew, cool and gentle, caressing Jarvia. She blinked back tears and wished she could see her husband once more. She wanted him to hold her, to tell her that everything would be all right. She longed to hear his voice and to see his beautiful blue eyes.

She should be thankful for the wonderful moments they had shared together; she should be grateful he had fallen in love with her. But at the moment she could only think of the years of love and joy that she would be denied.

She knew she had chosen correctly. Malcolm had been ordained by God to be king of Northern Scotland, to bring peace and unity to the peoples of the Highlands. Jarvia would not deny him his destiny.

The ard-righ neared. He raised his scepter. " 'Tis time."

The lur sounded for the third time.

"Aye," Jarvia said, " 'tis time."

"Lady," Arthur shouted for all to hear, "I play your song. 'Tis a lament because you must walk the Chamber of Fire. The Duncan will hear because the song of the pipes travels for long distances. 'Twill inspire you, lady, to come out on the other side."

"Aye, Arthur," she said.

"And, lady, I shall be waiting for you there. Then I shall be playing your song of victory."

"You are so sure I will live?" Jarvia asked.

"Aye, lady"—the lad's eyes sparkled with tears—"I'm sure. Clan Duncan wants you to be its lady."

The crowd shouted and cheered its agreement, but the people grew silent when Arthur began to play the soulful strains. If the feeling of impending doom had been noticeable before, it was oppressive now. Fergus held out his hand; Jarvia laid hers on top of it. The ard-righ, Rudie walking beside him, guided her into the entrance.

"I leave you here, lady."

"Aye, my lord king."

Fergus kissed her forehead. "I wish you well, lady."

"My lady," Rudie said, "may I offer you a blessing?"

Jarvia nodded. She bowed her head and closed her eyes, listening to the priest as he said a prayer and sprinkled water over her. She heard the beautiful but mournful sounds of the pipes as Arthur played her song.

"We take our leave now," Fergus sadly announced.

Jarvia heard the crunch of their boots on the rocks as they walked away, leaving her alone. She would not turn to see them leave. Slowly she began the upward climb, her footfalls blending with theirs as she entered the Chamber of Fire—the death chamber. She lowered her hand and ran it over the leathern pouch that Feich had given to her. She must succeed . . . she must.

"We have succeeded," Celdun argued as the warriors rode single file through the narrow mountain pass. "We set the trap and caught two of the varmints."

"But the biggest one is still free," Malcolm answered. He glanced at the two prisoners, one a Scot, the other a Pict, who rode between him and Celdun, bound to their ponies. Lachlann followed on his own mount. "Now to get Ghaltair."

As he spoke the words, Malcolm gazed ahead once more. In the distance, standing on the edge of a rock outcropping, he saw Cain, his scout. He urged his new white stallion to a faster pace.

When Malcolm drew abreast of his scout, Cain said, "Ghaltair's over the ridge about half a day's journey ahead of us."

Exhilaration filled Malcolm. He took off his helmet and brushed his gloved hand through his hair. He was so close, he could taste victory. Ghaltair—the man responsible for killing Thomas and framing him—was almost in his grasp. Malcolm would take great pleasure in bringing him back to the council for judgment.

"I know a pathway that will carry us out on the trail ahead of him," Cain said.

Celdun laughed. "We can set another trap and catch him this time. I like that idea, Malcolm."

"Aye, so do I," Malcolm said, "but we have to remember that Ghaltair is crafty. Lachlann and I took him unawares the first time we captured him, and we took a chance when we let him escape. 'Twill not be so easy to capture him a second time."

"Do you think Ghaltair has any idea that we're following him?" Lonnie asked. "Mayhap, my friends, we ourselves are being lured into a trap."

Cain shook his head. "I don't think so. He's moving much too slowly and is taking no care to cover his trail. He's so close to Pict territory that he thinks he cannot be caught. Besides, he has communicated with no one. He's alone."

"Why don't we stop to rest the ponies then?" Celdun suggested.

"Because we are too close to the border of Pict territory," Malcolm said, "and Ghaltair is smart enough to know that we cannot afford to cross over. The union between the Picts and the Scots is too tenuous." Malcolm shook his head. "We have to capture him."

"Are you aware that you are being followed?" Cain asked.

Surprised, Malcolm shook his head and looked over his shoulder. The thought that he had been too preoccupied with catching Ghaltair to think of anything else irritated him.

"I have been keeping an eye on him." Cain said.

"One of Ghaltair's men?" Tindell asked. He, too, looked over his shoulder. "The trap Lonnie spoke of?"

The scout shook his head. "I don't think so. It looks like one of our ponies. Whoever it is, he's riding fast."

"Lachlann, double back," Malcolm ordered, slipping his helmet over his head. "I do not want any unpleasant surprises."

The best-man nodded.

"Do whatever you have to do. We shall continue after Ghaltair," Malcolm said. "Catch up with us as soon as you can."

"Aye," Lachlann called and set off at a gallop.

"Lead the way to the shortcut, Cain," Malcolm ordered.

The company followed the scout. The higher the ponies climbed, the steeper and more narrow the pathway became, and the more impatient Malcolm grew. Victory was so close, yet so far away.

"Malcolm," Celdun called when they came to a small mountain stream, "we have to rest for a while. The ponies need to get their wind or they will be no good to us."

"Aye," Malcolm agreed, patting his stallion's neck.

As the men and animals rested and drank, Malcolm walked away from the group and climbed to the top of a large boulder. Impatiently he gazed into the distance. Today he was the hunter, and he smelled the scent of his prey. Ghaltair was almost within his grasp. Malcolm was eager to be on his way, but he also recognized that he had pushed the company and the animals hard. Cain was one of his best scouts; Malcolm trusted his judgment of the situation.

"Someone's coming," Tindell called out. "From behind."

Curious, Malcolm rejoined the others. Lachlann and another rider approached at a gallop and reined to a halt.

"Malcolm," Lachlann said breathlessly, "things are bad in the village. Brian has sent you a message."

The messenger slid off the pony and quickly related all that had happened while Malcolm had been gone.

"Hell's fire!" Malcolm exclaimed.

The man finished with, "Brian said you must come quickly, sire, if you are going to save your wife. Princess Jarvia is to enter the Chamber of Fire today."

Malcolm's desire to capture Ghaltair, to clear his name, to find Thomas's murderer, all paled when he thought of Jarvia dying in the fire chamber. Nothing, absolutely nothing, compared in importance to her. She was his life, his reason for living.

He strode to his stallion.

"Malcolm, we're not far from Ghaltair," Tindell said, grabbing his friend's upper arm. "He's just over the ridge. Think how sweet victory will be, Malcolm, when you ride into the village with Ghaltair as your prisoner. Let us capture him first."

Malcolm twisted away. "Nay, I shall return to Jarvia."

"Do not worry about the Southerlander," Tindell said. "If she dies, you have the other woman, the one called Gerda. She can give you a son."

Malcolm regarded him with contempt. "That is why I married Jarvia, but it is not why I return, Tindell. It is not why I want her to live. I do not care that she can give me a son . . . or any child, for that matter. She has already given me the greatest gift of all—herself. That is all I want from her." Malcolm swung onto the stallion's back. "If my wife dies, Tindell, I shall never know victory again."

"Malcolm, you cannot possibly arrive in time to save her," the old warrior insisted. "No matter how hard or fast you push your stallion."

The same fear plagued Malcolm, but he did not give voice to it. "I shall try."

"You are a fool to become so enamored of a woman," Tindell scoffed. "Ghaltair, the man who has almost ruined your life, is just over the ridge. You can return a hero with him as your prisoner. Prove to our people that we are going back to the glory of the old ways. Prove to them that you are worthy to be the heir to the High Seat of Northern Scotland."

"I have no time to be a hero," Malcolm shouted. "I am going home to save my wife."

"Is she more important to you than your duty?"

Malcolm stared at him for a moment. This was the first time he had put anything above his duty to his people. He smiled, then laughed. "Aye, Tindell, she is far more important. Far more."

The stallion raced up Labyrinth Hill, but he did not move fast enough for Malcolm. He was a driven man. Duty, country, honor, and Ghaltair were forgotten as he thought of his wife entering the Chamber of Fire. He could not imagine life without her.

Pulling to an abrupt stop in the crowd surrounding the entrance to the chamber, Malcolm leaped off the stallion. Brian ran up to meet him.

"Thanks be to God, you are here."

Malcolm pushed past him.

"I thought you would never arrive."

Long strides carried Malcolm toward the chamber's entrance. "Where is she?"

"She's in there."

"How long?"

"About an hour."

Fergus made his way to his son.

Fury welled up in Malcolm. "How could you have allowed this to happen?" he shouted, without slowing.

"You heard then?" Fergus asked, taking long steps to keep up with his son.

"Aye, Brian sent a message."

"She chose to do it," Fergus said.

"But you should have stopped it, my father."

Muireall, Catriona in her arms, rushed to Fergus's side. "Your father had no choice in the matter."

"None at all," Angus added. "Your wife killed Sybil. Murdered her."

"Not according to what I heard," Malcolm said. "But even if she did, Angus, my wife killed a traitor. After I save Jarvia, Angus, you will have much to answer for."

Angus snorted. "I have nothing to answer for, Malcolm. 'Tis you and your wife who are guilty of treason."

"Aye," Luthe said. "Your wife knew she had brought the shadow of death on the land. She is sacrificing herself to save your kingdom."

"Just as I am not," Malcolm said, and raced into the outer room of the Chamber of Fire.

Lonnie, who had trailed Malcolm all the way back home and had just now leaped from his pony to Malcolm's side, caught him by the shoulders. "You cannot go in there. You are thinking with your heart rather than your head. Like a man who has forgotten he is the future king of Northern Scotland."

"I am thinking like a man who is losing his very reason for living," Malcolm answered. He yanked the torque from his neck and tossed it to the ground. "My heart and soul are bound to Jarvia's. Without her I have no kingdom. If I cannot have her in life, I will be joined with her in death."

As Malcolm walked deeper into the stone-lined cavern, everyone but Fergus fell back in fear and trepidation.

Fergus ran after him. "I did not want her to enter the chamber, my son, but you must not follow. I have prepared you for the day when you will assume leadership of my kingdom. You are destined to bring unification to the Highlands."

But as they traveled farther into the smoke-filled chamber, and Fergus's words continued to fall on deaf ears, he fell farther and farther behind his son.

Malcolm started coughing. His eyes watered.

"Return, my father," he shouted, and plunged into the blackened, smoke-ridden darkness of the Chamber of Fire.

Jarvia took another step, her feet sliding on the narrow ledge. She could not hold on; she fell, screaming and clutching the huge, wet tartan about her shoulders as she plunged into the ice-cold waters of the deep cavern. The swift current caught her and pulled her down. She was tired; her lungs hurt; her skin was burning. She had survived the fire . . . thanks to Keeper Beattie's mantle . . . thanks to Feich's advice. She released the mantle from her shoulders and floated with the current. She rested for a while. Then she felt herself being sucked under.

Around and around and around.

She could fight no more.

She closed her eyes.

In the distance she heard a splash, then felt a sharp pain in her shoulder. She opened her lids to stare into soulful, golden brown animal eyes.

"Magda," she whispered.

With the wolf pulling her, she began to fight to survive once again.

Malcolm's chest hurt; his eyes and lungs burned. He could not see. He stumbled on. He had to find Jarvia. She had to be alive. She had to be. He could not imagine life without her.

His tartan was his salvation. Its protection saved him from the smoke, allowed him to plunge through the flames.

The water-filled corridor was a blessed relief, cool and clean and wet. He breathed more deeply.

He stayed well to the side, moving slowly and carefully over the rocks. He found the narrow ledge. Pressing himself against the tunnel wall, he kept going. He stopped and listened. He heard nothing except the crackle of the fire behind him. Step by step he forced himself onward.

Farther . . . and . . . farther.

He heard an animal's whimper. He stopped moving, one foot suspended in the air. He strained to hear. He heard the sound again. The wolf!

"Magda!" he shouted.

He waited.

Nothing.

He called again. Again he heard the whimper. Magda was there. So was Jarvia. She had to be. Dear God, she had to be.

With renewed strength he pushed ahead. He had to move faster. He slipped, searching desperately for handholds. He found a small rock shelf; his fingers dug into it just as his feet gave way beneath him, dangling over the icy water below. Inch by inch, pushing with his toes, with his fingers, he crawled back onto the narrow ledge.

Again he moved toward the whimpering sound. Ahead of him he saw that the path widened and became illuminated by a ray of light. Sunlight! And in that dim pool of light he saw his wife lying in a heap.

"Jarvia!" he shouted.

She did not move. Magda lay beside her, licking her face.

Malcolm ran to Jarvia and knelt beside her. Her clothing was wet and dirty and half torn, half burned from her body. He brushed tendrils of sooty hair from her face. He felt her breath warm against his fingers.

She was alive!

"My lady-wife," he whispered, "I'm here."

Slowly she lifted her lids. She tried to smile. "My love," she whispered. "I knew you would come for me."

"Aye, your love," he said. He kissed her softly on the lips. "My love."

She coughed. "You look a sight."

He laughed. "So do you. The most beautiful sight I have ever beheld in my life."

"Your torque is gone."

" 'Tis nothing."

"The torque itself is not," Jarvia said, speaking slowly, "but it stands for something wonderful and great. You, your land, and your people." She smiled weakly. "My lord of fire."

Her lids closed. Her head rolled to the side. Whining, Magda scooted closer and laid her head on Jarvia's breast. She nuzzled with her nose.

"My wife," Malcolm begged, tears running down his cheeks and dropping onto hers, "please do not die. Please don't. I need you."

Jarvia didn't move.

"I need you!" In those three words he shouted his anger, his love, his frustration . . . his helplessness. "By all that is holy! I need you, Jarvia."

Whining softly, Magda brushed her muzzle against his cheek; she licked the tears from his face. Malcolm scooped Jarvia into his arms and buried his face against her body. He cried as he had never cried before. Magda pushed closer to Malcolm.

Jarvia gasped and breathed in deeply. Her eyelids fluttered.

"Do not die, lady," Malcolm ordered.

Jarvia tried to laugh. "My lord, do not shout so loudly. You make my head ache all the more."

Magda barked. She wagged her tail and ran in circles around Malcolm.

"Aye," Malcolm said. "She is going to live, Magda."

His strides lengthened. So did Magda's. He moved around a bend of the tunnel, and cool, fresh air blew against this face. The end of the tunnel lay just ahead. In ten steps he was outside, breathing deeply, his eyes closed and his head held up so that the sun could shine on him and his love.

Tears still moistened his face. Magda sat down beside him, looking at the crowd of people who gasped and cried out their joy at seeing the three of them.

Crying also, Muireall watched her son as he stood with his bride in his arms. She held Catriona . . . and Malcolm's torque. He would be needing it soon.

"Both of them live!" Feich exclaimed. "All will be well for us." She turned and started down the hill.

"Will it?" Muireall asked.

Feich stopped, but did not turn around. "What do you mean?"

"The Northlander, the one called Michael Langssonn, is on his way to our shores to seek retribution."

"It won't be the first time we have dealt with Northlanders," she said.

"I cannot lose another son to them," Muireall said.

"You won't, lady. That I promise you."

And as Arthur blew on the pipes, Jarvia's song of victory filled the air.

The sun shone brightly on the day of Malcolm's and Jarvia's Scottish wedding ceremony. Both bride and groom stood in front of the dais in the Great Hall before High Priest Rudie. Between them sat Magda, attached to a gold-and-silver leash. Standing on either side were Fergus and Muireall. The queen held Catriona in her arms. For the time being the baby slept peacefully, but Jarvia did not think she would remain so. Witness to the ceremony were two of Malcolm's best-men, Brian and Lachlann. Standing with Brian was Sorcha; Gerda was with Lachlann. A small lad held a white pillow on which were laid an oak wreath and a delicate golden torque.

Rudie said, "I now bless the marriage union between Prince Malcolm mac Duncan and Princess Jarvia of Southerland."

Jarvia, caught up in the happiness of officially becoming Malcolm's wife in the eyes of these people, of knowing that both of them were safe and that he had been cleared of all suspicions of murder and treason, hardly heard the priest's words. When Malcolm nudged her, she rose with him and allowed him to escort her to her High Seat. Holding the pillow in front of him, the lad followed.

Jarvia sat down, and Malcolm lifted the oak wreath and placed it on her head. He reached for the small gold torque. Jarvia's breath caught as she gazed at the exquisite piece of jewelry.

When Malcolm leaned down to encircle her neck, she saw the light glint on his own torque. "My lady-wife," he said.

"My lord husband."

Warriors clashed their spears against their round, studded shields. Cheers and wild cries pierced the air. Never had a bloodcurdling cry sounded so wonderful to Jarvia.

"The Melodious Shields are sounding for you, my lady-wife."

Jarvia felt the warmth of tears on her cheeks, but she was laughing. Muireall stepped up and handed Catriona to her. Jarvia hugged her daughter; then Malcolm put his arms around both of them. The people cheered, the noise reaching such a crescendo that Jarvia couldn't hear what her husband was saying to her. But his smile told her everything she needed to know.

He was Chief Malcolm mac Duncan of Clan Duncan. Her gentle lover, her tender husband, her Highland warrior, her sovereign lord.

In her heart she had room for all of them.

Epilogue

Autumn colors brightened Malcolm's village as the people celebrated the end of harvest and the beginning of winter. Twilight encouraged them to hasten their activities and prepare for the procession of Samhain.

Jarvia smiled as she walked down the pathway from the Great Hall to the stables. Wearing her gold-and-silver collar, Magda trotted briskly at her side. Morag sat in front of her house and played with Catriona. Gerda, ready to give birth at any moment, stood in front of the corral and watched Lachlann as he worked with the ponies. Lucy sat in front of the weaving hut and trimmed lamps.

"Good evening, Lucy," Jarvia called as she passed by. "How goes the trimming of the lamps?"

"Very good, mistress. I am almost finished. We shall have a wonderful procession this Samhain."

"That's what my lord husband says."

Lucy grinned. "You and Malcolm will lead the procession. 'Twill be grand. Both of you in your new clothes."

Caught up in the excitement of the promised festivities, Jarvia asked, "Have you been in a procession before?"

"Aye, many times. We take our lamps and candles and torches. Marching through the village, we lead the spirits to their rest on Beinn Malcolm and leave them with the firstfruits of the harvest. Afterwards we return to the Great Hall and celebrate with the great feast of firstfruits."

Lucy breathed in deeply and looked about the village. Anticipation glowed on her face. She laid aside the lamp that she'd been trimming. "I am glad you are here, mistress. You have brought much happiness to the village. The gods are well pleased with you and Malcolm. Our harvest is bountiful, beyond measure."

"Ah, my lady-wife." Strong arms clamped about Jarvia. A bristly face brushed her cheek, and a hard chest pressed against her back. "Are you idling the day away with gossip?"

"Malcolm!" Jarvia exclaimed, her cheeks burning with pleasure. "Why are you not preparing for the harvest festival?"

"I am." His lips found the tender spot below her ear. "Our ponies will indeed be the grandest in the procession."

Jarvia turned in his arms to face him.

"This, my love," he murmured, "will be my happiest Samhain. 'Tis the time of year when all fires are made anew."

"I am sad about only one thing," Jarvia said. "That Ghaltair escaped your men. That would not have happened, my love, if you had stayed with them."

"I would like to believe that is true," Malcolm said, "but I do not worry about it. I do not want you to either. The council has declared him and those who ride with him renegades. He cannot escape for long, and at present he is causing no trouble."

Jarvia laughed softly. "And you did find most of the stolen cattle and ponies."

"Aye, we did."

"Recent events have been hard on Angus," Jarvia said. "Although the Scot prisoner said Angus was not involved in the plot, many do not believe in his innocence. I was shocked when his own clan elected a new chief."

"A few of his faithful clansmen still believe in him and continue to follow him," Malcolm answered.

He slid his hands down to her stomach. Jarvia breathed in deeply, marveling that his slightest touch could send such pleasure through her body.

"Do you think Angus and his followers will catch Ghaltair?"

"Angus has strong reason to pursue him to the ends of the earth," Malcolm answered.

"You have always believed in his innocence, haven't you?"

"Angus was gullible when it came to Sybil, but he is not a bad man," Malcolm answered. "Now let us cease talking about Angus, my love. Let us talk about us . . . about you."

"What about me?" she asked, pressing her buttocks closer to him.

He laid his palms against her stomach. " 'Tis still flat."

" 'Tis too soon for it to be rounded," Jarvia whispered. " 'Tis only twice that my moon has not come upon me."

"Aye, so 'tis." Putting his arm around her shoulder, he began to guide her back to the Great Hall. "Do you think it's time, my lady-wife, that we dress for the celebration?"

"Aye, my love."

As they walked, she looked up into the silver-blue sky and saw the glimmer of the first stars. She was lowering her head when she realized what she had seen. She raised her head to look again and laughed aloud . . . with joy.

"What is it, love?" Malcolm asked.

"An omen," she whispered, and pointed. "Look at the cluster of three stars, my husband. Our stars."

Malcolm listened as she told him about the stars. He smiled. Jarvia knew that although he might not believe this cluster was theirs, he would not destroy her belief in them.

To her surprise he said, "According to the Ancient Ones, stars are the fires of the gods."

"I believe that," she murmured.

"My lady," he said, "look closely at your cluster."

She did.

"Do I not see a tiny fourth star, behind the smaller one?"

Jarvia did not see a fourth star. She looked again at Malcolm. In the torchlight she saw the twinkle in his eyes and smiled. "Mayhap I do, lord."

"My lady-love, I believe it is time we made our fires anew."

"Aye, my lord of fire, 'tis time."

Author's Note

If you enjoyed reading Malcolm's story in *Lord of Fire*, you'll be pleased to know that Avon books will publish Michael's story, *Lord of Thunder*, in August 1994.

As a mother of identical twins, I have always been fascinated with twins. As an author, I promised myself that one day I would use them as heroes. Five years ago my dream came true. I began to plot the Lord Series—*Lord of Fire* and *Lord of Thunder*. My heroes would be identical twins named Malcolm and Michael because these are the names of my twin sons and because we are descended from Clan Malcolm and Sept Michael.

In choosing the names, I also chose the Scottish Highlands as the setting. The time of the series is the 600's—a period when the two primary populations, the Scots and Picts, were fighting for supremacy. Northmen from what are today the Scandinavian countries also began their southward migration into Scottish territory to stake their claim. While the first incursion of Northmen was recorded as having occurred later than the 600's, I'm of the persuasion that unrecorded migration began sooner. This seems reasonable since Northmen were sea travellers, traders, and settlers . . . and since many were ostracized from their particular societies for various crimes, even hunted down and killed. Starting new colonies was an accepted way of escaping punishment, as Leif Eriksson did, for example. I believe others, before and after Leif, did the same.

From this intriguing and exciting world of Highlanders and Northmen emerge Malcolm mac Duncan and Michael Langssonn. Their stories are filled with adventure and romance, tears and laughter. I hope you are eagerly awaiting the release of Michael's story, *Lord of Thunder*, this coming summer.

393